Cover Story

Also by Mhairi McFarlane

You Had Me at Hello
Here's Looking at You
It's Not Me, It's You
Who's That Girl?
Don't You Forget About Me
If I Never Met You
Just Last Night
Mad About You
Between Us
You Belong with Me
After Hello (ebook-only novella)

Cover Story

A NOVEL

Mhairi McFarlane

AVON
An Imprint of HarperCollinsPublishers

Without limiting the exclusive rights of any author, contributor or the publisher of this publication, any unauthorized use of this publication to train generative artificial intelligence (AI) technologies is expressly prohibited. HarperCollins also exercise their rights under Article 4(3) of the Digital Single Market Directive 2019/790 and expressly reserve this publication from the text and data mining exception.

This is a work of fiction. Names, characters, places, and incidents are products of the author's imagination or are used fictitiously and are not to be construed as real. Any resemblance to actual events, locales, organizations, or persons, living or dead, is entirely coincidental.

COVER STORY. Copyright © 2025 by Mhairi McFarlane. All rights reserved. Printed in the United States of America. No part of this book may be used or reproduced in any manner whatsoever without written permission except in the case of brief quotations embodied in critical articles and reviews. For information, address HarperCollins Publishers, 195 Broadway, New York, NY 10007. In Europe, HarperCollins Publishers, Macken House, 39/40 Mayor Street Upper, Dublin 1, D01 C9W8, Ireland.

HarperCollins books may be purchased for educational, business, or sales promotional use. For information, please email the Special Markets Department at SPsales@harpercollins.com.

hc.com

Avon, Avon & logo, and Avon Books & logo are registered trademarks of HarperCollins Publishers in the United States of America and other countries.

Originally published in Great Britain in May 2025 by HarperCollins Publishers.

FIRST US EDITION

Designed by Diahann Sturge-Campbell

Library of Congress Cataloging-in-Publication Data has been applied for.

ISBN 978-0-06-329257-4

25 26 27 28 29 LBC 5 4 3 2 1

For Kerry Jean Lister,
who knows how to live

1

"Ya suffering, darling?" Aaron said, at the sight of Bel.

"Shocking," she agreed, not even bothering to be offended that her hangover was that obvious.

Bel was pale and in sunglasses: a flamboyant, "film star at Cannes" oversize pair. She was juggling a tin of Appletiser, a large Americano and a steaming brown paper bag. There was a cheese puff twist in her pocket. Her scavenger's bounty told the whole story.

"Nibbles?" Aaron said, nodding at it all, referring to the nearby greasy spoon they'd anointed their favorite in Manchester city center. "We can't Uber Eats our Lemon Drizzle Cruffins, we need to mingle with the community," Aaron had said.

Aaron, north of England editor, was from Bury, and Bel, investigations editor, had moved from York for this two-hander journalistic experiment. Aaron had the regular churn pressure of headlines, Bel the long-form, deep-dive stories of greater resonance. Both of them thought they had the harder task.

"Yup, Nibbles. Workmen in brick-dust-covered Timberland boots, and then me. Buckfast at Tiffany's. Sorry not to get you anything, I didn't have any hands left."

"S'OK. I'm eating clean. Been in the gym already this morning, working on my *revenge body*," Aaron said. "Not sure who it's going to take revenge on yet cos my significant ex would call 998 if I was on fire."

Bel snorted as she took her seat, scattering her purchases.

"Try not to vomit with excitement in your condition, but it's new intern Christmas Day," Aaron said. "What will Santa have stuffed into our stockings? Can Cicely be bettered? And when I say 'bettered' I mean *worsened*, obviously."

Bel pushed her sunglasses up into her hair, wincing at the light. She dragged her cardigan over her shoulders, the old knackered one she left on her chair as a sort of comfort blanket.

"Hard to imagine a Cicely downgrade. They'd have to not turn up at all."

"Their not appearing would be an upgrade, sugar chicken."

A resentful third wheel had made for a strained atmosphere, it was true. All fresh hires in the newsroom down in London were now required to do this stint up here.

Despite it being buried in the contract that they could be deployed around the country, clearly none of them thought it would actually happen. Banishment to the windswept foreign territories came as an unpleasant shock. Bel's first editor at her weekly newspaper had announced that anyone under thirty in any profession should "eat shit and pretend they like the taste," but so far, there'd been no pretending.

"Is it a man or woman this time?" Bel asked.

She snapped open and gingerly sipped her drink, which would be the delivery system for two ibuprofen with caffeine once she could lay hands on them. Her desk wasn't the tidiest.

Oh God, her head. On a Monday. At thirty-four years of age.

Never, ever trust Shilpa when she suggested something like coming over for a "cozy Sunday pub roast," Bel thought. The mad bitch had them drinking coffee tequila shots from a teapot!

"Now we're both single and you live nearer, we've got to use these opportunities," Shilpa had hustled. "Plus, you renting a two-bedroom flat is a clear enticement to me. An incitement."

The last thing Bel remembered was both of them lying across the furniture, blasting Carly Rae Jepsen, agreeing they should go to Sri Lanka for Christmas. It was May.

Bel was trying to impress in a job she'd had for three months. Meanwhile Shilpa doubtless remained under a Chantilly cream–like cloud of 4.5 TOG Hungarian goose down in Bel's spare room in Ancoats. She was Stockport's most ungovernable textiles designer, enjoying her WFH privileges. Bel bet she didn't even have her eyes open, let alone her laptop.

"Or a third terrible thing: another demonic child intern," Aaron said.

Cicely, twenty-three, had eaten Perello olives from the tin like sweets, done less work than a cat and was a two-time victim of mysterious illnesses on a Friday afternoon. She wore baby-blue noise-canceling headphones at her desk, which felt like a low-key insult. Bel couldn't conceive of that level of confidence at Cicely's age and was rather glad she couldn't.

Cicely disappeared back down south after eight weeks of the twelve total she was supposed to spend in the Manchester office, without a farewell.

Bel and Aaron found out from their section editor, Toby, on the following Monday.

"She said, and I quote, the 'vibe was off,'" Toby reported in one of their twice-weekly editorial Teams meetings.

Aaron, who'd come from being the crime reporter at the *Manchester Evening News*, was still trying to get his head round the ethos. "Since when did the workplace involve the vibe needing to be on? I've been seriously misled about my contractual right to vibing."

"Interns." Toby shrugged.

After they got off the call, Aaron said, "I googled Cicely on a hunch. Her dad's on the rich list and her grandad's an earl. I wish the whole lot of them a *Saltburn*ing—"

That was where you got that level of confidence at her age.

"Today we have one *Connor Adams*," said Aaron, as if the name were in some way ludicrous. "Toby's notes say—"

The tinny mechanical *ziiiip* of the intercom interrupted him.

"And there he is. Brace, brace."

Aaron darted off to get the door, thundering down a steep, narrow flight of aluminum-ridged stairs that concentrated the mind when carrying scalding hot coffees.

It was a fairly insalubrious hole, this, an unkempt second-floor space with grimy windows looking down onto the busy thoroughfare of Deansgate. The walls were stacked with banker's boxes, the electric lighting buzzed, there was a tiny kitchen area of tea-bag-stained Formica. You could set-dress it as the 1970s without making any changes beyond the computers.

When Bel had been recruited by Toby and his boss Silas, clad in colored cord trousers with logo-ed lanyards round their necks, they'd swung on their chairs in the glass-walled office in London and outlined their vision. *It's about giving you a physical space to share, a nerve center of operations; the fragmentation of remote working is not the idea. We're building a hub, a new world. You're its Adam and Eve.*

"Eh, what a dump. Our Slough House," Aaron said, in his Lancashire accent, surveying the premises on their first morning.

Bel had feared a hypercompetitive or difficult character as her sole coworker. She was relieved instead to dumb-LOL with the terminally irreverent Aaron Parry all day. He still might be hypercompetitive—she was undecided on that—but, crucially, he wasn't doing it in a way that made the working environment inhospitable.

He gently made fun of Bel's professional pedigree.

"Were you . . . a successful podcaster?" he said, pressing a ballpoint pen into his cheek and pulling a satirical face.

"You say that like it's an oxymoron. I won a People's Choice Award, I'll have you know!"

This provoked a waggish grin.

"I'll give it a listen. Wassit called again?"

"*I Might Have a Story for You.*"

"Far be it from me to criticize, but—"

"Far be it from you, Aaron, so very far."

"*Might?* Why the qualifier? Why not *I Have a Story for You?*"

"Because it's not the phrase. People always say I *might* have a story for you. I don't know why, but they do."

Aaron gave her a look that said he preferred confidence to being arty.

"Here it is, the throbbing HQ!" Aaron said, leading a man a fair bit taller than him into the room—Aaron was about five foot four. "And this right here, the spider in the center of the web, is the one, the only, the legendary podcaster and all-round mega honey, Miss Bel Macauley."

"Hi. Connor," he said, in a self-confident staccato, extending his hand to shake.

Bel hadn't expected to be this formal and had unfortunately started on her fried egg and hash brown roll, putting it back down and hastily and discreetly wiping her hand on her leg.

"Nice to meet you."

Connor withdrew his hand swiftly.

He didn't look like a journalist. Or not an interning one, anyway. Older (her age? Early thirties, not the twenty-four-year-old she was expecting) and too well dressed: immaculate blue oxford shirt, black wool tie, police officer colors.

It sunk in that he was strikingly good-looking too, in a way that was certain to make him a self-regarding dick. Thick brown hair, dampened by drizzle, cut short but still long enough to rake your hands through. Puppyish eyes offset by strong cheekbones. Regency romance suitor via a partner at Deloitte.

His skeptical gaze flickered over her. Bel could not imagine a more explicit sense of *assessment* outside of airport security and swimsuit pageants.

His forehead creased, he was almost outright scowling. Bel gathered he was doing that thing when someone doesn't realize their face is conveying their feelings. Or maybe, even worse, he *did* know.

"You're not my pupil, it's not really possible to shadow investigative work. You're with Aaron, as your Work Dad," she said, reflexively having to assert herself, goad him a little, in the face of his evident disgust.

"Yes, I know," Connor said, his tone not concealing his offense in return.

He opened a stylish messenger bag and started organizing the spare desk. The casual mood of only moments earlier had completely evaporated, creaking tension in its place. Aaron widened his eyes at Bel and made a covert gun barrel to temple gesture.

Bloody hell, these three months would last forever.

2

If it was statistically proven to be a myth that it always rained in Manchester, why was it always fucking raining? Connor thought, as he checked the coordinates on Google Maps again and that his blue dot was moving the right way.

It had absolutely hammered down when he and his dad had arrived. The low, forbidding gray sky threw down water in quantities that felt personal.

He'd not wanted his dad to do the long round trip from Barking up to Connor's Salford Airbnb and back again, but he insisted. Connor didn't have the heart to say no.

His father was seventy-six now and Connor had been emotionally unprepared for how precarious and mortal things suddenly turned in that decade. Every interaction with his parents came freighted with the fear of how long he might have left with them. The loving sturdiness of their support became almost unbearable, with the growing awareness it was finite. When they sat in a companionable near silence eating ploughman's sandwiches in the front seats of his dad's Ford Focus at a pub parking lot in Knutsford, Connor felt like an elephant was sitting on his heart.

"You want to get a move on with any wedding or Mum and Dad won't be there," said his older brother Shaun, who could never be accused of peddling toxic positivity. Shaun's own nuptials, five years ago, had been at The Ludlow in New York. One of Connor and Jen's first dates, in fact. When it felt like Connor was showing her around his life, encouraging her to buy shares in it.

"Jen not coming?" his dad said, as they loaded the boot at the outset, bulging sports holdalls and a duvet, like Connor was a thirty-four-year-old freshman. Which was exactly as daft as he felt.

"Ah, no . . . she's got a friend's birthday this weekend. A thirtieth," he said, the prepared white lie.

In fact, she was at her parents', a "get myself out of the way" she'd arranged on purpose. Jennifer said she'd visit him in Manchester "in a couple of weeks, when you're settled in."

"It'll be more fun for a guest when you've got more than milk in the fridge and you've found a nice neighborhood place to eat. I'll send you a cute little succulent and you can call it Jenny."

Make it a spiky one, then.

She'd also done him a care package with "useful bits" in it, including an ironic champagne, and Connor deeply resented it in the way you did when you knew the offering was to soothe the feelings of the giver rather than gratify the recipient.

The whole point of her coming up now, Connor thought, was that things would be bare bones, chilly and lonely. It would be for him, not her. He knew she had no love for anywhere north of Leicester, or, indeed, Leicester itself. ("The only way to leave London is on a plane.")

But he didn't say so, as he wasn't sure he wanted her to come. He and Jennifer had quietly arrived at the hospice phase. You didn't try to actively treat the sickness anymore, only make the end comfortable. They loved their flat in Stoke Newington and it was nearly paid off, with Connor's money. She'd hate leaving the area she couldn't afford to rebuy in and he'd hate having to do it to her. So here they were. Withdrawing affection bit by bit and waiting for the other person to be the bad guy.

A tiny voice niggled at him: *She'll line someone else up first. Probably why she's not called time yet.*

Connor wasn't sure how much trouble they'd been in before he announced he was leaving his six-figure-salary job in the City for the significantly lower one in journalism, but it certainly put the big light on in their room, life plans–wise.

"I'm thirty-three. If we start a family, how are we going to afford it? We can't upgrade to more space unless we have the salaries for the next mortgage!" Jen had said, hands on superhero-blue Lycra hips, sleek as an eel in her running gear. She'd obviously hoped he simply needed to *say* he was going to give his notice, not actually do it. Also, interesting use of *we*.

"What use would I be as a parent if I was that miserable?" Connor asked.

"You aren't 'miserable'! You just aren't having fun! Which is most jobs. It'll be this job too, sooner or later. You like to feel ground down. If you didn't feel oppressed, what would you make sarcastic wisecracks about?"

Connor ignored this pretty horrific summary of his character, nature and behavior. Jen alone knew he'd been on beta blockers for stress and bursting into sobbing fits in the shower, by the end. He read a thing on relationship guidance about how the unsurvivable feature was contempt.

He stuck to the hard facts: "Your job pays as much as mine at the newspaper will."

"I knew you'd hurl that at me. I was doing this when we met, sold as seen. And I'll be promoted next year."

Translation: Jen was allowed to work in publishing, which she loved, for whatever it paid. She'd assigned him different obligations.

"I don't remember whispered pledges to love, cherish and stick to the higher tax bracket."

Connor thought she might have felt more shame than this at saying *You've got no utility if you're not on 100K-plus.*

But he couldn't say he was surprised. When love had flown, the comfortable lifestyle flying away too was going to concentrate your mind somewhat.

Last year, after he'd first told Jen he wanted to reinvent himself, she'd got drunk in the garden with her friend Libby. Connor heard her wine-laden voice carrying through the open window at 2:00 a.m.: "Connor's now going to be like a trophy wife. Great to have on your arm, lovely to show off, cos I know everyone wants to shag him. But fuck-all USE, you know?"

He was surprised to find it caused more clarity than offense. Why didn't he finish it with her? Because leaving his high-flying career, reassessing his whole criteria for success in life and retraining as a journalist had been enough upheaval.

Examining where he and Jen stood when the dust cleared was on the to-do list, but right when Connor might have had enough energy to tackle it, his dog died, and he got sent up north for three months.

His father waited until Connor was showing him out of his dismal lodgings to put his hand on Connor's shoulder and say, "Stop wearing your cares so heavily. She's a total fool to disregard you, there'll be women queuing up."

He winked.

Connor stood blinking in surprise as the door closed.

He knew his dad only intended to be encouraging. That his father would drive home congratulating himself on having steeled himself to speak up, rallying Connor's spirits.

Yet in fact, his dad had actually communicated: *Every last bit of resilient dignity you think you're showing is laughably futile; anyone can see your girlfriend likes you as much as a rectal bleed. And by the way, she's right about you languishing in self-pity.*

CONNOR TURNED ONTO DEANSGATE. He felt such a deep, dragging well of emptiness and sadness inside. Obviously he was down in general, but he wondered if he might be depressed again, the proper, clinical sort that doctors signed you off with. Could he get himself out of the Manchester internship on the sick, or would it be waiting for him on the other side of a return to work?

He knew the answer: whether he did or he didn't dodge the draft up here, switching careers, then getting his first job in his new profession and immediately disappearing on mental health grounds would give off every bad signal about whether Connor Adams and journalism were a good fit.

Shoulders back, deep breaths, positive attitude: first morning. *Three months, it's nothing, a term at university. Do you even really remember a specific term that felt long at university?* he asked himself, his own sports coach. *No? There you go.*

He located the anonymous doorway, pressed buzzer two. The contact he'd been given, Aaron Parry, answered: he was the absolute spitting image of the singer from the Arctic Monkeys, complete with black bangs and a lounge-lizard smirk.

Parry had come from the *Manchester Evening News*, apparently, but it was the investigations woman he was meant to take notice of.

Toby had said to him, in his public school drawl: "Absolute coup hiring Isabel Macauley. Really impressive girl. Have you heard her podcast? Oh, you MUST. Fabulous communicator, going places. Has a real knack for getting people to open up. Learn all you can from her."

The office was shabby, like a storeroom. Bel was sitting with her back to the door.

She had very long, treacle-brown hair, pulled up and looped back on itself like a collapsing bun, anchored by a large pair of sunglasses. Stray strands at the nape of her neck were pinned with tiny black butterfly clips, which Connor recognized as identical to the ones his mum had on the stems of her moth orchids to hold them upright.

As she turned to say hello, Connor felt a spasm of irritation at the likely motive for Toby's lavish admiration. Bel Macauley was undeniably pretty, in a way he could imagine had won her a legion of unimaginative admirers. Wide-set, bright eyes framed by clumpy mascara, a tiny, upturned nose and curved bow of an amused, expressive mouth. She bore an uncanny resemblance to a young Shirley MacLaine in that black-and-white classic romance that didn't seem at all romantic to Connor, and Jen insisted was her favorite.

And it was lucky she was the only person here or Connor might've taken her for the boss's rebellious daughter who'd just gotten back from Glastonbury. She was in a short blue cotton summer dress with a sailor bib neckline, black leggings that ended mid-calf, scuffed white canvas lace-up pumps on her feet. And a burgundy-glitter mohair cardigan thrown over the top of the ensemble. It was unraveling, one sleeve shorter than the other. It looked like Connor felt.

There was an absolute stench of hot egg emanating from the puck of soggy carb next to her keyboard.

"You're not my pupil, it's not really possible to shadow investigative work. You're with Aaron, as your Work Dad," she said, because of course the status humiliation had to begin straightaway.

"Yes, I realize," he said. *I'm not going to be begging you for advice. Unless it's on how to dress for a Just Stop Oil protest.*

Connor kept his eyes fixed on his screen in an atmosphere where he could actually *feel* the two of them exchanging pointed glances, and face pulling.

Bloody hell, these three months would last forever.

3

On a solid piece of guesswork, Bel rang the doorbell at her flat instead of using her key.

The fearsomely expensive duplex she was renting was a stunner. She'd dipped into her ISA to afford the first six months up front, with a discount because the last occupant had done a midnight flit and the owner—she could see why, at this rate—didn't want any vacancy. Financially wasteful, yes, yet Bel didn't feel it was a waste when she walked the twenty minutes home from Deansgate to her street in Ancoats.

She'd been reliably informed by Aaron that the fashionable area north of the city center was, in fairly recent memory, tatty, crime-ridden and neglected. "Rough as arseholes, doll face. The gentrifying Fairy Godmother has waved her magic money wand."

It was now a thriving, trendy bohemia: old mills converted into apartments like hers, small-plates restaurants with their names in swirling fonts on their picture windows. The sort of pubs that had fairy lights, skin contact wine and seasonal produce chalkboard menus.

Bel needed the sense of a fresh start, of being picked up and carried along by a different sort of life in her new neighborhood, and so far it had delivered in spades.

Her exorbitantly priced residence had exposed thick redbrick walls and original windows, burnt black timber, floor-to-ceiling white curtains that ran on heavy industrial-looking railings. It was very "boutique urban hotel," the recessed lights set to a permanent low glow, the dining room illuminated by a modern candelabra of industrial pendant lampshades on looped cord.

The heavy metal door swung open, Shilpa on the other side. Her long straight hair was in two plaits, a style that always provoked racially insensitive beery lads to shout "Pocahontas!" at her. She was eating a bowl of Frosties.

"I've got bad news, I'm still here," she said through a mouthful of cereal, standing aside to let Bel pass.

"Definitely looks like you're still here," Bel said.

Shilpa had been her best friend since they were teenagers. There was an anecdote she always told to best summarize the Shilpaness of Shilpa—indeed, it was the one Bel told as her bridesmaid at Shilpa's wedding. When they were nineteen and completely broke, Shilpa bought a wedding dress from a charity shop for a fiver, added a tiara and veil from Claire's Accessories and led them round local nightspots getting bought drinks all night.

When it came to real marriages, and a groom she met on a Ryanair flight, it lasted three years—Shilpa and Zachary were now divorced. "Did I superstitious-curse it with that fake runaway bride stunt?" she'd mused. Before concluding: "No, it was the raging incompatibilities."

"I am going to cut you a deal," Shilpa said now, putting her Frosties bowl in the double sink and vaguely waving the boiling water tap at it. "Wait, did you go to work dressed like that?"

"I didn't have any meetings today, no one can see me! Well, only my top half in the Teams meeting."

"Fair do's but your face still says 'open casket.' My deal is, I hang around for another evening but I pay for a huge takeaway. Like, colossal. The size where you can eat it tomorrow too. A Chinese banquet."

"Agreed," Bel said, collapsing onto the sofa. "Tell you what I did forget, dressing like this—the new intern was starting. One

Connor Adams, swags in with a nuclear winter attitude, sees my disheveled ensemble and gives me this look like . . ." Bel scrunched her nose up and pushed her chin down and reenacted an *ewww* face while scanning.

"Hahahaha."

"He went out on a sandwich run at lunch so we were free to gossip about him. Aaron tells me our boss Toby says he's had an unusual career path, used to work in the Square Mile. We googled him and he was in private equity, trading floor, a real *Wolf of Wall Street* type of world. God knows why he's slumming in journalism, his pay slips now must look like the tips they left in restaurants."

"Why's he not doing financial journalism at the *Financial Times*?" Shilpa said, flopping down next to her.

"Exactly what we said. Aaron's got a theory he's a mole, a plant for the pin-striped boys to do insider trading. Maybe we're the misdirection part of his CV. Also, he's handsome in a completely obnoxious way, so you can be absolutely sure he's going to fail upward so fast it'll look like the Rapture in a two-grand suit."

"*Is* he?" Shilpa paused, rummaging in a bag of Skittles she'd secreted somewhere in the sofa cushions. Bel personally preferred savory with a hangover. "Let the dog see the rabbit, please."

"Errr . . ." Bel opened her browser on her mobile, searched "Connor Adams investment" and brought up his old LinkedIn headshot. Ugh. He was even giving her an arsey look in that image.

She turned her phone to face Shilpa.

"Ooh, pass me my eclipse glasses! Retina burn. I wouldn't mind exchanging my rupees for a *strong pound* from him."

"Vomit to infinity." Bel shuddered, putting her phone down. "He doesn't need the ego boost of anyone fancying him. A self-saucing pudding if ever I met one."

She'd thought of their office as a two-person canoe, but if they had interns forever, it was in fact always going to be this: two people and a mulish interloper.

"This place is an absolute sex parlor, by the way," Shilpa said, casting a look at their surroundings. "I've loved hanging around enjoying it while you go to work to pay for it."

She paused. Bel knew what was coming.

"Heard from Anthony?"

"Nope. Relieved. Maybe he's finally got the message. Or rather, *not got the message* about where I live."

Bel sounded confident but she wasn't. She wasn't fooling herself, or Shilpa, yet the pretense felt necessary.

"If he finds a way to get in touch after this, I think you've got to do something about him," Shilpa said. "Prison door with spyhole's a good start, though."

"I have!"

"*Belly.*"

Bel had never consented to Belly, but nicknames didn't work that way.

"You have nuked all your social media, blocked him, changed your phone number and taken a job in a different city. If I wasn't personally convenienced by my best mate coming to live forty minutes away in an incredible apartment where I can crash regularly, I might have even advised you not to. But I'm a selfish little shit, as my ex-husband, Zachary, will tell you."

"There you go. In cowpats, daisies grow."

Bel pulled her shoes off her feet and tucked them underneath her. It was a defensive fetal position.

"Actually, he's not blocked on email. He can't tell if I've read them, so given they're long and rambling and make it clear he's off his nut, maybe I'm best off hanging on to them as proof."

"Proof of . . . ?" Shilpa trailed off, eyes widening. "So you do think it could end up with the police?"

"I don't know. I've never had relations with an obsessive harasser before."

"If he's not going to leave his wife, what the fuck is he even offering you? Lifelong mistress?"

"This is irrelevant given my period of insanity is over and I've reclaimed my brain from the Lost Property bin."

"I know that, I'm trying to figure out what he's asking you to do. Apart from the obvious."

"'Wait until my sixteen-year-old kid has left home' was the line," Bel said, her heart and bones heavy with self-disgust at even repeating it. "He didn't mean it. He *thinks* he means it. The weird thing with Anthony is he completely persuades himself before he attempts to persuade you, so he's like an evangelist preacher of his own fantasies."

"What if you forwarded the emails to his wife?"

They'd been round these houses before, but Bel didn't entirely mind retracing the route. She wanted the reassurance of running through it again, rehearsing her reasoning. Convincing herself.

"Assuming his wife doesn't know and hasn't accepted infidelity in the package with being married to Ant, which is a big assume. If I do that, ratting to his wife is going to give him legitimate cause to come after me. Imagine if she threw him out and he was free to pursue me 24/7."

Bel shuddered.

"I don't get it," Shilpa said. "I *really* don't get it. Does he think he's going to hassle you into you wanting him?"

Bel felt a little clammy.

"He's like a debt collection agency except I don't know what the debt is or how I'm meant to pay it."

"What a maniac. If he'd wanted to be with you, he could've. He ended your relationship with Tim."

"No, I definitely did that," Bel said, mouth dry.

Anthony was her manic episode, a shaming lapse in judgment and morals that he wouldn't let her forget. A horror film: *I Know Who You Did Last Summer.*

"Most people would be so embarrassed to beg and plead. What does he think he's achieving?! What's the kick, when you're telling him to get lost?" Shilpa said.

Bel shrugged, though she didn't feel casual.

"Intimidation? And control, I suppose."

"Yeah, well, he doesn't have that," Shilpa said, opening her phone to find spring rolls.

Bel thought that Shilpa's description of how Bel had handled it so far made that debatable. A voice in her head told her *it'll get worse before it gets better*, and she was ignoring it.

4

"Tell us about one of your podcast greatest hits, then, Macauley," Aaron said, in the 3:00 p.m. lull, the energy dip phase of the nine-to-five. And it was a Thursday: not yet the weekend, no Toby check-in until tomorrow. Outside it was no-jacket-required late-springtime muggy; in here it was a dingy sweatbox. The mood felt distinctly get a Diet Coke, doomscroll and piss about.

"Was it like MPs' expenses? Did a York MP claim for an ornamental duck pond and a load of dildos?" Aaron asked. "Or did you probe why Wetherspoon's chips are so many calories when you only get about six of them?"

Bel recognized the highly specific variety of teasing that Aaron was using with her, in front of a studiously unimpressed, blank Connor Adams. (He was a real charisma powerhouse. He'd worked in near silence since his arrival on Monday, except when asking Aaron for more to do. As Bel's mother liked to say, "Lucky he's got those looks, he needs them.")

To the untrained observer, Aaron's attention might look like mockery. In the world of journalism and in the north of England, Bel sensed it was a compliment.

He wasn't putting her on the spot so much as putting her in a spotlight, because he thought she could tap-dance.

"Erm . . . There was the one that was mentioned in the award," Bel said, then paused, aware this could still be a bear trap for making a boastful arse of herself. "Which was about the Ask for Amy initiative the police and mayor's office started. I'd seen the signs in loads of places back at home and thought, Has anyone stress-tested whether it works? So I did."

"What's Ask for Amy?" Aaron said. As he was a crime reporter, she was surprised he'd not heard of it—it had rolled out beyond York. Lovely male privilege.

"It's when a woman feels unsafe—a date's not working out or he's not who he said he was, you know. You ask for 'Amy' at the bar and the staff member unobtrusively goes to get the trained person on site who calls you a taxi or the police. It's a code for 'help me.'"

"Why d'you think it wasn't working?"

"It was a hunch that pub owners stuck the posters up in the ladies' with good intentions but were less rigorous about teaching every new bartender what to do. You know, we have fire drill practice because otherwise we'd forget the process in an emergency. I was pretty certain they weren't doing drills, so I did one."

"And? You were right?"

"It didn't work on most occasions. Some of the bartenders actually drew more attention by calling 'Oy, do you know an AMY?' down the bar and shaking their heads, nonplussed, at me. The whole point of it was it was supposed to be more discreet than saying you were in trouble. Anyway, it gave the scheme a kick up the arse so hopefully it operates the way it's meant to now."

"Whoa," Aaron said. "Well-done, crusader."

"Thanks. Except I made my brother Miles be my 'bad date' and he was really annoyed by getting barred by several pub owners until I went back and explained, hahaha. Even then one place said, 'Is he making you say this?'"

"And hopefully you didn't lose anyone in the pubs their jobs," Connor said, evenly but pointedly. Both Bel and Aaron looked over in surprise at him speaking. "For not knowing the protocol. Given I'm guessing it was their voices on the audio."

"Hopefully not," Bel said, startled at his input. "I wasn't calling out anyone pulling the pints. The venue needed to provide the training. It was the employer's responsibility."

"Not always how it works when a business looks bad, though, is it?"

Aaron looked from Connor and back to Bel, eyes wide, clearly delighted to have inadvertently kicked off drama.

"Right, but I can't control that."

Connor didn't reply and Bel realized she was annoyed.

"It matters more that women who feel threatened can call on help," she added.

"Of course," Connor said, mildly, with more maddening superiority.

A beat of tense silence.

"You know, investigative journalism with no risks isn't likely to be worthwhile," Bel said. "You can't safety-proof every aspect and anticipate every consequence. If people are getting something wrong, they're getting it wrong."

"Can't make a podcast frittata without breaking a few eggs," Aaron said.

"Sure. Though if they hadn't been given training or even told about it, they'd done nothing wrong," Connor said.

Bel was ready this time.

"Sorry, are you implying I'm against the working man or woman by demonstrating a scheme to protect women from harmful men isn't functioning?"

"I'm not suggesting that at all. I'm thinking out loud about how good some bosses are at divesting themselves of responsibility and letting others carry the can."

Sure, right, Bel seethed. Seriously, who was this guy?

"I could do with a better coffee than that moldy Kenco with Rice Krispies in it," Connor said after a minute, standing up. "Anyone want one if I go to Caffe Nero?"

"Ooh, Honey Iced Velvet Americano, cheers, mate," Aaron, who seemed to be like a wasp in a pub garden when it came to sugar, said.

"Bel?" Connor said.

"No thanks," she replied, prim. She felt certain her refusal had been correctly interpreted as: *The only thing I'd accept from you is an apology.*

"Oh," she said, as Connor opened the door to the stairwell, "forgot to say." She addressed both him and Aaron. "I've got a job tomorrow that's going to take me out of the office for the afternoon. So I'll meet you both at Platzki's at half five?"

She and Aaron had decided to offer every intern a Friday night drink and welcome dinner in their first week. Cicely had asked, "Is it compulsory?" and then declined. Connor was ahead in at least accepting.

"We'll get you a Black Cherry Vodka," Aaron said, and Connor nodded.

After Connor's footsteps thundered down the stairs, Aaron said, "Don't you be dumping me with him, Macauley!"

"I was explaining I will definitely be there even if I'm not here!"

"Hmmm. Look at this . . ."

Aaron was out of his seat and standing at Connor's desk. He held out a photograph in a frame next to the monitor, the size of a postcard. He turned it so Bel could see it—an elegantly gorgeous brunette, hair in a bob, smiled into the camera lens. Her arms were wound round the neck of a large shaggy dog. The hound—was it a golden retriever? Bel's dad was the dog person in their family, and he'd died fourteen years ago—had a pleasingly goofy expression, as if it too was smiling.

"Fookin' hell, a picture of your good lady on your desk! Does he think she'll do spot checks? He's definitely been to a school where they're all called Old Somethings," Aaron said. "Fair play, though, she's fit."

Bel might find Connor Adams repellent, but she had principles. Deriding someone's affection for their loved ones, or assessing the shaggability of said loved one, was not done.

"Aaron, leave him be. That's really nice. We should all hope to be worthy of a picture on someone's desk."

"My darling, if anyone displayed one of you, your portrait would be stolen within an hour by a randy thief."

Bel rolled her eyes and hoped his flirting was the automatic-irony type, and that he wasn't the randy thief.

Why did men have to make themselves problems?

5

The glittering skyscrapers of Castlefield juxtaposed against the redbrick of old Victoriana Manchester looked like science fiction to Bel, CGI trickery. In the city's building boom of the twenty-first century, spaceships had landed behind railway arches and viaducts. Her cab swept past this city center scenery then tightly packed terraces and, farther out, onto a highway and into the suburbs. It was three miles to Southern Cemetery in Chorlton-cum-Hardy, and Bel welcomed the chance to collect more geographical reference points.

Her youthful visits to Manchester were to nightclubs, and not heavy on drinking in the landscape.

Bel had prepared a lie about how she needed photographs for an art project if the driver asked her if she was visiting the deceased, but he seemed more interested in chatting on his hands-free in Urdu than any intention of his passenger. She idly wondered if he'd be able to give a decent description of her if she was about to disappear.

Bel phone-scrolled the intriguing email exchange that had begun earlier in the week. It was downright prime-time thriller stuff and she'd go as far as to say it gave her The Shiver. If you didn't recognize The Shiver, you shouldn't be in her profession, in her opinion. The Shiver was the rare, delicious frisson that you might've stumbled on something large and meaningful. Often The Shiver didn't pay off, but you needed to be alert to the possibility for the few times that it did. You maybe only got two or three genuinely bombshell leads in a career, if you were lucky.

In fact, recognizing The Shiver went deeper than bylines and exclusives. It connected you to the important truth that the world was always interesting, endlessly exciting, and all kinds of ripe, nefarious shit was afoot beyond the dull workaday veneer of energy bills, queues at the drugstore and traffic jams at rush hour.

The job was about facts, truth and verifiable reality—but it could still provide exhilarating, fast-paced narratives. Bel had begun her podcast to prove this. She lived in hope of a *New Yorker*-style long read that merited a nonfiction book and got adapted for film. Social responsibility was her other concern, yes, but oh God, the thrill of a proper yarn.

Bel people-watched Friday afternoon flashing past the car window: a young woman in patterned leggings on a homeworking jog, phone Velcro-strapped to her upper arm. Shoals of kids in sweaty, half-unbuttoned school uniforms giddy with escaping for the weekend. Men in short sleeves at picnic tables outside pubs. Two middle-aged women carrying a canvas holdall, one handle each, into a house with a SOLD sign outside it.

If life wasn't a series of stories and surprises for everyone, how many people were going to meet the love of their life tonight? Or alternatively, make torturous small talk with two male colleagues over pierogi, one of whom didn't want to be there?

But then Bel had always had a vivid, runaway imagination, her mother said. In the last year that observation had changed from charming to an indictment.

The email sender had scrambled his address, so it arrived without any clues to his identity beyond the moniker Grendel 505. Wasn't Grendel a monster in *Beowulf*? Bel thought. Encouraging.

Grendel 505

I might have a story for you. It's big and scandalous, and it might be very hard to prove. It could also lose me my job and see me exiled from what we can laughably call high society in this city, so forgive the cloak-and-dagger but I'm not going to give you my name for now.

Bel

Hard to prove is often my remit. Can you give me more details?

Grendel 505

It involves a prominent Manchester individual sleeping with their staff. I know politicians being extramarital cheats isn't a huge shock, but there's details here that make this really quite torrid. And I do know for certain what I'm talking about, given my proximity to said individual. Best to tell you in person. Could you get to Southern Cemetery at 3 on Friday?

Bel

I could, but can I ask why you want to meet in a graveyard?

Grendel 505

I need an outdoor location where we can't be overheard or recorded, or more importantly, seen together or recognized, and parks have too many people in them at this time of year. I know it's a long distance, but it also seems entirely safe in a way I can't think anywhere else is.

Bel

OK! How will I know who you are?

Grendel 505

I'll be the only balding fifty-year-old man lurking around notable people's graves on a weekday afternoon, with a look of nervous anticipation?

Bel

Fair 😊

Grendel 505
In case of any doubt as to identity, I'll wait by Jerome Caminada's headstone, which seems fitting. (Manchester's Sherlock Holmes of the 1800s, if you haven't heard of him.)
Bel
I hadn't heard of Jerome, I'm from York, please forgive me! See you there.

If Grendel 505 was a psychopath, he was the articulate and persuasive variety.

She was cautiously hopeful, foregrounding caution before hope. If he wasn't an active danger, Bel was still prepared for Grendel 505 to tell her—in the same tone you might say you didn't like the colors of the latest public transport livery—that the CIA were using air fryers as listening devices. For there to be a needle-scratch moment where she realized she was in a garden of the dead with a headbanger.

One of the first rules of journalism was "Anyone might be lying about anything, and for no reason. Trust nobody until they've earned it."

Bel's mentor and hero wasn't anyone she'd worked with, it was her late aunt Tessa, who'd blazed a trail through the tabloids in the fag-smoke-wreathed 1970s and '80s, going from newsroom librarian to reporter and subeditor. She'd no children of her own and had seen something in Bel, regaling her with inappropriate tales of Fleet Street from a young age.

As per established safety protocol, Bel had forwarded the email chain to Shilpa with *"work! NFS" (not for sharing)* and she'd made sure Share My Location and Find My iPhone were active too. It was daylight, it was a public place, there was a digital paper trail.

"Why don't you just tell people you work with where you're going?" Shilpa said.

"Because they'll nick your story," Bel said. "I've told you this. I don't discuss sensitive stories with Aaron. I use code words in our Teams meetings that are only understood by me and editor Toby. We all use Signal cos it can't be hacked. Paranoia reigns. But better paranoid than scooped."

"*Journalists!*"

6

The wrought-iron-gated entrance to Southern Cemetery was flanked by pleasingly Gothic turrets, though given the supernatural energy, Bel was relieved she was visiting in light-filled late spring, not the foggy, freezing, fading sun of winter. Inside, the Victorian graveyard had tree-lined avenues to make navigation simpler, but the space was still vast—moss-coated monuments and stone angels stretching as far as she could see, canopied by greenery. A recent rainfall had left leaves shining; it was peaceful and quite beautiful.

Bel saw her likely date.

He was standing with hands in pockets next to a tall, narrow headstone, under a distinctive mature yew tree with a trunk twisted into four sections. Grendel 505 was, as advertised, balding, the remaining gray hair shorn close, wearing fashionable, clear-rimmed glasses and a navy workman's jacket. He looked like creative, affluent Manchester—knew his way around design software and Pet Nats.

As she approached, Bel tried to assess how homicidal and unhinged he might be, based on these clues. If he was the fava beans and Chianti, upmarket mind games sort. She'd had cause to wonder about the varnish-thin layer of normalcy that covered lunacy a lot lately.

"Hi! Bel Macauley?" he said. "You don't have any pictures online so forgive my confirming your ID."

"Hello. Yes, I think it's better in my line of work if you can manage it."

This was true, and also not the reason she had no pictures online.

"I can imagine. I'm Ian," he said. "Shall we walk up the main path?"

"Sure."

"Don't want to be treading on anyone's head."

As they fell in step, Ian said, "Sorry for the gnomic correspondence and high drama choice of location but as I said, I couldn't think of any better way to keep our conversation secret. Even if I don't look it, I'm a long way off retirement and keen to keep my salary. This is all off the record, isn't it?"

His eyes darted toward her.

"One hundred percent," Bel said. "You have my word, and I have no way of taking notes."

"I'll be honest, I'm not sure I should be here. Not *here* here. I mean, risking my livelihood and my employability in the city I've made my home for the last thirty years."

He smiled a thin smile, and Bel couldn't tell how much of his pale complexion was Celtic genetics, and how much fear.

"I get it," Bel said. "I promise, by speaking to me you're uncommitted to anything. We can talk the issues through and decide to do nothing. I won't turn you over. Whatever we do decide, it'll be a joint decision."

This last line might be a slightly cosmetic version of the truth, but she understood the need for reassurance when your well-being was in the hands of a stranger.

"You're the investigations editor, so I'm thinking knotty, complicated stuff is of interest?" Ian said.

"Correct."

"OK. You know the general reputation and legend that is Manchester's 'big personality' mayor, Glenn Bailey?"

"Yes, of course."

"What's your image of him?"

"Ehm . . . very popular. Youthful and attractive, especially for a politician—you get those political-crush jokes. An ex-caner turned nighttime czar, then mayor. Has done loads of good things for infertility awareness as he couldn't have kids, and about sobriety as a reformed caner turned teetotaler. Bit of a folk hero feel. A folk hero in a designer plaid shirt, with a takeaway flat white from an indie coffee roaster permanently gripped in his left hand. Because caffeine is his one remaining vice."

The Mayor's love of coffee, a man who still needed a stimulant, had become a tabloid joke. A running meme photoshopped one into his free hand on his wedding day, shaking hands with the King, during minute's silences.

"That's roughly what I thought you'd say. He's my employer, I work in comms. Har har, right?"

Bel smiled.

"I've been around Glenn for ten years, one way or another, worked on his mayoral bid. And yes, he's immensely charismatic: energetic and tireless in his love and advocacy for the city, expansive in his vision. He did a lot of solid work with the gay community and, as a gay man of my vintage, I was impressed."

Ian took a breath.

"He's also a malignant narcissist whose addiction is seducing much younger women, preferably those who work for him. Caffeine is one of *two* vices." Ian exhaled. "You're not going to quote me, right? It's between us and the departed, here? He treats me like a consigliere. I feel like Mafia going to the FBI."

"It stays here."

Bel's heart rate sped up. She'd once heard a newsroom whisper that the Mayor played away, but she'd not given it much credence. GB, as he was colloquially known, had an image of being such a contentedly settled ex-raver, she suspected it was a wishful counter-take by envious men. The same way every woman's pinup A-lister was supposedly in the closet.

"I've known it's been going on for years. Men my age don't tend to be inner circle on the office sex-life gossip, but women would leave, suddenly. Certain organizations would be cagey about working with us again. Over time it turned out Glenn's whole ageist, insistent emphasis on hiring twenty-somethings, 'not old Dereks and Lindas, stuck in their ways,' revealed itself to have a different purpose. There's a particular way he can use his status with the less experienced."

"I know what you mean," Bel said.

"Anyway, I got my twenty-four-year-old niece, Erin, a monthlong placement at our office at the start of the year. I naively and arrogantly thought that, with me on-site, I could protect her from any untoward attention. I thought I had. Recently she confided she was briefly involved with Glenn and completely shattered by it. They'd swapped numbers and it only began after she left, so I had no idea. I wish I'd warned her he was a piece of shit, but somehow, I thought that was better unsaid."

"I'm really sorry," Bel said. Ian's voice had thickened and the guilt was palpable.

"I'm not proud of the fact I was overlooking it when it wasn't my blood, but none of the women had confided in me, you know? It didn't feel like my business, however uncomfortable the rumors made me."

Ian threw her a look and Bel opened her mouth to say *I am not an exemplar either* and then went with: "Don't worry, I understand. What exactly happened with Erin?"

A light sweat had developed under her clothes, and she pushed her hands into the pockets of her dress.

"His standard MO. I think. Says he's seen something special in her, wants to help her career. Gives her loads of great contacts and encouragement. Then when she feels obliged to him, he gives her the spiel he's been monogamous for decades but she's turned everything on its head, blah blah. Commences an intense love bombing. Then follows a brutal ghosting, once it's consummated . . ."

Ian took a breath.

"You can imagine it was agonizing for Erin to go into this with her uncle, but there was an even darker element too. This part is what finally shocked me into action and emailing you, really."

Bel was aware she was electrified and sympathetic; also, that she should be keeping every skeptical journalistic defense up.

"Erin said when she finally got hold of Glenn—to ask him why he'd dropped contact with her so dramatically, not with any expectations—he made it very clear he'd got what he wanted and they were done. And that he could weather anything she threw at him, but he had the ability to destroy her. He said she'd be discredited as some 'slutty young girl trying to use him for her fifteen minutes.' Especially as he'd leak photos of her, which she didn't realize he had."

"Nudes?"

"Yes. She'd sent them on WhatsApp as a disappearing message for safety—you know, where they immediately disappear? He said he'd screenshot them. She's not sure if it's true, but if he's unpleasant enough to bluff it, he's unpleasant enough to do it. He said they'd find their way online and no one would ever be able to prove where they came from."

"He threatened her with *revenge porn*?" Bel said, so shocked she briefly halted in her tracks, amid the eerie tranquility and tweeting birds. She tried to piece it together with the stoic, middle-aged man who'd smiled out of Sunday supplement articles about better special education needs care in local schools.

"Yep. He made it clear his ability to humiliate and expose Erin if she went public was considerable. I'd wondered how he took risks and always got away with it. I assumed he stayed friends with his conquests. Which he might well do, but, clearly, he's prepared for it to become hostile. Erin was so upset and shocked, she said she was physically shaking. Remember, this is someone who told her he'd never been unfaithful before. When the pennies dropped it was like a Blackpool one-arm bandit."

Bel nodded, face taut. She knew that sensation.

Ian paused. "The thing is, if he hadn't been my superior, if he hadn't been the mayor, Erin would've treated a forty-five-year-old man making those initial advances to her with extreme caution. He quite purposely used his position of trust to get past her defenses. This is about a power imbalance used to ruthless effect."

Bel's eyes settled on a lichen-covered heavenly messenger nearby, the statue posed with hand to face, as if deep in thought.

It wasn't a kiss-and-tell, Bel agreed. It was a story that shone a light on something larger, the kind she was always looking for. Bel's skin was goosebump chilly. She had The Shiver.

7

"Are you sure Erin won't speak to me? She and I could also have a completely off-the-record, no-obligations chat before we decide whether she wants to proceed," Bel said.

"If there was any chance of that whatsoever, you'd not be talking to her considerably less photogenic uncle right now. She's beyond mortified. Her firm belief is that if she goes public, it ends up defining the rest of her life and making her unemployable. Glenn said he'd, and I quote, 'salt the earth' for her here. Even if he was forced to cop to the infidelity, he'd likely tough it out as a moment of madness. If his wife stood by him, he could survive one indiscretion. And there's no way his intimidation about nudes could be repeated, without proof he'd said it. If she reported him for that and the police checked his phone, as said, it's possible he has none. After which she's made a powerful enemy. As you said, he's popular. Everyone loves Glenn, everyone knows him. His network is vast."

Ian sighed.

"That's why I worry I shouldn't be sticking my head above the parapet either, or persuading Erin it's worth reaching out. What's that line, *You come at the king, you best not miss*? I am loath to call the scummy, duplicitous fucker a king, but the fact remains, he can do anyone a lot of damage. He can make sure you mysteriously never get an interview, a callback, an invite to the event."

"I understand the stakes for you, entirely. Without your niece's testimony, how do you suggest I research the story?"

"I was hoping if I let you know it was happening, you might have some pointers. Sorry, I'm well aware this is frustrating. I've been awake at four in the morning taking heartburn medication with the fury of it so many times—I needed to feel I'd done *something*. Now I worry I've made you victim of that something and nothing."

He pulled an apologetic face.

Bel decided she liked him. She'd turn the puzzle over and over later, like a Rubik's Cube. Right now she couldn't see why even any disaffected enemy of this elected official would tell such a story if it wasn't true. The fact it was Ian's relative, and that she wouldn't go on record, made Bel feel near certain this was authentic.

"Don't worry about not being able to give me the story on a plate," Bel said. "You've got the tip, I've got the journalism. We collaborate."

"If it helps, Erin has said she'd do the interview if she was going to be believed. You know how there was a tipping point with Weinstein, where it was no longer a question of if, but how many and who?"

He saw Bel's expression. "I'm not suggesting anything non-consensual has taken place with Glenn," he said, hastily. "I feel sure, apart from anything else, their willingness when infatuated is key to the buzz. I mean the pattern of behavior."

"I get it," Bel said. "We would need to prove it's habitual. We ideally need evidence of his activities that can surpass He Said She Said. Do you think he knows you know?"

"No, I don't think so. You can imagine I wanted to slam him against a filing cabinet by his throat at first, but that was against Erin's wishes. I took a weekend to calm down and talked it through with her, realized it's a better play for him to have no idea. If you're going to plant a knife in someone's back, don't warn them with loud footsteps."

"Do you think his wife knows he's unfaithful? Or suspects?"

"Jemima? Hmm. Tricky. They met at a club in their twenties where he already had a rep as a hell-raiser; she's told me she liked that he wasn't 'safe and boring.' That doesn't mean she'd think this is exciting. He's on a long leash, given the number of times he stays 'in town.' Maybe even if it's a 'turn a blind eye' deal, she wants him at the price of that blind eye. I should say Erin feels terrible she was involved with a married man. Terrible, and very silly."

Bel nodded. "No explanations or apology needed." She could've added: *to me.*

"I could send you a list of other women I think he might've had dalliances with. But obviously, if you made contact, I'd need you to not say who'd put you on to them," Ian continued.

"Unfortunately, I think that's a nonstarter. If I start cold-calling his former flings, someone alerts Glenn very fast. They'd not even need to care about him to do it: they'll panic, ask him what he knows about it and what to do."

"Ugh, yes, I see that. Shit. There's me falling at the first hurdle of moving undetected." Ian looked queasy again. "Also, it occurs to me that if he realizes a journalist is on to him, he might well put the pieces together. Right now he doesn't think Erin's told me, but that would change quickly if he was looking for a newly made nemesis."

"He's not untouchable," Bel said. "It only feels like he is. That's what he wants you to think and why he went full Mob Boss on your niece. He's the one who's vulnerable to a huge takedown, not her."

In the quiet moment that followed, a large crow alighted on

a tombstone nearby and commenced a creepy, plaintive cawing, as if admonishing them, startling them both.

"This must be the soul of someone one of us knows; any suggestions?" Ian said.

"I'm going with my aunt Tessa," she said. "I'm surprised it isn't smoking an Embassy Regal."

Ian smiled broadly.

"I'm glad I pulled myself together and met you."

The crow looked at them and took flight, and Bel felt quite strongly at that second that there might be a God. She didn't know if He or She had passed judgment on her, but they were definitely, in the parlance of Aaron Parry, fucking with her a little.

They swapped numbers and Ian agreed to download Signal. "Safer than WhatsApp," Bel said. "I'm going to come up with a place we can meet with seating."

He glanced back at the headstones.

"Detective Caminada used to use a pew at the Hidden Gem church to meet informers. You could whisper while looking like you were praying."

"That's brilliant! But we might get bollocked for iPhone sounds and disturbing the reverential atmosphere. I was thinking more an out-of-the-way greasy spoon where we could meet early, before work?"

"Your plan involves sausages, so you win."

Bel beamed encouragingly.

"Is this how it usually works?" Ian said, sheepishly. "Trek out to be told I might have a story for you, but you can't tell it?"

"Every story is different, it's why I love my job," Bel said.

"Diplomatic, I like it," Ian said, with a bark of laughter, and Bel sensed he'd started trusting her. "Apologies, everyone," Ian added, glancing around at the headstones.

"Where does Glenn think you are now?" Bel said.

"Oh, I'm on long-booked annual leave! What better way to spend it? I've tried very hard to stay positive and normal."

"Keep that up. I'll be in touch," Bel said to Ian, extending her hand to shake, with the uncanny sense of their having witnesses.

8

Connor had just taken his seat at the Polish restaurant when he slipped his handset out of his pocket and saw the iconic HAVE A NICE LIFE message ping in from Jen on his WhatsApp.

Can you pick up?! Your brother's on my case. No one's dead (except you, if you keep not picking up)
Seriously Con, where are you to have your phone turned off this long?

He made his excuses to Aaron and Bel, who he suspected thought he was being London-grand or a deliberate saboteur of the occasion, or both.

"I have to make a phone call. Can you get me a . . ." He scanned the menu. "Zywiec? Sorry," he said.

"Pronounced *Jhuv-ee-etch* not *Zwetch*! Sure," Aaron said, as the ever-jovial antagonist.

"One of those, yes."

The restaurant was of the easygoing, rowdy variety: open kitchen, wooden chairs and tables and a jungle of artificial plants dangling above their heads. It was the modern hipster way, and yet strongly reminded Connor of Disneyland's Rainforest Cafe in Florida from when he was a kid. Just add piped-in cicada chirruping.

The legendary Bel Macauley was tonight in a belted navy dress with flared skirt and scarlet suede ankle boots. Her hefty quantity of caramel hair was again bird's-nested and coiled into a sloppy approximation of a bun, bobby pins stabbed at haphazard points in it.

The outfit looked to Connor still woefully closer to "Sunday brunch" than "Lois Lane" but it was leagues better than the *fell out of bed like this* look of Monday. Perhaps, he had to concede, being around women in Dries Van Noten trouser suits in finance had skewed his expectations. Aaron was no Cary Grant either: he kept a rolled-up black tie in his top desk drawer for "death knocks."

He pushed through the door, calling Jen, while dodging the already inebriated pedestrian traffic of a Friday evening.

"Hi, sorry for missing you. I was sent out on a knifing in Whalley Range," he said.

"I feel like I've had a knifing in my Whalley Range after half an hour on the phone with your brother."

"Haha. What's his problem? He's coming over?"

Shaun lived in Washington, DC, with his wife, Lauren, and announcements of his return to Britain were always like this: fiercely enthusiastic and out of the blue, demanding they drop everything. Shaun's incredible impatience and buoyancy of mood had brought him much success in life, but it was sometimes like dealing with a Yorkshire terrier on cocaine.

"Yeah, he wants to come over for one of his bacchanals. Just him, Lauren's busy. I explained you're not here and we're not . . . there anymore, you know?"

Connor had a jolt, wondering if she meant as a couple.

"He was going on about trying Soho Farmhouse? Yeah, no. He's not caught on to the change of pace."

Ah. Not there financially.

"I'll talk to him, don't worry. I could draw his fire and invite him up here. I know he'll have a meltdown at heading north, but . . . Gives me company."

"Yeah, that would work, actually," Jen said, with a note of relief, having clearly already considered this option.

Connor thought about their early days together and, wincing at the mini statement afterward, how hedonistic lost weekends with his brother and sister-in-law were a thing of the past.

If he was able to say *sure, book three nights at Soho Farmhouse, sounds good, charge it to my card*, like he used to, would this be going any different? Would it fix it? Yes and no. They'd been falling out of love anyway and this had merely expedited the process. But the fact remained, trips to The Ledbury were no longer available to oil the hinges—so subtracting them meant confronting how much they'd mattered.

He knew exactly what Shaun, never one to hold back with the blunt diagnosis, would say: You Can No Longer Afford Her. Once again, on examining his feelings there was no real pang of loss. Connor was more bothered that he'd previously been affording Jen, which, call him a rash idealist, wasn't how it was supposed to work.

"If Shaun's here soon, want to come up this weekend coming?"

"I can't this weekend because I've got a work thing on Friday night in Bloomsbury, a book launch. Weekend after?"

Three weeks since he moved up? You'd not mistake this for infatuation.

"Sure," Connor said, as they shifted to awkward chitchat for the sake of the other.

"Is everything OK?" Jen said.

"Yeah, why?"

"You sound like you're in a rush to go, that's all."

"I'm having dinner with my two colleagues. I get the feeling it's about as appealing to them as it is to me, but we're pushing through it anyway."

"Who are they?"

"Guy called Aaron from the *Manchester Evening News* and a podcaster woman called Bel."

"Belle? As in *Beauty and the Beast* Belle?"

"No, as in Isabel."

"What's she like?"

He was surprised at Jen still doing due diligence on proximate women.

"Umm . . ." Connor looked at her, in animated conversation with Aaron, and assessed what courtesy he owed her. He knew they were both mocking him behind his back; the photo on his desk had been moved. The thought of them sniggering at Maurice made his stomach muscles clench. "Honestly? Hard work."

A waiting call started blipping, with the caller ID: OH FFS IT'S SHAUN. Connor had forgotten he'd changed his brother's name to that in his address book during a drunken night out.

"Argh, Shaun's calling me, want me to take it?"

"Fuck yes, thank you! Speak soon, Con."

She rang off.

"Oh, THERE you are," his brother said, with the slight vocal muddiness of a transatlantic connection.

"Here I am. You've been harassing Jennifer?"

"What's going on with you two?"

"How do you mean?" Connor said, feeling motion sick, knowing exactly what he meant.

"I'm not getting warm vibes from your girlfriend of five years' standing, you know? I am getting a Talk to Connor one instead."

Connor sighed, pain in his chest. Knowing something was ending, and that it was better off ending, didn't stop it hurting. Nor, apparently, stop the mad urge to last-minute repair it.

Even if Connor could talk himself and her back in love again, he couldn't return to being the six-figure-bonus Connor she wanted.

"I'm up in Manchester, aren't I? It's tricky to make London plans," Connor deflected. "She says you're over soon?"

"Next month, thought I'd do a Wednesday to Sunday, stop off at Mum and Dad's after. How long are you in the grim north for?"

"Three more months. Well, two months, three weeks now," Connor said, savoring the countdown. "Why don't you visit me here? It's dull as fuck for me not knowing anyone. I'm renting a one-bed flat in Salford. You can sofa surf."

He grinned, tip of tongue between teeth, despite himself.

"Renting a one-bed flat in SALFORD? THE SOFA? What is this, WORLD WAR TWO? Are we like those Sealed Knot nerd guys, doing BATTLE REENACTMENTS? I'll get on the nice-hotel search. Better yet, you can. Shortlist me the best three you've seen from drinks in their bars and I'll get you a room too. I see why Jen thinks you've lost your mind. Gotta go."

Connor found himself dismissed with speed a second time inside a minute. He glanced over at Aaron and Bel, who were looking over at him, and both quickly glanced away. In that moment, being jostled by strangers, Connor felt exquisitely lonely.

He squared his shoulders and headed back into Platzki's.

"We've ordered some starters to share, hope that's OK," Bel said, as Connor picked up his beer bottle, muttering thanks.

As he poured the beer out into a glass, he was approached by a very heavily made-up girl with a mane of curled blond hair. She was surely only about twenty-five but had enough cosmetics and facial tweakments that Connor couldn't quite judge. Northern girls were a class apart when it came to high-maintenance presentation, he was gathering. Bel Macauley was an anomaly. There were two more look-alike girls in tiny Lycra dresses held together by metal hoops, standing behind her, looking expectant.

"Excuse me, has anyone ever told you—you look like the actor Aaron Taylor-Johnson? From the film *Kick-Ass*?" the girl said in a strong Manchester accent. Connor wanted to shrivel up and disappear into his own shoes, like a *Wizard of Oz* special effect.

"Do I? Thanks," he said. *Oh, the fucking HAY the other Aaron here was going to make of this.*

"You're a very lucky girl," she said to a horrified Bel, before smiling coquettishly, flicking her hair over her shoulder, and her Sugababes trio clattering to the door.

They left a stunned, aghast silence in their wake.

"If they think you're with him, who did they think I am?!" Aaron said.

"Our son?" Connor said, before he could stop himself, and from Aaron's face, he could see mocking his height was an absolute red line.

9

Bel hadn't witnessed a cold approach by an admirer like that for a very long time, she and Shilpa having aged out of going to the kind of places where men roamed like feral jackals in Superdry. She was reluctantly forced to award extra points for the fact that Connor's fangirl assumed he was spoken for, so there was no angle. Just pure worship of pleasing masculine geometry.

The funny thing was, Connor Adams looked hideously discomfited by the praise, rather than a foul-gloating jerk, as she'd have predicted. Bel toyed with the possibility he wasn't vain, then shook herself out of this gullible notion immediately.

Her ex, Tim, used to say everyone was easier on the opposite sex than their own. "You've the A to Z for your own sex but the other one you don't know the road layout, and you get lost more easily."

Here might be a prime example. It wasn't that Connor wasn't vain, it was that he wasn't grateful. His mild affront was likely due to a sense of: *Yes, AND? Go scrub my staircases in the north wing, wench.* Entitlement that could be seen by Google Earth.

A suspicion reinforced by his jumpy response to a phone call that allegedly couldn't wait—why did Bel get the feeling he was pretending he had urgent business, to make it clear he mattered?

"Putting you through to Air Force One now, hold for the President, Mr. Adams," drawled Aaron, as they both observed Connor scowling determinedly, gripping his handset, and Bel laughed.

A few moments later she saw Connor grinning in a devilish fashion and thought, Ha, knew it. Urgent my arse. His expression was disorientating, though, a stray flash of an entirely different person. One they certainly wouldn't get to meet. He stalked back in and she felt the strain of him trying to find a socializing gear. Bel knew it was good practice to suggest this *get to know you* to people who had no other contacts in the city, but she made a mental note to Aaron to suggest Friday was too big an evening to give away.

"What made you switch careers to journalism?" Bel said, over their panchkraut and potato pancakes, and then recalled, with a heart-rate bump, she wasn't meant to know this. "Mmm . . . Toby says you were in finance?"

Quick lie, good rescue.

"Yeah. I'd always wanted to be a reporter, wrote a lot for my university newspaper and so on," Connor said.

He pushed his chestnut-brown hair back from a classically good brow. Bel watched the muscles in his jaw move and wondered how many women he'd been mean to.

"Which university?" said Aaron, eyes as keen as a hawk's over the rim of his beer glass.

Connor looked like he spotted a trap.

"Bristol," he said, and Aaron flicked a look at Bel. Aaron would have preferred Oxford, Cambridge or Durham, to suit his prejudices, she felt sure. He was working up a case file, a profile of offending.

"But I graduated with a politics and history degree, was broke in a house-share dump in London, and my older brother persuaded me it was smart to take a trainee position in the City. He was a political adviser at the time, now a political consultant in the States. I did that thing a lot of people do, I guess, try a career on for size without really thinking you're choosing it. Then you wake up ten years later and suddenly, it's who you are."

Bel nodded.

"Was there a particular moment you realized it wasn't for you?" Bel said.

The waiter arrived with more beers, and Aaron added, "Do you prefer newspapers so far?"

To no surprise whatsoever to Bel, Connor ignored her and answered Aaron.

"I now have a lot less money," he said, smiling, and Bel reflexively smiled back and then wished she hadn't. He really got under her skin; blanking her question was just the latest microaggression. This sense he was better than his company radiated from him, and based on what? The personality of a microwave and the looks of a shit *Bridgerton* brother?

"I like it a lot. It's interesting, no two days are the same, you feel like you meet people and get involved in society, somehow. Instead of merely profiting from it. What about you, what made you go into journalism?"

"My dad worked on the *Manchester Evening News*," Aaron said. "Deputy editor. And my grandad."

"Oh wow, a nepotistic Parry dynasty," Bel said.

"Family trade. Beats selling Croc charms in the Arndale, eh?" he said. "I'm not going to make any money on wikiFeet. I've got talons like a barn owl."

"What're Croc charms?" Connor said.

"Things you use to Croc-jazzle your Crocs with trinkets," Bel said. "Some are supposed to look like weird little toes poking out the holes."

"Good God!" Connor said, and Bel couldn't help smiling: Connor in his immaculate white shirt, thick creamy material that looked like cartridge paper.

"What about you, Miss Macauley? Why journalism?" Aaron said.

"I always loved writing stories as a kid. I used to make a mini newspaper with stories about everyone in the family—even splashed on catching my diabetic uncle hiding Wispas in plant pots and got him in trouble. Got the taste for controversy. After university I got a job at the *Yorkshire Post* and they let me podcast in the evenings and weekends. As long as I offered them any stories I thought they might want first, which they generally didn't. Investigations have become my thing. So when you say I'm a blogger-podcaster, dilettante bullshitter who only self-identifies as a journalist, I've got my shorthand and done my apprenticeship."

She grinned and slid a glance at Connor, who remained stonily impassive.

"I know you're proper, I just think it's a cushy gig! Can you sign yourself off for, like, weeks at a time? I'd be in the casino," Aaron said.

"It only *sounds* fun and easy. If you do deep-dive stories there's more pressure to justify it all at the end. I've recently worked on an abuse in care homes story that took five weeks and went nowhere. I can't believe Mr. If It Bleeds It Leads here would be loving it."

As the waiter brought the bill, her phone rattled against her leg in her bag.

Shilpa
You out?
Bel
What's this, the girl version of "you up"? You're HERE again, aren't you? Yes I am out, with the gentlemen from work 💀
Shilpa
Got bored so came & worked in coffee shop here for the afternoon and then a sundowner called to me. Fancy a cocktail in Schofield's? BRING THE MEN. I'm a people person.

Oh God, Bel shouldn't have shown Shilpa that photo of monstrous Connor Adams. She should've told her he looked like Danny DeVito's Penguin. Shilpa liked to insert herself into the narrative—in this case, hoping the narrative would insert itself into her.

Bel could slip away, but she saw Aaron and Connor look at her expectantly: Aaron with hopes of a second venue, and Connor with the cynicism of *let's hear your awkward exit line*.

"My friend is out for a drink near here. Anyone want one for the road?"

Distressingly and unexpectedly, both of them claimed they did.

10

Shilpa had secured a high table in the chic, wood-paneled surrounds of Schofield's, arranged herself on a mid-century leather stool with one leg wound elegantly round the other. She was in a black silk jumpsuit with Chinese dragon appliqués, hair in long bunches, lips Ruby Woo red.

She'd been *working in a coffee shop*, had she? Bel pointed to the outfit and covertly flicked her off, behind the men's backs, as she introduced them all with courteous poise.

"*Very* nice to meet you, Shilpa," Aaron said, reanimating in the presence of an attractive woman.

Aaron was thirty-one and Bel imagined the plan was to acquire a Mrs. Aaron in a timely fashion and have some mini Aarons. For all the irreverent mockery, she sensed he was quite straitlaced traditional.

"My round, what's everyone having?" Bel said.

"Another Troublemaker, please," Shilpa said, with a head tilt smile, prompting Bel to shake her head and mouth *you* . . .

"Pint of . . . Guinness," Aaron said, wincing at the minimal row of draft taps. He had northern thrift, he'd explained to Bel, and *only my nan drinks things with glacé cherries.*

Connor flipped the menu open on the table. Shilpa gazed at his hair. Bel half expected her to plunge her face into it and inhale, Hannibal Lecter–style.

"Clover Club, if that's OK, please," he said.

"Good choice," Shilpa simpered.

"Sure," Bel said, feeling pathetically grateful for the ten minutes' peace this was now going to afford her at the bar, while they bashed fruit and swizzled mixtures with long metal implements.

"Take a seat, I'll come over," said a barman as she approached, and Bel said a gritted-teeth thanks.

"How long have you known Bel, then, Shilpa?" Aaron said, as they settled into their positions.

"Since we were fifteen and both got detentions. Bel was writing letters to her French pen pal, Rodolphe, while pretending to take notes in biology and I defended her. I pointed out she was doing work, because she was writing in *French*."

"'ow you say 'le penis, je'taime,'" Aaron said.

"With this story, you know both our natures," Bel muttered, and saw the odious Connor Adams smirking. *You don't know me.*

The bunch of chauvinism-based snap judgments Connor had made about Bel weren't the same as insight. Was Connor posh? His modulated, James Bond voice said maybe, but Barking didn't sound like an area with aristocrats.

"Bloody 'ell," Aaron said, looking past them. "That's Bryant."

They followed his eyes to a nondescript thirty-something man in a polo shirt with a group of male friends.

"Sorry, I have to say hello. Murder squad detective. One of my best contacts." Aaron pushed his hands into his pockets and wandered over, with his wolfish sort of insouciance.

"So, you're not going to believe this," Shilpa said, confidentially to Bel, as if Connor weren't present. "Tim and Zack have paraded their new girlfriends on Instagram. Together. A foursome, like." Shilpa did trout-pout lips and a peace sign with one hand, then mimed a face puckered in a kiss.

Bel's palms and underarms became warm. It didn't sound like Tim and she didn't want to assimilate this news with the intern watching her. "Ah, really," she said neutrally.

Bel's ex-long-term-boyfriend, Tim, and Shilpa's ex-husband, Zack, had become friends in the three years or so span when the relationships ran concurrent, Bel splitting with Tim six months ago and Shilpa and Zack, six months before that. On the unbelievably horrible day when Bel ended things with Tim, he accused her of "following Shilpa out the door."

She suspected that mistaken idea had partly fueled what sounded like this uncharacteristic fit of passive aggression from him, because he'd know Radio Shilpa would broadcast it.

Tim wasn't an extremely online person. He only ever used Instagram when he and his friends wanted photo evidence of reaching the summit at Scafell Pike.

"A champion two-man trolling, like something out of *Sex and the City*, and you missed it thanks to your policy of being invisible online," Shilpa said.

Bel was distinctly uncomfortable at Connor Adams gathering all these acorns about her. He was pretending to intently browse his phone and mind his business.

"Well, good luck to them," Bel continued, "I've got no right to complain."

"I exercise my right to complain. I think it's tacky, crass and uncalled-for. I don't want their antics rubbed in my face like a dog being toilet trained with its mess. Me and Zack said vows in front of two flavors of God. I've not so much as soft launched a Hinge date yet, out of respect for what we had."

Bel always forgot Shilpa's metabolism of alcohol: she took off like the Concorde, then hit altitude and started cruising at a level. They were currently in the "nose cone pointed upward, rapid ascent" phase.

"You could not follow Zack on Instagram, am I thinking too logically?"

"Yes, you are thinking too logically," Shilpa said. "Zack and I are locked in a fake-amicable follow-back to keep tabs on one another, while demonstrating we're not bothered. We're playing 4D chess, liking each other's posts immediately to show we're not pussies with each other on mute too. He's the first view on all my Stories. I at least try to wait until his have been up an hour."

"But why?" Bel said. *"You left him."*

She said these last three words in a stagy hush, which was ridiculous given the only person listening in was Connor, who could hear what she was saying with perfect clarity. It was more to communicate *can we not* to Shilpa, which was barely less futile, as Shilpa was in a vigorous *yes, we shall* mode.

"There is an aggravating aspect which may *pique your interest*," Shilpa said, tightening her jumpsuit belt, which Bel mimed throttling her with.

"My interest is stubbornly un-piqued," Bel said.

"Prepare to feast on your own words," Shilpa said. "Pique incoming."

11

"Connor"—Shilpa tapped his arm—"back me up on this. Do you follow any of your exes?"

Bel squirmed. She didn't want this man to know her middle name, let alone her personal life dramas. *Why oh why didn't she leave them at Platzki's! Damn her nice manners.*

"Uhm . . ." Connor paused. "Yeah, I think so? I've been with my girlfriend five years and I'm trying to remember who qualifies as an ex that I'm in touch with."

"Awww, how romantic. No one matters now, before her? What's she called?" Shilpa said, not missing a beat receiving the Has a Girlfriend information.

"Jennifer. To be honest, it's more that I'm casting back to my mid-twenties and I had nothing very settled before Jen. Yeah . . ." Bel was glad not to be in Connor's mind's eye as his brow furrowed with the effort of recollection. "One or two, I think?"

Was Bel imagining that Connor was being far nicer, and gentler of voice, to Shilpa than he'd ever been to her?

"There you go," Shilpa said, turning to Bel. "It's the etiquette now. But there's an aggravating factor . . . Ooh, thank you."

The barman presented her with her Troublemaker, from the tray he'd set down. Had she eaten? Bel wondered.

Connor sipped his Clover Club, said thank you to Bel and returned to pretending he had things to inspect on his iPhone.

"I know her. I know Zack's date! Nicky! She worked with him, she was the . . ." Shilpa made air quotes. "'Funny colleague frenemy.' Beware the Funny Colleague Frenemy, a wolf in sheep's clothing. *Oh, she sends me memes and calls me a wanker. Nothing to see here.* It made me wonder . . ." Shilpa paused, as Bel was weighing up how hard to tell her off later. "Think you also know Tim's date? Because that takes the absolute piss, if so. That's sending a declaration of war that shall not go unanswered."

"Who can say?" Bel said, knocking back a stiffening quantity of a Woo Woo.

"You, of course!" Shilpa said, fumbling her phone out and pausing. "Unless you don't want to see?"

Bel gave a performative sigh. If she snapped Can we save this until later? then she was admitting it was embarrassing and/or emotive. Somehow, in front of the coolly supercilious Connor Adams, that was unbearable. She wanted to maintain tough, bulletproof journo Bel.

"Show me, then we can change the subject."

Shilpa presented her screen to Bel with the image of a double date squeezing into the frame. The phone was angled to capture a restaurant table with four wines on it, everyone with that look of a kid on a camping trip, excited to be included. There were two familiar faces, the men's . . . *Wait, scratch that: three.*

"Fuck, that's Rhiannon!" Bel blurted, despite herself.

"I knew it!" Shilpa said, equal parts outraged and delighted at the vindication. "Who's Rhiannon?"

Bel gulped. "Childhood friend of his. Really lovely. We've been on holiday with her several times. We're still in touch, actually . . . or, we were. Shit!"

The hard liquor was hitting as the hard intel was hitting—it was a heady mix. She was calling up her memories of Rhiannon, of Tim's responses to her and vice versa, and reclassifying it all as slow-burn attraction. As something stifled by circumstance. Bel had spent so much time around them as long-standing platonic acquaintances, and all the while . . . ? Bel didn't want Tim back, but Shilpa was right, you could care without having feelings.

"The bare treachery! They've both acquired people we know, to get at us! And dropped this in a selfie bomb! If it's even *real*. The question is, do we respond with proportionate force? Also, Belly, I'm just going to say it because you never will, she's nowhere near as hot as you."

Bel muttered indistinctly as a new level of self-consciousness was unlocked, and Shilpa continued: "Connor, what do you think?" She turned her phone to him.

Oh GOD. "SHILPA," Bel hissed, properly furious-embarrassed now.

"What would I do if my ex was posting being with someone new, who I happened to know?" Connor said smoothly, and Bel was both utterly mortified and powerfully relieved at his deftly sidestepping the question.

"Yes. And she's your ex-wife. *Recent* ex-wife," Shilpa said, laying it on thick. Bel might remind Shilpa she'd said she and Zack were "as likely to reconcile as Johnny and Amber" by the end.

"Are the other women here your friends?" Connor said, inclining his head at her phone.

"No, *their* friends," Bel said, intervening before Shilpa could craft any more theater.

"Then, if I thought the ex was doing it to get my attention, I wouldn't give them any."

"Thank you," Bel said, finally having a use for Connor's chilliness.

"I'm going to avenge it thricefold. You can't let men go around freely doing psychological abuses on your apps," Shilpa said, and Connor smiled at her, amused.

Bel wasn't imagining it: the mind games–playing shape-shifter Adams was leagues nicer with Shilpa, and to prove it, stayed for another round that he insisted on buying.

Aaron rejoined them and regaled them with tales of Manchester's stupidest criminals. As an anecdotalist, he was a five-star performer and his laconic accent made it even funnier.

Despite the rocky start, Shilpa's pleasure in being there knitted them all together briefly, as if they were a quartet of old friends; she brought relaxed warmth where Bel was wary inhibition.

As they arrived back at her flat—because, of course, Shilpa had left "a few overnight things last time, just in case"—pleasantly but not excessively inebriated, Bel remembered why Shilpa always got away with her transgressions: she made everything fun.

12

Later, Bel lay awake and processed Tim and Rhiannon.

It was taking some getting used to.

It was ridiculous to feel this upset, really; Bel and Tim would be no more or less finished than they were already if he attended masked ball orgies, or lit church candles under an Isabel shrine and pledged a decade's celibacy.

What made Bel's stomach churn was that he must've known she'd find out this way, and knew it'd hurt all the more. It was a message, posted second class: *You don't deserve to hear it from me. Does it sting? It should.* Knowing that he was still sad and angry enough to do something spitefully out of character was painful. Someone was alive in the world and hating you, someone who used to bring you your morning coffee and call you "Mac the Wife." It *really* hurt. She'd made a good man bad.

Tim was the son of her mum's best friend; they'd grown up knowing of one another's existence. She, her brother Miles, Tim's sister Verity and Tim always called themselves "honorary cousins." It had burst into unexpected attraction one drunken family barbecue in their late twenties, when the security of falling for the nice guy who'd been there all along made perfect sense. But some part of Bel had always suspected she'd outgrow the size of what they had, and that gnawed at her. She'd let him play copilot, crashed the plane and run from the wreckage. If what she'd done wasn't cruel, why did it feel so cruel?

Not only that, there was collateral. It had been a fairy tale when it united the two families and a political nightmare when

Bel ended it. Tim's parents saw their son was in bits over it and responded emotionally; Bel's mother labored to support her daughter and absorb the fallout with stoic neutrality. Tim's parents had been exceptionally kind to them all during Bel's father's illness and death—Bel's family had spent several Christmas Days at the Hornbys when they were all too devastated to face their former, four-person rituals—and she desperately wanted to keep the peace. Tim was so burned by the loss of Bel that he vaguely resented her mum and brother Miles for still having her.

They'd finished last autumn and got through their first Christmas with the Boxing Day get-together, stuck to opposite walls, both too stubborn/principled to cry off. Bel had moved to Manchester at the start of the year.

They couldn't avoid each other forever, though—Tim's sister Verity was getting married at the end of the summer and they'd have to see each other then. It was nonnegotiable; her mother had secured a promise from Bel: *No cold war, you must both still be involved in family celebrations, set the precedent now.*

It turned out Bel would likely be tackling Tim and Rhiannon's big coupledom debut, and she was surprised by how daunting that felt. The Hornbys would form a tight and defiant mob, and Bel would be imagined to be getting her just deserts as they fussed over Rhiannon. There would be a schadenfreude of *Well, she broke his heart, but looks like karma did its job.*

Tim had completely and totally adored Bel, cherished the very bones of her, and she'd ruined it and devastated him by stopping adoring him in return. She knew no one would ever feel for her as he had, you couldn't recapture the innocent intensity of your first serious relationship. She didn't want him back, but she did still love him, and therein lay the paradox that left her crying in the dark.

ALCOHOL ALWAYS GAVE CONNOR INSOMNIA, which was why he'd given it up toward the end of the last career horrors, when he needed all the energy he could get.

He sat up, propped on pillows in the dark, illuminated only by his phone, and typed Shilpa's name into the Instagram search bar. He'd seen her surname, Gupta, when she'd shown him profiles on her phone.

Tonight had been grimly hilarious: Bel's accomplice had been a lovely girl, really easy to talk to, open and witty. However, unfortunately Bel clearly had not had time to deliver the Don't Bother With the Arsehole Intern, He's Trash memo, so she had sat rigid, awkward and lightly fuming throughout, until booze took over.

Why did she and Parry think the minor rank they pulled in that hole of an office was so important? Though Connor didn't doubt Bel would dislike him for all kinds of other reasons outside of it too. He could sense who she thought he was, some stuck-up, rich elitist, and that everything he said and did was interpreted as confirmation.

Ugh, speaking of Parry, he didn't know if Bel genuinely didn't notice or chose not to notice his drooling. Bel, periodically turning on her stool to speak to Shilpa, pulled the fabric of her dress taut against her chest, and Connor saw Aaron's eyes drift downward so many times he'd wanted to slap him himself.

Shilpa's online presence was predictably exuberant, though as she'd alluded, he could see no sign of her best friend in her available photographs.

It wasn't Shilpa he was interested in, it was this Tim, mention of whom had clearly blindsided Bel Macauley. He couldn't picture a Macauley boyfriend pick whatsoever, and 1:38 a.m. had a low bar for time-wasting curiosity. There was a reason he suited reporting, and Bel wasn't the only one who could conduct investigations.

Although Shilpa was the one who was supposed to be upset by their exes being coupled up, and Bel indifferent, Connor had a strong intuition the exact opposite was true.

Bel had changed color and Connor could see her frowning on it later in the evening, when she thought no one was looking.

He found a Tim Hornby in Shilpa's followers list and hoped, if he was the right perp, that he had a similarly loose approach to privacy. Sure enough, Tim's account was public, the most recent picture of a mid-thirties man in a khaki anorak, copyposing the stance of an Anthony Gormley statue. He got a firm sense of Bel's former significant other. He was good-looking in a lopsided grin, good teeth, friendly kind of way: the obligatory Neck Oil–drinking, Arcade Fire–listening, beard-haver sort of dude. Solid dad material, worked in the public sector and rode a Lime bike home from a lads' night out.

He was not quite who Connor expected, somehow, though he wasn't sure exactly why: Too goofily unassuming, maybe? Bel, by contrast, was all about assumptions.

Deep in the archives, Connor was startled to trip over evidence of Bel, dated four years ago. He got the feeling an embittered Tim Hornby on a deleting rampage had accidentally failed to expunge it from the record. It was a Christmas dinner party, paper crown hats, Bel's chin propped on her hand, eyes rolled upward: angelic. Tim gazing sidelong at her, the poor sod looking smitten.

@belmac was a defunct link. Wait, who was the fresh-faced farm girl next to her, name in the list of tags? Rhiannon? Wasn't she the interloper? Shilpa wasn't mates rates wrong. Your eyes went straight to Bel in the tableau, she was strikingly attractive: skin glowing like alabaster. Her combination of scoop-necked top and balcony bra a little distracting, even to a man of Connor's taste and maturity. Lovely cleavage, shame about the personality.

Connor left the page and idly clicked on his rarely used Facebook. He had been recently tagged with Jen, which led him to her profile. He paused: her green "online" dot was lit up—active? Jen went to bed very early and was an "out as soon as her head hits the pillow" person who liked to go for runs at dawn. Connor stared at it. It was the tiniest of clues and yet because he knew her so well, and the context so intimately, it felt quite a hefty one. Jennifer was awake late-messaging with someone, or doing research, like him.

He quickly shut the screen down and was left staring contemplatively at the shadows in a large portrait of a morose John Lennon in his rented bedroom. He was more curious about who Jen might be interacting with than anything. There it was, the hammer blow: if he could feel nothing about this, they were flatlining. He theoretically tried out various options of single men in their orbit, to see if, as per Shilpa and Bel, knowing the guy could stir anything up. Nope.

Would it actually make sense to finish things while he was up here and Jen was down there? Was it fair or desirable to let her travel for an ordeal of a conversation they could have on the phone? Would she make a thing of his having ended it by phone?

Could Connor face handling their finale while in this place of miserable, lardy-pastry perdition?

No, he was chickening out. Better to let Jen admit she'd met someone else, which would take the bitter recriminations out of it—then Connor got to be magnanimous—or wait until he was back in London to deal with it.

He startled at an eerie, monkey-like whooping out in the dark, very near his flat, and thought, with teenage petulance: I hate it here. He ignored the voice in his head that replied: *You hate it there too.*

13

"Don't you worry junk food is going to destroy your looks?" Aaron said to Bel, as she, unobserved, she thought, nibbled on her ice cream the following Wednesday. "My sister's always on about UPFs. She caused a ruckus telling her mate at a baby shower that the sugar in red velvet cupcakes causes cancer. It's that thing . . . hyper . . . what it's called?"

"Hyperactive?" Connor said.

"Hyper palatability!"

"Firstly, it's one mint Magnum," Bel said. "Secondly, nice sexism—would you say that to a man? Did you time travel here as an ad exec from Sterling Cooper?"

"It was a compliment in disguise, I'm only mithering," Aaron said.

"Yeah, wrapped like a tenner round a brick through a window." Connor was smirking. That sight roused Bel further.

"Also, bad science. Looking good as you age is genetics and sunblock. But *they* don't tell you that, because they can't charge you anything for the first or much for the second."

"Who's they?" Aaron said.

"Big Celery."

Aaron hooted with laughter and Bel was annoyed at herself for being gratified.

"I don't hold with your body being a temple. You should enjoy it. They wear out in eighty years, either way. Your body is a theme park," Bel said.

"A great ride," Aaron replied.

"Ewww. Can you send me the top six paragraphs of your motorcyclist death story? Toby wants to see if there's a longer piece in NHS response times in the northwest."

"Will do, doll."

What was all this newfound fuss over her being conspicuously attractive? Was Aaron trying to embarrass or intimidate her? Bel didn't think she was a sight, nor did she believe herself *owt special,* as Yorkshire had it. At the right time in her menstrual cycle, in obliging lighting, she could pass as reasonably enticing.

But she was no trophy girl—Connor Adams, for example, was certain to think she looked like a toe. She suspected Aaron was responding to the zoo-like captivity of their outpost office; she was the only lady panda he could mate with.

"Getting old is no sausage party, right enough. My dad always says the young never think they're going to be old, and only the unluckiest ones are right," Aaron said, trying on a philosophical air.

"Fuck," Bel said, putting her wooden stick down on the wrapper, "remind me never to risk the psychological impacts of 'having a snack' in here again."

Connor's mouth twitched a smile again. Bel couldn't tell if it was amusement or sarcasm, as usual. Laughing with her or at her.

"Hey, Adams," Aaron said, checking his laptop screen, "you're up. Reported threatening behavior incident in Victoria Park, some fucker with a plastic pirate's cutlass, the DI tells me. He's wearing a bedsheet as a cape and shouting about 'spreading the word of Saint Cuthbert's potency,' so sounds like a psych ward job rather than counterterrorism's. Fancy getting down there with your notebook?"

"I mean, 'fancy' might be overstating it, 'prepared to do it' more accurate," Connor said, finishing his coffee in one gulp as he stood up, opening his taxi app with one smooth movement in the other hand.

After he'd departed, Aaron said, "He's about as much fun as food poisoning on a ferry, but fair play, he's a hard worker. Every crap job I throw at him, he takes without arguing. Cicely woulda filed a harassment complaint if I'd asked her to go to Pret."

Bel noticed a notification from Signal, which turned out to be Ian confirming their meeting tonight.

It was the result of her prompt to him over the weekend. She was turning and turning the Rubik Cube's puzzle, trying to get the click. She'd sent:

Bel
Hi Ian. Quick Q. Where did GB take Erin for their private times together? Thinking he's too famous for hotels, unless he was hiding in cleaning carts?
Ian
I asked her, and her answer was extremely interesting. So much so, I think it's worth us meeting again.
Bel
You know I said rendezvous at a greasy spoon? How about the Hong Kong tearoom version, the Happy Valley Cafe opposite Strangeways? It's such a wild-card choice that it's surely unlikely we'll see anyone we know, and having done thorough background reading, I can confirm there's incredible toasted sandwich options.
Ian
It's as if you know me.

If she was honest, Bel half suspected that the mayor story would fizzle. Not through any bad faith, or untruth, but because Ian was rightly scared of being unemployed in midlife as a whistleblower. Erin would move on, or move away, as twenty-four-year-olds did.

Bel had it filed away for when something resurfaced, because one thing she knew for sure, men like Glenn Bailey didn't stop.

She'd ingested so much about the Mayor now, consumed so many newspaper reports and such a ton of social media, she felt less like an amateur sleuth and more like an obsessive fan. They were in a parasocial relationship.

Great day meeting the staff and patients at Wythenshawe Hospital

Pint of the 0 percent black stuff! Thanks to The Freemount. Much needed ☘

Honored to be asked to cut the ribbon on this new sports center which will be a fabulous resource for Heaton Park

When you reelected me I pledged to address the rise in antisocial behavior around Piccadilly Gardens

This refuge's work is vital for women and children fleeing domestic abuse

Every time, Bel squinted at the weathered, lean, trustworthy face beneath streaky strawberry-blond hair, and tried to put it together with a man who told a twenty-four-year-old intern he'd kept her nudes as blackmail.

14

Bel was aware that shifting from the acoustics of a cemetery to the highly confined space of the Happy Valley Cafe could seem illogical, if not reckless. It only had about two dozen seats and was one of those tiny "food people finds" that trainspotter bloggers would make a special trek out for. Its clientele was 95 percent local fans and curious passersby, and 5 percent restaurant bloggers taking flat lay photos of Spam and cheesy fries.

Its privacy was not in its social distancing, but in location and relative obscurity. When Bel entered and saw every other customer on this early evening service was Chinese, she felt confident she was right: the probability of a surprise encounter was very low.

She was shown a table, ordered a milk tea with red bean and waited for Ian. Only when he was fifteen minutes late did she consider he might be a no-show: except, she was absolutely certain Ian was determined to see this through if he could.

Bel couldn't help it, her storyteller's brain spooled forward to discovering he'd met with an untimely and accidental end: What would she do? *Get a grip! You're not a bit part in a major new BBC drama for the autumn, Macauley.*

All the same, Bel was pleased and relieved when he hurried in, with apologies about having been unused to the traffic snarl in this direction. He seemed anxious at the four walls, but Bel soothed him: "Look around. No one's interested in us."

They ordered deep fried chicken and beef ho fun and, with

Ian doing a safety glance at their indifferent company, he began, after a deep breath and in a low voice: "So. He took Erin to a house. Have you heard of a local businesswoman called Gloria Kendrick?"

"No, but I'm only recently in Manchester, as I said."

"OK. She's a property entrepreneur, reputation for ruthlessness, stinking rich. Lives out at Alderley Edge. Gloria is a friend, an ex-girlfriend of Glenn's going back to their college years. You can trace a lot of the most scummy, badly maintained rental housing in this city back to portfolios she's offloaded for millions, proper 'getting wealthy off misery' stuff. Nowadays her property interests are on the Continent, where you suspect regulations are more lax. As well as the McMansion she lives in here, she's got a house in Didsbury, and a wine bar nearby called Ci Vediamo she's gifted to her daughter Amber to run."

"Right . . . Didsbury . . ." Bel's knowledge of the suburb didn't stretch beyond *very wealthy leafy suburb, quite "media people."*

"Victorian detached, very nicely done out, an Airbnb otherwise, dressy hen do's and the like. The periods it's not hired, it's made available to friends and family. Enter one Glenn Bailey. I will send you the link."

Bel put her fork down.

"They know what he's doing? They're enablers?" Bel said. This was promising. The mark himself could be well protected but those around him, they surely offered potential ways in?

"Bingo. It takes a village to be this successful a scum bucket. The Airbnb bookings are managed solely by Amber, the daughter, who keeps an iPad just for the purpose, presumably to keep it clear and hygienic from prying bar staff eyes. It's under lock and key at the bar. If you can get into that iPad, you're going to find proof of Glenn's visits."

Bel quelled the rising tide of hope as she thought it through.

"Assuming he's not in there under a pseudonym and no money's changing hands . . . and proving he's stayed at the house isn't proof he's with women."

"Well, the plot thickens. Erin went there with Glenn three times. On the second night he got quite panicky about the doorbell being rung in the dead of night. When he went down to answer it, nobody was there. Probably local drunks, but guilty people are easily spooked. He summoned Amber and she said don't worry, we can check on it with Ring Video. Not only that, they told him they keep months and months of Ring footage, stored in the iCloud. A hundred and eighty days, she said. I'm guessing they think it's useful to keep tabs on the Airbnb visitors."

"This is on the iPad?"

"Yes. An iPad with rainbows on the cover. Glenn has been so, so careful but he didn't anticipate Erin witnessing this conversation. Get footage of Glenn arriving and leaving with women from that doorbell video, and you have your proof. I'm confident he's a frequent enough offender that you'll see him on more than one visit. Erin's trips were within the time frame. If you have that proof, my niece says she will do an interview. You've got the whole exclusive."

Bel now scanned round the room at weeknight diners digging into soup noodles, indifferent to their conspiracy.

"How am I getting into the iPad? Apple devices can't be jailbroken by the Feds."

Ian patted his mouth with a paper napkin.

"That I don't know. Ask her? Appeal to female solidarity?"

"Hmmm," Bel said. "A cold approach by a journalist accusing her of harboring a high-profile offender is going to get a very fast no. And once I've done that, she'll report back and they'll eventually work out who must've seen the iPad and talked to the press."

"Oh God, yes. That's an aim and fire at one's own foot. Let's not. You see, that's why I worry I shouldn't be attempting this."

"Don't worry. This is why we plan."

Bel frowned. There had to be a way.

"I suppose, being very basic," she said, "if I was seated next to Amber when she was putting the passcode in? Everyone has passcode protection but not many people are careful to shield those numbers in situations where they don't think anyone's watching."

"That might work!"

"'Might' is pulling a lot of weight there," Bel said. "My mission is to become Amber's friend, locate the iPad, get a glimpse of her opening the iPad and subsequently get access to this device to download footage to a second device, undetected. Within whatever time we have left on the one-hundred-and-eighty-day scrub and rerecord cycle."

"Reckon you could?" Ian said.

"I don't think I definitely couldn't," Bel said, grinning, and Ian grinned back. They too had a Fun Uncle and Mischievous Niece kind of spark. Nevertheless, Bel felt the guilt-squirm of what she'd be doing to this Amber. It was the Mayor and Amber's mother as targets, though, she told herself. As the up-on-himself intern said, she might've gotten bar staff sacked investigating Ask for Amy. If you only followed leads where you could 100 percent control the consequences, you'd not follow any.

"I have much belief in you. This dinner is on me, by the way. Also, I didn't know your age before we met. Amber is early thirties . . . ?"

"I'm thirty-four," Bel said.

"Perfect. I've been up close with the Kendrick dynasty at various fundraisers and functions. They're all social climbers, collectors. From what Erin says, I get the feeling they like fresh blood, people who look the part. Make yourself seem like a fun acquisition and I'd think you'd be invited to the regular lock-ins and part of the club in no time."

"Hmmm. But no one's trusting a journalist, whatever she says she's working on," Bel said. "I guess, if I wasn't a journalist . . ."

"You'd be undercover?" Ian asked.

"Think I have to. If I'm going to do an undercover job, doing it while I'm a newcomer in this city and virtually no one knows me makes sense. It's probably my one spin."

"I'm starting to realize just how big my ask is here, and I never thought it was small to begin with," Ian said.

"Talk to no one about this except Erin," Bel said, folding her arms and chewing her lip. "And please check *she* isn't talking about it either. For this proposal to work there needs to be no gossip getting back to Didsbury."

"Oh, I give you my word. Erin is extremely conscientious."

"Going undercover isn't illegal," Bel said, carefully, her food temporarily abandoned while her mind whirred. "But the ethical considerations to prove public interest are pretty significant. You have to be sure there's no other way to obtain the information. You need to show receipts, you need a strong reason to be digging in that spot. I know 'you need proof in order to get proof' sounds logically impossible, which is why newspapers don't send many people undercover. Or not that they admit to."

"I can see that. This is where I defer to your expertise," Ian said.

"Could we try to jigsaw together anything at all your niece has that would support what she's saying, obviously in strict 'need to know' confidence? Screenshots, anything circumstantial that links Amber and Gloria to Glenn. Debits at the wine bar if she bought drinks there. Messages she might've sent to friends at that time about the affair. I'll need that if I'm going to convince my editor."

"I'll explain to Erin and gather everything I can," Ian said.

Bel knew, in her bones, if she could get the sign-off from Toby—a substantial *if*—she was going ahead with this. It was high-stakes and terrifying and got her blood pumping, but more than that: if Erin's story was true, she had to do right by her.

"I hugely appreciate your adventurous spirit," Ian said, as they polished off a shared dessert.

"No worries," Bel said, realizing at that point she had long ago forgotten to consider Ian could be working some other angle. Aunt Tessa would be raising an eyebrow at her. "If nothing else, we've found out that white bread, condensed milk and peanut butter was the killer dessert we were missing in our lives."

"*Killer*'s the right word, I feel prediabetic already," Ian said.

"This Elvis is leaving the building," Bel said, hooking her bag over her shoulder. "Stay in touch."

15

"I can't help thinking Ring Video is going to furnish quite a few stories in the coming years. It's already being cited in divorces. Maybe this is the first famous scandal we break via doorbell surveillance."

At the end of a lot of talking on her part, Bel felt she should finish by holding her hands palms up and saying: *And that's our show.*

Instead, after a pause, she finished lamely: "Over to you."

"Hmm." Toby swiveled on his chair, as was his wont, in the rectangular frame of Bel's laptop, which was set on her dining room table. The meeting the following day was deemed considerably too sensitive for the usual office-based Teams session.

"You know, I never want to be 'The No Guy' as far as you're concerned, Bel. Very much not what I brought you in for, you know that. I asked for ambitious and you gave me 'ambitious' right off the bat."

Bel smiled and thought she didn't mind the "no"—this was always going to be a long shot—but a leisurely preamble to it might get on her tits. The same way defense lawyers felt it was a bad sign if juries returned quickly, Toby asking for a meeting within twenty-four hours of her proposing this project seemed to forecast a swift refusal.

One of the newspaper's lawyers was sitting in on their session—that's how she knew for sure it was a big ask. Albert Double Barrel (Bel had forgotten the precise name) was the kind of posh you didn't think really existed outside British romantic comedies hoping to sell to the American market. He wore a brocade waistcoat and often had a Tupperware with him of apple slices *from my orchard*. When Bel told Aaron this, he said, "Next time I'm in with him I'm going to tell him my Creme Eggs are from my chocolate hen."

"There's a high bar here, and we are tantalizingly close, but we haven't cleared it," Toby said. "If Bailey turns out to be a common or garden-variety one-off cheating husband, and we went to these invasive lengths to prove it . . . Well, sex scandals ain't what they used to be. You know, we live in the age of 'negotiated ethical nonmonogamy.' Boris moved into No. 10 without answering questions about how many children he has, or having got round to marrying the next wife. The danger is that the Mayor putting it about is greeted with a massive So What? His wife says 'actually, we've got an understanding,' and they become the first high-profile poster couple for polyamory. I can see the Twitter heat and backlash pieces now. Meanwhile, we've got IPSO up our arses demanding to know why our undercover reporter insinuated their way into innocent bystanders' lives and hacked their tablets, all to show that a married couple are unconventional. We're going after a rich family with the resources to sue, at that."

"But Glenn Bailey isn't simply sleeping with other women," Bel said, trying to keep the emotion out of her voice. "He's specifically preying on younger women where there's a power imbalance, lying, exploiting and discarding them along with the Durex. Women don't feel they can say no to the boss, or they trust them in a way that makes grooming much easier. You don't realize it's all been manipulation until, as Erin described, you are dispensed with. It might not be illegal, but it *is* immoral and abusive, and he's the mayor."

"I agree entirely"—Toby pushed his glasses up to rub his eyes—"but we have the word of a twenty-four-year-old who none of us have even met saying this, off the record. The only way we prove this isn't one lapse of judgment by the Mayor is your stab at espionage. And if we can't prove it, or find it's not true, it's a fuck of a risk. Undercover 101: you need to know you're definitely going to find the thing you're looking for. I feel like we're far from sure."

"OK, so . . . I thought you might say this," Bel said, hoping her gamble of holding this back would pay off. "I then took a different tack and thought, What if we treated the *enablers* as the target? I looked into Gloria Kendrick's business interests. In 2023, she and her husband were arrested and questioned on suspicion of fraud. The Kendricks were involved in a scheme where would-be investors were approached to purchase apartments in Ibiza off-plan, with the promise of charging high rents. The projects were never completed, investors lost a fortune. British police running a fraud investigation called Operation Foxhole teamed up with the Spanish authorities to try to nail them for it. The Kendricks' lawyers negotiated plea deals in return for suspended sentences. Sending you the links . . ."

She prodded her phone to ping Toby's phone.

Bel could see she had Albert Double Barrel's full attention now too.

"Glenn Bailey is legacy friends with her, and sure, none of us are responsible for what our old uni circle is up to, even politicians," Bel said. "But our mayor using one of her properties for illicit sex and therefore being wide open to blackmail? That's clear public interest. That's Profumo not only sleeping with a showgirl, but the showgirl also sleeping with the Russian attaché. I'd argue that if we find Glenn's staying there regularly we don't even need the girls for it to be a story. Why's he there, full stop? Then what happens when a Kendrick planning permission controversy crosses the Mayor's desk?"

There was a lengthy pause. Toby pressed and depressed his ballpoint pen with rapid clicks.

"What if we photograph him going in and out of this place? A lot easier."

"I thought about that too. Firstly, you'd need someone there every night of the month to catch him; secondly, Google Street View tells me the door is well shielded from the street, so you're going to get a grainy image of *man walks down public thoroughfare*. Thirdly, he's very jumpy, as you'd expect. If someone is snapping away taking his picture, twenty quid says he realizes, and he never visits the place again. He made Erin follow him after a fifteen-minute wait—he knows what he's doing."

"He's the full twenty-four-carat shit, isn't he?" Toby said.

"He's a real leading man love interest," Bel agreed.

Toby smiled and she felt it possible that he genuinely liked her, in a way he perhaps hadn't taken to Aaron, and this might help her case.

"What will you do if you befriend this Amber and get nowhere near her iPad? Trying to get eyes on a passcode is a tall order."

"I'll give up," Bel said. "The most underrated tool in the investigator's toolkit."

"Albert, what say you?" Toby said.

Albert put his snack box down and cleared his throat.

"I didn't like our chances when it was the infidelity alone because, as you say, we're not a tabloid, and playing away from home is covered under 'right to a private life.' But if he's taking undeclared favors from a convicted criminal, that's indisputable corruption. As Miss Macauley says, that makes the exploitative intercourse a 'nice to have,' not a necessity. Not nice to *have*, you know what I mean. I've got a four o'clock meeting, by the way, Toby, not to be a pain," he said.

"To be clear, as our lawyer, you're green-lighting this?"

"I am."

The virtual air between London and Manchester hung heavy, yet Bel felt confident she'd turned this around.

Toby sucked in a breath, and chair-swung again.

"All right. Six weeks maximum of being Amber Kendrick's new gal pal, with this as a weekly check-in. No covert recording devices for now, let's see if we can get hold of the RingVideo and get Mr. Bailey on the ropes. Stick anything you need on expenses, but don't take the piss. If Amber wants to bond during a holiday in Capri, steer her toward Las Iguanas fishbowl cocktails instead."

Bel laughed. She logged off, high on the fumes of unexpected victory. Still open on her screen were Amber Kendrick's Instagram and Facebook accounts, and the wine bar's website.

Now she had to become someone's new best friend overnight. Her mind wandered to Shilpa's winning familiarity in Schofield's Bar, as a collector of people, what Bel once called her platonic promiscuity. And she thought, *There's* your role model.

Actually, that gave Bel an idea.

16

Bel stared at herself in the mirror after a third reapplication of Lisa Eldridge's Sunday Matinée lipstick and repeated the internal mantra: *Yourself, but different.*

With no experience at creating alter ego identities, Bel decided her point of reference was her belief that the most convincing lies are part truth.

Ergo, Bella Niven (her mother's maiden name) wasn't some parody of an Amber Kendrick friend, but a special-event Bel with the volume turned up.

Bella was far more overtly girly and—*whisper it*—it had been quite fun to play fancy dress. Today she'd had a salon blow dry with heat-tonged curls pushed back from her face with a bejeweled headband. Her makeup, courtesy of a wedding trial session in Selfridges, was a full face with kittenish thin liquid eyeliner flicks and a rosy mouth. Her "It's a boy!" baby-blue nails and toes had been painted by a professional.

For outfits, she'd dug into the section of her wardrobe she thought of as special event and repurposed it to weekday. Ditto footwear. She practiced traversing the apartment in a pair of three-inch lace-up boots. Usually an "activity ring closing" walker, she'd have to become an Uber-to-the-door princess.

Finally, she'd rented a YSL bag on a thirty-day lease: the idea was she'd keep switching to give the impression of a sizable collection.

None of this was strictly necessary, of course, except Bel thought a costume would be extremely helpful when playacting. In order to behave differently, it helped to *look* different.

Her squeamishness about the deceit was kept hidden under these layers. Erin's interests trumped Amber's—yet who had made Bel the judge? Only Bel. Heavy was the head that wore the bejeweled headband.

She had also studied the women of Amber Kendrick's world, and this attire should see her fit right in. God bless those who set their social media profiles public—the harvest for Bel was plentiful. As with Glenn, she felt she'd already met Amber.

Her friends were shiny, spendy, rosé wine with ice cubes in glasses held aloft for the photo clink, Palma-villa holidaying, animal-print-wearing, Pomapoo dog– and Ragdoll cat–owning, noisy party girls.

Amber herself was a little sleeker and sportier than her glam squad coven: long balayage hair often worn pulled back, Grace Kelly severe, from small, balanced features, her long, stretchy dresses with cutouts showcasing a lithe figure, her feet regularly in immaculate Superga sneakers.

Bel wondered if it was because her friends aspired to a lifestyle, and Amber had always had it. If you're born into high-rolling, you don't need to dress like a WAG to prove anything. It could also be because running a bar involved being on your feet a lot.

Bel gleaned all this from Instagrams of Amber gripping an Aperol Spritz with a fluoro manicure, or posing in fairy wings, Burberry anorak and body glitter at Glastonbury, or hanging baubles on a department store–size Christmas tree. In a lineup, Bel could also now confidently identify her prematurely silver-haired fox boyfriend, Rick, usually seen with their pug, Gertie. The chatter in the comments between Amber and her friends allowed her to catch the tone, the mood, the jokes.

Bel felt she was learning a new language, one where she'd be using the upspeaking inflection.

Ci Vediamo was one of the more footballers'-wivesy bars in Didsbury, screened from the street by a ring of potted palm trees strung with festoon bulb lights. It had an outdoor pavement café area and inside, dark leather booths separated by sprays of ferns. A bar area, lit by a row of glass globe pendant lamps, ran across the back wall.

It was a brasserie by day, with a menu of expensive, high-protein girls' brunches of eggs, avocado and smoked salmon, the health mirage ruined by the ubiquity of bowls of their "house specialty" invention, smoked chili-tomato fries with aioli, which Bel was pretty sure the Spanish invented first and called patatas bravas. Accessorized by pint-size Bloody Marys, crammed with pickled chilies and leafy sticks of celery, as if three of your five-a-day could come from 11:00 a.m. alcohol.

All in all, it said the good life, large disposable income, *come and get accidentally wasted when it was only meant to be a midafternoon catch-up over flat whites.* The kind of place that was especially popular in lockdown: outdoor seating plus neighborhood-based binge drinking.

Also key for Bel in the Ci Vediamo layout was the table closest to the bar, its occupants inadvertently able to listen in on conversations between the staff and to be overheard in turn. There was a cash register—possibly with the iPad under lock and key beneath it—right above it. If you scanned the whole room it was probably the least desirable table for being squeezed in, and yet ideal for covert surveillance purposes.

Bella, also thirty-four (the less you changed, the fewer chances of a slipup, she reasoned) was a knitwear designer for a London company, who worked remotely—*thank you, Shilpa, for sending some relevant-looking documents.* And, rather like her inspiration, got bored of the same four walls.

So Bella had come up with an idea that she was going to work in different postcodes of the city to liven things up a bit, and June was Didsbury's turn.

All week, Bella had put in a couple of hours' stint a day at Ci Vediamo, sipping an iced macchiato (her alt liked milk: gone were Bel's Americanos) and tap-tapping at her MacBook Air, AirPods in but no sound playing. Observing out of the corner of her eye as the youthful proprietor breezed in and out and chatted to staff, waited on the odd table.

She and Amber had no interactions, though Bel felt her appraising gaze sweep over her a few times. It was a place with enough regulars that being new was noticed. This was why it was important not to attract attention until she had bedded in a little.

Bel repeatedly made her excuses at the newspaper's Deansgate office around lunchtime—"Working from home again this afternoon"—before nipping back to Ancoats to don her Bella costume.

Aaron made disbelieving noises, Connor maintained his couldn't-care-if-you-live-or-die-or-work-from-a-deep-ocean-submersible indifference.

Aaron pinged her phone by day three:

Aaron
Have you finally quit? Never known such a part timer 😊
Bel
I'm on a top secret op, thanks 😊
Aaron
You're in Topshop more like x

She knew what he was chiefly aggrieved about: he enjoyed Bel's company and despised Connor's and, in Aaron's mind, she was isolating him with a man *who's like a human desiccant. Human gherkin jar brine.*

Bel was waiting for a certain combination of circumstances to action the second part of her Ci Vediamo plan. After nine days' hard slog of pretending to be a well-heeled Wi-Fi scrounger, on a Thursday, at 5:45 p.m., those circumstances finally seemed to arrive.

Amber was inches away over Bel's shoulder, peering boredly at her phone. Bel prayed she wouldn't saunter off, and messaged Shilpa.

You're UP.

17

Bel's phone buzzed with a FaceTime incoming. She moved her sunglasses to her head and propped the phone on its pop socket, against a cup. She'd changed her plain rubber case to a hardcover one featuring a raven-haired anime girl eating ramen. She didn't really know what she was conveying with this choice, and decided Bella didn't either. *Just liked the aesthetic.*

"Hiiiii," she said, chin on hand, speaking at a pitch and volume where she hoped to immediately activate eavesdropping instincts.

"Hiiiii," Shilpa trilled back. Then, as if she was somehow sending the question up with her intonation: *"How're you?"*

(They'd practiced their ironic-yet-not-ironic mannered cadences. "Just a touch of vocal fry, not too much," Bel instructed. "We'll lose sight of whether we've gone full Paris Hilton otherwise.")

"You know your job is mad as shit, don't you?" Shilpa had said.

"Oh my God, babe, so much."

"Yeah, good. I'm working," Bel now said. "Well, working at this nice bar I've found." She picked up her phone and swooped it around for a panorama. "Yeah, in Didsbury. It's my Didsbo season. What's up?"

"So . . . Maya says she's not had your deposit for Cancún. Was checking everything is OK?"

"Ehm." Bel adjusted her sunglasses on her head and fiddled with her hair. "I meant to talk to you about that. I can't come,

I'm so sorry. I am sooooo skint. We'll do a lush lunch at The Ivy instead? Or go for Mexican food here, ha."

Shilpa left the stunned pause they'd rehearsed, in a read-through that had left them both hysterical, after ad-libbing. ("If you can't stop yourself laughing at any point, end the call," Bel advised. "It'll just look like you bitch-slap cut me off and I can call you back.")

"Sorry, but what the fuck, Bella? You're still doing New York in the autumn, but you can't do my hen?"

"I'd paid for those flights before you said where your hen was!"

"Oh, cos you thought my hen would be in Rhyl?"

"It's not personal, Shilpa, it's money!" Bel hissed, face warm with the peculiar exertion of the performance, which usefully looked like appropriate emotion. "I would if I could."

"Translation, getting pissed in Manhattan with those random idiots is more important than being with one of your best friends? More than something I'll only do once in my life?"

"Five-star hotel! Le Blanc Spa is crazy money. I know the other girls are stretching themselves too."

"Implying what? That *no one* wants to go?"

"I didn't say that, I mean it's expensive."

"If you couldn't afford it you could've told me, I could help. You can borrow it?"

"I don't want to get into more debt. I've got three weddings this year, it's breaking me."

"Three weddings, and how many hens? Two?"

"Yeah."

"So you're going on the other hens?"

"One's in the Cotswolds and the other is at Chloe's family place in France so the cost is way lower."

"Amazing! You're only sacking *my* hen? Wow, Bella."

"Shilpa, it's literally thirteen hundred pounds round-trip if I go in standard economy while you're all in business. I know your hen do will be absolutely lit, but you can't expect everyone to be able to absorb that kind of cost."

"Except I got engaged eighteen months ago and you could've been saving instead of buying YSL court shoes!"

Bel gasped. "Are you my financial adviser?"

"Honestly, I'm not sure I want you as my bridesmaid if this is how you treat me."

Bel widened her eyes.

"Um . . . we've had the dress fitting?"

"You're, what, a twelve? I'm sure I'll find another candidate."

Bel stared into her handset in feigned disbelief.

"Not sure that's how it's meant to work, but OK. Your choice."

"No, how it's meant to work is that bridesmaids go on the hen weekend. Enjoy the Cotswolds, and *France*."

Shilpa ended the call.

Bel picked her phone up, as if to be sure she was gone, and put it down again, mouth open. She checked her Michael Kors rose gold diamante watch (fifteen quid, Vinted) and hoped she was being seen. She extravagantly rubbed her temples, dabbed at her eyes with a paper napkin while exhaling.

She checked the time again.

"Excuse me," Bel said, flagging down a passing waiter and making sure her voice rang out clearly, "can I order a bottle of champagne?"

"Of course. How many glasses?" the waiter said.

"One, please," she said.

"Leo!" called Amber to the waiter. "No bill for it. On the house."

"Oh my God, thank you!" Bel said, turning as if seeing Amber for the first time. "That's so generous."

"Whole bottle. That bad, huh?" Amber said, nodding down at Bel's iPhone.

"Oh, you have no idea," Bel said, rolling her eyes extravagantly and shaking her head confidentially. "Have you ever had a friend get engaged, and the ring on her hand turns her into an absolute demon? It's like she's Bilbo in *Lord of the Rings*, if he went to Cartier. And Bilbo was being a massive bitch."

"Hahahahaha," Amber said. "OK, only condition for your comped bottle, you let me have a glass of it with you and tell me the story?"

"Deal!" Bel said, beaming.

"Got to be some perks for all the shit I shovel here. It looks nice outside—fancy taking it out there? I'm Amber, by the way."

"Great idea," Bel said. "I'm Bella."

"See you there in one min, Bella, I'll bring it out," Amber said.

Bel snapped her laptop shut, shoved it into her designer bag and picked her way carefully to an al fresco spot. She reapplied lipstick in a vintage Versace compact (£40, eBay), smoothed her ringleted ponytail and tried to calm the boiling sea inside her. A mixture of victory, anticipation and significant nerves.

Amber joined her and set down a silver bucket, white napkin over it and green bottle nestled in proper lumps of ice. She pulled two flutes out of the pockets in a cotton apron tied round her waist. "You pour it, just gonna grab my vape."

Bel carefully angled and sloshed champagne out in two equal measures and felt glad of the disinhibition it was about to create, though she needed to keep a check on inebriation.

Amber reappeared and sat down, crossing an acre of her bare, tanned legs in an ankle-length dress with a deep slit in it, and taking a drag on a Lost Mary, Watermelon Ice vape.

She picked her glass up, tapped, cried "Salut!" and drank.

"I could hear some of your conversation just now, and your friend sounded like *a lot,* if you don't mind me saying."

"Oof, is she ever."

Bel recounted Shilpa's fictional tantrums in colorful, amusing terms, and Amber snorted. They shared notes on hens, weddings and girl group holiday WhatsApp politics.

"Mexico! That's, what, a three, four grand spend on a hen?" Amber frowned, shading her eyes from the sun. "That is too much, in my humble."

Bel agreed it was. She tried not to congratulate herself too early on her prediction that drama and alcohol were key British girl-bonding rituals, ones that might fast-track a friendship.

(Shilpa had been awestruck when she outlined it. "If it works, Amber thinks SHE befriended YOU? You are so Machiavellian, Macauley! Like *Game of Thrones,* the shit stirrer guy, Lord Shitfinger." "Do you mean Littlefinger?" Bel said. "Wait, yes.")

And it turned out, Bel was absolutely right not to prematurely drown in pride, because a big fall was coming. A big fall in Tom Ford sunglasses and black Levi's.

Sipping her second drink, she glanced up, and with an immobilizing degree of horror saw Connor walking down the street toward them. A six-foot-tall, arrogant nightmare, slicing through her carefully constructed unreality. *Connor Adams.* What the fuck? This far from the office?! On a working day? On the day she starts playing her undercover role, properly?

It was such astonishingly bad luck, such an implausible comic beat, Bel took a few moments to absorb and process that this piece of cosmic ultra-fuckery was definitely happening. That this wasn't an uncanny look-alike, and that there was no arguing with it.

She couldn't flee the scene with a sudden loo trip: he'd seen her, she was captive and he would be within speaking distance any second.

Bella Niven had only a split second to work out what to do.

18

"Hi . . . ?" Connor said, hesitantly, as he drew level, removing his sunglasses.

"Hi yourself!" Bel said, in a voice that implied this was funny, in a way they both understood.

She could see him taking in her hair, makeup, the violet sundress with gold platform sandals, the whole "not working from home, in fact, pavement boozing" vibe, while not looking at all like Bel Macauley. Dissonant cues everywhere, confusion jangling like wind chimes. His knitted brow said: Was Bel some sort of grifting sociopath, using the "investigations editor" title to get wasted on the newspaper dime?

She had to leap, or it was game over.

"Amber. This is Connor. *My boyfriend*," she said, looking directly at him, enunciating clearly and confidently. She injected a note of shy girlish pride, inhabiting the role of A Woman Head Over Her Esska Heels: undoubtedly her most skillful acting yet.

Connor, understandably, stared at her in alarm, wondering if he'd misheard. Yet crucially, in the moments that followed, he made no response. Mute stupefaction was desirable—Bel could work with silence until Connor, she hoped against hope, caught up. It was a coin flip: surely he'd take some self-righteous pleasure in making her look ridiculous. She was at his mercy, and she didn't fancy his stocks of mercy were high.

"Pleased to meet you, Connor," Amber said. "I'm Bella's new BFF. Laurent-Perrier introduced us, hahahaha."

"I was hot-desking in there"—Bel nodded into the bar—"and got into a major Bridezilla spat with Shilpa about her hen do on FaceTime, tell you later," she said, with a theatrical eye roll, "and I needed a drink. This absolute babe has bought me bubbles to cheer me up." She paused. "What are you doing here?"

Her palms were now slick with sweat. Ironically, it was a question she'd like answered, just absolutely not right now. Connor hadn't been in the office this morning; she'd assumed he'd been sent out in the field.

"Checking out Didsbury House Hotel for my brother's imminent visit. He likes eyes on his options. I've got a day off in lieu today . . ." Connor hesitated. "Remember?"

"Oh, of course!" Bel said. "Looking forward to meeting him."

There was a tense beat where Bel realized the blindsided Connor couldn't risk saying anything else without knowing the terms of her batshit fiction.

"How long have you two been together?" said Amber, curiously.

Bel quietly panicked that whether consciously or not, Amber was registering it was quite odd for a couple not to share notes on their whereabouts. If it didn't bother her now, it might do later. It was too soon for unusual things to start happening. Bel had to bluster with enough force that it was forgotten.

"Erm . . ." Bel contorted her face, as if trying to do genuine calculations. "Where are we now, June? That's eight months, give or take? We met at a Halloween party in London. What a night that was, Con."

She let go a goofy dirty laugh, in her Bella mode. *Con. Well, quite.*

"Aww. Was it love at first sight?" Amber said, looking to Bel and then to Connor.

"Erm . . ." he said, with a look of consternation. Was he going to give up? *Sorry, I've missed a page here . . .*

"Difficult to say, thanks to the fancy dress," Connor said, after a throat clearing. "Harley Quinn costume. I was glad to find out the hair was a wig."

She had another rush of adrenaline, this time in relief flavor.

"I went all in," Bel agreed.

"Remind me what Harley Quinn looks like again?" Amber said.

O, fuck. Bel couldn't remember at all. Was she in a superhero movie? Supervillain?

She opened her mouth and nothing came out.

"Fishnets, pigtails, hot pants and a baseball bat," Connor supplied. "Reflective of Bel's complicated nature."

Bel gave silent thanks to him, and that she'd gone for a spin on her forename as her alter ego.

"Love it," Amber drawled, dragging on her vape pen and giving Connor an appraising, appreciative look. "What did you go as?"

"Gomez Addams," Bel said hastily, returning the favor.

"Mustache, pin-striped suit," Amber said. Her eyes ran up and down him and Bel had to concede, his being superficially hot was useful distraction right now. "Want to join us, Connor?"

Bel opened her mouth, but Connor was there first: "I'd love to, but apologies for not stopping, I've got a to-do list as long as my arm. Nice to meet you, Amber. See you later." He addressed his Not Girlfriend. He paused. "Call me if you need picking up?"

Bel was, for now, brokenly grateful.

"Sure. See you later, darling!" Bel trilled, trying to keep the tense relief out of her voice.

"Well, *well done, you*," Amber said, as Connor cleared earshot range, and Bel's heart rate started slowing. "He's *gorgeous*. Where did you say you found him again?"

"Soho. Liked it, clubbed it over the head and dragged it back north," Bel said, as Amber gurgled.

"He left his job?" Amber said.

"No, they let him move to remote, like me. He's in finance." Bel waved her hand. "*Please* don't ask me what he does, exactly."

"I'll never put you on that spot," Amber said. "When we've finished the bottle, I might make you tell me what he's like in"—she cupped both hands round her mouth to whisper—"*bed*, though."

"Oh, he's an earthquake," Bel said, with a knowing look. "Never had better."

Amber made an *oh my God* swoon face. Bel smiled, sipped from her flute and thought she'd be lucky to keep her lunch down.

"You run this place? That's so impressive, aren't you twenty-something?" Bel said, brightly changing the topic.

"Thirty-five this month! I own it, but don't admire me, I'm a rich kid. My family ran it first and my mum passed it on to me." She pushed a charm bracelet up and down her wrist, a distracted tic.

If Bel had thought Amber was any sort of soft touch, un-smart bimbo, an hour in her company had corrected that notion.

They talked Ci Vediamo, Amber's career history, Bel's concocted CV, which was in fact Shilpa's: a first at Manchester Met in Fine Art.

With Bel making sure she was at turns effortful, interested, funny, sympathetic, and Amber insisting they move on to piña coladas, the sense of spark was assured.

"This has been so great, I can't thank you enough," Bel said, when they decided it was time for Amber to check on her staff and Bel to find a carbohydrate.

Amber clutched her arm.

"Bella, you know what, you should come to my thirty-fifth, two weeks tomorrow! It's only here, private party. Boring, I know, but I can keep it open late as I like and I can't bear paying the markups at other people's. It's why I'm queen of the lock-in—I know how hard I'm being ripped off everywhere else, LOL. Why don't you come? Bring Connor? It'd be so nice to see different faces."

"That would be amazing, if you're sure?" Bel said, gesturing at the empties on the table. "I feel like I've totally taken the piss out of your hospitality as it is."

"Don't be a dick, it's my job. Give me your number . . . Do you have NameDrop? Put your phone next to mine, look, it's magic . . ."

In the second moment of blind panic during their encounter, Bel realized she had no idea if this would show her WhatsApp contact details as Bel Macauley.

"Oh, I had a security wig-out and toggled that off," she blathered. "What's your number?"

She tapped it at speed into her contacts, and text-pinged back BELLA <3

"Texts! Old school!" Amber said. "Got ya. So good to meet you—"

Mercifully, at that moment, Leo the waiter was at their side asking Amber to come referee someone querying their bill.

As soon as she was in the taxi home, Bel hurriedly scrolled to her WhatsApp. It was only showing as Bel but she changed her name to Bella anyway.

She saw her ghostly reflection in the taxi window and asked herself why she was scowling.

Befriending Amber Kendrick was, on the face of it, a raving success. It was just such a shame she'd pulled a joker at the last minute. Actually no, not a joker—the odds of that were far greater than what had happened to her. Two of them in a fifty-four-card deck.

A day in lieu. Had he followed her? No. That was paranoia, and when he saw her, it was like he'd caught her naked.

She was scowling because, firstly, Connor Adams was now going to have to be persuaded to become part of her undercover identity, passionately against both of their wishes.

And, secondly, because she had a resentful feeling that Connor's unwanted appearance had clinched the deal.

She googled Harley Quinn. The Joker's lover in Arkham Asylum. FFS.

AS THE UBER ENGINE IDLED IN MIDEVENING TRAFFIC, Bel looked at the phone in her hand again and noticed she had an unread WhatsApp.

Connor
Hi, are you OK? That felt like possibly some variant of an Ask for Amy. I wasn't sure if leaving you was the right thing to do but you have my number :/

Of course, and he had her number, a first-day formality. His profile picture showed him smiling, hair tousled; he looked totally different.

Bel conceded this was a more considerate first round of feedback than she'd anticipated. She'd vaguely wondered if he'd be utterly indignant, trapped into a flurry of lies, masculine pride affronted at being publicly claimed by a woman of lesser physical beauty than his own.

Bel
SORRY, and thank you so much for not blowing my cover. The explanation for it will need to be in person. Please not a word to anyone about this, especially Aaron.

Connor
Deal. I mean, we are end-to-end encrypted here . . .
Bel
Not as encrypted as our ends would be in the great outdoors.
I don't suppose you're free at the weekend?

19

For all the cloak-and-dagger and *having to find her in Platt Fields Park of a Saturday afternoon, so the Russians couldn't hack their telecoms* or whatever reason Bel was claiming meant they couldn't use their mobile phones, Connor had a premonition that this was going to turn out to be very little.

And moreover, he foretold he was going to be begged to withhold it from their employers. In their Didsbury encounter, Bel had seemed off duty as fuck. While Aaron teased her about Investigations being a racket, Connor hadn't thought it might be until he saw her looking super dolled up and swilling champagne.

My cover. Hmmmm. It was a very convincing one, yes.

To add to the cynicism, Aaron had told him Bel was from wealth. He'd not anticipated this with all the careless scruffiness, but of course that's precisely what should've alerted him.

"Oh, aye. Bohemian left-wing types where they don't put their heating on and have paintings worth as much as a car." "She told you this?" "Got a pal at the *Yorkshire Post*."

Of course Aaron was doing background checks on Bel, Connor thought. His unreciprocated crush on Bel was so poorly concealed, it was like Slimer in *Ghostbusters* pinging off the walls in excitement and leaving the office furniture coated in phantasmagorical goo. He sensed, on Bel's side, her alliance with Aaron was pure pragmatism.

"Why would she work here?" Connor scanned their dungeon in disbelief.

Aaron shrugged. "Maybe she felt a calling? I'd be feeling a calling to a poolside cabana in the Dominican Republic."

The awkward concept "successful podcaster" made more sense to Connor in light of this.

He checked Google Maps and Bel's Share My Location, and as he raised his eyes to the horizon, he saw her waving at him from under a tree.

He noticed on approach that she'd brought a checked waterproof picnic blanket and rucksack, the sight of which made Connor uncomfortable. Exactly how long was she anticipating they were going to talk?

If this was to launch some convoluted manipulation that no one could know she played hooky on occasion, complete with beseeching doe eyes to make him feel too bad to refuse her to her face, get it over with. *Let's not pretend either of us wants to split a thermos of Pimms.*

"Afternoon," Connor said, deciding he'd not take his shades off. Bel was in bug-like ones herself, and navy dungashorts that seemed better suited to people of an age to attend after-school clubs.

Her legs were outstretched and, as he sat down next to her, Connor's eyes were drawn by her small, pale feet, lost in clunky Doc Martens. Her toenails were decorated with squares of sky-blue polish that had obviously been applied long enough ago they were now floating oblongs, like a Rothko painting.

Jen insisted any color other than a caramel pink she called "nude" on nails was irredeemably vulgar. "I don't know why grown, professional women think it's a good look to be at the Barry M neons. They're for shoplifting while playing truant."

He felt sure Jen wouldn't like Bel, and wondered what Bel would think of her.

"I'm sorry to drag you out here on your weekend. This is a story where, if it leaks out that we're poking around, it vanishes," Bel said.

It belatedly occurred to Connor that it wasn't WhatsApp she mistrusted, it was him.

"I will keep this as brief as I can, I know I'm eating into your free time," she continued.

To his surprise, Bel went on to describe a pretty intriguing sting on the Manchester mayor, who was apparently a secret sleaze, consorting with crooks. He recalled Bel's work history and considered he should have given her a bit more credit before leaping to the most jaundiced conclusion. It was possibly somewhat dismissive and even sexist that he'd so readily thought she might be a frivolous lass on the sesh.

"It's a . . . sort of gray zone Me Too with added conflict of interest?" Connor said.

"Exactly," Bel said, looking impressed he'd got it in one.

"Toby knows about this?"

"I'd not risk undercover without sign-off."

"What does the Airbnb listing look like?"

"As Ian said, smart Victorian four-bed, supposedly sleeps ten if you're gullible or want a bargain. Welcomes parties. I noticed it has very little availability, which means either it's mad popular, or they aren't renting it to the public for some of the time."

Connor turned it over in his mind.

"What's the daughter called again? Amber? So Amber is in Didsbury, running this bar. That's what, four, five miles from here? What are you going to do if she bumps into you in your other life? Like I did?"

"I don't know many people here yet. If Amber catches me on a coffee run on a journalist day, I'll still be Bella. Aaron lives in Bury with his parents and goes straight home from work most of the time. Platzki's won't happen again until the next intern arrives." She paused. "This isn't going to work because I've eliminated all risk. It's *taking* a risk and hoping it pays off."

"And now I'm involved," Connor said, a statement and a question.

"Afraid so."

Pennies that should've dropped earlier for Connor dropped now.

"This is a request to join you in the make-believe?"

"Erm, if you want to. Amber's invite to her birthday party in a fortnight is for both of us. I think she took a shine."

"I'm only an intern reporter, I can't spend weekday afternoons getting shit-faced without Aaron getting me sacked."

"You don't need to be present during working hours. To be honest, now I've made the connection with Amber, I don't think I even do. It's about socializing. Which I appreciate is a pain in the arse given you're not being paid for it. I could pay you"—Bel swallowed and Connor could see her suppressing the grimace—"in a joint byline, if it all comes good. Very beneficial for the résumé."

"I'm not doing anything much else with my free time up here, to be fair. But is this not ethically grubby? She thinks she's got a pal, and you're plotting to steal her property and destroy the family name?"

"Yes, it is. She's been so friendly that the guilt is already giving me cold sweats. But I think if she's knowingly covering for a powerful, abusive man, that's worse, and this is the only way to find out. Also, I'm hoping it lands on her mother, not her."

Connor watched kids nearby kicking a ball through makeshift goalposts and arguing bitterly over the rule breaking.

"If I'm going to be involved, can I offer constructive input?"

"Sure."

"Getting footage from an iPad that you don't know for sure is there—either the iPad or the footage—and that you don't have the passcode for, then hoping to get enough time with it to access and copy the files . . . Do you mind me saying this isn't so much a long shot as a deranged moon shot? How bad was Plan B if this is A?"

He smiled, and Bel smiled back.

"I'm thinking take it one stage at a time. If I can get her to check something on the iPad when she's with me, I bet I can see the passcode. Everyone shields their pin from strangers, not their passcodes from their friends. She says she has lots of lock-ins. That could be the opportunity, everyone half sloshed."

"Let's say you do get into it. Months of recordings will take hours to download. You can't bung a memory stick in it and see a little red bar go to one hundred percent in three minutes flat, like in a spy show."

"Fuck! Yes. I need a tech guy like Bond has. Q?"

"You need a miracle . . ." Connor paused. "You *could* take the cover with the rainbows off and stick it on a second, identical iPad you've got on factory settings. Lift the information from hers overnight, then swap them back. Preferably before she goes to the Apple Store demanding to know why it's bricked."

"That could work!"

"About five impossible things need to happen first."

Connor wasn't going to flatter her by saying so, but he was quite impressed at the FaceTime hen-do spat, and the flirtatious chameleon he'd seen swilling Laurent-Perrier. That made him think she might just pull this off.

The northern leg of his internship had otherwise been pure grind. "Learn all you can from her," Toby had said. What did he actually have to lose by saying yes? Except his kneecaps, if these Kendricks turned out to be gangsters.

"Does this input mean . . . you're in?" Bel said, pulling her legs up. Those shoes looked like they could keep her anchored to the ocean floor.

"What am I agreeing to, exactly?"

"A month of attending functions as Bella Niven's boyfriend."

"I have a real girlfriend. What do I do when Jennifer is up next weekend? Keep her indoors the whole time with blackout curtains drawn? Hostage hood?"

"Oh, are you not still in the honeymoon phase?" Bel said evenly, and Connor caught it a second too late to laugh. She was too quick for him sometimes.

"Could Jennifer be your sister? Tell her due to an ultra-secret assignment, it's temporarily necessary. Please don't share the details, though."

"I tell Jen she has to say she's my sister because I've got another person up here saying she's my girlfriend instead, and I can't explain why. That's not going to go down brilliantly, I don't think."

"I don't know what else to suggest. Thursday was an unforeseen calamity. The only way I can think of dealing with it is trying to turn it into a win, and making us the M20 postcode's new It Couple. If you don't want any part of it, I'll have to ghost Amber. I think a phony breakup is too much narrative, this early on. I would trigger 'this doesn't feel right' sensations."

"Hang on," Connor said, "you'd have to tell Toby I'm the reason the story's sunk?"

Bel shrugged her shoulders. "I hadn't thought, but I suppose so."

Connor blew air out.

"If it's going to make me look like an obdurate, unhelpful cock to say no to the northern investigations editor before I've even left probation, then I've not got much of a choice, have I?"

"We would not want you mislabeled as an obdurate, unhelpful cock," Bel said, grinning, and Connor knew he should grin back instead of glowering, but this woman *would not stop* getting the better of him.

At least he knew how to locate the adult clothing section.

20

"I bought chicken yesterday that was labeled 'Space to Thrive,'" Aaron announced into thin air, the following Friday afternoon.

He could not encounter an extended silence without throwing a leading non sequitur into it, it seemed.

Bel had been trying to concentrate on a lead about the regeneration of Holt Town last week when Aaron had informed her "Strawberry Fanta is a devotional offering in Thai Buddhism, you know."

"My drumsticks and thighs have had a better life than we're having," Aaron continued, casting his eyes up at the stained ceiling. "Can any of us say we're thriving in our allotted space?"

"But then again our captivity will hopefully not end up with us coated in Aaron Parry's special spicy marinade," Bel said.

"You'd be lucky, darling," Aaron said, and Bel caught Connor making a *blurgh* face. She wondered if his repulsion was at Aaron being lascivious, or lascivious toward her specifically, and felt quite sure it was both.

Connor's girlfriend in his desk photograph was not merely attractive, as you'd expect, but a sort of luxury car advert, haughty beautiful. Bel could well imagine what he privately thought of the bad taste of slumming it undercover as Mr. Bel. She had a sixth sense he'd reconcile his girlfriend to it by stressing Bel was a bag lady.

No point sweating about all that now, it was happening. They'd sat on her picnic blanket, googled him and combed through all social media together, ascertaining Connor's Instagram and Facebook accounts were locked down as private. The visible bios had no contradictory information and girlfriend-free profile pics. As a great piece of luck, an out-of-date LinkedIn had him still working in finance.

"I'm not sure if we give them your real surname," Bel had said. "I'm of two minds, because if neither of us appears to exist online that's unusual enough to be a flag. If you can be on there but say you never check your accounts and are forgetful in accepting new follow requests, that might work better."

"What's your explanation for why you've got no presence?" Connor had asked her. "It's quite unlikely for a girl about town."

"I'm going to tell a lurid tale about a stalker ex in York provoking me to delete it all," Bel said. "Might pay ongoing dividends in getting out of being in photos, being tagged and so on. I already told Amber I was paranoid enough to turn NameDrop off, will keep that going. Plus nightmare exes are dynamite bonding material."

Connor nodded and she saw no hint he might've guessed it was real biography.

Bel snapped back to the present and saw an Anthony the Stalker email arrive. Usually she swiped to mark it as opened and saved the bilious detail for later. This time, she could see the line in preview was designed to spike her blood pressure and make her respond.

Hello Isabel, thought you should know I'm in Manchester today for an interview. The Ed has asked me to stop by your office and introduce myself later, in the spirit of Fourth Estate cooperation & connection. I'm letting you know in advance, so you can't claim I ambushed you. As usual, despite continually speaking into the yawning chasm of your petulant silence, I hope you are well. Ax

Her breathing became shallower. She knew Anthony had manipulated this: both the putative reason for the journey and calling in. She could see him, faux casual, loitering as he left the editor's office: *Isn't Isabel Macauley there now? Wonder how that outpost project is faring? Shall I put my head round the door?*

She rationalized: He can only pull this once, maybe two times, maximum. You can't Royal visit another newspaper's office every few weeks, using an alibi.

Why had he warned her and given her the chance of escape? She supposed because one, he wanted her to panic and fret and fire off a heated reply telling him that he couldn't, and two, had he surprised her, she might've exclaimed *GET LOST!* and as much as Anthony wanted to humiliate her, that might've humiliated him too. For all he knew she'd clued her colleagues in here—he'd know there was only a couple of them. Yep, this was why she'd gotten this feigned courtesy.

That Ant had to have war-gamed all this stuff out carefully was really quite frightening. It was a long way from normal. Had there always been a minority subculture of men like this that she was unaware of? Would he stop if she met someone else? Bel wondered at a world where you needed men to protect you against other men, patriarchy as Mafia racket.

Bel ground her teeth, palms sweaty. If she bolted home for the rest of the day, then she'd let him chase her out. Anthony would chalk that up as a qualified win and know he could simply try again. She felt sure he'd say so. *Well, Isabel, what bad luck not to catch you, I'll hope to be luckier next time . . .* It was better if he tried this and encountered some form of resistance.

But how, without either facing him down herself—a major win for Anthony, it was what he was hoping for—or tipping her colleagues off that this man was someone from Her Past?

She messaged Shilpa her worries.

Shilpa

He's issuing threats, isn't he? I mean, this is harassing you at your place of work. Can't you tell your bosses you want him barred, like in a pub?

Bel

I know how he operates: he'll have a real interview here, he will have suggested calling in to the editor. If I go nuts saying he's stalking me, I will end up looking nuts. And have to tell everyone what happened with my married ultra-creep boss.

Shilpa

Is it not insane that he's the married one and he's got you acting like you don't want this found out?

Bel

Honestly, it amazes me. I guess the thing is, if I made a formal complaint, it would be discovered by everyone we worked with in both cities, but not necessarily his wife. She never came to the office the whole time I was there, or any do. So 360 degree shame for me and probably nothing but a brag for him.

Shilpa

Ugh! I want him to get his arse served to him for this SO BADLY—who the fuck does he think he is?? OK, let's lock in: what's the goal, to stop him entering the office?

Bel

Ideally. Thought of his getting in here makes me itch. All he's doing is demonstrating I can't have any space that's safe from him.

She imagined his gloating, oily manner, the sense of danger, the skin crawl of him standing over her desk and Bel being forced to exchange pleasantries. Anthony doing whatever he could to hint at a special connection between them, while getting eyes on her coworkers for future email kompromat. Aaron guessing there was a story here, Connor's silent disapproval.

Shilpa
If you're using Aaron or Connor to get rid of him, tell them a lie about Anthony that motivates them to keep him out. You say journalists are always worried about getting scooped? Say he's a snake?
Bel
That is GOOD. Thank you. X

Bel cleared her throat.

"Erm, we're going get a caller downstairs in a bit, Ant from the *Yorkshire Post*. Says he's coming here to 'introduce himself.' Except I already know him. Can one of you two get it, and tell him that a major incident's kicked off and we're too busy? He's a proper snake. Always pinching ideas and passing them off as his own. He even got a reporter sacked once for following his suggestions then denying it."

Bel indicated the whiteboard on the wall, covered in scrawls about the current story leads (the ones that could be freely shared) and helpful hints from Aaron like: *DI CARTWRIGHT: RINSES YOU FOR KFC BUCKETS, BUT WON'T TELL YOU SHIT, AVOID.*

"He'll be slyly ripping things from that or snitching its gossip too."

"What's he even coming in here for?" Aaron said.

"Classic Anthony move. Friendly hello pretext cos he knows me from somewhere else. Like letting a vampire over the threshold."

"Aye, well, they have to be invited, don't they? And I'm not inviting him."

Bel had an ignoble notion that it wouldn't hurt to present it as a little white knight quest for Aaron.

"Exactly. Please block that cock. If you're able—he's extremely persistent."

"No worries. Consider it done, princess."

She sensed Connor's eyes on her and avoided his gaze.

When the buzzer went two hours later, Bel felt legitimately sick. Anthony was one floor away, and she had only Aaron's willingness to oblige her standing between her and an encounter with Anthony, with witnesses.

"This'll be that wrong 'un," Aaron said. "Allow me."

Bel pretended to be absorbed in her laptop screen in the silence that followed.

"Was any of that true?" Connor said, eventually.

"What?" Bel said, startled.

"Your description of this man to Aaron."

"Yes," said Bel, flushing with indignation. "I don't make things up."

A bit of a ripe claim in light of Operation Get Bailey.

"It's not like you to delegate a confrontation, that's all."

"Meaning what, I'm an aggro fishwife?" Bel said.

"No." Connor paused. It occurred to Bel he could be more antagonistic now she was relying on his help. "Why do you twist everything I say into the worst possible interpretation?"

"Well, what else did you mean?"

"Exactly what I said: you fight your own fights. I generally say what I think, I don't do snide double meanings."

"Nor do I."

"Wait," Connor said, in a lower register, "when you said there was someone back in York who made you—"

Footsteps thundered on the stairs and Aaron burst into the room. Bel felt twofold gratitude: firstly, at Connor's revelation being interrupted, and secondly, at Aaron being alone.

"Fuck me, what a tedious muppet!" he said. "You weren't

kidding. *Just let me say hi to Isabel and I'll be out of your hair . . .* No, mate. Not falling for it."

Connor and Bel shared a look that said Connor knew he was right.

"Superb work, Parry, well done," Bel said. "I owe you a pint."

"You're on, let's head down at half five," Aaron said, checking the wall clock. A pause. "Connor, want to join?"

"Thanks, but my girlfriend's visiting," Connor said, Bel felt sure, with relief.

"Ah, that's nice. What's her name?"

"Jennifer."

"Ah, the lady from your photograph." Aaron pointed with his pen. "Gonna show her the local sights?"

"Yep, full tour of the *Coronation Street* set booked."

"Really?" Aaron said.

"No, not really," Connor replied, as Bel laughed.

Half an hour later, it was Pub O'Clock.

"Have fun with Jennifer! Have a good weekend," Aaron called, and Connor muttered *thanks and you* before departing, with barely a nod in Bel's direction. She couldn't fault her undercover boyfriend for maintaining the persona on this side of the bargain, that was for sure.

When the door downstairs slammed, Aaron said, "That fuckin' guy is about as entertaining as the fireplace channel."

"Without the illusion of warmth."

Bel saw she had another email from Anthony. This time it was one line and made her even more nauseous than before.

If you're going to play games with me, Isabel, then expect me to play back.

21

Connor stood in the milling crowds in Manchester Piccadilly, hands in pockets, and waited for the electronic board to tell him the 4:33 p.m. from London Euston had arrived at Platform 7.

He'd have been apprehensive about Jen's visit as it was, but with the newfound necessity of asking her to moonlight as his sister, he was experiencing vague dread.

Thanks to Bel bloody Macauley, he was about to hand Jen a very large stick to beat him with. He'd not been willing to say: *Things are already drain-circling with my girlfriend. These antics are going to go down like the fucking* Hindenberg.

Bel bounced along in her irrepressible Bel Macauley way, and he could imagine she'd think Jennifer's objecting was clingy and basic. Except, he thought, 95 percent of all partners would think "What the hell?" if you told them they had to assume another identity while you Mr. & Mrs. Smithed it up with a colleague of the opposite sex.

He imagined Jen on her wine terrace in the small hours, tapping one of her "emergency cigarettes" into that turquoise gluggle jug that did part-time service as an ashtray, telling Libby she'd been banned from saying she was his other half.

As for the rest of their forty-eight hours together, he was going to play it by ear. They could do art galleries, shopping and mid-afternoon martinis and he could try to win her to Manchester—it depended heavily on her mood. When he examined his discomfort, he realized in a foreign environment he and Jen would have to spend proper quality time together. In the familiar grooves of home life you could benign-ignore. The prospect right now felt very make-or-break. They'd either rekindle some of their early days' enthusiasm, or end up having The Conversation.

Connor slid his phone out of his pocket to see if she'd sent any travel updates, or if Avanti West Coast were testing their runaway popularity.

He had a WhatsApp from Jen. He opened it to read:

If you miss me this weekend, here's something to keep you company. Feel free to return the favor x

Connor almost reeled back as a photograph of his girlfriend pinged into view. Jen was leaning on a sink, background unfamiliar: possibly a hotel. She was in full makeup, face angled to the side for maximum cheekbone, back arched, clasping her phone with the pearlized pink cover. The most striking thing about the image, however, was that Jen had no top on. Familiar breasts that he'd never viewed in pixel form before.

He and Jen had never swapped nudes. They'd met on a blind date set up by friends and ended up in bed together the same night. There was no lengthy digital wooing or fencing around each other, since they hadn't met on an app.

Plus Jen knew that Connor was opposed to nudes in principle. The whole idea of trying to compose images with your scrotum on show in a way that was supposed to inflame the recipient made him want to die. It also seemed reckless: if such photos of him existed, he'd certainly not be 100 percent sure Libby hadn't seen them.

So, even without the caption, he'd have known this wasn't intended for him.

JEN incoming flashed on his phone. His impulse was to throw it in a bin and run out of Piccadilly like some sort of

TikTok skit, except this viral comedy was one, his actual life, and two, desperately unfunny right now.

"Hi?" Connor said, having never wanted to answer a call less in his life.

"Oh God, Connor. I'm so sorry," Jennifer said, the mechanical noise of a train screeching behind her.

"I assume that's not for me?"

There was a pause.

"No."

Another silence, this time soundtracked by the tinny voice of a train announcement.

"See you in a minute, then," Connor said.

"Connor, I was—"

He pressed the red button and cut her off. In the five minutes left before she was due to disembark, he processed what this meant. Jen was having an affair.

They had definitively reached the end, and in light of the tragi-comic nature of the discovery, Connor was going to be able to set the terms and the tone. He tried to rapidly adjust to the idea of a third person in their relationship. Funny thing about an affair: it involved all of them, only with a third of the gang unwitting and nonparticipatory. This man was bound to know who he was.

When Jen appeared, she was dragging an aluminum Rimowa spinner case down the concourse, eyes screened by tortoiseshell-frame aviator sunglasses, her center-parted, highlighted brown hair now just longer than her shoulders. She was in a narrow-fitting denim jacket with sleeves rolled up, coffee silk lace-trimmed vest top, white jeans and cream-colored ballet pumps. She was coordinated like a cappuccino.

Connor had a pang of missing Bel Macauley's demented peacock razzmatazz, proving that the trauma of receiving another man's wank pic had attacked his cognitive faculties.

"Oh, Connor," she said, as she reached him, pushing her sunglasses into her hair, her taut expression making it plain she might sob in public.

"Let's save it for the bar," he said, as his greeting. "Shall I take that?"

She surrendered her luggage, accepting that, however nerve-racking she found it, dangerous civility was going to be his mode until they were somewhere more private.

He led her briskly, neither of them speaking, through the Friday evening hubbub to a pub called The Marble Arch. He'd researched it and judged it had enough northern character and original features that he wasn't being an Up From London, but with enough suave that it wasn't the Rovers Return either. He seized a table and parked Jen with her case.

"What're you having, vodka and Slim?" Connor said. He could see Jen think maybe she should buy them, and then realize a pint of guest ale wasn't going to rebalance anything.

"That's got the weekend off to a flying start, then?" Connor said, returning from the bar and setting the drinks down.

Still awash with adrenaline, he didn't know what note to strike. He didn't want to be gratuitously nasty, not least because he was more surprised than truly hurt. But he feared if he behaved like, as Shaun would call it, "a simp," and said, *There there, it's fine, we were done anyway so we might as well go up in flames,* it would make him despise himself later. He had a right to be angry—he should be angry.

But he wasn't angry. He was shocked and bereft, bewildered and queasy, in that particular way you were when you complacently thought you were going to choose the moment, and it was chosen for you.

22

"Who is he?" Connor said, cutting through the pointless apologies.

"Nobody. It's not serious," Jen said, tears sliding down her face. Connor was slightly worried onlookers would think the lovely brunette was out with her brutal captor.

"It's not serious but he's in possession of porny photos of you?"

"Hardly porn! You see as much on any beach."

"You're not on a beach, though. You're in his iCloud for all time. Have you got photos of him?"

"Y-yes."

"Can I see them?"

"Why?"

"Because I want to know what he looks like?"

"They're irrelevant and you're only going to mock."

Jen was hunched over her V&T in misery. This would be a gluggle jug tale for Libby, but there would be no schadenfreude.

"Maybe I won't mock, maybe I will be awed by the size of his bulbous salutation."

"See what I mean?"

"How did you meet?"

Jen sipped her drink. "In Spence."

"You met him in our local *bakery*?"

An odd crucible for a sexy liaison: tangerine-orange frontage, five types of sourdough and huge queues on Church Street of a weekend morning. Full of parents with toddlers called things like Myst and Dufraisne.

"Was he staff? *Here you go, one custard horn and also my custard horn.*"

"You know what, Connor, I appreciate I have fucked up badly but what is the point of ridiculing me?"

"The point is it's at least bleakly funny, and right now I will take bleakly funny over dwelling on how I found out my girlfriend of five years is shagging someone behind my back. I'm going to need a name and some details for him, I'm afraid. Do I know him?"

"No. He's called Francis and he's a personal trainer. We got chatting and he started joining me on my runs, going for coffee after. It started about four months ago."

"Is he single?"

A small silence and Jen said, "He lives with his girlfriend."

"Whoa. How did it happen? *That's enough about leg day, now let's try dick day?*"

Jen tucked her hair behind her ear. "Messaging, I guess, and it turning... more intense. He says he's unhappy with Victoria..." She trailed off.

"And you're unhappy with me?"

"Well, we've not been great, have we?"

Connor could see that as Jen hadn't foreseen Connor would find out, she'd done no forward planning on what she should disclose. It was like opening an overfull cupboard held together only by its lock, and the contents coming out in a cascade.

"We haven't. I didn't know we were sexting secret lovers, though. Did you not feel gross about it? If I'd not got it by mistake, you'd be sitting here with me getting his replies."

Jen covered her face with her hands for a moment.

"Honestly, nothing has made sense since it began. I've not been myself. I've just felt such a psychological mess, you know?"

Connor hadn't registered Jen was on her phone more and thought his lack of registering things full stop had played a part.

Shaun once said all infidelity starts with attention, too little of it in one place and too much of it from another. His brother could really try being right less often.

"Are you saying you've never thought about it? Other people? I wondered if . . . I wondered if you had."

"Nope," Connor said. "If I'd got to the point of wanting to sleep with someone else that much, I'd have told you."

"Look. It'll be completely long over when you get back. I'll finish it now and you can have access to my phone to see I'm telling the truth," Jen said, manner a little frantic, "I promise."

"Hold on," Connor said, being careful to modify his voice lest any drinker nearby tune in to the soap opera–worthy content. "You think we're not splitting up?"

He could see from Jen's stunned expression that she really didn't think this was terminal if she didn't want it to be. Connor was going to have a lot to think about in the coming months of dreary solitude up here.

"You don't want to even try?" she said. "Unfaithfulness can be a reset opportunity."

Connor rubbed his eyes. "Oh, please, can we not with the therapy phrases. Let's not find out it was your Father Wound."

"It can be worked through, long-term relationships are work."

"I don't want to try, Jen. You've taken three weeks to bother to visit, because you preferred to be vigorously nailed by Franco Manco the PT. I take it there was no book launch?"

Jen cast her eyes downward. "You didn't ask what book it was. What does that tell you, Con? I've not needed to invent cover stories—you had no interest."

"That's called *trust*," Connor said, trying to exclaim in fury at a low volume. "Are you for real? You think your lying to go bone some other man reflects badly on *me*?"

"Sorry," she said, but her tone and face were sullen. When the mortification of this faded for her, Connor realized her dominant feeling would be one of resentment that she'd given him the upper hand.

"There's no amount of Relate sessions that's going to fix this for me. When would you have told me about him, if ever?" he said.

"I don't know. I still love you enough to try, that's all I'm saying," Jen said, raising limpid eyes to meet his. She was trying to guilt him and it wasn't going to work.

"You said it yourself, things weren't good before this. You hated me ditching my career," Connor said.

"Have you got any idea how hard you were to live with during the worst of it? You barely spoke to me."

"I know. I'm sorry for that," he said. "I was keeping my head above water and everything else had to take second place. But you should've been glad I quit, then. Instead you actually told me not to."

"I worried about how we'd make it work with a mortgage and kids, that's all. You were so unhappy that all you cared about was escaping. I was worried you'd still be as depressed afterward."

"What you mean is, you thought the problem was probably me, so it might as well be rich me."

"You know what? With all your razor-sharp insights, I get the feeling you just don't like me very much anymore." Jen put her hands up. "I know, I know—I've got no right to complain as things stand."

"No, you haven't," Connor said, which was an easy dodge. "Where did you have sex with him?"

Jen cast her eyes to the table. "Hotels. Never at our place if that's what you're asking."

"How many times?"

Jen swallowed.

"Um . . . four."

Somehow, even though Connor hadn't felt what a partner ought to feel throughout the conversation, the specificity of four was woundingly graphic. He felt like he'd been in the room.

They stared at each other until Jen looked away.

"I guess I should start looking for somewhere to rent?" she said.

"Yeah. No rush for leaving. It's not like I'm using the flat again until August."

Connor's napkin-level math in the past told him he could pay Jen her share from it and still afford the remaining mortgage.

"While we're doing practicalities, there's no point you coming back to Salford and there's only one bed. Why don't we check you into a hotel near the station after this, go for dinner and you can head back south tomorrow morning?"

"You don't have to go to dinner."

"We need to eat, and I'd rather make this amicable, if we can."

Jen slugged the last of her V&T and nodded. They went through the tasks mechanically, Connor watching her ask at the Britannia Hotel if they had any rooms left for tonight and the receptionist's quick look to him that said *got lucky, eh?*

After they were seated in Erst, Connor, wishing he'd not made a proper dinner reservation, said in a low voice, "Oh, I almost forgot, in all the excitement. If we get approached by a girl called Amber this evening, you're my sister. I'm doing an undercover assignment where I'm supposed to be dating a colleague."

He'd been so concerned at saying this, and it was such a nothing burger after the missent bare boobs.

He palmed the stone from a Gordal olive and took a swig of Negroni.

"What? Which colleague?"

"Bel."

"Why would she need you to be her boyfriend?"

"She was working undercover and I walked into the situation and she was forced to introduce me as her bloke. I promise you, she's sick about the fact. Not least because she doesn't want to share credit for the story."

"Newsflash, *Bel* is using this to pull you."

"Ha. I promise you, Bel would not pull me out of the way of a speeding truck."

"What does it entail? Making out with her?"

"No, of course not. In name only."

It was strange, Connor thought, how Jen didn't really want him anymore, but didn't want anyone else to have him either.

"Do you find her attractive?"

"Why? What does it matter?" Connor said.

"I don't know," Jen said. "I hate the thought of you with someone else, Connor. I've spent five years fending off the competition. I don't want to see whoever she is coming in as I'm leaving."

Connor thought Jen might be trying flattery as a last bid—there'd been no fending he was aware of.

"Well, be reassured the only desire Bel Macauley creates is the longing to be out of her company."

JENNIFER TURNED TO HIM, eyes shiny with natural wine and real emotion, outside the Britannia lobby.

"I know I've behaved appallingly. But I didn't realize how totally out of love with me you were, until tonight. Carrying on when you knew you didn't love me anymore wasn't right either. I know what you're like when you're devastated, because of losing Maurice."

Connor pushed his hands into his pockets. *Do not take Maurice's name in vain to minimize your shittery.*

"I'm the bastard because I haven't been horrible to you about this?"

Connor had expected her to be bowled-over grateful he'd not gone crazy. He realized now that Jen's ego didn't like that he'd coped, that she'd been denied him storming and raging about his jealousy. She'd wanted him to fight for her, over her.

"If you'd been sent a dick pic tonight, intended for another woman, and I said you're ultimately in the wrong for not loving me enough, how would that go down?"

Jen sniffed and shrugged. "I've never been able to out-argue you, Connor."

"'Night. Safe journey tomorrow," he said, giving her a quick, tight hug, too brief for either of them to feel anything.

Forty-five minutes later Connor was once again sitting up bare-chested in bed, doomscrolling alone, finding Francis the PT in Jen's friends with ease. He looked like Joe Wicks trying to be punk rock. Willy-flashing goon.

Now they had reached the end, he thought about his and Jen's start and could see them in totality. He was playing the part of a somewhat spontaneous North London playboy in their early years—*Hey, I know we've only just met, but want to come with me to New York for my brother's wedding?*—and he'd found it an exhilarating escape from himself, at first. The fact it wasn't really him was the buzz. No wonder, really, Jen felt that he was mis-sold goods.

She was, in fact, entirely correct in her parting words. He'd stopped caring about her when she hadn't cared he was suicidal. He'd survived that experience, but his feelings for her had curled up and died. They were a good-times romance, untested by crisis, and when bad times arrived they had discovered they weren't compatible sharing a nuclear shelter.

23

Bel suggested she and Connor meet for a pre-match drink elsewhere in Didsbury, and walk to Ci Vediamo together. Otherwise they'd have to snap into a loved-up mode they hadn't practiced and quite possibly couldn't pull off, as soon as their shoes hit the pavement outside the cab.

Appearances were everything here, so Bel had bought a dress for the occasion: a strapless black mini with marabou-feather trim along the hem, plus sheer tights and black stilettos, which she had to balance on carefully, as if she were on ice. Her hair was in a big bundle of salon-created updo with artful wisps. The lip-linered brick-pink lips and false-lashed eyes she did at home.

It had been witty in the planning and felt fairly ludicrous in practice, not least because it was straining to be sexy. Bel accepted her usual half-arsed style was a form of protection. If you'd not tried that hard, no one could mock your effort. She was strangely vulnerable, and more so when she was plus-oneing with terminally judgmental Captain Cheekbones.

When she walked into the carpets-and-wooden-beams pub she'd chosen, Connor had a table and a pint in front of him. He was in a light gray, thin wool sweater, his hair shorter, sideburns still rakish—and, unhelpfully, he looked like an enhanced version of office Connor.

He got up to insist he buy her wine, but not before Bel caught a look of extreme despondency on his face before he'd seen her. Was an evening in her company that much of an ordeal? She knew the likely answer.

"Did Jennifer have a nice visit?" Bel asked, once they both had a beverage, and Connor momentarily looked wrong-footed that she knew that much.

"Yes, thanks."

"What did you do?"

"Nothing too strenuous. Dinner at Erst in the Northern Quarter if you know it? Yeah, it was really good."

As predicted, even without anyone listening in, it was tricky to find topics that were sufficiently innocuous. As they drained their drinks, Bel's anxiety that they weren't about to magically transform into relaxed, fizzy chemistry made her snap.

"Connor, I'm worried it's not going to work if there's *this* between us," she whispered through gritted teeth, flapping her hands at the air.

"A pub table?" Connor said.

Bel hadn't eaten much through a combination of butterflies and the pressure of a tight dress, and a large Sauvignon Blanc had landed fairly hard.

"The obvious frost of arseiness," Bel said. "The touch of cold arse in the air."

"How do you mean?"

She smiled. "You tolerate me at best."

"Whereas you're super keen on me?" Connor said, with a sardonic look.

They stood up to leave, Bel picking her way carefully across the carpet.

"When you see two people in close conversation, you can immediately tell if they're involved or not," Bel said, as they emerged into the street. "The body language, the eye contact, the way they lean in when they talk. If they're new, it's all intense. The whole 'nobody else in the room' feeling."

"Your point is . . . ?"

"We've been going out eight months and we recently moved in together, you've come up north for me. We're serious, but we're in the first flush of love. There's still going to be the *crackle* of"—she cleared her throat—"electricity."

"Electricity?" Connor repeated dully.

You are going to have to act like you fancy the shit out of me, are you up to that considerable acting feat? was embarrassing enough to hint at, without Connor blanking her like this.

Bel plowed on.

"I'm giving you explicit permission for any physical contact during this evening. Anything that a couple would do. You'd not worry about putting your hand on your girlfriend's knee. If it feels natural, do it."

"Right."

Connor's flat monosyllable made it clear she had offered a Snickers to someone with a severe peanut allergy.

"I assume vice versa is allowed too?"

"I'll probably cope," Connor said.

Yet she didn't feel she could grab for his hand. If she didn't have the courage when no one was watching, how much worse would it be when they were?

"This is what I mean!" Belle hissed. "The chilly sarcasm. All great as office enemies, but I'm worried it's going to knacker us cosplaying lovers."

"We're not enemies!" Connor said, looking surprisingly offended.

"I wouldn't call us friends," Bel said.

"We're colleagues," Connor replied.

"You know how corporate team-building weekends do trust exercises? What's our equivalent?"

Connor sighed and put his hands in his pockets. They couldn't arrive like this, Bel thought. You wouldn't believe they shared a Netflix login, let alone knocked boots.

"OK. My bra size is 34DD. I think they're holding up quite well but if I was on top and lights on, I'd definitely be self-conscious enough to keep my shoulders back, like . . ."

Bel stopped and gestured a tension in her chest, performing an impression of a heavy-lidded, coital gaze, mouth gone slack. She dropped it and grinned again.

"I don't bother with waxing because I'm too lazy. I bought one of those at-home hair removal IPL things. I am worried with my styling skills it looks like a gerbil's been in a fight."

Bel glanced over and Connor was grimacing. He actually *grimaced* at the notion of her nude. He was so not her kind of person: pube jokes were life.

"Sorry, what's the point of this?" Connor said.

"It's the private stuff you'd know if we were seeing each other. I'm breaking down our barriers."

"I don't think they're likely to ask me to draw a picture!" he said, with distaste.

Could he give her a tiny bit less of the I Am Repelled by You Physically and Other Ways Too vibe?

"I'm fast-tracking a sense of intimacy between us, through the cold-water shock plunge of sensitive information."

"How do you imagine this will help? Are we walking into a Mr. and Mrs. Quiz, round one: 'Is he circumcised?'"

"Are you?" she said, brash with nerves.

"Fucking hell! *No.* I don't much want to talk about private stuff as prep if that's OK? I feel a man doing it to a woman would be taken very differently too."

Oof. That hit home, he was right.

"All right, apologies," said Bel, holding her "New Jersey wife" red-manicured hands up, trying to sound breezily unbothered.

"I don't think chatting about our genitalia brings 'ease' in British society," Connor said, and although he was at least smiling as he said it, Bel was suitably mortified.

Sharing the state of one's depilation, only to be firmly put in your place because you were grossing out the listener, was not a pleasant sensation. They walked the rest of the distance in silence, with Bel feeling, thanks to white wine pissedness, self-beclowning and apprehension, borderline tearful.

Connor turned to her as the fairy-lit palm trees appeared in the distance.

"We'll be fine."

He took her hand, and having not anticipated this whatsoever, Bel felt self-conscious at it revealing she was sweating. She was having a bout of extremely ill-timed stage fright.

They joined the hubbub of the bar and immediately got "And who are you?" from not only the door police, but other guests.

"Hi! We're the 'first day at school' ones here—we only met Amber a fortnight ago. Well, my girlfriend did, I'll let her tell the story," Connor said. "Connor and Bella . . . A Peroni is great, thanks . . . One of these?"

He lifted a Prosecco from a passing tray and handed it to her, clinked.

"Amber's popular, huh? I'd not get a third of this turnout." He paused to gently and affectionately brush an artful wisp of Bel's sweepy fringe out of her eyes. "You look really great, by the way."

Bel was a mixture of brokenly grateful and completely stunned. Where had Connor been hiding this easygoing look-alike the whole time?

24

Connor was so sad. He could try to find a more macho word, a face-saving alibi, but his counselor told him to name and sit with his feelings more often. He was sad, and knowing he and Jennifer had run their course and were better off apart did not stop him being sad.

Yesterday evening, probably steeped in Friday rosé, she'd sent him one of those long-ass messages it took three full-screen-length scrolls to read, starting: *Connor we can't leave it like this*, which it turned out translated as *I won't be dumped like this*.

He didn't want to send a reply that could be misread (or read aloud to Libby while doing A Voice) so he called Jen up and said, using purest Stoke Newington self-help speak: "It's honestly better if we shift into the acceptance phase and accept bargaining is over, or we are retraumatizing ourselves." She cried again, but conceded. He cried once they'd rung off.

If Connor was going to sit with his feelings, he was also going to sit with a drink, and he got to the pleasantly lo-fi Didsbury dad pub Bel had nominated early enough for a sly pre-pint, returning his empty and replacing it with a second drink before she arrived.

Bel Macauley walked in looking like something from a 1980s advert for dark chocolate. This was not a derogatory thought: He could hear his brother Shaun reviewing her appearance with "WOOF." It was a power move, in Connor's grudging opinion, to scrub up that well and mostly choose not to. Maybe the Aarons of this world irritated her too much, which was understandable.

He couldn't tell her he was having a low day, or why. Connor knew that false friend, alcohol, was soothing it and possibly soon going to make it worse. But tonight he had to pretend to be a sociable, happy person with a girlfriend in front of strangers, so needs must.

He'd been expecting to coast on Bel's buoyant, can-do Belness, but she was unlike herself: preoccupied and agitated. It seemed to peak as they got up to leave, and she started fretting they weren't going to fool anyone.

With a jarring lack of timing, she apparently thought this was the moment to point out they didn't like each other very much, and Connor bit down his indignation. *She'd asked him to do this, so WTF? Now, really?*

It got worse when she announced they needed to "break down barriers" and Connor tuned in to a description of . . . *oh God, herself unclothed, and during sex, what?*

He had to quickly arrange his face to convey a defensive *yuck* because, in fact, he was ashamed to discover he didn't feel nonchalant. Blame the beer, perhaps, or how good her exposed, chinawhite collarbones looked in that dress, but Connor's mind's eye reflexively served him an image he had *absolutely not asked for and did not want* of her astride him, him clasping her bare hips. Her attitude toward him would be completely altered when he thrust . . . *NOPE! No. There will be no fantasizing thrusting, stop right there.*

He'd thought he was currently out of commission in this regard, and he'd never spent a second considering what Bel Macauley was like in the sack. Yet with her making that *experiencing pleasure* face, an unmistakable lightning had gone right through him, with a particular and shaming emphasis in his groin. Fuck's sake, men were simple creatures. He didn't even find her *attractive*. Well, objectively . . . yes, she was attractive, not remotely his taste, though. Too . . . too *much*.

As she tilted at asking for a description of his junk, he emphatically shut her down. As if visualizing hate-sex with Bel was going to help anything whatsoever here, except the rate his therapist could charge when he went back to London.

She fell quiet again and Connor felt guilty. He'd said he'd help, he should help.

He took her hand. It was very soft and slightly damp, and he realized he'd been unfair: never thinking for a moment Bel would be nervous. The previous eight minutes of conversation suddenly made sense. They'd been transmitting on different wavelengths ever since they met, he might've at last tuned in to a signal he understood: she wanted looking after.

That much he could manage.

He led her into the bar with an air of assertiveness, getting them drinks, fielding inquiries about their identity with a lively confidence. Bel was staring at him as if he'd produced a turtle-dove from a top hat.

Had she honestly never worked out that her and Aaron treating him like an unwanted nuisance, laughing about him to bond, might not have brought out the best in him? That you might get back what you give out? Clearly not.

He'd seen a glimpse of a different side to Bel Macauley with the strange episode of the former colleague calling in at Deansgate, a man she evidently couldn't face.

If she had a stalker—he had to assume it was too great a coincidence that it was part of her invented persona—it didn't seem at all Bel not to dispatch him with some salty home truths.

Ci Vediamo was awash with a kind of hedonism that Connor rarely dipped his toe into anymore, and he didn't doubt there were *frequent trips to the restrooms* going on. The volume of the music, the units consumed and the clearly maxed capacity meant he and Bel were more clinging to each other as if aboard a ship in a storm than chatting.

"I'm going to get us a couple of those things," Bel said to him, and gestured to a row of dangerously red lowball drinks in the distance, with wedges of watermelon on the rim. These cocktails were on the right-hand side of the bar, by the till, and he intuited what Bel meant was "getting eyeballs on the iPad area."

"Have at it."

Connor, tipping beer bottle to lips, watched the whirl of the room and felt drunker than he had for a good while. He was single. He'd have to keep repeating this to himself until it sunk in. Dating apps? Oh God, no. Going on dates, full stop? Starting again from the beginning? He had no appetite for any of it. There should be a word for this liminal state: not still in a relationship, not yet single. He felt predatory eyes upon him, and deliberately looked away.

ACROSS THE ROOM, Bel had been intercepted by a late-twenties, hipsterish man with a mustache, stubble and collar-length hair. Not a good combination, Connor thought. Worked for Kevin Kline in 1995, and no one else ever. Bel had found an arancini ball and cupped it decorously over a napkin as she dispatched it. He liked that she ate with such gusto.

He watched with an academic interest as Mustache Man tried his moves, pretending that the effort of leaning in to hear what Bel was saying required him to unthinkingly put his hand lightly on her waist.

As she spoke animatedly, eyes cast upward to emphasize a point, his eyes slithered down her chest.

Bel seemed unperturbed and could handle herself, and essentially it was none of his business. Yet, Connor thought, he was meant to be acting like she actually was his girlfriend. By Barking pub rules, he should be ready to throw a chair.

Mustache Man had wiggled his way close enough to accidentally bump chests with her as they both laughed at something, hand then on the small of her back.

Oh, OK, this guy was taking the piss. Connor put his beer down and squeezed a path to them.

"Need a hand with those, darling?" Connor said, taking a glass from her and giving a pointed look to her suitor.

"Nice to meet you," Bel said to Mustache Cad, accepting her summons.

Back in their original location, Bel whispered into his ear, "Ted's a waiter here. Good recruit for gossip. The iPad drawer's *not locked*. I've seen the actual iPad, it's there."

"Oh, that's why you were flirting with him that hard, was it? That's your excuse for your TED Talk? *I know which drawers should be locked.*"

Bel hooted and Connor grinned and it might be the first genuine laugh they'd shared.

Connor looked round the room, and then at her mouth, no doubt thinking things a lot of people had thought, looking at that mouth. Music pounded. *You were a stranger in my phone book . . .*

He slid his hand round her back, pulled her toward him like she was his to manhandle and kissed her exposed neck, at the curve with her shoulder. He felt Bel's body go rigid with shock. He had a strong intuition he'd dished her back a version of what he had felt on the way here. It was a sleazy liberty, yes, but he'd been told to.

"Was that electricity?" he muttered, as they disentangled.

Bel caught up with the moment and wound her arm round his waist in a casual gesture of ownership. There was that bolt of lightning in Connor again, and he discreetly shifted so there was no risk of crotches touching. He didn't want it receiving any missent memos. His senses were still full of the brush of her skin, and the scent of her perfume.

"Oh God, you're here! You came! Thank you so much for coming!" Amber shrieked, suddenly at their side.

25

Was that electricity? Connor's whisper reminded Bel he was doing this by special request. She needed her pathetic body to catch up. It felt like he'd pushed a key into her ignition and, with one swift twist, her engine coughed into life.

Although she'd given him this pass, she'd never thought he'd use it. For a surreal second, when Connor pulled her toward him, eyes locked on hers, and the Arctic Monkeys' "Knee Socks" blasting out, she even thought he was going to kiss her. She discovered she had no chill about it whatsoever. Undercover revelation: it turned out kissing someone was still going to feel like kissing, whatever motive you've ascribed to it. As Connor wasn't single, she wasn't sure the politics of it were very sound. Fortunately it was her neck his lips brushed, as Bel tried to ignore how good it felt.

There would be no daydreaming of the pushing of keys into ignitions, no thanks. This wasn't real—and anyway, Connor might be good-looking, and smell nice (sort of spicy oranges? Almost Christmassy), but he was also awful.

Awful, and yet able to dramatically improve for a special occasion? Bel hadn't worked out how she felt about Connor morphing into this approachable, considerate doppelgänger. She was grateful and relieved, and wondering which version of him was the real Connor.

Amber seized on them excitedly: "You're here! You came!" She was in a pink Birthday Girl sash across an off-the-shoulder black dress, ushering her boyfriend, Rick, over. "Meet Bella and Connor, my new favorites!"

The blokeish silver fox, Rick, in band T-shirt and wooden bead necklace, was pleasant enough, though, Bel got the impression, less interested in novelty people than his girlfriend. He made nimble excuses to talk to guests he knew.

"The food is so good," Bel gushed.

"Thank you! It's from the Italian restaurant round the corner. Are you a food person?"

"Only in the sense I'm greedy and I enjoy cooking a lot."

"Wow, as in you cook for guests? I'm so shit. I will only touch the deep-fat fryer here in an emergency. I get huge anxiety in hostessing if it's my food," Amber said.

"It doesn't bother me," Bel said. "I think if I'm going to go to trouble at the stove I want as many people to know about it as possible, ha."

"Would you let me join the Bella Supper Club?! I would *love* that," Amber said.

"Of course!"

"Where's your place again?"

Bel had a sense of losing control of the direction of travel.

"Ancoats. One of those duplexes where everything is distressed brick and uplighting and downlighting."

"Like a converted loft–type place? I have such a thing for those, being from the suburbs."

"It's so swaggy but my rent is criminal."

"Oh my God, I'd love to nosy around! Would you cook for me? Is this too cheeky?"

"No. Absolutely," Bel said, looking toward a studiously blank Connor. She was cheerfully scribbling out a check she had no idea how she'd cash. "Bring Rick!"

As she said it, she thought, *Whatareyoudoing*. Just say yes now, like it's not a thing, and then kick it into the long grass?

"Any chance you're free next weekend?" Amber made prayer

hands. "I've got cover on the Saturday which literally *never happens* and we said we should do something good with it."

"Um . . ."

Bel realized she was experiencing a high-performance collector-networker in her natural habitat. She was trying to make an overnight friend for a purpose; Amber did this as a hobby, if not a living.

Did Bel bluster her way out, or did she grab the opportunity and cannonball from the diving board? How large a problem was it for Amber to know Bel's address, versus the sense of trust engendered by having them in her home? Toby said she had six weeks.

"I think so?" Bel said, stalling. "Con, can you remember?"

Connor produced his phone as if to check a diary, squeezing the button at the side to bring the display up. With a lurch of sickening dread, at that moment, Bel saw he had a sun-dappled photo of Jennifer the Girlfriend as his lock screen.

Oh. Holy. Fuck. How had they not noticed this during the Platt Fields planning? They were so absorbed by what they found *on* his phone, they didn't examine the artifact itself.

Amber had seen, for sure. Connor had effectively held it under her nose.

"Who's that?" Amber said, in confusion, darting a look at Connor and then Bel.

"Connor's sister," Bel said, in a panic, and then realized she'd in fact made it worse. *Sure, everyone in his part of London has a romantic portrait of their sibling on their handset.*

Amber's look of confusion increased and everything they'd worked for now hung in the balance. Bel heard herself say, "She passed away."

"Oh God!" Amber's hand went to her mouth. "I shouldn't have asked, I'm so sorry."

"No, it's fine, you weren't to know," Bel said, reaching out to touch Amber's wrist in reassurance.

Connor was stonily unreadable throughout the entire exchange, but as soon as Amber moved on, he said to Bel, "Let's go."

His manner felt ominous.

THEY HAD PRE-AGREED that they'd taxi together back to Ancoats, debrief and Connor would journey onward to Salford. They French-exited into the balmy night (was it still a French exit when 99 percent of people didn't know who you were? Maybe simply an exit).

The taxi driver was blaring a Ministry of Sound CD and making conversation about local crime, so their debate was delayed.

As they entered her flat, Bel threw the lights on and she saw Connor's eyes widen at the interiors.

"Cup of tea?" she said, apprehensively.

"No thanks. What on *earth* was that?" Connor said. His tone was combative.

"I'm sorry," Bel said, "I improvised."

"No shit. My *dead sister*?"

A late-arriving thought, one that should've arrived earlier for Bel: What if Connor actually did have a dead sister? Her skin prickled.

"I didn't know what else to say. She'd seen your girlfriend's picture. It was either that or it looked like incest."

"What do I do next time my girlfriend visits? What with her now not only supposed to be someone else, but also not alive?"

"I have no idea," Bel said. "Fuck. Sorry. Could you visit her in London instead?"

Connor ruffled his hair and cynic-laughed. "Why did I have a premonition that it'd be up to me to fix this through sacrifice?"

"I'm not telling you what to do."

"What else do I do?"

"I don't know! You're assuming I just said what I said with some sort of nefarious plan, as opposed to just blurting the first thing that came into my head."

"And if I decline to murder my girlfriend, you'll go to Toby and say the story is sunk because the intern is both an idiot and a wanker?"

Bel was bewildered by this interpretation of what had happened. Why would she run him down to their boss? Connor Adams had, above all, a terrible victimhood complex.

"Why are you behaving like I inflicted this on you? I wasn't trying to paint you into any corner, I was reacting in the moment. You left the photo there. This is not a single-parent fuckup, we both had a hand."

"Yes, except the entire 'lying about who we are in the first place' situation is borne of you."

"You knew the deal! I notice you've not explained what I should've said. Who were you going to say your girlfriend was?"

Bel put her YSL Niki bag down on the kitchen island, metal hardware straps clattering like a bicycle chain. She opened the cupboard and picked up a water glass, proffering it to Connor. He shook his head.

"I don't know what you should've said," Connor said. "I know I'm not putting Jennifer into witness protection to service a story to benefit you, that probably won't even come off."

"Great. Thanks. It's your decision to walk away—but stop acting like I've suddenly persecuted you."

"You genuinely don't think I have any right to be upset, do you? You don't care what goes back to Toby. I *need* this job. I don't have loaded parents to fall back on, and I can't treat it all as a jape."

Bel's heart leapt into her throat.

"Loaded parents? What the fuck is that supposed to mean?"

Connor glanced at their surrounds. "It doesn't seem to me like you'd be in huge trouble without your salary."

This was sufficiently personal that Bel decided unless he disclosed a deceased loved one, she was going to assume he was simply a massive arsehole.

"You know absolutely nothing about me. You've disliked me since the first second you set eyes on me. You're not exactly hard to read, I'm sorry to break it to you, if you thought this was an elegant facade." Bel waved a hand in front of his face, knowing she was losing control, and not caring. "You've been practicing kicking off about petty stuff; now you've finally found a mistake you think you can attack me with. It's so perfect that it was only me covering for YOUR error. But hey, why let logic affect things when you're massaging the chip on your shoulder?"

"I don't dislike you. That's a total invention on your part simply because I haven't fawned over you, like Aaron or Toby."

Oh, please! She might've guessed: the problem was her expectations and her ego.

"How would you describe your attitude toward me?"

"Neutral," Connor said. "Completely indifferent."

"If this is neutral, I'd hate to see actual animosity."

"You know what? This is main-character syndrome," Connor said. "You have to invent this . . . *grandiose antipathy* on my part, because someone simply not caring either way about Bel Macauley is too much for you to process."

"I'm a rich kid, now I'm egomaniacal—"

"How would you describe your attitude to me, from the start?" Connor said.

She didn't want him to win but she had nothing better: "Erm. Neutral."

"Exactly."

"You don't like that I've stood up for myself in the face of your I'm So Important and Special I've Got to Establish My Superior Mind Mr. Darcy energy."

"As opposed to your I'm So Important and Special I'm the Feisty Girl Who Wore Converse Boots With My Prom Dress energy."

"You know what, you can leave," Bel said, walking over and holding the door open.

"Agreed," Connor said, striding past her.

At least she no longer needed to wonder which was the real Connor.

26

"I thought you weren't risking Sunday seshes with me," Shilpa said. They had seen off roast beef with horseradish cream and salted caramel choux buns in the Gothy Victorian splendor of The Edinburgh Castle Pub's first-floor restaurant. They were now nursing large red wines in its downstairs snug, the unseasonal "thick velvet curtains and pillar candles on saucers" decor suggesting a séance.

"That was before I spent a Saturday night with Connor Adams," Bel replied, satisfied they couldn't be overheard.

Today she was in a Bel outfit of billowy black linen strappy maxi sundress over striped T-shirt, and her Doc Martens. She wished she'd been dressed as herself for their confrontation, not a dolly bird.

"He might've felt like an idiot and externalized it!" Shilpa said, having earlier heard of his wrongdoing and revealed herself as a *Free Connor* campaigner. ("Your passion for justice for people with strong jawlines is truly inspiring," Bel said. "Shilpa Gupta QC." "I just hate to see wrongful convictions. Imagine him sent inside, banged up . . ." Shilpa made a rabbit face. "STOP," Bel said.)

"Whatever he felt, there was no excuse for turning on me like that. Plus, I know his getting dragged into it was my fault, but doing what he did was about the worst outcome for me possible."

Which reminded Bel of the unhinged promises she'd gaily made to Amber about having her over for a couples' dinner. Hopes that Amber might have forgotten in the party whirl were dashed by a *Is that on, should Rick and I bring anything?* message earlier today. To which Bel responded: *Just your beautiful selves and maybe a bottle of red at 7:00 p.m.!*

In terms of following any plan, she was joyriding a Cessna plane in an electrical storm at night, playing Nine Inch Nails and swigging from a bottle of Wild Turkey.

She didn't even have a "boyfriend" to produce anymore. She recalled the secret shivery joy of his embrace. Ugh. Who *was* that guy? To think she'd felt supported by Connor. She'd had more than enough of men pretending to be one thing and turning into another. Apart from anything else, it really attacked her belief she could read people.

"Do you think Ant will try to come to your office again?" Shilpa said, unknowingly picking up on her thoughts. "What is the 'expect me to play back' threat going to mean? Are you SURE you can't tell York CID?"

"I don't think they'll intervene on florid emails," Bel said. "And no, he won't come back, he wouldn't risk Aaron stopping him like that again. He'd think it was undignified, he's always drowning in pride. I have no idea what he thinks he can do to me. Maybe it's barring me from his office. I've got to hold my nerve, I guess. The whole point of him saying it is for him to live rent-free in my mind."

Shilpa made a face of revolted disbelief.

Bel again pondered the alternative: a message or a phone call where she explained to Anthony, in articulate terms, how much this upset her, and what a repugnant creep he was being. When she had tried this, it had bounced like rubber arrows off the ten-story stone wall of Anthony's towering self-image as a Nice Guy, and his unshakable belief that she was in love with him. Telling him different was converted into reinforcing this delusion, so arguing with him was like feeding kibble to a kibble-powered gremlin.

"You know what? I knew he was completely wrong for you from the start," Shilpa said. "When you said, 'He can be quite quiet and serious, he is very sensitive and might take a joke the wrong way.' You should be able to introduce your friends to your partner and know they'll 'get' them because you do. And vice versa. That's part of how you know they're the one—you can't wait." Shilpa frowned, no doubt recalling Zack. "*One* of the ones."

"Oh God, did I say that?" Bel said. She had mentally scrubbed the memory of the frenetic upswing phase where she believed she was going to live happily ever after as Mrs. Anthony. What she in fact needed was psychotherapy, Kalms, a hot bath with a romance novel and an assertive conversation with Tim.

"Yeah. It made me think that if you have to make lots of excuses for how they might behave, they're definitely not the one."

"Amen to that, sister."

"Is he stopping you being on dating apps? He's searching for you on them, isn't he?"

Bel nodded: she was sure he was.

"Dating apps are stopping me being on dating apps but yes, it's a headache for the future because I am sure my seeing anyone else would set him off."

"How can he think he's a good person and not a walking workplace misconduct with a stupid goatee?"

"From my experience of life so far, I think everyone thinks they have reasons to do what they do. Bad people are always other people. Even serial killers think they're misunderstood shock-tactic campaigners."

Bel walked back to her apartment arm in arm with Shilpa, making a mental note that if they were seen, she'd need to say they resolved Cancún.

They decided on large mugs of builder's tea and a comfort watch of *Clueless*, taking up horizontal positions on the couches, legs hooked over armrests.

"Paul Rudd completely takes the curse off the whole 'is her ex-stepbrother' thing, doesn't he?" Shilpa sighed. "I would totally inbreed with him."

"Perhaps I should've gone that route with Connor's 'sister' on his phone."

"Wait! You don't think that was why he kicked off; he has a dead sister?!" Shilpa said.

"I very much hope not"—Bel grimaced—"but even if he does, he could've said so."

What made her fearful this was right, was that there was something about the heat of Connor's reaction, his sense of injury, that she was missing. Could it simply be protectiveness of his girlfriend?

During Cher's date with Christian, the doorbell rang. They exchanged a worried look. No deliveries on a Sunday afternoon.

"Oh, if that's Anthony, I am going to DEAL," Shilpa said, sitting up like a meerkat.

"He doesn't have my address," Bel said in a hush, though as she said it, she wondered. She paused the film, stood up and patted Shilpa's leg to indicate *stay there*.

The sitting room area couldn't be seen from the doorway, the kitchen island was in the way.

"Lie low. Only intervene if it is Anthony and he Maces me or something."

She crossed the apartment and looked through the spyhole.

"Oh, seriously. I don't need any more of your crap," Bel said, after wrenching the door open to him, as much in tense embarrassment and edginess as aggression.

27

Connor removed his spendy-looking sunglasses. He was in a burgundy jacket and it was a shame he was odious, given he looked pleasant. God had stuck a nice face on a turd. A Colin the Caterpillar white chocolate smile on a log.

"I totally understand why you don't want more of last night. Can I come in for a minute?" he said.

Bel frowned and yet stood aside to let him enter. She could see why he hadn't simply called her, no way would she have answered.

"I want to offer you an unreserved apology," he said.

Bel said nothing. Probably an image-saving ploy from a man so obsessed with his career advancement. *Don't tell management, we can work something out.*

"I was completely out of order. To give you some background, which isn't an excuse, I've not been open about my circumstances. Jen and I broke up last weekend."

"Oh," Bel said, in genuine surprise.

"I found out she's having an affair via her sending me a nude meant for the other guy, which arrived as her train was pulling into Piccadilly."

"Wow!" Bel was authentically taken aback now. She thought of Connor as a man with his pick, never a man being mistreated. For a brief second it occurred to her they were both guilty of operating on insufficient information about the other.

"Yep. Add to the fact I thought I could cold-turkey my citalopram prescription six weeks ago, and the fact I'd had a skinful. You saw where it ended up. You were quite right, you did nothing other than try to cover for my howling fuckup. I hit some sort of psychological rock bottom aided by Italian lager. Then took it out on you."

"So." Bel paused. "Your basis for having a go at me was 'how can my girlfriend visit me now?' and you already knew she wouldn't be visiting you?"

"Yep," Connor said. "I was fighting about it in principle. I was being a dick."

"I see the dick but not the principle."

"I woke up this morning and replayed what I'd said and was pretty appalled at myself. After a gym session and a lot of self-recrimination, I thought I'd at least drag my self-loathing arse out and apologize for being obnoxious."

He cleared his throat. "The ad hominem stuff about loaded parents was especially over the line. Sorry."

Bel thought he might've blushed.

"From Aaron, I assume?"

"Yes. He was being gossipy but not nasty. The weaponizer was me."

"Whatever backgrounds we're from, let's agree we both work hard and don't want to get sacked?" Bel said. "I've never asked about your upbringing. It's got no bearing on anything."

"Agreed. That was the 'chip on my shoulder' you identified, because being the intern aged thirty-four sometimes does a number on my self-worth."

"OK. Apology accepted, I guess," Bel said, stiffly. She had to accept it, given the groveling. It was inconvenient to her prejudices that she thought it was sincere too. "Sorry about your girlfriend. The photo you have at the office made me think you were very loved-up."

"Ah, that's never been about her, really. My dog Maurice died at the end of last year and he was the love of my life. I know having pictures of late pets on display is somewhat open to ridicule, so it was a way of smuggling him in."

"Oh. Right."

Bel was duly disarmed. Connor had now admitted to: being dramatically cucked, needing antidepressants and mourning a dog as his true love. Bel conceded he had bared a fair amount of soul. He'd not expected to be forgiven with some stilted formalities or awarded points just for turning up; this was material she could use against him. The strategy underlying his approach was clear: he was showing he was willing to trust her, in return for being forgiven. He had judged it right: she'd not tell Aaron any of this.

Connor looked at his feet.

"You might've already spoken to Toby, or Amber. Or you might not want to work with me anymore. But I'm willing to carry on with our couple charade, if you want me to."

Bel's mouth opened, and she said, "I've only confirmed to Amber that our dinner's on, I'd not said anything about you."

Connor smiled up from under his brow.

"You are truly jazz freestyling, aren't you? You'd confirmed it anyway?"

"It was a placeholder, yes, while I figured it out."

"Dare I ask how we're throwing a dinner party? And where? I didn't think letting them know where you lived was part of the plan."

Bel found she was actually relieved to have someone else to brainstorm this with. She'd never wanted Connor involved, but it was a bonus to have someone in her corner.

"I've fretted about this, but my rent comes up for renewal in eight weeks. I can always bounce on if I decide the Kendricks knowing where I live is too hairy."

"You'd do that? It's pretty amazing," Connor said, looking round, then their eyes met as they mutually recalled last night's take on that.

"As you might've alluded to, it's nice but it's ruinously expensive so there would be an upside to being forced to relocate. I don't see how else we could make somewhere else look inhabited for one night. Even if I got an Airbnb, she's a Superhost. She might recognize the listing."

"Fair point."

Bel folded her arms. "Shall I give you a quick tour, so you know your way around ahead of Saturday? Shilpa's here, by the way. Shilpa, show yourself."

"Hi, Connor!" Shilpa said, sitting up on the other side of the kitchen.

"Oh, hello! Good to see you," Connor said, and Bel noticed he seemed authentically pleased at her presence, despite Shilpa obviously having overheard his climb-down. Was he fundamentally decent, or did he have a soft spot for her? Both felt unlikely—it was one or the other.

Bel walked Connor round the sitting room, the dining room, the ground-floor guest bedroom with en suite, then they clanked up the metal spiral staircase to the primary bedroom.

Bel was glad that Shilpa was downstairs, as showing Connor the king-size bed they were meant to share was a little disconcerting. *Here's where we don't have the earthquake sex that you don't know I boasted about—kill me now.*

"Very large en-suite bathroom back there," Bel pointed out.

"Man, this pisses all over my digs in Salford, I can tell you that much," Connor said, hands in pockets. He politely made no move to firsthand inspect the bathroom, which Bel was quite glad of given there was a box of heavy-flow Tampax on the loo cistern and tights, like shed snakeskin, on the floor.

"Would you be all right to bring a few things for the bathroom and the wardrobe and so on, on Saturday? Theatrical props? We don't need to go overboard but if they ask to look round, we'll need some set dressing—a bottle of aftershave and a toothbrush."

"Of course. I'll set Saturday aside. Means I can help with the shopping or cooking too."

Bel mumbled thanks. Keeping track of Connor's fluctuating morality gave her seasickness.

Downstairs again, he said to Shilpa, nodding toward the freeze frame, "*Clueless?*"

"Yes!"

"*Do you like Billie Holiday? I love him*," he said, proving he not only knew the film but the dialogue in the specific scene.

"Hahaha! Impressive," Shilpa said, eyes like pinwheels.

"My ex loved it," Connor said. "First time I've called her that, feels odd."

"I know what you mean," Shilpa said, trying for "empath" and gravitas despite the fact she was in a Gap adult romper and her hair was in space buns. "You're welcome to stay and watch it."

"Oh, thanks, but I've got a hot appointment with the Hotel Gotham. My brother is an embarrassing swag lord and he wants me to go make a booking for his forthcoming stay *in person*."

Bel was grateful for Connor's smooth refusal; they weren't friends, and she had no interest in the pretense either. They had been air-clearingly honest about where they stood. It didn't change the fact that where they stood was not close.

As he was departing, Bel said, "By the way, I didn't wear Converse boots to my school prom."

"Oh . . ." Connor said, catching up with what she meant, and looking suitably chastened. "Cookie Monster pajamas with heels?"

Bel hated that she laughed. His audacity!

"I was so 'feisty' I didn't go. Let me guess: You were Prom King?" she said.

"Er. Reluctantly."

"Hahahaha. See you at the office."

Bel wasn't saying she needed to establish her dominance in their farewell, but it didn't hurt either.

She closed the door. There was half a minute's pause.

Shilpa hissed, "Oh my GOD. He's so gorgeous and lovely!"

"You took *lovely* from that? I took *not as bad as I thought* at most."

"And he's *single*?!"

"Convenient, not exciting."

"Erm, it's absolutely highly pertinent. The market will be abuzz with the news he's back on it."

"Is there a man market that stretches from London to Manchester? Like an old trading route with stagecoaches?"

Shilpa rested her head on the edge of the sofa like a watchful dog.

"Did you really not have any moment when he was pretending he was your boyfriend when you thought, *Nnnggg*, this is hot? Did you hold hands?"

"Nope and nope!" Bel lied.

Shilpa rolled onto her back.

"I would like to have the kind of fling with him that sees us both publicly condemned by the Pope."

28

"We are fighting thirty degrees Celsius in a densely populated, built-up environment, trapped in an office the size of an Argos pet carrier, with broken air con, and THIS fucking thing," Aaron said, pointing accusingly at a desk fan, which rattled lethargically from side to side and seemed to only move the hot air around. "It's like stirring porridge with a baked baguette."

Bel snapped open the makeup compact she'd bought as Bella, and did a futile ladylike pat of her face with a pressed powder puff. She looked as if she'd been swimming.

Aaron had tied his black "death knock" tie around his head, like Mark Knopfler in Dire Straits. The usually buttoned-down Connor had gone so far as to roll his sleeves up, adopting a "pilot forced to fix the engine himself" energy. Bel found herself curiously distracted by the way his white shirt had gone slightly transparent, and his dark brown hair was glossy with sweat.

She retasked herself to transcribing her interview about a rescue package for Salford Lads Club, a two-hander between herself and Aaron: he did the splash about the anonymous benefactor saving the day, she dug into the Grade II–listed history.

The Mayor story buzzed in her brain like a bee: it was hard to think about other projects. It was hard to believe the man laughing and joking on a Manchester tram as lead item on Channel Four News last night could be brought down by people who couldn't achieve adequate workplace ventilation.

"By the way, gang, email's incoming, but we've got orders to go to the Northern Media Awards at the end of next month,"

Aaron said. "At the Town Hall. We've not been nominated for anything because we've not been here long enough, but Toby says they've still paid for a table for us. We have to go and get our faces seen and lick all the right arses."

Bel and Connor glanced at each other in slight alarm, given they didn't at this time want their faces seen. Furthermore, Bel knew her old paper might have a table at these awards. She'd have to do some background digging about who would be at it.

"Not how Toby put it, obviously," Aaron continued. He did a good impression of Toby: "*Ingratiate yourselves, network your damn tails off. I want everyone reeling with the triple-threat force of your charm offensive* . . . All right, mate, I'm not cracking out the cookie-dough-flavor lube. Connor, you're gonna need to hire a tux."

"Believe it or not, I own one. I'll have to get it sent up," Connor said.

"I do believe that. Bel, buy a new dress. The Mayor's going to be there, Shagger Bailey himself. And they've got some nob 'ead actor hosting."

Bel, heart rate increasing, was careful this time not to look at Connor.

"The Mayor's a shagger?" she repeated.

"So they say." Aaron shrugged. "There's a right Bailey groupie lot around him, isn't there? Word is that GB likes his bananas green. Not illegal green! Like, Leonardo DiCaprio girlfriend–age green. The old dirty bollocks."

"Isn't that worth a story?" Bel said.

Aaron snorted.

"Er, I bet the *Chicago Sun-Times* wanted to run the rumor that Al Capone was on the tax fiddle but there's this thing called proof. Also, he'd probably have shot ya."

"I guess. Bailey's married. Seems a bad fit with the dignity of holding high public office, et cetera."

"True, but you're kind of allowed to play away as long as you keep it on the down-low now, aren't ya? We'd be kink shaming or some such. Weird, cos that's how it used to be with, like, Kennedy and Marilyn Monroe in the 1960s. We're going backward. Not to sound like a massive feminist."

"Careful now," Connor agreed.

"Funny how the values of every era protect men. The house always wins," Bel said.

"Hey, Macauley: Take one for the team and honey trap him?" Aaron said. "If a woman complained about him cracking on to her, that'd be a story."

"I'm not a green banana, sadly. I am a lightly brown spotted banana."

"I can't believe he's that fussy," Aaron said, pulling the tie from his head and drying his face with his arm. "Right, devastated to abandon our hot-sauna three-way sex party but I've got to go interview an unconventional imam. Laters."

When they heard the door to the street bang shut downstairs, Connor said, "Can we go to these awards?"

"Looks like we have to," Bel said. "Let's be smart and keep an apex-predator-level awareness of where the official photographer is in the room. Try to dodge being on anything they'll put on a website."

"Copy that. And what if we end up face-to-face with Bailey?"

"Again, let's try to avoid him. It wouldn't be the end of the world but if he comes into Ci Vediamo afterward and recognizes us . . ." Bel made a gritted-teeth face. "The Town Hall is a big space, he's a celebrity and we're nobodies. Shouldn't be too difficult."

Connor nodded.

"All true and yet this has a 'best-laid plans' feel to it."

"Hmm. Agree. If we skip it, though, it has to be one or the other of us. Both of us having a reason not to go is too suspicious."

"That'd have to be you—I don't have the seniority to pull tactical sickies," Connor said.

"Tell you what, I'll run the problem for both of us past Toby. I feel I already know what he's going to pick regarding *establishing the paper's presence with Manchester's finest* versus *Bel's wacky caper* he's humoring, however."

"Yeah."

"Interesting the shagger thing is now fully Out There in the gossip sphere, isn't it? I always trusted my source but it's still good to get it countersigned."

"Yes, though as Aaron points out, you need aggravating factors to make it reportable."

"I feel sure they're there. This isn't about a high sex drive, he's a callous Jekyll and Hyde."

"Agreed."

They worked on in a comfortable enough silence, Bel concentrating until she disconcertingly saw a WhatsApp arrive from her ex, Tim. He had her new number, but she'd given it to him as a courtesy, and it had only rated a thumbs-up reply. This would need to be special circumstances. She opened it with apprehension.

Hi. Thought you should know I had a weird message from an Anthony Barr at the Yorkshire Post *asking for your mobile number. Said you were friends at the paper and he couldn't get you to answer an email and tell him your new one. I pointed out he could call your office number, and he said oh yeah and went away. Amazing skills for a journalist. Whole thing felt off.*

Bel began shivering like a cold dog while simultaneously almost levitating with rage. Anthony contacting Tim, who didn't know they'd been together the night before she and Tim separated? A tanks-on-lawn move and it was a taunt to Bel. It was sadistic toward Tim, this wide-eyed asking for fake assistance from the unwitting man whose girlfriend Anthony had wooed. And getting her mobile number, without her consent? It was bait, but it was bait she couldn't ignore.

Cheers, appreciate you passing that on, useful to know—I'll sort.
Hope you're well. Bx
No worries.

"Everything OK?" Connor said.
"Yes, why?" Bel said.
"You look like George W. Bush on nine-eleven when he was interrupted reading *My Pet Goat*."
"Oh, got to make a call to my bloody internet provider is all," she said, shoving her sunglasses on and marching out, gripping her iPhone like it was a stun grenade she was about to use in combat.

Downstairs, pacing the pavement, she pressed to call the *Yorkshire Post* reception.

She knew she had to use this anger, surf on its superpower.

"Hi, can I speak to Anthony Barr, please?"

She simmered some more while she listened to the hold music.

"Bel, how are you!" Anthony said, deliberately loud, upbeat. The *I'm broadcasting this on the newsroom floor, your approach to me has been made known* volume. With a strong note of triumph. He'd finally done something sufficiently provocative that he got contact.

"Can you explain why my ex-boyfriend has had a message from you asking for my mobile number?"

"Oh, is he your ex? I wasn't sure. Apologies."

Bel bit down the one-syllable, hard-consonants word she wanted to throw at him for this. He knew perfectly well—she'd told him the day the split occurred. But telling bare-faced untruths was one of Ant's "exhaust your opponent" tactics.

Bel had learned that if someone is prepared to swear black is white, knowing you know they're lying and not caring you both know this, you have nowhere to go.

29

"I had an interesting tale for you about the John Rylands Library and thought it'd be great to chat it through with a Manchester publication."

"You could've called the office number here," Bel said.

"Assumed you'd not want the story nabbed by whoever answered."

"Because you weren't capable of asking for me specifically?"

"You'd not have taken my call! Haha. You won't even see me when I'm fifty feet away."

She imagined Anthony playing coquettishly with the telephone cable, swinging on his chair. All this to soothe his wounded male psyche because she didn't want him anymore, on terms almost nobody would accept.

But that was Anthony: he thought he had her on the hook and could keep making the tasks harder. Bel had walked away, and that couldn't happen: *he* chose when it ended.

This dysfunction now being vividly inflicted on Bel—it was somehow her responsibility to resolve his Reduced Empathy Disorder.

Sorry your mum didn't pick you up from your crib enough, go get therapy.

The way he got gratification from this harassment was so loathsome, Bel worried it bordered on psychopathy.

"You don't have my number for a reason. You know that. You need to back off and stop acting like a creep, or . . ." Bel had not been able to control her emotions in contacting him, and here the lack of planning made her stumble. "Or I will have to start letting other people know what you're doing. I don't think that'll go well for you."

"Sorry, are you making threats toward me, Bel?" he said, pitched nice and clear for anyone around him. He'd anticipated this.

She wanted to scrub her skin off at the thought he was relishing it, with an audience at his end.

"Yes. Fuck off," she said, and ended the call.

She turned to see an embarrassed-looking Connor, passing her on his way out.

"Awful customer service," he said, with an apologetic, wry smile.

Bel trudged back up to her desk, put her mobile down next to her open laptop and sat morose, staring at a larger blank screen and a smaller blank screen.

This was a big sign that read: GET REAL: THE ANTHONY PROBLEM ISN'T GOING TO GO AWAY ON ITS OWN. She had no idea how to fix it, none.

As she'd said to Shilpa, if she told on Ant to his wife, how could she do that in a way that stopped him? Apart from the fact she had no means of directly contacting her, who knew what would happen after the disclosure: *Your husband (who I had intimate relations with) is stalking me?* Pretty wildly unsympathetic as far as pleas for help went. If Anthony and his wife had patched it up, telling her would mean Bel launching missiles on herself—it would be the end of her leverage, and guaranteed he'd tell Tim.

That was what Ant's message to Tim was really about: showing Bel he could do that. She technically had nothing to lose there, except she did.

She was wrecked at the thought of hurting Tim further, of reopening wounds that had barely begun to heal and wax-sealing his claim he'd not known the real Bel. He'd tell his parents.

Bel's mother had been holding them back single-handedly, like a storm-battered Gandalf with his staff, insisting it wasn't fair to take sides in a no-fault breakup. She would be unable to defend a daughter who'd cheated and lied about it, and, on top of that, cheated with somebody so malignant as to tell Tim after the fact.

On every analysis, telling Anthony's wife was impossible, and Bel assumed he'd figured this out. The other route was informing the editor of the *Yorkshire Post* about his emails, imperiling his salary instead. Except she'd have to also tell Toby—you didn't enter into a form of litigation like that and not clue in your new boss. The prospect of that Teams meeting made her want to shrivel up and die. Journalists were gossips by nature and he would become the keynote thing known about that Bel Macauley up north. She'd said relatively little to Anthony in return in messages when they were involved. But she was sure he could still find sensitive, out-of-context WhatsApps if he wanted to act like it was six of one, half a dozen of another, hazing the cops, like that *Baby Reindeer* series.

This was Anthony's power over her. The gun to her head was: *If you reveal I'm pursuing you like this, then everyone you work with, your family and your friends and your ex, will all find out about your sorriest sex life transgression.*

Bel's phone lit up again. She wanted to bash it with a stapler.

Ian
Miss Macauley, you have an admirer here. Two, actually. Erin tells me that Amber Kendrick posted a bird's-eye view photo of the partygoers at her recent thirty-fifth. Someone asks who you are (face obscured, nicely done). Amber says in the comments: my "gorgey" (ugh the hideous neologisms of social media!) "new friend Bella." You are a master of your craft. Bloody good job! Ian.

Bel
Ian, you're very kind 😊 *Thank me when we've nailed the bastard.*

Bel opened her dummy no-followers Instagram account on her laptop, created for snooping only, found Amber's profile and the image in question. In addition to being part of a panorama of dozens, Bel's face was turned away from the camera; a dark-haired man had his face buried in her neck. Thankfully, neither she nor Connor was identifiable.

Ian had intended to pay her a compliment, yet Bel shuddered.

She couldn't help but think a master of her craft would (1) have noticed a photograph being taken and (2) currently not be being outsmarted by a cheating married man.

Bel
Connor, a quick heads-up: my contact re: GB has messaged me to point out there was a party photo on Amber's Instagram and we're in it, she mentions Bella. We're not recognizable tho! 😄

Connor
Yeah I saw that one being taken, hence the hugging to bury our faces 😊

Oh, perfect. Connor had been savvier than her too. And while Bel knew he wasn't fondling her out of any native attraction, it was still sobering to discover it was prompted entirely by necessity.

What a two of clubs kind of day. Fold.

30

Connor wondered if any journalism assignment between now and his retirement would ever be as weird as this one. Turning up at a glamorous apartment with toiletries, a couple of suits, his gym trainers and a coat, intended for one evening's display only. The very Manc-sounding taxi driver said, "Got serious, 'as it?" nodding up at the address and down at Connor's clutter, and he said, "Something like that."

He was dreading tonight, somewhat. It was one thing to perform an assumed identity in the melee of a party and another to lie directly into two people's faces all evening. As if a dinner party with strangers would be easy at the best of times, and this one would require him to safety check his every utterance as it left his alcohol-marinated brain via his mouth.

Bel answered the door, music in the background, St. Vincent, maybe? Her hair piled up in a mound on her head and wound round, like rope on a bollard. She had a dab of flour on her cheek like she'd been styled as the kooky girl in a sitcom.

"Before you give me one of your looks about my outfit, I will be getting changed," she said, wiping at her face and gesturing at her baggy T-shirt and clinging leggings, with a striped apron over the top, tied tight enough to cinch her waist. Connor could imagine, in fact, with the way it simultaneously concealed and revealed her figure, that some men would be very into it. Luckily he wasn't some men.

"One of my looks?" Connor said, mildly perturbed.

"Yes, one of your Dear God Who Got Her Ready winces."

"Wow, now my face is in the dock for silent crimes," Connor said, and she laughed.

He'd kept it together, but actually he was unsettled. She was right in what she'd said last weekend—he'd been way more obvious dispensing disapproval than he thought. And if it had been so evident, Bel's hostile response to him might be more . . . explicable?

"Will what I'm wearing be OK?" He gestured to a navy sweater and black jeans.

"Absolutely."

"I'm going to unpack my scenery props," he said, as Bel returned to a large lump of meat in a double-handled roasting tin on the kitchen island.

"Do it," she said, wielding a pepper grinder. "Treat the place as if you live here. Make a mess."

"You want me to piss on the floor by the loo? Message understood."

Bel guffawed. It occurred to Connor she enjoyed laddish humor in a way women he'd previously known had not. That was journalism for you, coarsening to the soul. (He could hear Aaron saying, "Ponce." And Bel saying, "Chauvinist." Both justified on this occasion.)

Connor stamped up the spiral metal stairs and unzipped his duffel bag in the immaculate bedroom. The exposed red brick in this place made him feel like he was in a late-night members' club, and territorially marking a female colleague's sleeping quarters with stray possessions was deeply odd.

Bel's bed was a football pitch–size piece of furniture with a black headboard and a collection of about eight jute-colored pillows of varying sizes, arranged in rows, hotel-style. The wrinkle-free coverlets were in shades of "shingle beach." A trio of framed black-and-white photographs above depicted quintessential Manchester scenes of yesteryear: kids on cobbles playing under gas lamps; grimy, smoke-belching chimneys; the one of Ena Sharples in a headscarf standing on a balcony, looking out over a monochrome 1960s Salford.

He knew the decor wasn't Bel's choice, but what a strange and somehow appropriative juxtaposition: industrial poverty as style accessory in your grand-and-a-half-a-month shag pad.

Connor wandered between the built-in wardrobes and the bathroom, depositing relevant bits and bobs.

"Your en suite," Connor said, appearing back downstairs to the scent of lemon and garlic in the air. "Astonishing. It's huge. I always think of wet rooms as smaller spaces and you've got some sort of beautiful tiled sanatorium. With a walk-in shower and copper slipper bath."

"Nuts, isn't it," Bel said, wiping hair out of her face with her elbow. "It's the distressed silvered mirrors I like best. They take six to seven years off you."

"You're free to be impressed that I've chosen a side of the bed and left two books, cuff links, a spare watch and a *glass of water* on the table. Impeccable staging."

"Oh, the glass of water. Chef's kiss," Bel said.

"I went for the bulkiest clothes so if they snoop the wardrobes on a tour, it looks full."

"Yeah, it occurred to me on a quick scan they'll not be assessing 'my things versus man things' ratio so a few pairs of shoes and a suit and tie, we're good."

"My thoughts too. No need to turn it into my mate Dave's flat, which is like a terrorist cell's hideout with a PlayStation."

"Hahahaha."

"What's the plan for this evening?" Connor said. "Both meanings. I could do with a sitrep on the iPad, as well as the menu. What can I do to help?"

"OK, if you want to get a seat here . . ." Bel ushered him onto a stool at the kitchen island. She set down, in turn, a chopping board, knife, a packet and two jars. "Cut this cheese into cubes, then these peppers into strips, and we can bung olives on the cocktail sticks and call it pinchos. Pile 'em up and I'll find the serving platter."

"Got it."

"As for the main plan, the mission tonight is to try to get them to talk about the Airbnb. It's not impossible they'll say 'hey, don't pass it on but the Mayor uses it as a bonking shop,' and boom, there's the story. There's the baby delivered into our lap."

"Not impossible but also mad on their part? As facilitators?"

"Yeah, but it's gossip. Never underestimate how much people like to gossip, something I learned doing the podcasting."

Bel's phone on the counter started flashing. She mouthed *Amber* and answered.

"*Hi there!*" Bel's body language had changed. Connor remained impressed at her versatility.

"Uh-huh . . . eesh, tricky . . . oh God! That'd test any guest's popularity. No, definitely, bring her! I'll risk my soft furnishings and Connor will love her . . . Honestly—promise, she'll be on his lap all night. Yep, seven, see you then."

She rang off.

Connor frowned.

"I'm being pimped out now?"

"Gertie, their pug dog, is suffering terrible separation anxiety and did a dump on her babysitter's Persian rug as they tried to leave. I said you knew dogs and you'd take it all in your stride."

"You've offered me up to be shat on?"

"Your view of the Manchester internship experience in a nutshell, am I right?"

Connor laughed. "You said that, not me."

God, he'd had no poker face *at all*.

31

Bel put the roasting tin into the built-in wall oven with a satisfying snap of the spring-loaded door and pulled her watch round her wrist to check the time.

"As for the other plan, I'm not doing starters. I'm with Nigella, I think they make everyone feel too formal," she told Connor. "My unfailing method for dinner success is start with cocktails and plates of small salty things. Then a hefty main where you can serve yourself second helps, and a dessert that kids would eat. So it's Greek-style leg of lamb and vanilla ice cream with rum-soaked spiced sultanas. Obviously, I'd give hypothetical kids teetotal ones."

"Isn't that how Danny, Champion of the World, drugs pheasants, rum-soaked dried fruit?"

Bel barked with laughter. "OK, didn't expect that feedback."

"Sounds amazing anyway," Connor said. "Tonight's dinner represents a major upgrade for me. I've only been cooking things that can be topped with fried eggs and strafed with hot sauce."

"*Strafed*. Good word."

"I didn't only go into journalism to be Aaron Parry's bitch-boy," Connor said.

Bel grinned. "Why did you go into it? A big change from what you were doing before."

"Oh, well . . . there is the sanitized shorter version which I think you had in Platzki's, about finance being the wrong fit. The longer version, which I'd rather we kept within these walls . . ."

"Of course."

"It's a horrible, cutthroat environment where hair dryer bollockings are what you're expected to withstand in return for the monthly paycheck. After a particularly stressful quarter, a colleague jumped out a third-floor window. Up until then I'd bought into this idea that buckling was for the weak and it was to be endured. When someone lost their life I thought, No, this is dysfunctional to the point of evil."

"Fuck!" Bel gasped, pausing while pushing ice cubes out of a rubber mold.

"You know, my colleagues had multiple banking apps on their phones. When they got bawled out they'd go to the toilets and look at the balances in all these apps to remind themselves why it was worth it. Hoarding piles of gold like dragons. I got through Eli's funeral on Grey Goose and beta blockers and I started to think, you know, maybe being well-off isn't worth this. A spiral into clinical depression and the citalopram followed. I had a few months off and did a course, rediscovered what college Connor wanted to do." He paused. It felt good to be honest. "Jen and I are collateral from that. She wasn't as keen on Connor 2.0. Or a return to Connor 1.0, however you want to see it. Is this the right size?"

He pointed at the cheese.

"I'm sorry," Bel said. "Yes, they're ideal. Size of a dice."

"Would you mind if we did a quick-fire round on each other's life and times?" Connor said. "I'm slightly concerned that total ignorance might find us out, over the course of an evening. Like, do you have any brothers or sisters?"

"One, my younger brother Miles, thirty. Lives in York. We get on well. He's a children's party entertainer, believe it or not."

"Really? Is that a thing you can full-time be?"

Bel curled the skin from an orange with a potato peeler and threw it into two lowball glasses.

"Yes, if you've got a Rowlf the Dog costume, boundless energy for dealing with noisy under-tens, are a member of the Magic Circle and have a girlfriend Yasmin willing to chauffeur and DJ. He gets loads of work from weddings, when they want kids present but not involved."

"I'm jealous, frankly. What a joyful career."

"You, siblings?"

"Apart from my dead sister?"

Bel grimaced. "Erk."

"Are we calling her Jennifer? How did she die?" Connor asked.

"You decide."

"This is the most tasteless and disrespectful conversation imaginable and I am going with an aneurysm in Sainsbury's two years ago."

Bel nodded.

"My phone's got a picture of Maurice on it now, by the way," Connor said. "Sadly genuinely passed away. Erm, moving on, my elder brother Shaun, who lives in DC with his wife, Lauren, works for a senator over there."

"He's the one who's visiting soon?"

"Next weekend, in fact. He chose Hotel Gotham in the end—remember he had me scouting Didsbury? Shaun's unlike anyone you'll ever meet. Astonishing forward momentum, messianic levels of self-belief. Will analyze and summarize you to your face and, even worse, is usually accurate. This makes him sound awful but he's great, if alpha dog mental, and I love him a lot."

Bel registered minor surprise at Connor being this unguarded and warm.

"Does this mean I'm meeting him?" Bel said, placing a drink by Connor. "Old-Fashioned. Sip it or it'll blow your doors off."

"I'd not thought about it—can you? I'm staying with him so I'll be in the city that weekend. Might make sense for the cover story."

"Cool. Parents?"

"Two, Stuart and Elaine, both retired teachers and very nice people. Still in Barking. Shaun has tried to help them move to somewhere more retirement villagey, but they're settled. You?"

"My dad died when I was twenty, my mum Bridget is in York. She's a GP's receptionist."

"I'm sorry about your dad," Connor said.

"My dad's side is where the money comes from," Bel said. She had decided to reward openness with the same approach. If they'd mirrored each other's disdain in the past, maybe it was time to harness that habit for positivity. "My paternal grandparents were 'own land' wealthy. But my parents have always been firm that they'll make our lives 'comfortable, not idle.' Miles and I have always worked, but we've been free to make more risky choices because we had them to fall back on. We went to state school. My mum works because she thinks she should and she enjoys it."

"You don't owe me explanations, I was completely out of order," Connor said.

"It's OK, I want to be open about it. Thing is, people think you're blithely unself-aware about being a 'rich kid,' and I'm not. My dad gave me a lot of confidence but maybe the source code of that confidence was being well-off. So there's all sorts of advantage you can't unpick. My conclusion is you can't choose the privilege you're born with, but you can choose how you live." Bel glanced around. "Not that I'm slumming it! I'd had such a bad time before I left York I needed cheering up."

She had said too much and shot Connor a look she hoped conveyed *let's not dig into that*.

"Trivia round, what perfume do you wear? It's unusual," Connor said, interpreting it correctly.

"Oh," Bel said, feeling her skin pinken with self-consciousness that he'd got that close, and noticed, "Malin + Goetz Dark Rum."

"Booze as a scent? I like it. Jen always wore jasmine something or other."

Bel decided it wasn't the moment to share Shilpa's conviction that "bitches wear jasmine. Not all jasmine wearers are bitches but all bitches like jasmine. Scientific fact."

"How are you bearing up regards Jen?" Bel said, carefully.

"Shamefully well. It should be a lot more difficult than it is and it's now obvious I had been shuffling 'breakup' down the to-do list for months, if not a year, and I shouldn't have. She called me out on that, in fact."

Bel hesitated. "She called you out? Didn't she send you the bombshell nude?"

"Yup. Jen got over the ignominy of the misfired topless selfie very quickly and then it became a savage indictment of my lack of caring that she was lured into sexting with the other guy, when minutes away from seeing me."

"That's . . ." Bel paused.

"Say it."

"An inspiring degree of self-esteem," Bel concluded. "I want to 'match her freak,' as they say."

Connor burst out laughing. For an unwary split second she thought she saw Actual Like on his face.

She bolted upstairs and changed, reappearing as Bella with hair in a long plait over one shoulder, bright red lipstick and matching shift dress (£25, Vinted). (There was something peculiarly freeing about trying on someone else's taste, even if that person didn't exist, Bel observed.)

"You look really nice," Connor said, and sounded genuinely approving, brushing the last of his Old-Fashioned from the corner of his mouth.

"Of course you think I look nice, I'm dressing completely differently to my own taste."

"You could find the coded insult in absolutely anything I say, couldn't you?"

The doorbell rang at a punctual five past seven. The food smelled great, the lighting was glimmering-perfect, the music was the right level, candles lit, glasses out, their eyes lightly spangled by cocktails.

If only this wasn't a sinister masquerade . . .

32

"I've never seen Gerts like this with anyone other than Rick," Amber said. "Duchess Gerts, you're such a flirt!"

It had been established that Duchess Gerts (1) loved Connor, (2) loved cheese and lamb and (3) was sufficiently happy that she retained sovereign control of her bowels, for the time being.

Though Bel worried for Connor's Levi's if that changed, given she was now perched in his lap like a baby, worried eyes and flat nose peering over the edge of the dining room table.

Connor had happily scooped her up after she pawed his leg, and now they were a devoted couple.

The necessity of bringing their pug was, in fact, an extraordinary stroke of luck: fussing over a small creature was in the British DNA—Connor was a dog person, and Gertie absorbed any anxious oxygen in the room in an instant.

Despite the concealed apprehension on the part of the hosts, when Amber, Rick and airborne-in-arms Gertie clattered through the door, Rick bearing an entire box of bottles of red wine, the evening had effortless momentum.

"I didn't know if you were wine *people*, you know? When Bella said bring red, I panicked and fired up the Wine Society site and bought anything expensive and French."

"You'd think I'd know, running a wine bar, but we sell a lot of rosé—that chicken wine!—and cocktails." Amber shrugged. She was slinky in a long bias-cut silk skirt, shoulder-grazing hoop earrings and her trademark slicked-back Grace Kelly hair.

"Girl dinners," Bel said.

Rick wasn't standoffish as Bel had originally thought, simply stretched too far by the number of introductions when they last met. Bel was disarmed by him apologizing instantly: "I'd stopped taking information in by the time we met, I'd gone fugue state, hahaha."

He was the creative director at a marketing agency and said "don't make me explain" and Connor said, "What if none of us talked about employment all evening? *Forced* ourselves."

Bel offered them Old-Fashioneds, and they were off.

If you were going to playact, it was helpful to have an alluring stage, and Bel's showy flat helped her feel as if she and Connor were the Gatsby aspirationals they were imitating. Bel spoke of a holiday in the Hamptons that Connor hadn't attended and he described a sports car he once owned and they made separate histories sound entwined. Bel realized she and Connor didn't have a single photograph of themselves together and thought, All Amber needs to do is ask to see a picture, and we're cooked.

"Do you own this place? It's absolutely lush," Amber said, looking up at the candelabra on braided cord, after she and Rick had eaten a gratifyingly large amount of Greek lamb and potatoes, amid much praise for the cook.

("So good, Bella leaves me in the dust with her abilities," Connor had said, and Bel glowed before remembering all compliments tonight were voided by the treachery.)

"God no, I don't know what it would cost but think it's well beyond our means," Bel said. "The rent is steep enough."

"I've still got my flat in Stoke Newington and I rent it out," Connor said. "My plan is a property pension. Do you two rent or own?"

Oh, bravo, Bel thought, clocking what he was doing. She got up to clear plates.

"Mmm, need another drink for this! Ha." Amber set her glass back down, which Connor refilled. Rick's wines were strong and fruity and tasted to Bel like some potent fairy-tale sleeping draught. "I live rent-free in my flat in Didsbury but that's the nepo baby thing I mentioned, Bella. And it's tiny. I know, diamond clogs too tight."

"That sounds ideal!" Bel laughed. "Nepo, not the clogs."

"It might be if my mum wasn't . . . my mum."

Rick wore a look of practiced neutrality, a war vet's stare, having clearly heard this speech many a time.

Bel made an uncomprehending face. Connor made no eye contact while whispering sweet nothings to a bewitched Gertie, cleverly taking the pressure off.

"You don't get on?" Bel said.

"I call Gloria 'the tractor' because she rolls over you and crushes you, no matter what you do. She's got a Wikipedia, if you're nosy, and it's not easy reading," Amber said. "But, I took the freebies, didn't I? So I should shut up. As my mother regularly reminds me."

Bel had an urge to fill the quiet that followed and instinctively held back, while Massive Attack soundtracked the brief pause instead.

"There's a bigger place in Didsbury she might let us have one day but it's an Airbnb for now. I call my life 'the big carrot and the big stick.' She needs someone reliable to run Cee Vee and that's me. I'm not allowed to go get another job, on the hook waiting for the house. I should've said no when I was twenty-one, but now I'm used to the disposable income and I'm not skilled to do anything else."

"We're not exactly badly off, though," Rick said, rubbing an eye. "Let's not wash our stained underpants in front of the nice new people, eh?"

"I know." Amber sighed. "I'm being honest."

It struck Bel they were collectively a good few shades drunker than they thought.

Bel smiled. "Please don't fret about underpants washing. We've all got family dramas."

"Some of our underpants are more stained than others," Rick said, and Bel laughed.

"I worry you're all triggering Gertie," Connor said.

"Do the Air Beeb guests behave themselves?" Bel asked. "We thought about it for Connor's flat but worried we'd get the lager lads."

"Mostly pretty good, actually. They're not the problem." Amber dropped her voice. "It's my mum's friends having affairs and swinging and so on I can't hack." She mimed two fingers to her throat. "All meant to be respectable and married. Me and Rick call the house the Waitrose Brothel."

"Whoa! There I was thinking Boomers behave better than us! What, do they book in saying they're having a bunga-bunga party?"

Amber helped herself to another scoop of ice cream and added the sultana garnish.

"Damn you for making this, it's too good." She spoke through a full mouth, hand held over it. "It's always euphemisms about working in the city and 'need somewhere to stay overnight' but here's the thing: Ring Video Doorbell. Had to set it up due to the numbers of robbing scrotes. Unfortunately for them, I know who they're turning up with. Get the alerts on my phone so it's like . . ." Amber made a face of mock surprise. "Why's 'Uncle' Brian with someone who isn't 'Auntie' Angela? Aargh."

Bel pantomimed amazement.

"If your mum does give us the house, I'm gonna ask for a deep professional clean," Rick said.

THEY MOVED TO THE SITTING ROOM, positioning Gertie on a beanbag. Bel had an urge to drag the chatter back to the Airbnb again, but this had already been such a win, she knew she shouldn't be greedy.

Rick asked to use the loo. Bel was glad she'd done two full sweeps of the place to make absolutely sure she had no personal belongings lying around that could contradict her persona.

"Through the bedroom over there." Bel pointed him the way.

"You know, you two are SUCH a fit pair," Amber said, surveying them in open admiration.

"Aw shucks, as if," Bel said, not least because she felt sure it was Connor who'd provoked the approval.

"My friends were all *who the hell were THEY*, like, swoon."

"Probably Bella's manners around the bagna càuda," Connor said.

"Honestly," Amber said, "they said your body language was so in tune and you were clearly, like, the male-female versions of each other. Couple goals."

"Ugh! I sincerely hope not," Bel blurted, and luckily a completely honest response played as flirty humor. Connor shot her a look, because, of course he knew this.

After they discussed the merits of pedigree dogs versus the puppy that Connor bought in a pub who became Maurice, they realized Rick had been gone an unnaturally long time.

"I better see where he's got to," Amber said. She returned moments later, looking stricken, with the news: "He's passed out on the bed."

"Is he OK?" Connor asked.

"Yeah, he's breathing fine, he's just comatose, I couldn't wake him," Amber said. "Oh my God, this is mortifying. I was telling him to slow down on the vino!"

The three of them went to inspect the patient, lying crossways on the king-size divan, feet in red-and-white trainers dangling.

"It must've looked too enticing," Bel said. "Maybe sit him up a little, because airways and all that?"

Connor helped Amber heave Rick to a more upright position against plumped pillows, with some difficulty.

"Yeah, he's a dead weight," Connor said. "Want me to make some black coffee?"

Bel looked at the prone Rick, his eyes screwed shut and mouth contorted as if in disapproval. He reminded her of a petrified bog cadaver she'd seen on a school trip. It didn't look like Nescafé Gold was going to get the job done.

"How are you going to administer it, intravenously?" Bel said.

"State of him!" Amber groaned.

Bel glanced at Connor: his widened eyes seemed to be trying to wordlessly communicate a message she might be able to decode if she'd not been drinking.

"He sleeps like he's had a general anesthetic at the best of times," Amber said. She shook his shoulder. "Rick! Rick?"

He didn't stir.

"I can call an Uber but how am I going to get him into it?" Amber said.

They gazed upon a slumbering Rick and assessed the impossibility. He *might* magically come round in half an hour, but . . .

Amber turned to Bel. "Would it be the most massive inconvenience if we stayed over? I am so, so sorry, this is beyond embarrassing."

"No problem!" Bel said, not missing a beat. "Will Gertie be all right?"

"Yes, she'll be fine if she's with us. I can take her out for a wee. Are you sure this isn't horrendous?!"

"Hush, I've got a guest room for a reason. There's the en-suite bathroom and . . . hang on, I bought a three-pack of toothbrushes the other day, I'll get them for you."

Amber's words of lavish apology and gratitude followed Bel up the spiral stairs, as she heard Connor being solicitous about Gertie being brought her beanbag.

It was then that a pissed-up, prematurely triumphalist Bel belatedly translated Connor's alarm. Their staying meant he had to stay too.

33

Shit, Bel mouthed silently at Connor, as they stood facing each other, in shock.

They were trapped.

"At least you'd chosen a side of the bed," Bel whispered. She handed him a spare toothbrush. "And I thought to hold this back."

Connor walked over to the canary-yellow Roberts Radio on the shelf nearby and tuned it to a soporific burble of BBC World Service.

"Have you got a key for this?" Connor said in a low voice, gesturing at the door's lock.

"Um . . . I think so?" Bel reached up and felt along the top of the doorframe.

She handed it over. "Here. Why?"

Connor took it from her and turned the lock, leaving the ornate heavy metal key in the door.

He inclined his head at the ground floor. "You mean it's not even occurred to you they might be doing this on purpose?"

Bel was momentarily stunned.

"What? Why . . . ?"

"I mean, it's an admirable lack of cynicism," he hoarsely whispered. "However. Everything considered, you should be more wary."

"But Rick's spannered!" Bel hissed.

"We *assume* he's spannered," Connor said. "They're near strangers and now they're nonnegotiably under your roof for the night."

"He's our generation's Laurence Olivier if he's sober."

"I'm not sure 'lying down and closing your eyes' is quite as hard as you think it is. Anyhow, he's probably drugged like a Roald Dahl pheasant. Glad of the lock."

Bel shivered a little. Connor was several things, but he wasn't stupid. What if he was right? She'd not wanted him anywhere near this undercover escapade and yet, without him here, she'd have gone to bed, inebriated, in an unlocked room, not thinking anything of it.

If one of the first rules of journalism according to The Tao of Aunt Tessa was "anyone might be lying about anything, and for no reason," then she'd mislaid this wisdom at a crucial moment. Bel was so sure she was taking Amber in, she'd not considered it might be the reverse.

"I'm afraid it gets worse," Connor said. "I didn't bring a T-shirt. Would you have anything that might fit me?"

"Oh God!" Bel said. "Erm . . ." She'd thrown the splattered one she'd cooked in into the wash. "Let me check but I don't think so. I only have one extra-large one."

Bel rummaged in a drawer and produced a baby-doll-fit Bruce Springsteen T-shirt, emblazoned with *Born to Run*.

"Do you like The Boss?" she asked, holding it up, then couldn't help laughing, to Connor's rolled eyes.

"Jesus Christ, why is that a child's size? *Newborn to Run*?"

"It's the skinny design that shows off your rack!" Bel hissed. When she was nervous she went sassy, she couldn't help it. Masking.

"Looks like I'm showing off my rack either way. Um, I'm sleeping in my pants, then, are you OK with that?"

"What are my options? You in my leggings?"

"I'm glad you're finding my enforced nudity so funny," Connor said.

"This is a trauma response," Bel said, and Connor finally laughed.

They negotiated changing in the bathroom, Bel going first. She pulled on her pink cotton grandad pajamas and decided to keep a bra on, as swinging free here felt far too intimate.

As she washed her face, she thought, Am I really going to platonic bed with the arsey intern? Is this what this sodding "jape" has come to? She allowed Connor had far more to resent here.

Bel said perkily "All yours!" and once Connor was in the bathroom, wriggled to the far edge of the bed. Thank goodness it was massive. Not massive enough for this not to be hideously awkward, of course.

After a moment's worry it looked like seduction, she dimmed the lights. As well as the side-table library lamps there was a recessed LED yellow-glow that ran under the skirting on a separate circuit. It was enough illumination that you could see your way to the loo, but not too intrusive for sleep.

Bel plugged her phone in to charge and stared determinedly at the handset as an underwear-clad Connor exited the bathroom on the periphery of her vision and climbed in next to her. From the scant amount she saw of his abdominal definition, she could tell Shilpa would be growling.

There was a moment of quiet where they lay there in mutual disbelief.

"Oh God, this is nightmarish," Bel whispered, to ease the tension.

"*You're* not topless," Connor muttered.

"Sorry to break the news that I am," Bel said, and was rewarded with Connor shaking with laughter.

"I worry about you a little, you know," he said. "You didn't consider this downstairs could be a put-on, and now you're unexpectedly in bed with a male coworker you barely know. What's the next intern going to stumble into? Hitchhiking in a cheerleader's outfit by moonlight? Infiltrating the Taliban in a joke-shop mustache?"

Bel laughed and Connor smiled, sighed and put his arm above his head. Bel didn't pay any attention to his arm, his bare chest, or the way his muscles moved.

"I'm able to trust you implicitly on the basis you not only do not find me attractive, but actively abhorrent," Bel whispered.

"You love exaggerating. Our generation's Vivien Leigh."

It might be the school trip silliness affecting her, or the claret, but she sensed firstly that Connor was warming to her, and, secondly, her surprise that he'd echoed her nearest and dearest. "Bel's flair for the dramatic," her mother said.

"This bork aside, an amazing evening, I thought," Bel said. She had to be careful. They were at a distance, two doors in between, where they'd not be heard speaking at normal volume, let alone sotto voce. Yet comparing notes with the marks still on the premises felt both reckless and unkind.

"For sure, talk tomorrow?" Connor said, reflecting exactly this discomposure.

"Yes. For now I will only say I have an unforeseen issue, and it's not you in gray Calvin Klein underwear."

"Oh my God, they ARE Calvins! You pervy little spy!"

Connor was definitely sounding sweeter on Bel than he ever had, and while Bel was grateful, what a time for it to arrive.

"It was a guess! Settle down, no one's objectifying you. My issue is, Connor: I like Amber and Rick."

"Same," Connor said.

34

Bel had said *night* and lain awake in taut self-consciousness for some time. She was, as far as she knew, a silent sleeper, but it was extremely hard to relax with Some Guy from Work, feeling exactly the same, an arm's length away.

When she woke, lightning was flashing outside the window in blue-white bursts while rain pelted the window. Downpours in this city had to go the extra mile to be considered torrential and yet it was truly biblical, the kind of ferocity where you felt it could do damage, break the glass.

As Bel got her bearings in the low light, she saw Connor was sitting up, awake. He turned to her and put his finger to his lips.

He leaned over and whispered directly into her ear: *"Someone is on the stairs."*

Bel brushed her hair out of her face and tried to get a measure of the situation, amid the jump-scare special effects. There was a rumble of thunder and another huge crack of lightning.

Why? she mouthed back at Connor and he shook his head.

She could see his alarm and she abruptly grasped the stakes. There was absolutely no respectable reason for anyone to be creeping up those spiral steps, when calling out or ringing Bel's phone were easier options. And if the intention was to knock and wake them, why the stealth?

"Get your phone," Connor whispered.

Bel nodded and pulled it out of the charger.

"Is it on silent? Good."

There was a gap in the wuthering outside and Bel heard it

then, the recognizable sound of a carefully light cat-burglar footstep moving up another two or three places, the metal creaking, getting nearer.

Bel focused on the door handle and realized that it moving was the clear cue to panic. Then, they could be sure this was some sort of fuckery. The person (or people) on the other side weren't to know it was locked.

The rain blew in a gust. There was another couple of footsteps, this time moving faster, obviously trying to use the weather as cover. Bel was suddenly so scared about their intentions, she moved next to Connor and pushed her arms round his bare middle. Her need for complete solidarity in the face of potential impending evil was greater than concern at how pathetic this was.

His skin was hot—and instead of recoiling from her as she thought he might, Connor drew her closer. He put his arm round her shoulders and almost distractedly smoothed her hair in reassurance, a reflexive muscle memory from girlfriend protocols. It told Bel his level of anxiety was as high as hers, that inhibitions between them no longer mattered. There were, as her father liked to say, no atheists in foxholes. Wasn't Operation Foxhole the sting that caught the Kendricks?

"What are they trying to do?" she whispered, as if Connor would know.

If Amber and Rick knew who they were, and wished them ill, then the wine coma was a fake-out? Were they going to trash the place, take photos of them sleeping and say "we can get to you anytime"? She thought of herself in that Teams meeting downstairs, producing Gloria Kendrick's wrongdoing with a gleeful flourish.

It was white-collar crime, and Bel had arrogantly and snobbishly not considered they might be into *crime* crime. If you were fine with people losing millions, you were probably fine with them losing anything.

"I don't know," Connor said. "Whatever happens, I'll play along like I've just woken up while you keep your phone ready, OK? The door's heavy. Does that door lock too?" He gestured at the en suite and Bel nodded. "Go in there if you need to."

"Got it," Bel said, and felt herself break into a sweat. What a conversation. She assumed Connor meant *to call the police—* except to say what? *There are people I don't know in my house, I let them in and gave them toothbrushes? Now they're skulking around and freaking me out?*

"It's OK," Connor said, "I won't let them do anything, all right? You're safe."

She squeezed him a wordless thanks. Thank God, Connor was here. Bel would've probably woken with a face looming over her.

She could hear the steps again, this time closer, and Bel felt her body go into fight-or-flight, the adrenaline ready to launch her from the bed.

They held their breath. Bel realized time had slowed, that every second was now elongating as a little eternity.

A strange snuffling followed, a plaintive, keening sound, and a scratching at the door.

"*Gertie! Gertie! Come here,*" they heard Amber hiss.

Bel and Connor both went limp in each other's arms—with relief.

The dog made a few more futile muffled honking noises of objection and there were the acoustics of a lovelorn, confused Gertie being retrieved and carried back down the stairs. This time the progress was slower and more labored as Amber balanced her weight.

As Bel's heart rate started descending accordingly, she had to reckon with the fact she was entwined around Connor. For a fleeting moment she noticed she could quite happily stay as they were. No, worse: she wanted to expose as much skin as he had, and sense his heart rate bump again.

"You were a hero there," Bel said, in a whisper, as she withdrew her hands from his midriff, and the inhibitions came rushing back.

"I wasn't and I'm glad I didn't have to be, but thank you," Connor said, at the same pitch.

"Better safe than sorry," Bel said, knowing she was wittering inanities to ease their having hugged and petted each other. The fact that the cause of their fear wasn't real didn't mean they could undo the moment of tenderly clinging to one another. They'd both exposed something about themselves: Bel's willingness to seek his support in an emergency and Connor's willingness to give it.

"I guess, though who knows what either safe or sorry will end up looking like here."

"Are you regretting saying you'd do this?" Bel said.

"No. The thought of you going it alone is terrifying."

Bel squeaked a laugh.

"Yeah, but my stupidity is my responsibility, not yours."

"True, but once I knew what you were doing, I'd have it on my conscience if I left you to it."

"I thought you were only concerned with what our bosses would think," Bel said, genuinely surprised.

"Yes, it's impossible I could have any nuance or complexity, in your mind. Dickhead intern pursues dickhead goal."

Connor said this in an amused tone but they were swapping real information. After this jarring experience, a small bloodletting was occurring. It was underscored by yet more gales of rain.

"I'm only going by what you said . . ."

"People are actions and words, aren't they."

"Look, I thought you had a bit of an attitude at the start, that was all. I didn't think really badly of you," Bel said.

"Ha! And you didn't have an attitude?"

"You can't keep doing this, you know, the playground argumentative technique of 'I know you are but what am I?' As I remember it, I said *oh hi, new intern* and you looked at me like I was Rasputin's bloated river corpse."

"I think the operative word here is *looked*. Are you telepathic?"

"What were you thinking, then?"

A pause.

"I don't remember but it wouldn't have been critical."

"Sounds like your brain needs to tell your face."

"Wait, *I'm* the one who's immature?"

Bel giggled.

"I love that seconds ago we were afraid for our lives and now we're bickering. We're like a straight-to-DVD buddy cop movie," she said.

"Doubting I have a conscience mere minutes after I prepared to save you from the consequences of your own actions is very you, huh?"

"I didn't doubt that!" Bel said. "I was trying to figure your processes out. I'm insanely grateful."

"Night," Connor said, with a world-weary intonation, turning over.

"Night."

All Bel had intended to do was say a heartfelt thank-you, so that had gone brilliantly. After five or so minutes of feeling guilty, Bel said, "Connor?"

Silence.

"In case there's any doubt, I appreciate you being here so much."

There was no reply.

35

Bel
MORNING (sorry, feels odd to message)—our guests left at dawn, Amber's texted me, will fill you in shortly. I'm making breakfast for whenever you're ready but you're off-duty regards The Double Act. Feel free to have a shower if you want one.
Towels in there too. Just don't nick my Springsteen tee, I saw you coveting it. Bx

Connor rubbed the sleep from his eyes and reread Bel's words. He could smell frying bacon and hear music downstairs. He was embarrassed to discover he'd slept through Bel waking and getting up, and not only that, he'd kicked the sheet off in the post-thunderstorm heat, lying face down in his underwear.

Oh well. If ever there was a bed partner who'd decline to ogle his arse, it was Bel Macauley.

He pondered that he found her infinitely easier to deal with when they dropped the pretense: not with company, but with each other. She had unexpectedly clung to him in their mutual terror last night, the soft squish of her breasts pressed hard against his rib cage and the dark rum perfume-smell of her hair in his mouth and nose again. Connor had been completely disarmed by her vulnerability and stroked her hair in nervous auto-response, as if they really were seeing each other. He'd had time to notice she was wearing a bra, and the modesty of it was unexpected. He'd thought of Bel as confident to the point of careless. Maybe the underwear was about finding him deeply off-putting—the bed share was pretty agonizing.

When it became clear that the threat was simply an incontinent pug dog gone rogue, he and Bel had nearly sobbed with relief. Connor was disturbed to discover his survival energies didn't exactly dissipate but converted into a briefly powerful urge to further reassure Bel with his presence. He even kidded himself there was half a minute when she felt the same, that if he'd crushed his mouth against hers and started feverishly unbuttoning the silly pajamas, she'd have let him. Bel would have been utterly revolted if she knew—and frankly, Connor was too. Apart from anything else, he was supposed to be trustworthy.

Why couldn't his libido behave normally? Had the slow death with Jen messed him up? He was no longer able to fancy a nice, appropriate woman who liked him back but instead yearned for an emotions-free hookup with a spiky adversary who'd punish him for his weakness.

It was embarrassing to stifle the surge of unwanted lust and it had probably made him a little more caustic than necessary after they disentwined. Though she did restart the jibes about him being coldly careerist, which was pretty galling when he'd been ready to do anything to protect her.

When Bel whispered in the dark about how sincerely grateful she was to him, Connor had opened his mouth to reply and then, as the seconds ticked by, he couldn't find the words or the pitch. Any response was either too flippant or too loving and it was easier to pretend to be asleep.

He decided to enjoy the superior facilities given he'd had no choice to be here. He stood for a cleansing five minutes under hot water in the rainfall shower in her en suite. Connor didn't lock the door on the basis Bel knew he was here and would rather permanently lose her eyesight than expose herself to a full-frontal, yet it still felt like alien behavior.

Connor appeared down in the kitchen in last night's clothes, with damp hair.

Bel, hair in a topknot and hoodie over her pajamas, face flushed from proximity to the grill, slid a coffee toward him.

"I didn't know your preferences so I've made both brown and white toast. The sandwich is a bespoke self-assembly job."

She set down plates of food in front of him, HP brown sauce, ketchup and a butter dish, handing Connor a fork so he could spear the rashers himself. She'd cooked them properly: the fat was copper-colored, not burned. Connor thanked her and inwardly conceded, without saying as much, that Bel might be a nice friend. Her acquiring Shilpa made more sense, if Shilpa liked brunch.

As Connor buttered wholemeal toast, Bel read from her handset, out loud:

Morning Bella, the monster (Rick, not Gertie) awoke at 6 and we've decided to get ourselves gone—so embarrassed, I'm so sorry. Let me know how we can make it up to you, assuming you ever want to see us again. Rick is blaming the "boozy raisins" hahahahaha. He looked like a boozy raisin more like. And sorry to Connor too . . .

Bel trailed off and glanced up.

"She says more about you, but I'm not sure I can bear sharing it."

"I deserve to know, information is power," Connor said, smiling, as the brown sauce fart-squirted as he squeezed the bottle.

Bel sighed.

I'm sure you know this, but Connor is such a catch, he has a personality as nice as his looks. The way . . .

Bel cleared her throat. Connor saw a new flush appear on her neck, and he started regretting forcing the disclosure.

. . . the way he looks at you, like you're magnetic to each other, is so sexy. Just flagging you can never break up and destroy my faith in love.

Connor blinked as he absorbed the idea he was looking at Bel in any particular way.

"Top marks on the acting. Take a bow, the real Larry Olivier," Bel said, stiffly.

Connor was surprised to see Bel was discomposed. He'd have expected her to shrug this off with a derogatory joke, and the fact she didn't made him worry he *was* gazing at her. Connor flashbacked to last night's clinch and thought, Oh no, did Bel pick up on anything untoward there? The idea he had a thing for Bel was sodding ridiculous and both Bel and his penis needed to be clear on that.

"It's very much a joint effort," Connor said, with a forced lightness, making a start on his sandwich. Bel got paper towels from the cupboard and passed them over.

"I've said we'd love to go to a Cee Vee lock-in. It's time to try to put ourselves near the iPad."

Connor nodded, mouth full.

"Work-wise, regards the investigation, to recap: We've had corroboration of Glenn Bailey's reputation and the rumors from Aaron," Bel continued. "We've heard direct from Amber that the Airbnb in Didsbury is Gloria's property, and a den of ill repute. It feels as if the story's coming together. Now all we need to do is prove one of the visiting shaggers is Bailey."

"Ah, the small matter of the iPad. I think robbing a bank vault in a Ronald Reagan mask would be easier."

"Yup. We're going to need a strategy. It might be worth us finding an excuse for you to get out of the office to attend a meeting next week with Toby," Bel said.

"Sure," Connor said. "I dread having my stupid face on that screen somewhat. I know it was, uh, happenstance, but I still feel a huge idiot for having ambled into your story."

"Oh." Bel blinked. "I never told Toby that, actually."

"What? Really?" Connor said, pausing mid bite. "Why does he think I'm involved, then?"

"I told him I thought the undercover sting would work better as a couple, and that I'd witnessed how conscientious, willing and methodical you are. I requested to have you come in on it with me."

Connor was slightly stunned.

"Why did you do me that big a favor?"

Bel folded grease-coated tinfoil into the bin, stamping the pedal to open its lid.

"You were doing me one—and, in general, I think colleagues should boost each other. A rising tide lifts all boats, as they say."

"Right. Thank you," Connor said. "What would you have done if he'd said no?"

Bel gave a small smile. "I know you're conscientious and methodical, and I can learn from that. In turn, can I introduce you to the 'calculated risk'? Also. I thought it was probably better not to confess to a fuckup, straight out of the traps."

Connor smiled back and sipped his coffee, thinking that the risk of Toby saying no to Bel Macauley was lower than that of a mere mortal.

It in no way diminished the impressive gracefulness of what he'd just learned. It wasn't only that Bel had been so helpful to him. She'd done it without letting him know, so not making him feel indebted or collecting the brownie points.

He finally conceded that he had underestimated Bel Macauley.

"Wait. You knew you'd done me this good turn when I was insulting you about how you were going to make me look stupid for the phone screen mistake at Amber's party?"

"Oh? Yes."

"I was a huffy man-child," Connor said. "While you were too dignified to put me in my place. Sobering."

"Now you know how I feel when Amber's gushing about how you're"—Bel did air quotes, though her hands were now in oven mitts—"'the most good-looking man she's ever seen.'"

"Did she?!"

Bel paused the exact amount of time to elicit the biggest possible laugh: "No."

36

Bel had hung two pictures on the wall of the office on Monday morning, clambering onto a chair to reach the cobwebbed hooks and canvassing a nonplussed Aaron and Connor's opinions on whether they were straight.

With these homely touches she was, as Aaron readily told her, lipsticking a pig. On the other hand, given they had to spend many hours of their lives in here, Bel insisted that refusing to improve it was self-defeating.

"I'll ask Toby if there's budget for a jungly floor plant too," Bel said.

"Aye, you do that, petal," Aaron said. "But when I said I needed a woman's touch, I didn't mean this."

"Ta-da!" Bel said, standing back, once the decoration was deemed spirit level.

One was a modern print with MANCHESTER lettered along the top, in the style of 1920s travel posters. It depicted an imposing Art Deco limestone building on King Street which used to be an HSBC. Its windows were lit and walls shadowed to look like New York at dusk.

"*Only Murders in the Building*," Aaron said. "In Manchester, murders outside the building too."

"It does look very 'Manc-Hattan,'" Bel agreed.

"That's that ponce hotel now, isn't it?" Aaron said. "Hotel Gotham. Prices to give you the meat sweats."

Bel and Connor exchanged a momentary sidelong look: he

and his brother would be there this weekend. They wordlessly agreed it served no purpose to tell Aaron this.

The second artwork was a moody, misty wash of rainy gray blue, dappled with yellow-white lights, a view of barges on a Manchester ship canal in 1912. Romanticized toil and pollution.

"It's by a French Impressionist called Pierre Adolphe Valette; he painted a lot of urban, postindustrial Manchester," Bel said to an aghast Aaron.

"It's a bit fookin' gloomy, isn't it?" Aaron said. "We could've had a Stanley Chow of Oasis; instead we've got miserable girl paintings."

"A miserable girl chose 'em, what's gonna happen?" said a completely unoffended Bel.

Bel was gradually learning that Aaron, like many reporters of keen instinct who thrived on big breaking news, was a crisis addict. Quiet days saw him pacing his cage, metaphorically. *Starting some shit* with the other bodies present was Aaron trying to give his brain the dopamine of danger.

"You 'didn't do much' at the weekend and nor did Connor, the Refrigerated Intern," Aaron said, when he and Bel were alone for an hour that afternoon.

"Mmm?" Bel said, pretending to be only partially paying attention, when in fact she had fully caught Aaron's snaky innuendo and was playing dumb.

The trouble with reporters was they had a feral intuition. Bel and Connor were no friendlier to each other in the office than they ever had been. Nevertheless, something intangible had shifted, like air pressure in a cabin. Perhaps it was because Bel and Connor pointedly didn't interact; either way, Aaron's senses were tingling.

"Did you do much?" she asked Aaron.

"More than you two," he said. "The didn't-do-much twins."

"What are you suggesting?" Bel said. "We were 'didn't doing' each other?"

"Whoa, why would your mind go THERE?" Aaron said. It was absolutely where Aaron's mind was, and where Bel's was supposed to go. Phase Two of his game: *Funny how you brought sex into it, isn't it?*

Anthony had seriously reduced Bel's tolerance for male mind-dickery.

"Is there a different subtext I'm missing?"

"I'm just wondering why there's an echo in here," Aaron said, and Bel screwed her face up like *what the hell are you on?*

In actual fact, Aaron's instincts were spot-on: Bel and Connor were deterring him with the same blandishments, for the same reason.

For the first time, Bel wondered how Aaron would cope if Bel really was involved with Connor. The fact that would never happen while there was breath in her body—or Connor's, for that matter—didn't mean she should discount Aaron's reaction. If it could manifest in a different time, with a different man, she should nip it in the bud.

Aaron had established an intense bond of loyalty between them, making it clear from the outset that if she needed her back covered with the bosses, he had it. Yet Bel was realizing it came with strings. Anthony's dark shit had further made her allergic to male attitudes of ownership.

If Bel was seen out with Connor and his brother this weekend—and Aaron had many pairs of eyes, in his direct messages—it would quite possibly not go well for her. She didn't technically need to socialize with his brother, and Connor's invite was only made offhandedly, by accident. Yet Bel felt compelled to meet this Shaun Adams. Connor had become a riddle she couldn't satisfactorily solve—she'd long since lost the straightforward peace of mind that came with simply thinking him a condescending wanker.

His stories of leaving the City, his readiness to protect her from threats she'd created, dammit, his *love of a dead dog* (Amber had tried to ask about him, what was he called, Malcolm? Maurice! And Connor, to her amazement, had teared up. She thought she might've seen Amber fall in love a little.) had left Bel without a working sat nav for him.

Also, a voice whispered, and she tuned it out: *You have thought a lot about the idea he looks at you a certain way.*

Bel turned her attention to a newly arrived email—she'd been on a fishing trip to find out who was on the guest list for *Yorkshire Post*'s table at the Northern Media Awards.

Her contact gave her three names, none of them Anthony Barr, but that was no guarantee, of course. Anthony was plenty sly enough to suspect Bel would check and do a last-minute swap-out.

Bel had sternly instructed herself this was a risk she'd have to run in attending. He'd had a disproportionate impact on her life as it was; time to feel the fear and do it anyway.

She listlessly clicked on Instagram to be served a reel of Glenn Bailey judging the best kebabs in the city. Some social media manager had to edit him dunking fries into polystyrene pots to The Lightning Seeds.

Bailey was "tellygenic," easy in front of a camera, shaking hands with thrilled customers and making new fans wherever he went. He had what was called the common touch.

"That research, is it?" Aaron said, and though he was idly ragging on her, Bel quickly clicked away.

"Trying to avoid the thankless trudge of digging into an onshore wind farm controversy."

Connor reappeared from a job, rumpled in his blue shirt in the July heat, and Aaron turned his mithering attentions to him.

"Not to pry, Adams, but is all OK with your beautiful fiancée?" Aaron said. "I notice your photo's gone. Or do we need to check if the cleaners are on the rob?"

He gestured with his pen at the space on Connor's desk where his framed portrait of Jennifer once stood.

"Oh yes. We split up," Connor said. "She wasn't my fiancée."

"God. Sorry to hear that," Bel said, pleased with herself for not missing a beat in responding to information she already had.

"Thanks. Not a huge deal. It was a mutual decision and we're both fine with it," Connor said, looking directly at Bel.

"Aye, sorry," Aaron said. He paused. "So we're a trio of singles?"

"Unless you've met anyone," Bel said, and Aaron regarded her coolly. He knew something was being kept from him. Bel could tell Aaron had started building a case. She should warn Connor of this.

Bel needed to not be distracted by office politics tittle-tattle when bigger issues were at hand.

Once both men were on phone calls, she slid her iPhone out.

Bel
Ian, we should meet for a catch-up this week if you can risk it, but also, I'm going to shoot my shot: can I request you bring Erin? Not to apply pressure, I just think it'd really help for us to meet each other.

A reply after fifteen minutes:

Ian

I've spoken to Erin and she's agreed to join. She's becoming a devotee of your podcast archive. And I think your cameo in Amber's Instagram made her realize you are both serious about this, and very good at what you do!

Bel

😊 *I'm definitely at least one of those things.*

37

"It's nice enough weather to sit in the garden and yet we probably shouldn't for reasons of privacy, should we?" Ian said, answering the door at his immaculate terrace home.

"Could compromise with kitchen and open windows," Bel said. "Serious hydrangeas. Your garden is incredible."

She gestured at the explosion of blooms, the flowers a beetroot-stain pink. Ian's fenced front plot, window boxes and hanging basket had the well-controlled wild abundancy of a good gardener.

"Oh, thank you," Ian said. "I can give you a cutting when you leave."

"There's no garden at my chic city address, I'm afraid, but thank you. Someone did vomit in my shared hallway the other day, though, and the other residents were insistent they could 'tell' it wasn't resident vomit. That's as wildlife watching as we get."

Ian guffawed.

"Then you can have them for a chic city vase."

Bel stepped into a narrow hallway in red ankle boots, the space made narrower by a trail bike and a coatrack with old-fashioned umbrellas propped in it.

For their third meeting, Bel had the lightbulb she could simply go to Ian's house. He lived in Sale, so Bel decided to get the tram after work.

On her way, she squeezed in among the commuters, her mind turned to how on earth they could pull off the iPad stunt. Connor's skepticism was merited, and Bel was starting to sense the limits of what her brother called the "it'll be reet" approach.

She'd begun to very vaguely toy with a backup plan, but *plan* was dignifying it. *Death or glory reckless self-immolation with 2 percent chance of coming off* was probably closer to it. There was a disconnect between her devil-may-care methodology and the trust that had been placed in her, and when she wasn't rationalizing herself out of it ("This was Ian's idea!") Bel felt it.

Ian's home was exactly as she'd have predicted if she'd thought about it: spider plants on full shelving and mid-century modern furniture with toothpick legs: sofas and chairs a seal dark gray, crocheted throws and rugs, a riot of bright color.

There was an Aaron Parry–approved Stanley Chow print of Mrs. Merton hung above an original fireplace in a dining room with a chunky wooden table and an old-style stereo stack, a spotless galley kitchen beyond. Fastidiousness and warmth. (Bel had politely declined a lasagna with Ian and Erin, feeling it crossed a line into socializing. "Probably for the best," Ian said, "my plant-based-diet niece is forcing a butternut-squash filling upon me.")

"Take a seat and I'll put the kettle on. Unless . . ." Ian checked the time on a wall clock. "Sun's over the yardarm. Can I tempt you to a wine, or are you driving? Do you drink both white and red?"

"Yes, you can, no, I'm not and yes, I do. I can drive but I haven't got a car, just as well with where I'm living at the moment," Bel said, taking a seat at the table.

"Right in the thick of it, Ancoats, I think you said? I love those old converted cotton mills. I envy you and I put in a shift in the 1990s, but I'm too old for it now. The quiet burbs have a sudden allure when you hit forty-five."

Ian placed a glass of white wine in front of Bel and she outlined Amber's thirty-fifth, adding illustrative details about fake boyfriends and overnight stays.

"Lord in heaven," Ian said. "It'd make several podcast episodes at this point. With cliffhangers."

The doorbell rang. "That'll be Erin."

Ian's niece entered the room with a look of trepidation. She was small, in a black cord jacket, with henna box-dye-red shoulder-length hair with chunky sections bleached white, and a punky amount of eye makeup. Bel would've guessed her age as late teens, twenty at the oldest. She should've been babysitting Glenn's nephews and nieces, not fodder for his fantasies.

"I'm Bel and you must be Erin . . . so good to meet you." She stood up and reached out to shake Erin's hand, and she mumbled a hello.

Aaron's line about green bananas came back to her and made her feel sick. Erin made Bel feel like a protective older sister. She had protectiveness to spare: her brother Miles was six foot by their mid-teens, and very popular, so he'd never needed it.

"Wine?" Ian said, waggling the bottle at a visibly affrighted Erin.

"No thanks, Coke Zero if you have it," she said.

"I have it because you drink it, dear niece." Ian stage-whispered to Bel, "Gen Z don't drink."

As Ian plinked ice into a glass in his fridge-door ice-maker, Bel smiled at Erin.

"Investigations editor, that's such a cool job title," Erin said, dumping a tasseled bag onto a spare chair. "Like you work at the *Daily Planet* or something."

"Yes, it's a big vote of confidence in me I've now got to justify," Bel said.

"I love your podcast," Erin said, "I've just finished the one about the estate agent murders in 1996. The story your aunt worked on."

"Oh, thank you! Tessa's are big shoes to fill. Well, in real life, small shoes and always stilettos."

Erin smiled and looked awed and shy, though she'd spoken with quiet confidence. Bel cast her mind back to how being twenty-four was to be full of such contradictions.

"Really appreciate you meeting me and sorry it's for a crappy reason," Bel said.

Ian put a soft drink in front of Erin and said, "I've got to phone my mother, so I thought I'd leave you two to speak in private for a while."

"Say hi to Gran," Erin said.

He disappeared upstairs, as Bel turned to Erin, who looked like she wanted to disappear inside her jacket.

Bel could tell she needed to keep talking until Erin relaxed enough to contribute.

"If it's easiest, I'm going to tell you what your uncle told me, and you can interrupt and correct me, or add, when necessary," Bel said.

As Bel described her time in the office, Erin said, "When Glenn spoke to me, it was like a celebrity noticing me. He *is* a celebrity . . ."

Erin's self-loathing radiated from her and Bel understood it instinctively. *You don't only deal with hating them, you hate yourself. Your self-image as someone who'd see through those kinds of tactics takes a battering.*

"He made you feel valued and noticed," Bel said, nodding. "You'd been anxious in a new environment and here's this magic person saying it's going to be all right . . . it's like a holiday romance, isn't it?"

"Exactly," Erin said.

(Erin was twenty-four; how did Bel fall for a lowlife flatterer at thirty-four?)

"When he got in touch after I left and said he'd love to help me with career next steps, I believed him," Erin said. "But he said not to tell my uncle in case he got worried about correct procedure and nepotism, you know? *There's rules around interns.* That was the massive warning sign but I wanted to think he liked me. We kept meeting up, he's giving me all this advice. Eventually he said he *likes me* likes me and somehow at this point I've caught feelings for a forty-five-year-old man. My *dad* is fifty-four."

Erin made a blow-out-cheeks puke face.

"Is there nothing on your WhatsApp that could prove he flirted, or that you kept making plans?"

Erin took a tiny bird-sip of Coke and shook her head. "Pretty much nothing. He was very careful. He'd always ring me back. At the time I was all *oh wow, he's so keen*."

Bel nodded.

"You went to the Didsbury Airbnb three times total? All in April?"

Erin nodded, fiddling with her jacket sleeve.

"Ian said that Glenn threatened you over nude pictures," Bel said. "But you're not sure if he has any or if it's a bluff?"

"He does have them," Erin said, eyes suddenly shiny.

Bel reached out and held her forearm.

"It's OK. You did nothing wrong by sending them. Nothing at all."

"I didn't send him nudes. I didn't tell the truth about that," Erin said, shaking her head. "Sorry. It was so cringe telling my uncle about what happened that I gave him a different version. I didn't know if I'd ever want to tell the real story so it made sense to simplify it at the time. I mean, it's true he shouldn't have them, and he has them."

"Oh?" Bel was lost.

"What happened was . . . Glenn hinted about sending some. But there was a big scandal at my school with a girl who ended up on everyone's phone so I've always been too scared . . ."

Bel stayed silent.

"Glenn, erm . . ." Erin played with her glass with small, bony fingers, nails painted in dark blue glitter polish. "He took photos of me sleeping."

Bel sucked in a sharp breath.

"When I met him to ask why he'd stopped replying to me, he showed them to me on his phone. Like, *if you cause trouble for me, Erin, I can cause trouble for you. Don't think I haven't got insurance.* I nearly threw up," Erin said.

"He took nude photos without your knowledge or consent and then used them as blackmail? Was he actually unashamed about this?" Bel gasped.

"It was as if I'd been made redundant and might go to a tribunal and he was telling me *well, if you do that, the company will defend itself to the full. Here's what we have on you.* Emotionless." Erin was pale.

"I mean, that's criminal, surely? You could report him, get his phone confiscated . . ." Bel said.

She knew Bailey was a nasty piece of work but this was the first time she thought he was the full sociopath.

"Even if I could stand the shame of other people seeing those pictures, and even if they believe me that I didn't know they were being taken—you know what he's like. He'd have the police officers laughing and joking with him and taking a jar of his homemade pickles home with them. *Great with sausages,*" Erin said, throwing her hands up, doing a Glenn impression. "He has so much goodwill to draw on and who the fuck am I? Sorry to swear."

"Never apologize for swears to me. Very true. Wish I trusted the police more than that, but I don't," Bel said.

"I really appreciate what you're doing," Erin said, rubbing her nose and its tiny jewel stud. "I'm not being difficult about the interview, I'll tell you anything you like, if you can get proof he's going to that house. I can't cope with the idea that I might put myself out there and then look like an idiot fangirl who thought a one-night stand mattered, and nothing would change. As I said to Uncle Ian, I'm totally grossed out that I did it, so how can I expect other people not to be?"

"I get it entirely. I think you've been extremely brave doing this much, and other women would thank you for it," Bel said. "When did you meet Amber?"

"When Glenn had dragged her out at one in the morning when the doorbell kept ringing and he was panicking it was someone who knew he was there. She wanted to show him the footage to prove it was some drunk stumbling around, so she brought that iPad. She seemed embarrassed, she didn't meet my eyes . . ." Erin paused. "Do you really think you can get into the iPad and get those recordings of Glenn?"

"Honestly, I have no idea. I am going to give it my best shot," Bel said. Erin nodded.

"Knowing someone believes me, someone proper, it's meant a lot," Erin said, and Bel felt like a fist was gently squeezing her heart.

IAN SAW BEL OUT, so they could briefly speak, one-to-one.

"You know what makes me so angry?" he said, as they stood at his gate. "Erin hasn't had much experience of the world of work yet, the world full stop, really. And that fucker has taken her optimism and her self-confidence and all the . . . brightness she should feel in her youth. Why should the start of her story be dominated by him? How dare he vandalize her youth for a few meaningless encounters?"

Bel put her hand on Ian's arm. If she'd ever thought she'd maintain an unemotional professional distance, that was long gone.

She thought of Ian discovering that his boss had taken sneak shots of his unclothed niece.

"We're going to get him. We're going to give Erin the power of putting out her side, and we're going to stop the next Erin ending up a Bailey victim. He thinks Erin is his victim too—but he'll find out she's his mistake."

"You're a credit to your profession," Ian said.

"I will settle for being of use to you." Bel smiled.

Bel departed home on the tram with a renewed sense of furious purpose, a greater degree of apprehension than ever before and four hydrangeas, their damp stalks in a twist of cling film.

38

Shaun's flight was inevitably delayed, so Connor checked into Hotel Gotham by himself, all liveried bellhops in those flat usher hats, dramatic lighting and maximalist, glitzy Art Deco clutter. He was quite won over to the *Murder on the Orient Sexpress* look they had going on. His room—Shaun had enjoyed the irony of it being the Bank Manager's Suite—had a zigzagging geometric black-and-white carpet and vintage travel chest as coffee table.

In London he'd have found it insufferable but up here it was playful larks. There you go, Manchester, Connor thought, I can learn to love you, all I need is a five-star accommodation in a £600-per-night suite. Or spacious-interiors appeal on a par with Bel Macauley's place, which was probably a £1.2 million proposition. God, maybe he WAS a shallow Finance Bro.

Shaun
Good news, my phone's finally got a signal. Bad: only just landed. Get dinner and I will see you for the strong liquor part of the evening, after a shower.

Connor was going to inform his brother that he and Jennifer were no more tonight, but he'd not yet told their parents. This two-hour wait, with only a ginger kombucha and a bag of wasabi peas from Itsu he'd acquired en route, seemed the time.

There was something hilariously, poignantly incongruous about sitting on the emperor-size bed with leather headboard, peacock feather–print bolsters and furry throw to announce his newly single status. This sybarite's coital lair was not designed for cuckolded losers.

(That was a point: What the hell was Aaron needling him over Jen's departure for? Connor had a fair idea: Aaron's Bel infatuation had now gone supersonic, and he thought an unattached Connor was some sort of threat. Albeit Aaron being laughably wide of the mark, Bel ought to be wary there. In Connor's experience, men who wanted women that much and didn't get them could turn vengeful.)

His dad answered their landline at 7:00 p.m. on a Friday night, in his parents' solidly reliable way. Connor made the announcement of his separation in a low-key "such is life, we're both fine" manner. As a bombshell, it had lost most of its power, given his dad had assumed they were over when he dropped him off, sans life partner, in Salford.

"Oh no, what a shame. I'll get your mum," his dad said, and Connor smiled into his iPhone.

He'd decided to keep the Jennifer nude snap farrago from them. It would only embarrass and scandalize them and turn Jen's reputation to dust. He didn't need that and she didn't deserve it. Plus he had his brother for the gory postmortem.

"Your dad says you and Jennifer are splitting up," his mum said. "Are you all right?"

"Yeah, I'm fine. The writing had been on the wall for a while and we're keeping it very civilized, Mum. She's staying in the flat until I leave here."

"Why not come back home for a weekend and let us look after you?"

"That's a lovely offer and I have thought about it, but I've only got a month left here. I don't think I'll ever return to Manchester again without good reason so I might as well stick it out."

A month. That was quick. It had dragged, now it raced. He didn't feel as gleeful as he expected to.

"You must be isolated up there without knowing anyone and going through this," his mother said.

"I was, but my show-off brother's about to blow into town..."

Connor rang off, promising to send photos of the room and him and Shaun, and signing off on his mother sending Jen a consolatory WhatsApp message.

Connor had no interest in eating deconstructed fish and chips solo in the hotel restaurant so decided he'd have a soak in the gold rolltop bath, tipping White Company bubbles into the gush from the tap. He was glad there wasn't a prospective lover observing him getting into it as, in fact, clambering naked into a high-sided tub was comically ungainly.

Once immersed, the sounds of the street far below, he felt a potent combination of hopeful, lonely and absurd. You were supposed to have someone in here with you, holding a glass of something expensive and cold.

His mind wandered to how Bel Macauley often wore her hair slung up, as if she were keeping it clear of bathwater. He pictured her opposite, gazing at him skeptically. He recalled her emulsion-white skin, her bare collarbones. His imagination added suds-coated, floating breasts. He banished the vision before he was bobbing about with a tragic erection inspired by a combative coworker who would retch if she knew.

He'd started listening to her podcast, which was undeniably good. Her gentle northern accent and sparky, personable nature made her a very likable presenter.

He needed to neutralize this persistent wrong-think about sexing Bel up by acquiring a wholesome crush in London, but how did he find such a thing when he wasn't even there?

Later, in the bar, through black-lacquered doors, Connor

nursed a Pisco Sour and thought, Yeah, no, I'm not downloading the Hinge app. For what? To enrage Jen when patrolling and reassure himself he could still pull? That wasn't what he wanted reassurance about.

Shaun grabbed him from behind and kissed him on the head, saying, "Here he is! Charging it to the room, I bet."

Connor stood up to give his brother a hug.

His years in the States and his American spouse had given Shaun's accent a transatlantic lilt—one of the few things he was embarrassable about. Possibly because he was the king of being in control, and it wasn't a conscious choice.

"Here you are," Connor said, sitting down, inspecting his brother's appearance. "You look annoyingly with it for a man who's done long haul."

"That's good, then, because I feel like a Ziploc bag of hot dog shit."

Connor felt aglow at the sight of his brother in this city where, as his mother had observed, he knew almost no one, while simultaneously being painfully aware of how much he missed out on, with Shaun living three and a half thousand miles away. Perhaps Jen had a point about his incurable melancholy.

Once Shaun had a beer, Connor broke the Jennifer news, including how the discovery was made.

"Fuck!" Shaun said. "You got this photo right as she's arriving?"

"Right as she was arriving. I actually felt sorry for her more than anything."

"Mmm hmm," Shaun said, "that's very you."

"The real shocker was she wanted us to go to counseling and carry on. It was very difficult to see our path back to happiness. I think she was determined to make me the quitter."

"Jennifer's an acquisitive person. You're a prize, and she can't bear to willingly surrender a prize. It's not that you have value to her, it's that you have value to others."

"Shaun," Connor said, rubbing his eyes and laughing, "I know your whole thing is you don't sugarcoat anything ever, but could I ask for the merest icing dusting?"

"Are you conflicted about it ending?" Shaun said, dangling a Padrón pepper by its stalk into his mouth. He'd covered half the table in speculative side dish orders. "Also, you say you're not harrowed but you're thin. Eat something."

"Ripped, I'm *ripped*."

"If you say so."

"No, I'm not conflicted, but . . . humans aren't machines. *The woman you spent five years with was a thunderous nause* is quite hard to hear." Connor tried a cauliflower fritter and spoke after chewing: "I still feel defensive of her and wish you'd liked her more. I knew you were never bowled over by Jen, but you got along."

"We did get along. I just thought she was wrong for you. We all did."

"Oh, great!" Connor said. He was playacting more bothered than he was. Now the files had been declassified, he was self-conscious, yes, but also curious. He'd never thought his family were mad keen on Jennifer, merely respectful of his choice, and that had been enough.

"I appreciate it hurts," Shaun said. "Equally, do you want me to say you just lost the best thing to ever happen to you, drive to North East London right now with a boom box and stand under her window?"

"No, obviously," Connor said. "I look back over our five years and try to see why she and I ever thought we were a good fit. By thirty-four I should've figured out my kind of person."

"You were aimless back then, and she had purpose. It was a situational attraction, it had a time and a place. A lot of people turn those errors into marriages and kids so you're lucky, really."

Connor explained they'd have company for dinner the following evening. Checking they were speaking in total privacy, he briefly explained the undercover op, his intrusion into it, who he was meant to be.

"That sounds a heck of a gig." Shaun lowered his voice. "No offense, but you're an intern? I thought you'd be doing golden wedding anniversaries and cats up trees."

"I would be if you'd not sent me to check out a hotel in Didsbury."

"You're here twelve weeks in this city and you're trying to get its mayor fired? You fucking journalists, I swear to God."

Connor grinned and Shaun shook his head.

"This Bel Macauley must be quite formidable," Shaun said.

"Oh, you have NO idea," Connor said, with a grimace.

He suddenly felt exposed, even rattled, having sailed through discussing JenGate. He'd not prepared a party line on Bel. If he revealed any confusion or ambivalence, Shaun would leap straight into dissecting it. Connor wasn't ready.

"Why are we spending Saturday night with her, then?"

"Because I bloody have to, don't I," and Connor, aiming for rueful jollity as he said it, feeling both ungentlemanly and something of a fraud.

39

What outfit would Connor really hate? Bel thought, with a smile, surveying her wardrobe. I seek a How Dare You Show Me Up Like This impact. She no longer wanted to go tonight and needed her clothes to convey it.

She'd abruptly gone off the prospect after Connor messaged *I know I dropped my brother visit on you a bit, no worries if you've got better things to do! Very much extra to requirements rather than essential.*

Unthinkingly, with innocent enthusiasm and the warmth of a return exclamation mark, Bel insta-replied *No, I'd like to meet him!*

Then the ripple of typing dots, three times, starting and stopping. Bel frowned. It wasn't hard to give her a time and a location. Then it dawned—she was supposed to take the hint and politely back out. Having not gotten the outcome he'd angled for, Connor was now tying himself in diplomatic knots trying to both act pleased and hint again, always a tricky, highly skilled maneuver.

Sure enough, his fourth—fourth!—bout of typing resulted in:

OK cool, want to join us for food? Thinking about optics—it doesn't make sense I'd take my brother out for dinner on a Saturday night if he's come this far, and leave my girlfriend at home? But if you want to do drinks-only I'm happy to come up with a rationale, not as if we're likely to have to use it. Up to you!

This time, she read his regret perfectly clearly. A no-worries-if-not that reeked of hoping for a cancellation from the other party. If he didn't want her there he should've swallowed it and borne his error nobly, as she did when he tagged along to Schofield's. Take the hit and let her erroneously believe her company was welcome. Bel was surprised by how put out she was. It wasn't like her to fret over minor slights, especially from people who weren't important to her.

She supposed she thought they'd reached a friendly détente, over bacon sandwiches, the morning after the night before. Dare she say it, she'd enjoyed his company and thought it was mutual. So it made her feel like she was being Undercover Conned too.

Bel briefly agonized about whether to fake-find something she was doing after all, but it would be so lumpenly obvious.

Food sounds good, Bel eventually replied, coolly. *How about I ask my friend Shilpa to join? Four is always a better number.*

Given it was too late to back out, better to seek reinforcements.

Sure. Will forward details.

Chilly. Great. What a win, Connor, now neither of us wants to be there.

Shilpa arrived with the eagerness of Road Runner in a deep red vinyl coat with a white shearling collar and cuffs, taking advantage of Manchester's cold snap this weekend, even in high summer. It was completely OTT and suited her incredibly well.

"Do I look like Whore Santa? Love your dress!" she said to Bel.

Bel had gone for ankle-length navy cords, a smocked bodice with a tiny-yellow-flower print, long sleeves and frilly cuffs, and clompy lace-up boots. It was "Amish wife meets petulant sixth-former." She felt sure Connor Adams would think it was provocatively unattractive.

"Thanks. It's going to be loathed by male eyes, isn't it? Excellent."

"I don't know, it makes your boobs look nice. I wouldn't underestimate them."

If Connor Adams had ever thought about her mammaries, except possibly to find a fault, Bel was Liza Minnelli.

As they walked to the restaurant, 10 Tib Lane, just beyond the Town Hall, Shilpa wrestled her phone from her flamboyant coat pocket to show Bel an Instagram: "New 'shit ABBA' has dropped."

Bel laughed as she saw a photo of two bearded men, a blonde and a brunette.

Zack, Nicky, Tim and Rhiannon were on a weekend away in Galway, rosy-cheeked in walking gear and brandishing pints of Guinness in a proper boozer.

"It is very double-dating cozy. I hope they had an argument over Tim burning out the clutch in the hire car and everyone's simmering," Bel said. "He always did drive like Jason Bourne."

Shilpa stuffed her phone back in her pocket.

"Sick of it. Zack wouldn't walk as far as Nisa Local for some Monster Munch when he was with me. Also, I posted my favorite courgette pasta and Zack commented 'serving . . . a custodial sentence' and sorry, he does NOT retain rights to mock my cooking."

Bel suppressed more laughter as she could see Shilpa was genuinely upset.

Bel chose her words carefully. "How bothered are you really? I don't mean that in an accusing way. In a 'I thought your feelings for Zack were deader than Geronimo the dead Alpaca' way."

Shilpa sighed.

"I thought we were playing by the same rules. I'd never have done this to him. He's made me feel stupid for thinking we still had an understanding."

"I know exactly what you mean. But we left them and they have male egos and here we are. They've done it precisely to make us feel like this. We got everything we wanted. We have to let this hurt a bit for as long as it hurts a bit."

"Yeah. I think getting everything I wanted is my problem," Shilpa said, removing a strand of her loose hair from her lip gloss. "Divorce is an utter shit show. I know Zack was scared of being single and I wasn't, because I wanted out so much. Now he's happy and I'm alone and it feels like the gods are saying 'suck it, bitch.' I am not meant to get divorced. As my mum said, it's yet more white behavior from me."

"Yes, except Zack rushing into something fast might not work out and you, taking your time to repair, probably will. I mean, you don't even know that he *is* happy. This could be an empty gesture to get back at you, as you said."

"True," Shilpa said. "But you think Rhiannon's real?"

"Oh, Tim and Rhiannon are definitely real. I realize, with hindsight, she might've been waiting for him, and that's spooky. Good luck to them."

"Tonight is what I need," Shilpa said. "Connor's brother's married?"

"Married, lives in the States, and you're *not* getting together with someone who would keep Connor Adams in my orbit, *thankyouverymuch*."

"Imagine if we did a retaliation selfie with them!"

"My employment prohibits, I'm relieved to say."

10 Tib Lane, a low-lit, unfussy yet fashionable "big plates and little plates" restaurant, had been chosen by Connor.

He was at the table, against a wall of copper-green distressed plaster, wearing a dark blue shirt, raising a hand to say *over here*, his chestnut-brown hair and strong bone structure immediately distinguishable and striking. Shilpa would gnash her teeth at the banned selfie.

"Evening. Nice dress," Connor said to Bel, mildly, and if he was trolling her, it was too subtly done for her to tell. So, 1–0 Connor.

Bel carefully took a seat opposite Connor's brother: not as tall and stockier than Connor, with the same dark hair, cut shorter, and, she soon discovered, far more amenable. If he'd heard anything negative about Bel, it didn't show.

His work in Washington was fascinating and Bel was soon deep into the intricacies of the US political system versus the British civil service, and the culture shock of marrying an American.

She'd thought Connor's "alpha" descriptor could mean "potentially overbearing" but the only time she saw it in action was when Shaun said, "Shall we get the whole menu and see if there's anything we want to reorder? Cool, that's sorted."

She wasn't about to complain about the sort of commanding masculinity that ended up with double portions of Pommes Anna.

When Shaun went to the loo, Connor and Shilpa were in an involved conversation about how Shilpa wooed her ex-husband on a budget crossing to Berlin. The way Connor's body language transformed with Shilpa into that of someone open and sweet-natured, who smiled easily and often, was truly enraging, Bel thought.

He was leaning back, absently ruffling his hair as he spoke, gurgling at Shilpa's remarks. *I mean*, Bel fumed inwardly, *I've never even seen that many of his teeth. Literally if not metaphorically. I've never seen his face do that.* Why did he inflict sullen, guarded mode on her, specifically?

Connor unexpectedly glanced over at her and Bel was fully caught out, staring at him with an intent expression. He stared back, frowning: very clearly thinking something and communicating it. Bel felt a reverberation between them. The strange thing was, until now she'd have interpreted his expression as *don't window-shop what you cannot afford* self-regard. But it didn't feel like that. It felt like . . . ?

Shaun returned. Shilpa went to the loo in turn, leaving the three of them together.

"Fuck me," Connor said, looking at his phone. "Sorry, dirty laundry—but I'm quite drunk. I told my parents that me and Jen had separated. My mum wanted to text her to say she was sorry. I've had a message from Jennifer raging that I told my parents our decision was mutual. *To be clear, I didn't want to break up and you did.* I didn't tell them about the other guy or the nude she sent me, out of consideration for her privacy and image. And she's got the balls to say I've defamed her by not saying I dumped her? Now I've got a message from my mum asking *do I know how much Jen wants to make it work.*"

"Jennifer's actually given you a gift here," Shaun said.

"She has? Enlighten me. It's got a layer of wrapping."

"Can you have the slightest doubt you made the right decision? She thinks she's defense but she's working for the prosecution."

Bel laughed and then said "Sorry" to Connor and Connor said, "No, he's right. I hate Shaun's propensity for being right."

"You know something I've discovered in life . . ." Shaun said.

"Here we go." Connor sighed.

"Some people—and I don't mean bad people, all sorts of people—have no interest in changing their behavior in order to seek better outcomes, and the condition is lifelong. Once you realize you're dealing with one of those people you can make an informed decision about how much energy to give them."

"I'm going to put that in my Notes app," Bel said, eyes wide.

"Could I convince everyone to have a post-dinner cocktail?" Connor said. "The bar here looks nice. Tell you what, I'll see if there's a table free before we move."

"I'm going to answer for Shilpa as a yes," Bel said.

He chucked his napkin down and stood up.

"He's not usually like this, you know," Shaun said, nodding after his brother, once Connor had gone round the corner. "In his attitude to the Manchester branch of your enterprise."

"How do you mean?" Bel said, suddenly riveted. She'd never thought Shaun would break rank. So Connor *had* been slagging the northern HQ; she might've known.

"He's not usually this closed off and jaded. The real Connor is too trusting, if anything. He sees the best in people and tries to take on their problems and fix them. But he picked the wrong career and the wrong woman and it broke his spirit. You're meeting him in the plaster-cast healing mode. Actually, that analogy works well. He's currently got a hard shell round him while the bones mend. But it's not part of him."

"OK. I will bear that in mind," Bel said. She paused. "You mean there is a whole easier, parallel-version Connor I haven't met? Fuck."

Shaun burst out laughing so loud it startled her.

"He's been that bad? I mean, he's a bossy, opinionated little shit, that part's forever."

"He's not been *that* bad, and I wasn't perfect either," Bel said. "I think because he didn't want to come here, he took it out on us a bit. I mean, he didn't turn up acting like he wanted to make friends . . ."

"Therefore he's not made any?" Shaun finished.

"He's got an ardent fan in Shilpa," Bel said, smiling.

40

"Do you know about Connor's colleague committing suicide? He leapt out of a window. He'd lost millions on a deal. Absolutely horrific," Shilpa said, as they tottered up Oldham Street, arm in arm, anticipating shoes off and kettle on.

"Oh yes. Have you been in your Emily Maitlis mode?" Bel said.

Shilpa's ability to turn small talk into a searching interview was well established.

"You know that Connor wrote and delivered the eulogy to, like, two hundred people? No one else at his company would do it because they were bastards and Eli wasn't well-liked. Connor did it for Eli's parents' and sister's sake, and it was so moving and well written that everyone applauded."

"He told you this, did he? *Bit* self-aggrandizing—"

"No!" Shilpa said, genuinely stung on his behalf. "Well, yes, in that I asked 'What did they think of it?' and Connor said 'I think it was OK because they clapped and cried but I've not been to enough funerals to know if that happens often.' He still goes to see Eli's parents every couple of months."

"Hmmm. I'm glad if Connor Adams has a higher self—shame we've had so much of his lower self."

Yet as she said it, Bel felt shabby. His brother's input had mattered. Even she had to admit at this point the books more than balanced: Connor might not be to her taste, but he had his virtues.

"Why are you so hard on him?!" Shilpa said, then stopped in her tracks. She turned to Bel, eyes wide. "Oh."

"What?"

"*Oh*."

"Oh no—NO," Bel shrieked, seeing Shilpa's sparkling delight. "No no no no. Shilpa. That is a conspiracy theory on a par with the CIA building the pyramids."

"I can't believe I haven't seen it until now! You don't hate him, you hate your boner for him!"

"You are a rank fantasist and delusional romantic who has seen *La La Land* way too many times."

They resumed walking.

"So if Connor said 'Isabel Hilda Macauley'—"

"If you tell him my middle name I will fucking kill you, can we be clear?"

"If he said 'Bel, this pretending to be together. It's made me want you to bounce on it all night long,' you'd feel *nothing*?"

"I'd think, all things considered, he was pranking me."

"Oh my God, stop dodging! If he said 'Surprise, I've got an idea: *You bounce on it all night long,*' you're telling me you'd feel *nothing*?!"

Bel flashed back to That Look earlier. Her insides started to liquefy. It felt like . . . a dare. He was daring her.

Bel cleared her throat. "It'd feel like being challenged to a duel."

BACK AT THE HOTEL after Connor ordered the one-for-the-roads they'd regret tomorrow, Shaun said, "That was a great evening, I don't know what you were grousing about. Your journalist Girl Friday, 'thorn in your side,' by the way? She's dream woman material."

"Bel Macauley?" Connor said. "*Bel Macauley*'s a dream woman? A cheese dream more like."

"Funny, smart, ambitious. Very cute. Seems a genuinely nice

person. Literally, only some sour old direct competitor in her professional field could find fault."

"Oh, haha. Bel's pretty, I'll give you that. And nice company for an evening. But add: frequently dresses for work like she's plotting to climb a motorway gantry, full of herself, snarky, exhausting. The hubris of being born with a silver spoon. I promise you, the distaste is wholly mutual."

"You two really get across each other that much?"

"She and her sycophantic sidekick Aaron needlessly opened hostilities with me on day one because she's imperious, conceited and arrogantly thought she had me sussed out on sight. She's too used to men going giddy at the Bel Macauley schtick. The scruffy, sweary indie movie heroine thing, Winona in *Heathers*. My polite indifference to her appeal was reconfigured as me being a pompous wanker."

"She was very interested in you."

"I bet. The way a boxer wants to know their opponent's weaknesses," Connor deliberately snapped back before his real reaction could settle on his face.

Bel had started to provoke a new emotion: insecurity. He'd hedged and caveated her invite tonight to make declining easy, as he'd wanted to be absolutely sure she wanted to come.

And That Look she was giving him, what was that about? He'd glanced up and she was unexpectedly staring at him with this . . . discontentment . . . and if it didn't sound insane, which it did . . . *longing*?

It gave Connor a feeling he'd not had since he was a kid in the school gymnasium, and someone had hard-pushed him off the climbing frame onto the crash mat. He could've looked away but he chose not to. If she wanted something from him, she could let him know.

He wanted her to let him know.

"You think she lacks integrity?" Shaun said. "Would she turn you over?"

"No! Not at all," Connor said, recalling the good turn she did him with Toby. "Annoyingly."

This was why he'd dodged: he didn't actually know what he thought of her.

"Well, I don't know why or how you've turned her into Irene Adler to your Sherlock, then. She's the most intriguing person you've introduced me to in forever," Shaun said.

"Ugh. If I'd known you'd take to her I'd never have risked introducing you. This is like annoyance squared."

Their drinks arrived. Shaun paused with glass to lips and made the face he always made before he dropped one of his "Et tu, Brute?" lines.

"I put it to you that the only thing you don't like about her is that you don't think she likes you."

41

Bel opened her door to Connor the following Thursday afternoon and despite the relative solemnity of the occasion, a make-or-break professional meeting, she ended up hooting.

Connor was wearing a "just say it" comedy hangdog fury look. His hair was as wet as if he'd been standing under a showerhead. His jacket was drenched, and his skin glistened with moisture, as if he'd run a marathon.

"Ahahahahha," Bel offered as greeting.

"Oh, fuck you!" Connor said. "Going home to London can't come fast enough."

"London, our famously rainless capital," Bel said, standing aside to let him in. "You southern boys, seriously. Have you heard of a thing called an umbrella?"

"It was sunny when I left Deansgate!"

"Yeah, Manchester does that, I've learned," Bel said.

"I thought the Gallagher brothers' huge anoraks up here were a style thing but they actually serve a purpose, don't they?" Connor said.

He unbuttoned his jacket and peeled it off. You could wring it out like a dish cloth, Bel thought.

"I'll put that on a radiator for you. Wet white shirt, is it? As predicted, actual Mr. Darcy," Bel said, before her brain could halt her mouth. Connor, rather winningly, blushed.

"If I said that to you it'd be harassment," he muttered.

"It would be, because the patriarchy says my nipples are ruder than yours," Bel said. "Take it up with them."

"This escalated quickly," Connor said, eyes wide.

"I'll get you a towel," Bel said, before awkwardness could develop.

She returned with one from the spare room, pulled a chair out from the dining table and whacked the kettle on.

Her laptop was open and ready to start their conference with Toby and Albert the lawyer in ten minutes' time.

"The next Didsbury trip is on, then?" Connor said, rubbing at his hair.

After a period of silence from the Ci Vediamo direction—which Bel was right on the verge of finding concerning—Amber had gotten back in touch, and with strenuous apologies.

She and Rick (sans kenneled Gertie) had been on a last-minute holiday to Santorini. Instagrams confirmed. There was a holiday dump of beaded thong sandal–clad feet resting on whitewashed balconies and slab-size blocks of feta on fries next to his 'n' hers sunglasses on the check tablecloth, set to a clip of "GREECE" by DJ Khaled. Bel was glad the psychodrama of advertising yourself like a commodity online was one she could skip.

You & Connor have to come over. How about late drinks lock-in at CV? I need to pay you back for that MESS with Rick. Gertie will be over the moon to see her boyfriend too. How are you fixed for a week on Saturday?

Bel had responded positively and alerted both Toby and Connor they needed a hasty Teams meeting, hence today.

"Your brother was great, by the way," Bel said. "Did he have a good trip?"

"Oh yes, he did, thanks. He's on to London now seeing my parents. He bought them a sack of gifts in Selfridges food hall and went to the football museum."

"I see what you mean about his being incisive. I felt cleverer just talking to him."

"Right? He left me by handing over this card in a sealed envelope with the date I leave Manchester on it, with strict instructions not to open it before then. It contains a prediction, apparently. Like some sort of cheap magician."

"Wow. You'll have to tell me what it says. *Should've bought an umbrella*, probably."

The wall clock hit the hour and Bel clicked the link to join the meeting room.

"I can't overrun today, I'm afraid, I've got tickets for *Operation Mincemeat the Musical*," Toby said, as the glass-walled office sprang into view on Bel's MacBook.

Sure, sure, this is only lives, careers and our arses hanging in the balance, Bel thought but didn't say.

"Hi, Connor. How's the Manchester posting going?" Toby said.

"It's gone in unexpected directions," Connor said, nodding toward Bel, then Bel saw the shadow cross Connor's face because he'd made it sound like they were sleeping together.

Bel assumed a businesslike tone and outlined the lock-in, the whereabouts of the iPad, the general intention to plunder.

"I'm going to ask Amber if I can book the York family in for a stay there because my apartment won't be big enough. I'm hoping she gets the tablet out and I see the passcode. Then, after that, one of us lifts it. Connor had a smart idea we could take a factory settings iPad, put their cover on it, let them think it's bricked overnight while we swipe the goods from it, then put the original back."

"Whoa, whoa, whoa," Toby said, putting his coffee mug down with a bump.

Albert Double Barrel had woken up too, like the dormouse in the teapot.

"Nobody's taking anything off the premises. That is the criminal act of theft."

"We'd return it ASAP," Bel said, but she was hot under her clothes. This was a Jenga block tumble; she knew it and felt it instinctively.

"Steady on there, Woodward and Bernstein," Toby said. "'Intention to return' isn't mitigation when stealing something, or everyone would use it. And I'd rather you didn't make that case in a magistrate's court, in the name of working for this newspaper."

"We can't upload up to a hundred and eighty days of doorbell footage while we're in the bar, though," Bel said. "It's going to take about two hours. Right, Connor?"

"Yes. Obviously, if it's only recording when motion-triggered, it's not six whole months of tape but it's still a lot. It'll take at least two hours, I reckon. We can erase the fact we've uploaded it so they'd not know we have it straightaway."

"Then you have to figure that out *in situ*, I'm sorry," Toby said, leaning forward on his elbows. "We're out on a limb here as it is, hoping the strength of the Ring Video evidence will negate the manner by which we acquired it."

"But we're robbing that?" Bel said.

"Copying sensitive data and pilfering an expensive thing are two different activities; neither is without risk but one is far greater than the other," Toby said. "Albert, this feels like your purview?"

Albert coughed into life.

"Yes, that's correct. With the doorbell camera we could argue if she left the device around and open in your presence, then it is tantamount to photographing a page in an open diary. It's snooping, yes, but in the public interest. Once you remove the device from the premises you have simply stolen her property."

"Which I can't do?" Bel said.

"Which you can't do," Albert confirmed. "We are bending the law, not breaking it."

"Right," Bel said, chewing her lip. "This limitation might've been useful to know from the outset. Still, limitations make you more creative."

Much as Bel wanted to howl, she had to accept the compound error. Until Connor raised the time frame for copying the footage, Bel had never thought of logistics much beyond accessing the iPad.

"We do this not because it is easy . . ." Toby began.

"But because we thought it would be less hard than this," Connor said.

Toby chortled and Bel realized he'd never thought this was going to work. He'd been playing along so the plucky podcaster gal felt she still got to try things.

"Oh, and you two, have a fab time at the awards tomorrow! Schmooze your butts off, please. That table cost an arm and a leg but it's worth it for presence, I think. But it'll have none without you working the room and pressing the flesh."

Bel said *sure thing, we'll be belles of the ball, no pun, speak soon,* smiled a false smile and hit End Meeting. She closed the laptop to be sure.

"Ugh! No concern for how impossible our task just became, much excitement about us eating toad in the hole with the presenters of Smooth Radio North West. The real Operation Mincemeat: we're dead in the water."

"How do we pull this off?" Connor said. "The undercover sting, not the toad in the hole."

"Spoiler: We can't. We're screwed. Totally," Bel said. She saw his surprise that she didn't have a work-around. If she wasn't so gutted she might've been flattered.

"Really?"

"Even if I manage to see Amber's passcode, and we make a grab for the iPad, the idea we can hide it for hours while it's uploading to a second device? I know you think I am a vainglorious dipshit," Bel said and Connor smiled, "but even I don't think that's feasible. That is beyond the bounds of credibility."

"I can't go to the loo, get it on my way past, hide it in the men's somehow?"

"But if it goes missing right after I've asked Amber to look at it . . . ?" Bel said. "If they hunt for it while we're still there and find the upload in progress?"

"Yeah. Sheesh. What do we do? We're committed to the lock-in as it stands," Connor said.

Bel tapped her pen on the dining room table.

"We carry on and hope the answer comes to us in the meanwhile."

"Ah, the old Bel Macauley approach of *It'll be all right on the night*?"

"More or less."

"Toby told me to learn everything I could from you. I'm certainly doing that."

"Oh, really?" Bel said.

"Yep." Connor counted off on his fingers: "Hope is a plan, starters make people uptight, and Big Celery control the media."

Bel laughed. She was grateful to him for responding to this setback with good humor. She didn't feel humorous.

The number of people who believed Bel could achieve something she couldn't was now totaling five. Or six, if you counted Bel herself, which after that encounter, she didn't.

42

The Victorian neo-Gothic facade of Manchester Town Hall was lit with a garish blue-and-purple NORTHERN MEDIA AWARDS banner strung across its entrance and a red carpet leading to the arched doorway.

A lone paparazzo was half-heartedly loitering, even though the only famous people here were the Mayor, and the actor who was hosting and a former *Strictly Come Dancing* contestant duo handing out the awards—Marcus Rashford wasn't going to suddenly appear among the pallid hacks.

Bel's heart was in her mouth as she emerged from her minicab in an emerald-sequin cocktail dress she'd acquired as a Bella Niven choice (admittedly her Vinted habit wasn't wholly justified by her needing to kit out her doppelgänger). It was one-shouldered and she'd added dangly fake diamond earrings. A YouTube tutorial on how to do your own chignon had qualified success. The look was Best Supporting Actress nominee at the Aldi Oscars meets Rutshire wife-swapping party.

As she painstakingly traversed St. Peter's Square at half speed in heels, she could see Aaron. He was early, sucking hungrily on a vape pen, his quiffed dark hair smoothed into place with pomade.

"Macca, you look properly stunning," Aaron said, looking her up and down. "The stuff of instant marriage proposals."

"Thank you. You look pretty damn good yourself, Parry."

Aaron pretend-tightened his tie in a Morecambe and Wise gesture.

"That's good, because I feel like a total nob."

Bel cast a glance at others milling around. No sign of Anthony. He'd surely not bother with somewhere this busy? *Keep calm, carry on.*

"Let's get our heads into the social-climbing zone," Bel said. "Given Connor won't be here in a few weeks' time, it's up to us to work the room. In the nicest possible way, and I say this with envy, Connor is irrelevant here."

"Speak of the swaggering irrelevant devil . . ."

Bel followed Aaron's sight line. *Jesus Christ.* She'd never seen someone suit a tuxedo in the real world before. Bel thought of them as either ill-fitting hire attire at weddings at golf clubs or straining against the circumference of a Tory grandee, and certainly naffer than a good two-piece suit.

And yet. Here was Adams carrying off black tie as if he'd been born in it, one hand in his pocket as he strolled up to them. It was as if he were going to walk the red carpet at the Venice Film Festival or play high-stakes poker in Montenegro with an arms dealer. Connor had additionally acquired a five o'clock shadow that was thinking about becoming a beard and set off his jawline beautifully.

All in all, he was outshining his company to a brazen and impolite degree. Bel knew it couldn't be her "straight woman weakness" goggles as Aaron was visibly sick as a parrot.

"You look like one of those hen-do strippers who's going to cook dinner in an apron with his bum out later," he said in greeting to Connor.

"You look like a Buddy Holly tribute who's going to sing 'Peggy Sue' on the Cunard Line," Connor said.

"Not to sound like your mums, but I think you both look great," Bel said, diplomatically.

"Not all of us already owned a custom-made tux like Jordan

Belfort here, eh," Aaron said. "This cost me a hundred fifty quid from Ted Baker."

"It's always extra to get the legs taken up," Connor said, and Bel had to stop herself barking with laughter.

"Enough flirting, you two!" Bel said. "We have to present a united front tonight, please."

"Let's do our *Peaky Blinders* squad strut, then," Aaron said. "Can someone cue up 'Red Right Hand' on their phone."

They joined the flow into the building, Aaron immediately and vocally running into his former *Manchester Evening News* pals—"Gareth, you twat, you can't be nominated unless there's a category for Biggest Email Not Opener"—breaking up their threesome.

Bel held her dress clear of her feet on the grand staircase up to the Great Hall and picked her way with extreme care.

"I'm not going arse over tits in front of dozens of my peers whom I respect. And Connor Adams," she said.

"Charmed. Do you know these steps are low-rise for women in Victorian dress? Bustles and the like?" Connor said, gallantly slowing his progress to stay abreast of Bel's and offering his arm. "Shaun made me do the history tour."

They cast eyes up at the towering stained-glass windows.

"Hmm. You'd think a hundred years later we'd be in trousers," Bel said, accepting the arm.

"Did anyone stop you wearing trousers this evening?" Connor said, and Bel gave him an *oh, fuck you* eye roll.

In the main space, despite their general indifference to a back-slapping corporate jolliness, they oohed and aahed. It was lit by chandeliers the size of monster truck wheels, scatterings of stars projected onto the vaulted ceiling. White tablecloths were set with all-white flower arrangements on long gilt stems, and with white taper candles.

They found their place cards at a table distant from the stage, as befitted people with no nominations, and got lightly battered on table red wine and bonhomie and ate salmon mousse, chicken in mushroom sauce and lemon tart.

The ceremony was mercifully brisk, engraved shards of Perspex on plinths dispensed to this year's shining lights of northern media amid waves of applause.

After the plates were cleared and Connor's internship proved fascinating to the other women at their table, Bel slunk out of her gold seat and approached a handsome young Indian photographer brandishing a Nikon and snapping stray angles.

"Excuse me, excuse me, hi." Bel tried for her most ingratiating smile and baby Marilyn voice. "My work requires me not to have photos online, so would it be all right to ask if you could keep me out of any candids tonight? Oh, thanks so much, I *really* appreciate it."

"Are you a secret ethics and standards inspector or something?" the photographer asked, flirting.

"Ha! Something like that. I'd have plenty to inspect, right?" she flirted back. *Needs must.*

"If you're in any of the backgrounds, I'll delete it. Shame, though." He winked.

They shared a secretive smile and Bel thought, That's sorted, then.

Bel grabbed her glass and circulated, talking shop with the relaxation that came with free Malbec, and watched Glenn and his entourage in the distance.

She witnessed the cult of personality that Ian referred to: Glenn was the center of a group that revolved around him. How could he look so normal? How could men who did such things present as the nicest guy in the room? It even made Bel doubt herself, calling to mind Erin, the things said, trying to map it onto the tall, engaging blond man who laughed easily and often.

Bel turned away until she felt a tap on her shoulder.

"Excuse me, are you Bel? The Mayor would like to meet you," said a woman with ponytailed hair in a suit, one of those curly wires running up the back of her neck to her ear.

"Me? Are you sure?" Bel said, suddenly feeling far more sober. Fuck. What if he *knew*? She recalled Ian saying the Mayor had people everywhere.

"He's over there," the woman said, and as Bel followed the line of her hand signal, Glenn Bailey raised a glass to Bel, as someone tugged at his sleeve.

She told herself if she was about to receive Tony Soprano whispered threats, it would only invigorate her to carry on. Bel navigated her way through the crowd.

"Hi, hello! You're Bel Macauley?" Glenn said, as she reached him. He extended his hand and Bel shook it. Bel blanked thoughts of where the hand had been.

"Forgive me for being a little starstruck here, your voice has been the only sound in my ears for weeks."

"It has?" Bel said. The idea was extremely startling. She was the watcher and Glenn was the wildlife and here he was, shining a torch on her. She had been completely caught on the hop. Was he on to her? She sweated under sequins.

"Your podcast series is wonderful. I love the way you've mixed those famous story backgrounders with your own investigations. I've told everyone in my office to give it a listen. A real reminder of what journalism could and should be."

Glenn was handsome in a weathered way, deep-etched lines and good bone structure.

"Thank you," Bel said, mind racing to come up with a reply. "I was lucky that my late aunt gave me a lot of contacts for the legacy stories. I'm kind of a nepo baby, ha. Tessa was a big star on the *Mirror* in the 1980s, and when I said I was her niece, people answered the email."

"I was going to say, the guy in Sunderland reminiscing about the Ripper and Wearside Jack tapes was a real coup. I'm sure your likability plays a big role too. It's not how you get contacts and opportunities, it's what you do with them once you have them."

Bel smiled and said thanks and thought, *Oh, you're good*.

Fortunately, Glenn was claimed by another guest.

"Bel, I'm sorry this has been so brief, another time!"

Bel made a polite face of gratitude and reeled away with genuine gratitude she'd not had to come up with more to say.

Strange times: Had Ian never summoned her to Southern Cemetery, *the Mayor loves my podcast* would've been a feather in her cap with her bosses. And she'd have thought he was impressively knowledgeable beyond the responsibilities of his office.

"Wow, that's a special recommendation," said a gaggle of people from a weekly paper who'd been standing nearby, shamelessly earwigging. "What's your podcast called?"

"Thank you," Bel said. "It's called *I Might Have a Story for You* but it's on hiatus at the moment."

It was quite something for Glenn Bailey to take second place in the award for "man she least wanted to come face-to-face with at this event," yet she turned round, and there was the first, smirking at her.

43

No one bothered to talk to Connor once the table formations dissolved, despite a few inquisitive glances, and he was fine with that. Being unknown came with freedom, the luxury of lurking.

He liked to think he was a good people-watcher.

His friend Paige once said to him, "For a beautiful person you're unusually good at making yourself invisible, and you know why?"

"No, but I'm happy with the descriptor," Connor had said. Paige was gay and often cheerfully told Connor her opinions about him, as a non-stakeholder.

"Because making yourself invisible is to do with curiosity and lack of ego, and not looks. It's a state of mind."

Across the room, Connor observed a man in his mid-forties or so, handsome in a "trendy geography teacher" or "noir author" way: black-rimmed glasses, neat features and auburn hair, with a goatee. What Connor principally picked up on was that this person was staring intensely at Bel. At first Connor thought he might be imagining it, too sensitized to scrutiny because of his and Bel's shadow life. They had been warned of a network of spies.

Bel was in animated conversation with a woman and two men, telling a story that required her to swing her Prosecco flute around and make emphatic facial expressions. They were beguiled, the Bel Macauley Effect in real time.

She'd done one of her sartorial caterpillar-to-butterfly transformations again. Connor had noticed men noticing her, and Bel not noticing at all. This was something different, however.

Every time Bel moved, this man's line of sight moved with her. The heaviness of his gaze as he stared at her was like that of a dog in undergrowth tracking a squirrel.

Eventually the man saw his opportunity and approached her. Connor watched their exchanging opening words in rapt fascination. This man's manner: smug, confidential, excited. Bel's demeanor: like someone had thrown a drink in her face.

Her response to him decisively confirmed that Something Was Up. Connor had never seen her like this, her whole posture completely altered. He was the sole audience for this little tableau, a two-hander play.

Wait! Was this *the stalker*? From York? The one she'd used as biography and obviously expected Connor to treat as a fiction, except he turned up at their office? Also, wasn't he from her last paper, so it'd fit with him being at these awards? Oh . . . Connor was already intrigued and now it was like he'd leaned down and found the key jigsaw puzzle piece on the floor.

Bel looked so hunted in this interaction that it activated a protective instinct. The man put his hand on Bel's upper arm and she flinched. Connor was baffled too. Macauley was one of the most forthright people he'd ever met. She had no difficulty standing up for herself. Not in any abrasive way—but she wasn't a wilting damsel needing rescue, a rare hothouse flower. If someone needed telling to go bum themselves into the middle of next week, she'd gaily do it.

Why did this individual look as if he intimidated her so much? What did he have on her? Had Bel done something so terrible this guy could hold her for ransom? Was the ransom . . . sexual? One thing Connor was certain of, there'd been some sort of personal entanglement.

He watched as a nervy-looking Bel said something to goatee guy with a bright, fake smile and walked away.

Connor saw Bel move onward through the rabble decisively toward the far end . . . the exit? She was leaving? Oh, he didn't like this at all. Not only was the party much less interesting without her, this man being able to chase her out felt all wrong.

It got worse: after glowering at her departure, the man swigged the rest of his drink, set it down and moved with purpose in the direction she'd gone.

He was following her? Was this an agreed pursuit between two people playing games? *You go first, I'll wait a minute*? He felt reasonably sure it wasn't. On impulse, Connor wove his way through the crowds and followed both of them.

It took him a couple of minutes outside the Town Hall to spot them, a dozen paces away: their distance from the building was exactly as it would be if Bel was fleeing into the night, and goatee guy had intercepted her.

Connor could overhear what he was saying as he drew nearer. Bel's arms were folded, her expression taut.

". . . Isabel, all I'm asking is you give me an hour of your time. I really don't think that's much to ask . . . Why are you so obstinate about this? What are you scared of?"

Connor took a deep breath. It was never wise to interfere when you didn't know what you were interfering with, he thought, but here went nothing.

"Excuse me?" Connor said, interrupting, startling them both. "Sorry to cut in—Bel, there's someone inside I'd like to introduce you to."

"We're busy," the goatee man snapped.

"I wasn't talking to you," Connor said. He addressed Bel again: "All right if I borrow you?"

It was an Ask for Amy: if she wanted this other conversation, it was well within her capabilities to tactfully dismiss Connor.

"Sure," she said, politely obedient, and Connor relaxed a few degrees that he might've judged this right.

"Who the fuck are you?" the man said, and Connor was surprised at talk this aggressive from someone who looked like he taught Year 7s about oxbow lakes.

"Is this my replacement?" the man continued to Bel, who, with these words, looked as though she'd mentally teleported far from this place and left her body to deal with it.

"We're colleagues," Bel replied, voice flat.

"Our conversation is more important than you, then," the man said to Connor. "Can you give us some privacy?"

Whoever this was, Connor suspected he'd done something bad enough to justify the smack in the mouth he fancied giving him.

"I think Bel can decide that," Connor said.

"Isabel," the man said, in a beseeching tone, gripping her upper arm.

Without knowing quite what gave him the right, Connor reached out and detached the man's hand. He then stuck his hand out for Bel's. She accepted it, stepping forward.

"*Colleagues?*" the man repeated, staring down at the hand-holding. "You know who I am?" he said to Connor.

"Are you someone important in northern media?" Connor said.

"I'm the one who came before you," the man said.

What a weird, possessive remark, and why wasn't Bel kneeing him in the ball bag for the emphasis on *came*?

"Good for you," Connor said, eyes widening in a *who cares, you lunatic?* way. "Enjoy the rest of your evening."

Connor led Bel through the door, feeling goatee man's eyes boring into them like lasers. Connor moved his hand to the small of her back and without discussion they went up the steps and into the throng.

"Who am I meeting?" Bel said.

"Oh, no one. Sorry, I thought you looked like you wanted assistance."

Bel gave him a wonder-struck look. She slipped her hand back into Connor's and squeezed, then let go.

"Thank you for that. Seriously. Thank you, Connor."

"No problem," Connor said. "Are you all right?"

"Sort of," Bel said, sounding as if she might cry.

"Were you trying to leave?"

"Mmm hmm."

"But that prick stopped you?"

"Yup."

"Want to leave now with me as escort, and I'll punch him if he gets in the way?"

"*Yes*," Bel exhaled, smiling. She still looked powerfully miserable, dependent on Connor's direction; it was so unlike her, it was almost disorienting.

"Follow me," Connor said, decisively. He was enjoying being heroic protector, though he didn't like to admit it. He felt like she might faint and if so, he would scoop her up and carry her out in his arms.

They did a small circuit of the room and then looped back to the exit, Connor cutting sharp left to avoid goatee guy if he was still hanging around outside, but he suspected that they'd shaken him off if he'd followed them back in, by their walking in a circle.

In the muggy evening air, Connor said, "Taxi rank's round here, I think?" and Bel nodded, still uncharacteristically meek.

Connor was going to hand her into the hackney cab like some sort of Disney prince with a horse and carriage, and instead he found he couldn't let her go.

"Fancy a nightcap?" he said, braced for her to make a "sorry,

I'm tired" excuse to be the fuck away from men in dinner suits angling for her attention.

"That'd be great, actually," she said.

Connor felt a rush of joy that he told himself was the relief of being accepted when you feared you were being annoying.

"Where to?" the driver asked, as Connor slid the door shut.

"The Edinburgh Castle Pub?" Bel said, to a nod from Connor.

As the taxi stop-start-picked its way through busy streets, Bel said, "The Mayor asked to meet me, I don't know if you saw. He loves my podcast."

"Really?" Connor said. They both cast eyes at the driver, indicating to each other this exchange would stay anodyne.

"Real fan of investigative journalism," Bel said. "Made me feel like I was the only person in the room. That's some rizz. The funny thing was, he was telling me he was my fan and I felt I was recruited into being his fan."

"Huh. Good to know he likes investigative journalism," Connor said.

"Right?" Bel said. "He praised my likability. Little does he know I'm going to get more likable still."

She held on to the grab handle as the taxi took a sharp corner and grinned.

There was the Bel he knew, so what on earth had happened just now?

Connor realized he was dying to find out who goatee shit was. He'd never really thought about Bel's love life beyond that half-arsed digital stalking of her other ex, but he vaguely imagined a trail of broken hearts.

Bel was the kind of woman that men thought half of their music collection was about.

44

Connor had pulled the tie from the neck of his shirt to look slightly less conspicuous in the witchy, atmospherically lit hubbub of the pub and there was no getting round the fact, Bel thought, as she watched him at the bar, he looked Old Hollywood heartbreaking.

She indulged a surprising moment of perving on him, letting herself pretend he was her date. On pure aesthetics, Connor was impressive, but more than that, his swooping in to save the day with Anthony was downright spectacular.

He was attired like James Bond but she'd not expected Connor to act like him too.

In turn, Bel hadn't expected to behave the way she had: she'd been paralyzed. She'd ordered herself not to be intimidated by Ant, reasoning he couldn't make a scene in a crowded room. Yet she'd hidden from herself that she had been playing a game of odds in her head. A Surely He Won't Go That Far game, and every time he proved that he would. She couldn't lose again.

Once he had appeared, she didn't know how to handle it. Losing her shit with him both risked attracting attention and sustained his delusions that they were sexy pyrotechnics. Being calm and courteous wasn't sufficient deterrent—he used that as a welcome, to insinuate himself. Simply removing herself from his presence was all Bel was left with, and even that failed as he haunted her every step.

Then Connor was simply there, calmly cutting Anthony down to size and extracting Bel, as if he were her paid protection officer.

Connor made Anthony insanely angry but Connor, with no stakes here, wasn't riled in the slightest, so the power balance shifted with ease.

How Connor had figured it out, she had no idea. No doubt she'd pay for his help with a worsening of Anthony's antagonism, but it was worth it for Connor taking Ant's hand off her arm as though he were an autograph hunter with Lady Gaga.

When she told Shilpa, her ovaries would explode.

"Do you mind me asking who that was?" Connor said, as he put a gin and tonic in front of her, a red wine for himself.

Bel didn't mind. She wasn't at all sure of the wisdom of Connor as her audience, for various reasons, but one strong factor in his favor was that he soon wouldn't be here. Connor had seen what he'd seen. What the hell.

"Anthony, who you met there, was on the news desk and then a section editor at my last paper in Yorkshire . . . it's a long story, you're sure?"

Connor saluted her with his glass.

"OK. Not long after I was hired, he took me for a drink to talk about how I was getting on; he was a cheerleader for my work. He persuaded the big editor to accept me doing a podcast in my spare time. It was all very mentor-and-student. We'd keep going for lunchtime pints. Inevitably, of course, we got to talking about our private lives. I told him about my long-term boyfriend, Tim—the wheels were coming off at the time. I didn't say anything too disloyal, but it became obvious I was at a crossroads and unhappy."

"You lived with Tim?" Connor said.

Bel nodded, took a deep breath.

"Yeah, we'd been together since our late twenties. Oh God, I am so disgusted by myself even telling you this . . ." Bel said.

"You don't have to," Connor said.

"I know, but I want to, I've got a compulsion to spare no detail, if you can stomach it. It's better if I own it . . . Eventually, Anthony's 'agony uncle' routine turns into more. I'm starting to fall for him and he's sending email love letters, persuading me we have this huge, star-crossed"—Bel waved her hand—"meeting of hearts and minds going on. I wanted to believe I was in love. I wanted a reason to leave Tim. 'The next person is here, it must be time to go,' you know? It was so hard to finish it when Tim was desperate to stay together. He begged me to go to couples counseling. Ant's married with a teenage kid, but he says that his marriage is over and he's been looking for the courage to get out of his situation too. I'd never, ever have interfered with a marriage, but he told me it was functionally over in every respect."

"Of course he did," Connor said.

Bel took a breath.

"With hindsight, it was a technique. If my problem had been that Tim liked partying too much, Anthony would've positioned himself as Mr. Steady. He found out what I wanted and he became what I wanted. A getaway-car driver."

Bel played with a beer mat and dropped eye contact.

"It builds and builds and I let myself be persuaded into going to a hotel bar for an evening together to 'talk about the future'— and Connor, if that wasn't unfaithful enough, of course I know what else is going to happen. He's giving me enough deniability to go along with it. Anthony waits until it's all hand-gripping and intense and 'we could make this work' to reveal he's booked a room for 'privacy.'"

Bel took a sip of her drink to steel herself.

"I'm not a cheater by nature, though maybe everyone thinks that. Ant was like this big hit of dopamine in misery. Tim and I were arguing bitterly and I wanted to force things to a decision one way or another by doing something decisive. I started to believe I could follow Ant's lead. That he knew what should happen next, and that he'd fix everything. It was total cowardice, and karma has rightly been kicking my arse black-and-blue ever since. I tell Anthony he can't touch me until I've told Tim it's over—how arbitrary is that? Then my 'red line' ends in a Superior Double room, giving my boss—who's wearing his wedding ring—a blow job."

She cast an ashamed look up at Connor and shook her head in a way that said *judge me*. He gave her a steady look in return that said he wasn't going to.

"Anthony leaves at one a.m. so he's not spent the night away to alert his wife, which should've been a huge tell . . . The next day, taking the hotel bar promises seriously, I believe we're both telling our other halves that we've met someone else. I mean, we have to. Because as far as I'm concerned that shouldn't have happened and that can never happen again while Ant is with his wife. I'm naive enough to text Ant and ask, 'When is it going to be OK for us to call each other?' The admin of both of us turning the keys on the submarine. Ant calls me straight back and it's lots of shifty mumbling about how now's not quite the right time. But he's super keen to 'meet and talk' again. And I know in a second . . . it all fucking hits me—"

Bel's voice cracked and she deftly wiped tears away from carefully applied makeup.

"Ah shit! Sorry, sorry . . ." she said.

"No need whatsoever to apologize to me," Connor said, kindly, putting his hand on her arm.

"Absolutely loathe being a weeper," Bel said thickly, with a smile, as Connor murmured, "Don't be silly." She cleared her throat.

"I found out the Never Leaving His Wife men must all start like this: promising you the earth and then you realize the earth is in fact a pyramid scheme, a scam. *Make this initial upfront payment to secure the deal.* My damaged intellect finally woke up—*this is an older guy who wanted a belt notch, he told you what you wanted to hear, no one's leaving anyone.* Except I was honestly intending to leave Tim. So having seen through Ant, I still have to face what it tells me about my relationship. I go home and tell Tim it's over. He's devastated. He's sensed the Anthony complication. Tim points out I've been on my phone constantly, jumpy, distant. He asks, 'Are you sure there isn't anyone else? Swear on your mum's life,' again and again, and I say no and no and no because there isn't—but what a shitty person that makes me. There hasn't been a day since when I've not wanted to slap myself if I've thought about it."

Bel's tears threatened to make a return and she swigged her drink as an antidote.

"I deserved it, though. I deserved to have to tell Tim we were done, not with someone else lined up and waiting for me, but with flashbacks to deeply regrettable oral sex in Hotel Du Vin with a man who declared it 'super.'"

45

"I think you're being incredibly hard on yourself," Connor said.

"I think I'm going easy on myself! I did that with someone else's husband, and broke my ex's heart, and I'm making out like it's my ordeal. It's my main-character syndrome you identified."

"It was *your* ordeal," Connor said, in a gentle tone. "Breakups in serious long-term relationships are always really hard. Of course you agonized about it. If you'd been less of a person you wouldn't have. You were fragile. And fuckers like that guy? They can sense fragility a mile off."

"Thank you, but I think I emotionally destroyed Tim. Our mothers are best friends, his family is almost my family. His nice parents, who've known me since I was a kid, sent me a letter telling me exactly what I'd done to him, which was an incredibly hard read."

Bel choked up again. She couldn't see that her falling out of love with this Tim wasn't sadism, it was just a shame, Connor mused.

"In that case, sorry, they aren't *that* nice," Connor said, firmly. "His parents? How old is Tim?"

"Same age as us."

"He shouldn't have Mum and Dad playing HR department in his breakups, then."

"Maybe he didn't know."

"Men who let their parents do that *always* know."

"He didn't have to protect me, he didn't owe me that."

"He did owe you that," Connor said. "You owe basic respect and decency to your partner, even when they break your heart. What he knew about your character didn't disappear when you said you wanted to end things. Caring isn't about self-interest."

Bel looked at him as if she had never considered this before and was genuinely taking it in. There might be some bonding going on. Connor had a sudden powerful conviction, the sort that tended to turn up in low-lit bars with strong drinks, that if he could fix her sadness, it'd fix his sadness.

"Tell me this, is Tim so hurt he's now forever alone?"

"No, he's with Rhiannon."

"There you go," Connor said. "You had to get out of the way to let that story happen. The complication of the other guy was a burden you chose to spare him, and you're carrying that burden very heavily yourself. Let the guilt go. The very fact you feel this much guilt is proof of who you are."

Bel let out a deep breath she'd been holding, eyes still glittering with tears, and said, "Thank you."

"You know I'm right. For once." For some reason, he discovered he'd momentarily give anything for her to find him attractive, even though he knew she didn't.

"I would love you to be right this once." Bel smiled. In the candlelight glow, she really was quite beautiful. "Tonight you saw a scene from the grotesque epilogue. Could you take another drink?" She nodded at his glass.

"Yeah. Let's have our grotesque epilogue be tomorrow's hangover," Connor said, and found himself trying the sort of winning smile he'd not deployed on a woman for a long time. Bel beamed back.

He sat, face propped on palm, while she was at the bar and didn't check his phone. He wanted to absorb the moment and the pleasure of the company. He'd not talked like this with anyone for a long time. He'd not seen a version of himself, reflected back in someone else's eyes, that he liked.

It was as if his appetite had returned after a sickness. He'd started to think it had gone for good.

46

Connor realized that going through a tough time wasn't the issue, it was letting it change you permanently. He'd lost sight of how Enduring Hardships Connor was a sharper-edged, less tolerant character. That Connor went in expecting the worst of everyone, wearing it as his armor.

His job had been a bloody battle, and he and Jen had been locked in a gladiatorial state of mutual enmity. A doom spiral, where whatever lever you pulled, you were going down into the sea. He'd forgotten he was someone else before.

"Thanks!" he said, as Bel placed a fresh Chianti in front of him and a Dirty Martini in a coupe in front of her place, as she swung herself back onto a stool.

Connor raised his glass in thanks. "Martini at this hour, you're not here to play."

"Hell no."

"Grotesque epilogue. Go."

"OK . . . Ant, as said, dodges the leaving his wife part, says their son needs him at home for another however many years and so on. I split with Tim, I apply for other jobs, avoid Anthony like the plague at the office, leave his messages on Read. Anthony turns this 'coming to my senses' into a narrative where I ghosted him. I'd toyed with him on the explicit understanding we'd not be *together* together straightaway and then changed my tune in impatience. I'm the heartless bitch who led him on. Go figure."

Connor made a face. "He sounds somewhat unwell."

Bel fished the green olive out of her drink and ate it, daintily spitting the stone into a napkin and folding it away. Connor tried not to think about her lovely mouth doing something quite different, and with him, his hands wound in her hair. It gave him a little spasm of want so intense he'd have to park it for examination later. He pictured her with Anthony and felt a spasm of something else, something painful. Jealousy . . . ? No, it must be revulsion; the man didn't deserve her.

"I thought Ant was winding me up at first, it was such extreme projection," Bel said. "It was like arguing with a pigeon. He says that I exploited his compassion, hahaha. That the hotel room was intended for talking only, *I mean!* Yet I seized his dick. It goes from that bewildering bullshit to really quite obsessive, rambling messages about the grandness of our passion. You give up pushing back on someone that deranged."

"Did he really think a woman ten years younger than him, with options, was going to agree to be an Other Woman for however long it took to get his shit together?"

"I think he's an obsessive manipulator. First, he manipulates me into letting him be my confidante, then agreeing that we're in love and ultimately into doing what I did. He was puppeting the sad girl from work so effortlessly. After that, I'm supposed to be manipulated into being his bit on the side. When his manipulation of me fails he gets angry, but he can't admit that's why he's angry. Instead he turns it into 'I don't like how this makes me feel, and if I don't like how I'm feeling it must be your fault and your intention.' He's recast me as this brutal femme fatale. It's like he's living inside a story because 'Bel realized I wouldn't leave my wife so she wouldn't consent to full sex on a semi-regular basis' is too ignominious and, you know, *on him.*"

"Didn't you tell his wife? If you're single and he isn't?"

"No. I thought about it, of course, but what am I going to say? 'I've had a thing with your husband and now he's hassling me, can you do something about it?'"

"Yikes, yeah."

"I'm not ruling it out, though. I'm not ruling out having to report him for harassment. I've had dozens of emails from him in the last eight months and I've never replied to one."

"It was him at the office the other day, wasn't it?" Connor said, and Bel nodded.

"He's been trying to get my mobile number out of Tim, posing as an old friend from work. I know it sounds daft, given we've split up, but honestly, Connor, if he tells Tim I will be in pieces. Tim would be absolutely enraged and broken and it would set off a bomb between our families—his family would move to a full war footing with me and I'm going to Tim's sister's wedding soon."

"I get it." Connor nodded.

"Then Ant turns up at Deansgate, as you say. I'm worried about the pattern of escalation. Speaking of which, the email about you is here," Bel said, checking her phone, and Connor's jaw dropped.

"Emailing now?!" Connor pulled back his sleeve on a Patek Philippe vintage watch, a gift from Shaun. "It's almost midnight."

"Yep." Bel scrolled her handset. "Do you want an excerpt? They're all in this mad, melodramatic tone. Shilpa calls them his Batman-villain monologues."

"Go on," Connor said, eyes wide. "This sounds like a bid for a sectioning, to be honest."

"*Dear Isabel*," Bel read aloud.

It has been devastating to me, since we parted, to discover how vicious you can be and yet I am not too proud to admit that this evening has emotionally demolished me. I assume you and that AI generated matinee idol are involved with each other, despite the claim you are merely "colleagues" as we once were. Do you know how the thought of you with someone else affects me? Do you care in the slightest that I'm lying here, tortured by visions of the two of you together? I wonder often if you know what you do to me. If I visited your apartment now, would he be there? Unlike me, does he get to undress you, to know what it's like to . . .

Bel stopped reading with a sudden gulp mid-sentence, looking up at Connor with evident embarrassment.

"God, sorry! I had no idea that was going to take a swerve into soft-core. Fucking hell. What is *wrong* with him?"

Connor looked appalled and Bel misread why. "You don't deserve to be dragged into this sordid mess of my making and I shouldn't have shared that—"

"I'm glad you told me because I want to help. I know I'm trying to plot the coordinates of a fever dream, but calling you vicious—why would you tell Anthony if you were seeing someone?"

"Right?! Because we're in love, you see? But I'm so fearful of the size and power of that once-in-a-lifetime love, I'm running scared of it. Moving to Manchester, my private life, my aversion to having anything more to do with Ant—it's all one giant displacement activity. He's trying to make me face up to it or else I will ruin both our lives with my denial."

"Bel, I don't want to upset you but this is really worrying," Connor said. "He's got to be staying over in the city with these awards, hasn't he? He says 'apartment' there—does he have your address?"

"God, no! I can't see how he would."

"That sounds like a threat to me and a hint that he does have it."

"Oh," Bel said.

"Can I read the rest of the email?"

"Erm. If you want to."

Bel surrendered her phone, wincing. Connor scanned Anthony's furious fantasies about Connor's access to Bel, with a stomach-turning twist that Anthony was sure Bel was thinking of him at crucial junctures. Connor hated Anthony anyway but if he was going to claim Bel's mind was straying during the sex they weren't having, it was personal. *I can promise you, in this entirely theoretical coupling, I would command her full attention.*

It was followed by entreaties to meet Ant to "lay all our cards on the table."

He handed her iPhone back.

"At the risk of making your evening go from bad to very bad to even worse, how would you feel about me kipping in your spare room tonight?" Connor said.

"I wouldn't mind at all, but why?"

"He's got a whole night here tonight and he hoped to spend it with you. He's a stranger to boundaries and dignity. This guy is going to come round."

47

"Can I ask you something, and please don't take it the wrong way," Connor said.

"Like all people asked that, I am immediately going to identify what the wrong way would be and take it—and, moreover, assume that was how I was meant to take it. Go ahead."

They were drinking cups of builder's tea at her kitchen island, trying to sober up, amid moody illuminations. There was no way of turning on the lights in this place that didn't look like you were planning a seduction or a party, so Bel didn't try.

"How did Ant ever impress you enough to pull you? I can't imagine it. I know he's only mid-forties but even the young-fogy thing . . . ? That said, I've never met a guy you like so I have no idea what your type is, and I'm running my mouth as I'm pissed. Also, I sound like I'm victim blaming and I promise I'm not. I suppose I'm saying: What's he like when he's not like that?"

Bel smiled and sighed. It occurred to her Connor was very easy to talk to, really. Her senses were martini-fugged, true, but she wasn't sure why she'd ever thought he wasn't.

"Ugh. I know. First, imagine me in my state of avoidance of knowing I had to end things with Tim. He had our mums saying they couldn't wait to be co-grandmothers and I'm secretly crying in the bath I'm so unhappy. Then, secondly, Ant is known as the 'loveliest guy' at work. Ask anyone at his paper. They'd say 'would do anything for anyone' and 'goes the extra mile for interviewees,' sending them cuttings, checking back in on them. He's very well read and pops over to your desk to lend you something he thinks you'd like. I remember one bloke saying, 'He's an old-school gentleman—you don't get many of those anymore.'"

"Thank fuck you don't," Connor said.

Bel stirred her teaspoon in her cup.

"Haha. It's an insurance policy so that when he goes off the rails in private you can't match it up with Public Anthony and he has all these defenders who'd refuse to believe it of him. He is 'what if gaslighting was a man?'"

"You know what this means, though," Connor said. "He has things to lose by his behavior coming to light. Not only his marriage—his living with his kid, his salary. He has his reputation too. He's been bluffing you. He's doing this because he feels confident it'll stay between you, and if not, his word counts. He's been depending on your greater embarrassment."

"What are we going to do if he does turn up?" Bel said.

"I hold him up against the wall by his throat while talking like Batman to the Riddler, that kind of thing? I'll be honest, I hadn't thought it through beyond thinking I might be useful."

As much as Bel guilty-pleasure-liked the idea of Anthony facing off with Connor, she felt it wasn't the way.

"He'd probably file an ABH charge against you. Imagine the police interviews and the official statements. Loads of exciting interacting, and with him role-playing the wounded party."

"Wouldn't that mean the background would come out and be bad for him?" Connor said.

"I think he'd get a kick out of my having to decide if I was going to talk about what brought him to my door. He'd give evidence at a magistrate's court here in Manchester and pull favors at the *Yorkshire Post* to not have it covered and his wife would never know. He'd make sure the office buzz was *Hear that Bel Macauley mucked around with poor married bedazzled Ant and then when he had the temerity to ask why, got her new fella to lamp him. She's not as butter-wouldn't-melt as she seems."*

"I refuse to believe he has this much power when he's the one with more to lose," Connor said.

"We're journalists. What would we do with this story as journalists?" Bel said.

All of a sudden, a plan came to her. It was simple and powerful and she couldn't see a downside. She explained it to Connor, then they tested it out.

Connor said, "I have to admit this is better than hitting him. Its only flaw is it needs two people to execute it."

"For now, I have two people."

As with many planned-for calamities, Anthony failed to show.

"He's our millennium bug," Connor said as Bel handed him a clean towel the following morning.

"I'm still so grateful for you staying," Bel said.

She didn't know how much Connor's failed prophecy had been due to her winding things up and their being wankered, but it was incredibly considerate of him all the same. Also, she'd needed to stop playing the Surely He Wouldn't game. She was happy to lose this round, if this was losing.

Connor had a shower in the downstairs en suite while Bel made scrambled eggs on toast.

"Apologies for no bacon, I didn't expect to have a guest," she said, passing his plate over.

"You mean you didn't think you'd get lucky at the Northern Media Awards?" Connor said.

"That reminds me. I've had a text from Aaron wanting to know 'where you and Adams got to.' We're on the horns of a dilemma there."

Connor paused, fork in eggs. "You mean . . . ?"

"I might tell him we're working on a story. He's going to be unbearable otherwise."

As Bel got up to put the plates in the dishwasher, the doorbell rang. She went rigid and she and Connor stared at each other. Connor nodded at Bel and went to the sofa, where he was out of view of the doorway.

Bel steeled herself, counted to five before she walked over. After all that, it'd probably be a guy in a DHL tabard.

She yanked it open. It was Anthony. Standing there in a waterproof walking jacket with an expectant smile, like he was collecting for charity. She shouldn't be surprised and yet she could scarcely believe it.

"What the fuck are you doing here? Where did you get my address?" she said.

"Ha. Good morning to you too, Isabel," Anthony said, in a wry yet affectionate way, as if he were her father and she a rebellious teenage daughter ruining the family brunch. *To what do we owe the pleasure?*

"Do you think you can normalize this by using a patronizing tone of voice?" Bel said.

She had to be careful: the plan required her to keep her temper.

"I think you and I passed 'normal' way back, didn't we?"

Anthony wasn't only unashamed, he was buzzing. He thought this pursuit of her was incredibly exciting, Bel realized. He bewailed the lovesick agonies that he'd convinced himself he was experiencing, but it was surface tension. And as he knew himself to be a Good Guy, it wasn't abusive. There'd need to be an abuser for that.

"There is no 'you and I,' this is harassment and you're a stalker."

"I've come to see you this morning precisely so you can't say my intention is to intimidate you. I come in complete peace," Anthony said, holding his hands up.

A lie. Anthony had no impulse control. His being here meant he fully intended to turn up last night, exactly as Connor predicted, and hadn't dared because of Connor. Anthony had taken this morning as second best, gambling she might be on her own. He'd not been able to bear going back to York empty-handed.

"Stalking refers to a *time of day*?"

"I have tried in vain to have a sensible conversation with you, offered coffee to chat this out. I come up against a wall of silence or this flapping panic that I might access feelings you don't want to acknowledge. So lover boy's not stayed over . . . ? Well, well," he said, craning to see past her.

"Do you think it's OK to turn up here uninvited? You honestly can't see how far off the map of acceptability this behavior is?"

Bel was biting down her urge to scream in rage. She wanted to say "you don't care how scary this is for me?" but he'd love that: scoffing at it and saying how on earth could HE scare her, while getting a crotch-thrill from how it made him a dangerous rake.

He was obsessed with her—because he couldn't have her—and it was conceptually impossible that she wasn't obsessed back.

"I think it's unacceptable to sleep with someone and ghost them, Bel. I'd have dropped you in turn except for the fact I know you're a much better person than this. I know for sure how much we feel for each other. You can fool me to a point with this hurtful routine but you can't fool me about that. In fact, it's exactly how I know I'm right."

"I didn't ghost you. I told you I was no longer interested in having anything to do with you. What you imagine is keeping the faith is, in fact, refusing to accept someone else's decision."

"When the realities of my other responsibilities became real for you, responsibilities we'd discussed at length, I might add, you ran away."

"No one's asking you to abandon your responsibilities, Anthony. No one."

"This is what I mean! The stonewalling! Dear God . . ."

"Do you understand what"—Bel couldn't say "breaking up," it made her want to wire-wool scrub her skin, and they were never together to break up—"something 'being over' means?"

"Do you deny you cut me dead when I wouldn't instantly walk out on Julie and Jacob, even though I explained to you that Jake's move to sixth form college is a delicate time? The irony is, I'd be the terrible person you paint me to be if I said 'oh, myself and this younger woman are besotted with each other, you'll have to fend for yourselves.'"

Bel steeled herself. Temporarily tolerating this sanctimonious, oleaginous, morally back-to-front shit was the price of getting to the other side of this nightmare.

48

"Your marriage is entirely your business—"

"Give it a rest," Anthony spat, with a flash of real nastiness. "Blah blah, 'your marriage,' playing the innocent. If it's all my business then why ever get involved with me?"

"Because I was extremely messed up at the time, at the end of a serious relationship."

"You admitted we were in love. I have messages from you saying you loved me."

Bel clenched her jaw. She struggled to think of something more repulsive than claiming ongoing rights to intimacy with someone. Anthony was like private browsing on a dodgy site and letting a virus into your computer.

"I was wrong. Feelings change. We didn't know each other."

"Oh, I know *you*, Isabel. We're twinned souls."

"That is mental, arrogant and romanticizing that you're not taking no for an answer. If you knew me you'd know how much I don't want to hear from you."

"Look"—and she could see Anthony switching gears to *let's drop all this silly belligerence, I idolize you* nice cop, and she felt sick—"we didn't give this a chance. We were absolutely sensational together and you know it. I understand why your pride was hurt that I wouldn't leave Julie straightaway. Any man would jump at the chance of being with you, and you had the bad luck to fall for someone who was saying *hold on while I figure a few things out*. My situation is more complex than yours because I'm ten years further down the road. Leaving is a process, not an event. You took it to mean I don't care enough, and I want to assure you, I do."

"I don't want you, Anthony. I don't want anything to do with you. I don't know how many times you can be told that before you accept it."

"I'd probably need you to not have kissed me like your life depended on it. I'd need you not to have pushed me onto the bed and put me in your mouth in the first minutes we were ever alone together in a locked room, to believe it. This talk of my 'stalking' you? You *devoured* me."

He was smirking as if this was waggish wit, as if he wasn't simply trying to humiliate and nauseate her. How was this supposed to work? Was he going to heckle, insult and mortify her into being in love with him?

But of course, Bel's perspective was a blank to him.

Anthony was a psychopath, Bel thought. Not the knife-wielding sort (though right now she'd not bet her house on it) but a misaligned, insidious, suburban, low-grade psychopath who was so bored with his staid life and the vanity version of himself he successfully passed off as that he'd invented this erotic thriller he was starring in. He'd cast Bel as his leading lady. His mediocre male misogyny helped seal the deal: imagining that she existed only in relation to him, that he was irresistible, that with his quicksilver intellect he was outfoxing her.

Maybe future generations would have a label for his genre. Meanwhile Bel would have to live forever in the knowledge that one got past what she imagined were her sophisticated defenses.

"Thought that would give you pause. You want me to forget what that evening was like, but I won't and I can't. I know you can't either."

Don't forget the mission, Bel told herself. *He wants you to lose control.*

"I regret that happened. It will never happen again. Are you going to stop?"

"Stop what?! You have walled off all routes by which to contact you!"

"Stop the emails. Stop pestering people I know. Stop shit like this, turning up at an address you've purposely not been given."

"I knew that man wasn't your partner, by the way. Last night. I knew it was a little theater. He is not someone you'd choose. He's a 'Chad Thundercock'—Jake taught me the lingo."

"Are you listening?"

"No. I'm not, because you are wrecking both our lives in a fit of pique. I'm in love with you, Bel, and you're in love with me. I want you to think about what we could have if we both admitted that. *I've* admitted it, however inconvenient it is, quite frankly. It's pretty obvious at this point it's ruining my life. Can you admit it?"

"Anthony. I am telling you, plainly and clearly, I no longer want any contact with you. That is not going to change. You are at my home after finding my address out by some underhand means, you have tried to extract my mobile number from my ex-boyfriend. Obsessively seeking contact with a woman who does not want it is harassment. I will go to the police if there is any more behavior like this from you, anything at all. I have kept scores of emails as evidence. Do you understand that? Final warning."

Anthony sighed.

"You go to the police and I'll counterclaim you're harassing me. I'll describe what's passed between us, that we've had an affair. That I won't leave my wife and you're reporting me as revenge. Who do you think will come out of it looking vindictive, the single woman or the married man? You think the police will be interested in refereeing a lovers' tiff? Still, all publicity for your work, I'm sure. A bit of notoriety can't hurt."

"Even though you know that's not true?" Bel said. "You're threatening me that you'll say something that's untrue to the police?"

"I'll defend myself to the hilt before I'll let myself become a victim of Isabel Macauley's willingness to chew men up and spit them out. This was a game of bait and switch on your part and my crime is to represent the consequences of what you've done, instead of taking my punishment like a good boy."

"That's a yes, you'd lie? Because I'm not stalking you—you're stalking me."

"I'm saying, if you decide to publicly and professionally embarrass and damage me, I'll make damn sure the same happens to you."

"Even if it means lying?"

"You're lying about everything anyway. You're lying to yourself most of all. Quid pro quo."

"And you don't care about the effect of this on me?"

"When have you ever cared about the effect of this on *me*?"

Connor emerged from behind the kitchen island, making Antony physically startle, and spoke to Bel.

"I think that will do it. Please don't make me listen to any more of this mad idiot."

"Have you got enough?" she said. That felt like a line in a film.

"Oh, more than," Connor said. He tapped at his handset and adjusted the volume.

Anthony's disembodied voice filled the air.

"*. . . love with you, Bel, and you're in love with me. I want you to think about what we could have if we both admitted that. I've admitted it, however inconvenient it is, quite frankly. It's pretty obvious at this point it's ruining my life.*"

Connor switched it off.

Bel turned back to a frightened-looking Anthony.

"There we are, Connor has got a video of our whole interaction. I'm willing to have that replayed in a police interview, or a court, or in front of your wife. I stand by everything I said. Do you feel the same?"

"Fuck you," Anthony said to her, a mask dropping. "Seriously, fuck what a horrible person you are, despite this . . . 'responsible feminist' persona."

"Thought so. Bye, Anthony. For good this time."

She slammed the door. She turned, leaned against it and heaved shaky breaths as her pulse rate descended.

"And *scene*," Connor said. "For the avoidance of doubt, you were magnificent."

49

"I'd like some credit for not sticking my head up and interrupting: 'How did you know my name is Chad Thundercock? How much fucking research have you done, by the way?'" Connor said, and there was a second before Bel collapsed on the sofa in helpless laughter. "The temptation was crippling.

"You know he's halfway to Oxford Road right now," Connor said, "and he's thinking, She's KEPT my emails? *Still got it*."

Connor made a finger guns at his groin gesture.

Bel shrieked, "Oh, fuck you, Adams! That makes me think I'll get an email tonight."

"Fifty quid says you don't. I was right before and I'm right now. Accept that I keep being right."

Something about their trouncing of that crazy Anthony combined with the fact he was a ridiculous little popinjay was now making both Bel and Connor mildly hysterical, as the adrenaline left their bodies.

"I can't believe he's decided how I feel about him, on my behalf. That I don't get a vote," Bel said. "Saying 'Your rejection proves you are in turmoil over me'? It was 'no means yes and yes means yes.'"

"You did so well to keep calm. I couldn't quite believe it," Connor said. "I've never heard anyone Flat Earth like that. 'You love me,' 'No, I don't,' 'That's exactly what someone in love with me would say.' *Twinned souls*, haha. Like twinning Paris with Little Shitlingham."

He'd unguardedly called Bel "Paris" and hoped she'd not notice. Actually, he was trying not to notice.

"Stomach-turning, isn't it? You see why I said it's pointless to argue with him? Everything you say is more wood thrown onto the fire."

"I think the man is an absolute danger," Connor said.

"God, it feels good to have a witness. Shilpa has supported me every step of the way but you actually *heard* how he talks to me when he thinks we are alone . . . How the fuck did he get my address? Work wouldn't have given it to him, it's not online anywhere." Bel pulled at the neck strings on her hooded top.

"When he wanted your phone number, didn't he go to your ex-boyfriend?" Connor said.

"Yes, but Tim doesn't have my address here."

"Then he went to someone else close to you who wouldn't know who he is."

"Oh . . . God."

Bel did some rapid texting.

Her phone lit up with a reply. Bel read aloud: *Oh dear yes— months ago. A nice man called from the Yorkshire Post for a chat, said your old team wanted to send 'good luck in Manchester' flowers to you and for it to be a surprise. Should I not have told him?*

"Utter bastard! *My mum*," Bel said. "So he had my address from the start but he didn't want to give it away easily, must've thought he'd use it to best effect when he was *in* Manchester. I can't believe you sussed it all from his using the word *apartment*. Astonishing, really."

"I'm actually disturbed that I can get inside his thinking. You said he left you at one a.m. last time. I assumed someone who can't afford nights away from his spouse when he's booked the hotel room was going to treat a legitimate reason to be overnight in the same city as you as gold-dust rare opportunity. He'd have anticipated you walking away from him so his backup would be to make sure he knew where you lived. I know any normal person would think that's blatant stalking, going to completely freak her out, etcetera. But, news flash: he isn't normal."

"What fucks me up is finding out what a normal-presenting person can persuade themselves is justified, if it's them. Principles disappear. I feel sure if a stalking and harassment story landed on the paper's news list, Ant would condemn the perpetrator. But once it's him doing it, it's noble Anthony's quest."

"Not *that* normal-presenting. The midlife crisis goatee is a huge red flag. He looks like Mr. Tumnus."

Bel started laughing again. Connor loved how it felt to make her laugh. He remembered when she thought he was carved from a block of ice.

"His poor wife . . ." Bel said. "Imagine how controlling he is with her."

"Awful, but she's beyond your help and probably wouldn't want it if you offered it," Connor said.

"Yeah."

"Anyway, if you feel safe now, you have a weekend to have. I should get off." Connor stood up. "I've sent the video to your number and to your email."

"Oh, thank you so much," Bel said, standing up too.

Connor had no "things" to get so he picked up his tuxedo jacket and said, "High-end-walk-of-shame look here."

Bel smiled.

"Connor. I hate asking for this, on top of everything else. In fact, I hate asking for it full stop."

"Yes?"

"Can I hug you for a second? I need to be reminded of sanity, friends and allies existing right now. Not that cuddling the intern is bloody sane."

Connor grinned and put his arms round her.

"You're using me as your emotional support animal? My exit interview from Manchester is going to be lurid."

"Exactly." Bel giggled, weakly.

Connor felt the heroic-protector glow return. That Bel had historically been so spiky, and had so little real need of him, made it all the more rewarding. Oh God, he hoped that wasn't Anthony Brain thinking. Some straight men really did ruin being a straight man for everyone else.

He was so pleased for Bel that her elegant takedown of Anthony had worked, at no cost to her. Had it gone awry, Connor had been entirely willing to, in Aaron's parlance, twat the fucker.

"Tell me Ant's stopped now? My peace of mind is going to take a while to come back," Bel mumbled into his lapel.

"Put it this way, if he doesn't, your version of events is now unassailable. He'll be blowing up his own life, not yours."

Bel looked up at Connor, eyes cartoon-cat large.

"I can't bear people finding out I was stupid enough to suck him off, though."

They both shook with laughter again. Connor couldn't bear the thought of it either.

"I hate to undermine your main-character syndrome, but getting involved with someone and later not knowing what the fuck you were thinking is a pretty common experience."

Bel squeezed her eyes closed and Connor smoothed her hair, the way he had during the bedroom storm. They had come a long way, for sure. He wasn't certain they were friends, exactly; Bel's word *allies* was more accurate. They trusted each other.

"You know what Ant and Glenn Bailey have in common?" Bel said, quietly.

"Stamina?"

"They both think the cover story about themselves is so convincing that no one would ever believe there's a whole other version that they're inflicting on unsuspecting women. Ant saying I'd end up looking like the problem if we both went to the police was probably right. They think they've pre-invalidated complaints."

"One down, one to go," Connor said.

"Yep," Bel replied, but she sounded uncertain, and Connor didn't blame her.

50

"My plant's here!" Bel said, childlike-delighted at the colossal paper box blocking the stairwell. Toby had agreed the decor budget could stretch. She wrestled with the cardboard to free a potted palm in an earthenware urn. It turned out to be too heavy for her to move. After she'd made some comic straining noises and managed to wheel it an inch, the leaves shaking violently, Connor got up and moved it to the corner of Bel's choice.

"Ta-da! It needs a name."

"Like draping Christmas lights in a squat," Aaron said. "Like a Bagpuss beanbag in a crack den. If it makes you happy, though. Got some more good news for you an' all, Bellatrix," Aaron said. "The photographer from Friday's do has emailed the general address for the office saying he met a woman who didn't want to be in the photos and he doesn't know her name. Gotta be you?"

"Oh yes, that was me," Bel said, brushing earth from her sleeve as she sat down. "I asked him to respect my zero-imagery-online policy."

"Well, well, in that case . . ." Bel realized too late that Aaron had laid a little mousetrap and she had nibbled the cheese. "He wants to ask you on a date."

"Piss off, seriously? What?" Bel said. She blushed a hard red as if they were in school, which was not like her.

"I quote: 'She was lovely and I'd like to see if she fancies a drink, if that's not too forward.' Bet I could get the horny little toad sacked from his picture agency for it."

Bel had no comeback, also unlike her. Somehow, the involuntary troubled look that passed between her and Connor complicated things. Why did she care what he thought? She did, for some reason. She also realized she'd blushed because Connor was here.

"How does that make you feel, Connor?" Aaron added.

"Me feel?" Connor repeated.

Oh, fuck.

"Aye. If someone was hitting on my woman I'd not like it very much."

Connor frowned—he was back in Office Connor mode—and left a You Haven't Intimidated Me–length pause.

"Bel isn't 'my woman.'"

"That's surprising, then, cos on Friday my mate saw you *holding hands*," Aaron said, with an accusatory flourish, looking to Bel. "And then you got into a taxi together and left early? Sudoku and a mug of Knoops hot chocolate, was it?"

"God Almighty, do you have people monitoring CCTV?" Bel said, genuinely a little shaken. The hackney rank was several minutes' walk away and out of sight of the Town Hall.

"How long have you lived in this city? And how long have I lived in this city? Speaking of mugs," Aaron said.

"There's a tangled explanation for it and none of it involves what you think it involves," Bel said.

"Aye, does it not?" Aaron said. "Try me."

"Tell you what," Connor said, somewhat terse, "I'll do the coffee run and you get Aaron up-to-date? I don't think my contribution would add anything."

"Good idea," Bel said, with relief, as Connor opened a filing cabinet and rifled in the petty cash.

It would be easier one-to-one. Also, she didn't know if Connor had enhanced powers of intuition or just really needed a flat white but Bel knew Aaron's irritation with her would contain things not suited to Connor's ears. Actually, on reflection, she suspected Connor was principally fuming at the idea Aaron had rights to know who he was sleeping with, and she didn't blame him.

Once the door downstairs had clanged shut, Aaron looked to Bel.

"This should be good," he said. "Your faces just now! As transparent as a jellyfish's arse."

"You know the man from the *Yorkshire Post* you spoke to the other day for me, Ant? Trying to get up here to say hi?"

"Yeah?"

"He's actually got an unhealthy fixation with me. He tried to hassle me at the awards, Connor happened to see it and intervened. Ant assumed we were a couple and it was effective to play into it to scare him off," Bel said.

"Mmm. Chivalry isn't dead. Adams worked all this out by telepathy and had the confidence to stride over, did he? You know what, Macauley, I didn't think you'd ever treat me like a fool."

"I said it was a tangled story and you've only had the first part."

Aaron made a hands-up *enlighten me* gesture.

"A month ago I'm undercover—"

"*Undercover?* All right, Spy Cop."

"Indeed . . . and Connor barges right into the middle of it by pure chance. I had no time to warn him, so I tell the person I'm with that he's my boyfriend. In saying this, I simultaneously alert him to the fact I am up to something. It worked like a dream in the few moments I used it, and then obviously we had to see it through. He's been having to playact our being a couple at evenings and weekends ever since. So his helping me out at the awards, which was unrelated—it didn't come from a standing start. I haven't told you about the undercover thing because as you know, I'm not supposed to tell you what I'm working on until I'm actually typing it. Toby knows all about it. He signed off Connor having to come on board."

"And Connor's also *come on board*?" Aaron waxed an imaginary mustache.

Bel shook her head at him. "I should warn you that, thanks to Ant, I have dramatically low tolerance for men thinking they have license to attack me over nothing right now."

Aaron swung on his chair and twirled his pen.

"Who were you 'playacting' to when you left early together?" Aaron said.

"No one. I was antsy and so Connor saw me home. Via the pub."

"So, in other words, you were racing off for a late drinks date, for no reason?"

"No! . . . Well, yes, but . . ."

"Thing is," Aaron said, "I have a couple of points to make. The first is, office romances hit different in our line of work. How many times did we sit here and rip it out of that guy"—he nodded toward the stairs that Connor had departed down—"all the while I'm thinking you're on my side, I'm on your side, we're speaking in private—"

"We were! We are!"

"Hang on, I haven't finished. As you said, 'who knows what' is power in this business. If I don't know you and that guy are banging, then I'm going to conduct myself differently. It's not fair to let me think one thing, treat you one way, and then you two be pillow talking. You can tell me you don't pass things on, and I'd believe you, cos I know you're one of the good ones. But I still want to make my choices knowing if there's a bcc on my email, if you know what I mean."

"Fair enough. But you're referring to me and Connor being romantically involved, which, once again, *we are not*. Luckily your surveillance doesn't extend to my bedroom, but in absence of that, you'll have to take my word for it." Bel paused. "Also, if we were, why would I not just say so? As you said the other day, we're all free and single."

Aaron made a *not for me to say* shrug.

"Because he's a right arse and you don't like to admit you're shallow enough to go for a fit arse?"

Bel laughed.

"You know, being forced to get to know Connor much more than I would've chosen to otherwise, sorry to say I have some feedback notes for us."

"Oh yeah?"

"Yes. He knows he wasn't friendly on day one but we were somewhat 'you can't sit with us' mean kids, and we outnumbered him. Therefore his defenses went up even more. We've got to make interns feel welcome in future.

"That leads me to my second point. Remember our take on Cicely? What would you think of me if you later found out I'd been slipping her a length? Wouldn't it make you think I wasn't exactly who I said I was?"

"Maybe it would, but mainly because she was twenty-three." Bel paused. "I don't think an office where you're running someone down, gossiping and mocking them, and then getting off with them in secret is the sort of office I want to be founder of either. That's not what this is. But in your position, I'd have thought what you thought, because the truth is bizarre. Instead of falling out over it, why don't we treat this as a chance to write our constitution? Today's law says: Interoffice relationships with colleagues are OK if they're consensual, nonexploitative, age appropriate and not manipulatively covert. However, all interns will be treated with welcome and respect and not as potential conquests. Both of us will disclose to the other if we're seeing someone. In return . . ." Bel felt this clause was vital: "Neither of us gets to complain if all the conditions listed have been met."

"All right, agreed," Aaron said. "You know—you're all right, you are."

He smiled a smile that Bel hadn't seen before. Aaron might be experiencing a newfound sense of responsibility and respect for female agency. Or he might be delighted about the imminent change of intern since he found out she was a twenty-five-year-old ex-gymnast called Lexi whose nickname was Flexi Lexi. Hard to say.

"Isabel's filled me in," Aaron said to Connor, as he reappeared with a tray of cups. "I retract my accusations regards your knocking boots."

"Good, thanks," Connor said, putting a cup down in the mess on Aaron's desk. "One bejazzled Americano."

"So, this pretending to be a Mr. and Mrs.?" Aaron continued.

"Yes?" Bel said.

"Who do they think you are—your marks, I mean? You can't be journalists?"

"They think I have my best mate's job, textile designer, and Connor's still in finance. Luckily he never got round to changing his LinkedIn."

"How does it work that yer boy's all over the awards gallery, then?"

"What?" Connor said, head snapping up.

"The Northern Media Awards. Bel's suitor obviously thought you were photogenic too. Offer him a throuple."

He turned his laptop round and both Bel and Connor got out of their seats to look.

Aaron had clicked an image where a group were chatting and Connor was among them, seen in profile.

"Fuck," Connor said. "I was so sure I was avoiding him!"

"Captioned, I'm afraid," Aaron said, enjoying himself somewhat, picking another image and opening it so they could see *Connor Adams, reporter* in the small print.

"Bollocks!" Bel said. "I'll call the press office, ask them to take them down."

"They've gone out, though," Aaron said. "It's in the *Manchester Evening News* and on all them I Love Manny Instagram accounts."

"They'll use ones of the celebrities, surely?" Bel said.

"Nah, they've run Shagger Bailey but this too cos their reporters are in it. Blame yourself for being a pretty boy," Aaron said, opening a browser window to show them the local paper's website.

Bel and Connor exchanged a worried look. "I'm sorry," Connor said. "You told me to duck and weave and turns out I was shit at it."

"Not your fault, it can be really hard to tell. My last paper accidentally outed loads of affairs in panorama pictures of bars and restaurants."

"What you gonna do?" Aaron said.

"Pray," Bel said.

51

A mere week left to endure and Connor would be home. Back to the floor-to-ceiling-windowed open-plan office with beeping security arches and laminate passes, the Underground, his fancy local with onglet and Café de Paris butter on the menu instead of chips and gravy. And less rain.

The *Tinker Tailor* half-light ramshackle office on Deansgate with its dusty storage, art prints of mythological Manchester and a pot plant called Jason Not Orange would be a hallucination, an anecdote, a reference point.

If he saw Bel, it would be across a packed conference room, their doing a mutual startled wave of recognition and later a quick bout of that sort of British non-conversation when you knew someone but didn't know them. *Hi how are you yeah good thanks you not bad thanks it's been ages wow yeah.*

It made Connor wistful, even sad. He'd compiled himself a Manchester bands playlist so The Smiths could be partly to blame. He could hear Shaun saying "you obtuse miserabilist motherfucker."

There was the small matter of the undercover gig concluding first, with what seemed destined to be a trombone slide and a wet-firework fizzle.

They arranged a drink in the same quiet, timber-ceilinged Didsbury pub which had hosted their previously fraught encounter. Connor recalled it being the tearful stage of Jennifer separation. They had progressed swiftly to irritation, where she was regularly updating him on why a rental she'd viewed wasn't viable. *Sure, condolences, but pick one, you have two weeks.* Is what he didn't say.

This evening, Bel had arrived before him, sat in a Jessica Rabbit–ish strappy red dress, hair in loose waves swept back with clips, chin propped on palm. She smiled broadly at the sight of him and there was a tiny yet perceptible lurch of excitement in Connor's stomach that he had provoked the smile. He relished the prospect of her company, even in straitened circumstances? That was new. Amazing what imminent departure could do for your mindset.

"Even though I know you'll be in character, it still comes as a surprise," Connor said, checking they spoke in solitude, taking a seat in front of his waiting pint.

"Bella Niven is my Sasha Fierce," Bel said. "I see that the straightforward girly look makes more sense to your basic boy brain. I feel like I'm nine and my mum helped get me ready for a birthday party."

Connor winked at her as he lifted his glass.

"If this doesn't happen, tonight . . ." he said. "Are we just disappearing, as far as our new friends are concerned?"

"You dump me, go back to London. I need space and the space need turns out to be indefinite," Bel said. "In my fiction I'm distraught enough to do some friend shedding from the Connor era."

"Ugh. Sorry for dumping you," Connor said, brushing beer foam from his mouth.

"It's OK. It was awful for me, though. You'd never actually properly finished with your ex and I caught you messaging her saying Manchester was temporary."

"Why do I have to be that bad?! I would never actually do something like that."

"Yeah, that's what I thought," Bel said, shaking her head, curls bouncing, and Connor felt significant disquiet. It turned out a conscience was a heavy burden even in make-believe.

Bel looked downcast and Connor added, "Ghosting them full stop feels slimy."

"It really does," Bel said. "But we went up in a hot air balloon of lies and now we have to get down again without breaking our legs."

"And if they've seen the awards photos?" he said.

"You've been helping out a business writer at the *Manchester Evening News*, he wangled you an invite. They miscaptioned you."

"That feels a stretch, to be honest."

"I'll jump in with lots of *ooh could see you as a reporter, the Clark Kent look nnnnggg* and you say something slighting about the wages and I reckon we'll paddle to dry land."

"Hmm. Can I say I'm glad this is our last outing?"

"Agreed." Bel tipped her white wine to clink his lager.

"Connor," Bel said, after a loaded pause. "I'm going to take it. The iPad. It's not going to happen otherwise."

"What? You can't," he said.

"It'll be nothing to do with you. We'll say we hid it and uploaded on-site."

"But we made it clear that was impossible."

"No, *they* said it was impossible, we didn't. If Toby wasn't superhot on the *how* before he's not going to ask for an in-depth postmortem once we've got the goods. We hid it behind a cushion. If the worst comes to the absolute worst and it comes to light, I'll make it clear you had no idea and I went rogue. I'll take the full rap if the bosses ever find out, but they won't."

"Bel, you could end up not only losing your job but with a criminal conviction. Making you much less hirable in future.

Don't be a dick. You're not doing this under your own name on a podcast. This is a 'bringing into disrepute,' gross misconduct situation for a national newspaper."

"I don't believe for a second the Kendricks would pursue someone *overnight borrowing* an iPad that far. Why bring attention over so little? Plus, if we've found what we think we're going to, then none of it matters."

"The problem here is you're saying A will happen, then B and C. It won't. A big unexpected is coming, because it always does, and then you're going to be left holding a stolen tablet you were clearly told you couldn't steal. You don't have the protection of the paper to do this."

"I know this. Call it my aunt Tessa's DNA. Fortune favors the brave. Or call it my rich kid golden parachute DNA, you can't offend me."

"I was going to say. Much as I don't want to revisit why I value employment . . ."

"Look, go now," Bel said. "I could say we've split up already. That might work, actually: if I go in being teary, it's a distraction."

"Absolutely not," Connor said.

"Why?"

"I'm not leaving you to do this alone."

"Connor, you are an immensely good and honorable person . . ." Bel looked him in the eye as she said this. They both knew it was from the heart, and a newly held position on the matter. "And I thank you so much for it. But you don't owe me this."

Connor swallowed a lump in his throat.

"Nevertheless. I decline to bail. I just don't want to spectate the premature end to your shining career either. Or sit down to a banquet of consequences with you."

"I'm going to pretend to get completely smashed. That should give me enhanced eccentric roaming rights. Then I'll go back first thing tomorrow and say I took the iPad when I didn't know what I was doing. I'm going to tell Amber I'm hideously embarrassed but I have this light-fingered habit when under the influence. It's a real thing, Tim's grandad used to nick random items constantly. He didn't have a mental condition or anything, he just loved half-inching stuff."

"It is a mental condition. It's called kleptomania."

"My point is, *whoops, sorry, here's your thing back* within hours of it going missing is hardly something you're going to call Greater Manchester Police about. Especially if it's a device you don't want them looking at. You can hide the fact we uploaded Ring Video memory, right?"

"Yes, but—"

"If I give the iPad back, while groveling, explain to me how there can ever be a police complaint. They'd need to report it at two a.m. And unreport it at ten a.m. They will only know of the data theft if we find something newsworthy in it."

Connor let out a heavy sigh.

"Twenty-four-year-old Connor would be like *wooh, yeah, you're right, this is watertight*," he said. "Thirty-four-year-old Connor says *fuck around, find out*."

"Thirty-four-year-old Connor needs to rediscover his optimism."

Shaun had said similar. He felt sure he didn't mean like this, though.

"I'll do it all," Bel said. "The only thing you have to worry about is a drunk girlfriend. You've handled one of those before, right?"

"Know what, Bel? Don't take this as a compliment. But you're without precedent."

52

They'd ersatzed their way through Amber's thirty-fifth party well enough but Connor loathed the lock-in, for multiple reasons.

The hostess herself was effusive as usual, clad in a teal cheongsam dress and silver trainers, but as before, the number of guests meant her time was spread thinly.

Amber had her hair cut into a simple blunt bob she could tuck behind her ears, which provided Bel with a reason to coo and fuss.

"Why have I never noticed you're the spit of Riley Keough?" Bel said.

"Oh, extra picklebacks for you!" Amber said.

"I would have to know who that is before I could notice it," Connor said, as they found a table, and Bel said, "Derp, she's Elvis's granddaughter."

"If I was Elvis's granddaughter I would one hundred percent have kept my grandad's surname," Connor said.

"Not everyone is as status conscious as you," Bel said.

"Oh, we're back to that again, are we?" Connor said, with an eye roll but no animus.

Slider burgers and trays of shots appeared, on the house. Connor had only ever been to lock-ins at his local at Christmas, where it was free rein of the jukebox and an honesty bar with cash and coins in a pint pot until 1:00 a.m.

Connor would have disliked the cokey braying noise of it all anyway, but this time he had more to worry about. Bel was truly committing to the bit.

She was throwing B-52 "bombs away" shots down like there was no tomorrow. Keeping visual track of her working the room, he felt like a harried father with a kid at Soft Play. An analogy he'd not be using with Bel unless he wanted to be called a putrid patriarchal Finance Bro.

When someone had warned you they'd get quite pissed to look very pissed, it was extremely difficult to gauge how actually pissed they were. When, eventually, she returned to his side, leaning her head on his shoulder, Connor said, brushing her hair out of her face and tilting her chin, "We can go home, you know."

"Can we?" she said, looking up at him, as if this was news.

"Yes," Connor said, not knowing which reality they were in. Then, in case it *was* reality, added: "You have nothing to prove."

Bel looked at him as if she was assessing his meaning.

"Know why I didn't go to my prom?"

"Ha . . . oh God. Why?"

"Bunch of girls at school bullied me really badly. Rich girl tall poppy thing, you know, because I got good grades. They turned the boys against me too, I only ever had Shilpa. If I'd gone to prom they'd have made me . . . what do you call it? . . . the 'main character' but in a bad way. So I went to see my aunt in London instead."

"Oh man, and I said that stupid Converse trainers thing. I'm so sorry."

"S'OK. Loved visiting Tessa. It was the making of me," she said, picking up her Porn Star Martini now, having to concentrate to keep the liquid level.

Connor saw Bel in context for the first time. He'd thought, attractive, go-getter, well-shod background—and bristled that the "outsider" temperament was a pseud's pose.

All of a sudden he understood that adult Bel, because she was accepted, felt like a successful impostor. That's why she carried off the Bella Niven assumed identity with such aplomb: Bel Macauley was one too. Hadn't Connor been doing the same in his last career and relationship?

Minutes later, when Connor came back from a trip to the men's, he found Amber in his seat, iPad in front of her. He was grateful Bel initiated this in his absence.

"She could do the week starting the fourteenth," Bel was saying, reading from her handset. "If that's any good?"

Amber flipped the case open and Connor watched Bel watch her index finger jab rapidly at the keypad.

"We've got someone in on the nineteenth, looks like . . . Sorry."

"Never mind. Another time!" Bel said.

Rick deposited a glass in front of Bel and said to her, "Slainte. May you die in Ireland."

"Did you know Rick's family was Irish? *Are* Irish?" Bel said to Connor, over the raucous din of Chappell Roan and many conversations.

"Can't say I did. Bella, slow up on the Porn Stars, eh?" Connor said, cloaking his genuine concern in Persona Concern.

Bel downed the glass's contents, turned to him and clumsily kissed his cheek, a near enough miss that he smelled passion fruit. "Don't worry about me."

"Easier said than done, darling."

She laughed and hiccuped.

"Do you have an 'unbridled joy' setting? Like, do you ever abandon yourself entirely to the moment?" Bel was staring intently at his mouth, as if she was thinking hard about Connor for the first time. He had a feeling he knew in what way too.

"Yes, I do, thanks," Connor said, firmly instructing himself not to rise to this.

"Er, your dress needs sorting," he said, pointing to a pink animal-print bra that was on show to a greater degree than intended.

"S'from Zara," Bel said. "My dress."

"Very nice," he said, then gestured at his neckline and nodded his head. "Pull it up?"

Bel didn't respond and Connor leaned over and proprietorially tugged the fabric back into place. He was extremely glad she'd not done this alone.

"Jus' going to the loo," Bel said, in a semi-slur.

Ten minutes later, Connor registered: still no Bel/Bella.

"Gonna see where my girlfriend's got to . . ." he muttered, but no one was listening.

"Bel?" He rapped his knuckles on the door of the ladies'.

Nothing. He gingerly pushed the door open and went inside. Both cubicles unoccupied. He looked nervously up at an open window, which even though the dimensions made it borderline feasible, surely to God she'd not pulled herself through?

Had she done a runner? He slipped his phone from his pocket: no messages. If she was with it enough to do a midnight flit, she'd be with it enough to alert him. It was disconcerting. What if she'd been caught red-handed . . . by who, though? He could see Amber and Rick in the group as he walked back down to the main room.

On an impulse, he peered over the bar as he passed it. Bel was sitting on the floor, head resting against the bottle fridge.

"Bel—la? What the hell are you down there for?"

She looked up at him. She was hugging her bag on her lap. (Bel had told Connor previously it was a "squashy quilted tote that's roomy but not out of place"—"squashy quilted tote" being as new to his brain as Riley Keough.)

"The room was spinning, so I sat down."

"Yeah, that's not the most hygienic place to choose. Nurofen-and-water time for you, I think."

He coaxed her to her unsteady feet, Bel smoothing her dress over her behind and making her way back into the restaurant.

"Bella has entered the floor-sitting phase so I'm going to take her home," Connor said, seeking out Amber and Rick. "Thanks for a great evening, too great for some."

Amber threw her arms around him.

"Thanks for coming, you guys, so good to see you."

Once they were clear of the sight lines of the bar, Bel stopped leaning on Connor and walked with noticeably enhanced powers of balance.

"This is like watching Kevin Spacey lose the limp at the end of *The Usual Suspects*," Connor said.

In the taxi, Bel nodded her head toward the bag on her lap to indicate: *Got it*.

Connor wished this felt triumphant, but he'd been hoping she wouldn't manage to swipe it.

"That was some performance," Connor said.

"It went Method, I'm pretty shit-faced," Bel said. "I kept the objective in mind."

As soon as they were through the door of her apartment, Bel said, handing him the iPad, "I put the code in my phone calculator so I couldn't forget it. God, imagine if I've got it wrong and we have a useless iPad we still have to give back!"

Connor sat at the dining table, opened the cover and tapped the code as Bel read aloud. The tablet rippled into life, a page of apps.

"BINGO," Bel said.

"God, this feels disgusting."

"Your disgust might reroute when you see our mayor looming up, many times over, like a badger in your bins."

"True," Connor conceded.

"We can leave it uploading overnight while you crash here, and then you can review the footage tomorrow while I go to Didsbury," Bel said, running a glass under the kitchen tap. "You don't need to be here, pressing buttons?"

"Yep," Connor said, squinting hard at the screen.

"Thank God, cos I need painkillers and sleep," Bel said.

"Good work tonight," Connor said. "I admit, I didn't think it could be done, but Irene Adler in Zara comes through again."

Thanks to Shaun for the reference. She was a criminal, so . . . Connor was too far in to back out, but he was deeply uneasy.

"It still might be not be done."

"Might be not be done?"

"I did say I needed sleep."

He cleared his throat.

"Bel. I'm so sorry about the prom thing. I was out of order anyway but knowing what I know now, I'm properly ashamed."

"Prom thing?" she said, frowning.

Connor saw she couldn't remember their conversation at all.

"Never mind."

53

Bel left Connor eating toast in front of her laptop, watching January's comings and goings from the big Victorian in the ironically titled Honour Road.

"How big is the Tesco delivery the baby shower got? There's me thinking they were sober affairs . . ." Connor saw she was dressed, bag over shoulder and phone in hand. "You going now?"

"Sooner I get this over with the better," Bel said. The taxi beeped downstairs and Connor seemed wrong-footed by the speed she took off at. Tessa had told her: "If there's a difficult thing to face, face it fast."

As the car reached the outskirts of Didsbury—pavement tables, awnings dripping with last night's downpour, mock Tudor red bricks—Connor messaged: *Free for a quick word in private if I call? Still in taxi?*

Bel replied yes and yes. The driver had earbuds in, Perspex glass between them, and she judged it low-risk.

"Hi. He's not on here," Connor said.

"What?"

"The Mayor. There's tons of unknown couples of varying ages, and sometimes younger women on their own, but absolutely nothing of Bailey."

"Are you sure it's not that you're not recognizing him? Have you searched in April, when he was there with Erin?"

"End to end. No mayor. I am hazy on what Erin looks like, but don't think she's on it either. You can see for yourself when you get back. There's a thing called Event Delete where you can go in and scrub specific sections from Ring Doorbell recordings. They must've been extra careful and done that. Or your sources have been spinning you along."

"No way," Bel said, bringing Erin in Ian's house to mind. "Not a chance."

"Afraid those are your two choices."

"*Shit*. I've got the prospect of being handcuffed on arrival at Ci Vediamo and now I know it's for nothing."

"How far away are you?"

"Two or three minutes max."

"OK, in five minutes I'll drop you a WhatsApp saying hi. If you hit any emoji reaction to it at all I'll assume all's good. If you don't respond I will take it that it's not so good, and come over."

"Ha! Connor, that's so considerate, but what would they do? Set Gertie on me?"

"I don't take your gung-ho approach to risk, so there we go. Five minutes. Keep your phone close and don't forget to check, because I'll take forgetting to mean the same thing as an SOS until I know different."

"I won't. Thank you."

She was grateful for Connor's caution, even if it increased her anxiety. She had no idea how Amber would take this. Bel guessed she'd be gracious in the moment and more irritated and suspicious the more she thought on it. If so, that was fine; Bel only needed the moment.

Bel got out of the taxi and looked up at the tall narrow blue neon letters that spelled out CI VEDIAMO, taking a deep breath of crisp midmorning, late-summer air. The palm trees outside were draped with fairy lights as yet unlit, like cobwebs, the tables and chairs not yet out. She pushed on the door that was usually wedged open.

Ted with the mustache was behind the bar, cleaning glasses, Radio One booming out from unseen speakers. There were no customers.

"We've only just opened if you want to take a seat and I'll bring the menu? Coffee machine's waking up."

"It's me, Amber's friend. Bella."

"Oh yeah, hi there," he said, as she drew closer.

Amber appeared, in a vest top and velour tracksuit bottoms.

"Hey, good morning, what are you doing here at this hour? How's the head?" Amber said, throwing a tea towel over her shoulder.

"Head is so-so, my knapsack of disgrace is worse."

"Knapsack of what? Hope that's not a euphemism."

"I can't remember anything from about ten p.m. onward. However—I can't entirely blame alcohol for my 'stealing for no reason' tic, that comes from Grandpa Bob. When he died they found his garage full of fenced goods. I am absolutely crucified over this . . ."

Bel balanced her bag on a bent knee and opened it, Ted and Amber watching as if she were about to pull off a Mary Poppins stunt.

Bel produced the delicate coupe glass from her bag first, between finger and thumb, and placed it on the bar.

"Must've thought this was pretty," Bel said.

Ted guffawed. "Congrats on not breaking it."

"It gets much worse," she said, yanking the iPad out and placing it next to the glass. All three of them stared at it, as if it might talk.

"I am so incredibly sorry and embarrassed. I woke up with beer fear and then thought, Why on earth do I suddenly own an iPad? You must've been looking everywhere. I think it's completely intact. Wish I had a reason for what I did, but as said, I have no recall. I woke up in my clothes on the sofa this morning. Connor said I refused to come to bed."

"Oh, THAT'S where the iPad is! I was about to accuse the staff," Amber said.

Bel throbbed with relief.

"Oh my God, that's terrible," Bel said. "No, all me, one hundred percent Madam B-52. If there's any damage done to it then you have to bill me, but I woke up clutching my bag like it was a baby."

"Hahahaha. When we were at yours, Rick passed out and slept over due to *raisins*. Don't sweat it."

"Yeah, but that's not committing crimes."

"I dunno, you didn't hear the farting."

Bel and Ted laughed. This would be a 5/5 outcome, yet it was a Pyrrhic victory.

No, Connor had to be wrong, he had to be. He'd scanned too fast and jumped to the worst conclusion. He did have a fatalistic streak, after all.

"Come say hi to Rick, he's got a funny Gertie clip on his phone . . ."

Bel followed Amber down past the ladies' and the men's, past a gilt-framed print of Marilyn Monroe in a white fur coat, and on the floor, a Henry Hoover, to an office at the far end of the corridor.

"Bel's here, she's brought us glassware and the iPad back that she borrowed," Amber called.

Rick was behind a desktop computer, a landline phone and other workaday bits and pieces indicating it was the admin nerve center.

Amber ushered Bel into the room and, behind her, turned the lock. There was a split second when Bel thought, Wait, why would you lock the door? and then a split second that followed when she wondered why Rick wasn't smiling at her.

"Hi," she said to Rick, and . . . nothing.

"I had Find My active, so I knew the iPad was in Ancoats," Amber said, evenly, and yet not in the same voice she'd used in front of Ted. "I wanted to see what excuse you'd use. I didn't expect 'I've got pickpocket genes' or whatever that was but you do go the extra mile with the bullshit."

"W-what?" Bel said, feeling the pulse in her neck.

"Ever notice how you only need one small thing to be out of place, and then everything else starts falling *in*to place?" Amber said.

54

Amber tilted the desktop screen to face Bel.

"Even with the Ancoats info, I still didn't suspect you at all. Not my nice new friends. My *very new* nice friends. Told Rick it must be a mistake. But because a valuable has gone missing, I watched the CCTV. And then I think, That's weird, why is Bella walking less drunk when she's out of the bar? I mean, it could be the fresh air sobering you up but it pings something in my brain . . ."

Bel saw the hours-old fuzzy black-and-white image of herself and Connor and didn't take it in.

Why was the door locked? Was there still a way to spin this? Had Connor messaged yet? Bel felt every inch of her arrogance and sloppiness and stupidity, yet there was no time for that right now. *Think, think.*

"A lot of things are out of the ordinary, I realize. How we met, your having a fight on your phone in the bar. Your interest in the iPad last night, right before it goes astray. I'd looked for you on Instagram in the past but you told me you weren't on there. Because of a 'stalker ex,' was it? Yeah, I'm sure he exists. And Connor's page is locked down, he never accepted my follow request. So I finally got round to googling you both, and *guess what!*"

Bel adjusted the bag on her shoulder and fought the urge to pump the door handle while screaming, *What would Tessa do?*

"I assume your name's made up because I can't find you, but here's Connor, at a press awards, and he's a journalist. If he's a journalist, then you are too. I can see which newspaper you work for. This has all been about getting to my mother, using me? Fucking amateur hour, Bella Not Bella."

"No!" Bel said.

"What did you want on my iPad, then?"

Bel hard-swallowed. *Fuck, fuck.*

"I'm trying to gather evidence on the Mayor. Glenn Bailey. He's sexually abusing young women who work for him."

"Oh, right. What would that have to do with us?"

"He stays at the Airbnb."

"Nope. Where's your proof of that?"

"The Ring Doorbell. You record everyone who visits."

"Riiiiight," Amber said. "Rick, you remember the Mayor of Manchester visiting our Airbnb? Booked in right after the prime minister and Ryan Giggs?"

Rick shook his head. Bel wondered if she had been given bad information. From the meeting in the cemetery, she'd taken Ian's word as gospel. Maybe Tessa would be telling her that her Act Three problem was in fact an Act One problem.

"That's what you wanted from the iPad? The doorbell camera?" Rick said.

He and Amber had obviously spent a lot of time pulling this apart but their analysis hadn't gotten that far.

Amber folded her arms.

"How's that gone for you? The Mayor on there?"

Bel could see absolutely no advantage or point in lying.

"No. He's been deleted, I assume."

"Oh, you assume?" Amber said, volume increasing. "You've assumed a lot, all told."

"Can I tell you why I'm going after the Mayor?" Bel said. Here it was, the "backup plan," which was barely a plan or any sort of backup. Also known as "shit or bust."

"You might understand why I've done what I've done if I tell you."

"It's nothing to do with me. I don't know what you're talking about. Do you, Rick?"

Rick gave Bel his assassin's mute stare.

"He's not only manipulating women who work for him into bed. He blackmails them to stay quiet by taking nudes when they're sleeping and only showing them afterward. Saying he'll release them if they make his behavior public."

Bel paused. Amber and Rick were both silent.

"He's the full Me Too monster and he's doing it in your house. If you help me, not only have you done a net good to women and society, you're not complicit and you can't be blamed."

"Whoa, you're *threatening* us now?"

"No!" *Oh God, THINK, Bel.*

No atheists in foxholes and it didn't pay to be slow-witted in them either. "I'm saying I've fucked this up and I don't blame you for hating me, but Glenn Bailey is going to be outed one day, by someone. I'm proof of that. One of his victims will go public, others will come forward. He's got a lengthy past in the city's nightlife, so probably a flood. And when they've finished asking how could he behave like that and get away with it for so long, they'll start on Who Knew What."

Amber regarded her, blinking. "So you are threatening us."

"I'm being realistic. You don't want to be mixed up with him."

Given Amber was already mixed up with her parents, this might be the wrong approach.

"You know, it's pretty incredible to lie and wheedle your way into someone's trust using a false identity, get invited into their lives, steal their possessions to trawl their private information. Then turn round and say 'hey, if you don't want everyone to think you're a cunt, lend a hand in digging me the dirt I failed to find.' You must think we're stupid. The stupid couple who run a bar and only know how to free-pour Tanqueray."

"That's not what I'm saying at all!"

"And I bet you also think we're stupid enough to let you walk out of here having had a bit of a rant at you."

"I don't think you're stu—"

Amber's menacing control broke.

"Shut up, Miss Alias! Tomorrow morning first thing I'm going to call your editor and tell them we're making an official complaint against you and them for what you've done. Invasion of privacy, taking our property, false identity, whatever the fuck—I don't know what the official terms are. Then I'll find some press standards–type watchdog and tell them too."

"Please, Amber. We're not enemies here."

"Yes, we fucking are. I don't know your name but I have Connor's and that'll do. Becky Something and Connor Adams."

"Connor's only my boyfriend, go for me, not him."

"Even though he's a reporter?"

"That's how we met. He didn't want to do this story and begged me not to. It was, I swear on my life, a mistake that he walked past that first day we met. I'd have said I was single otherwise. It's nothing to do with him. Please, report me. I'm Bel Macauley. Investigations editor. Look me up."

"You really are mad about him, aren't you? A criminal couple, like Bonnie and Clyde. Fred and Rose. But no, sorry. He was by your side every step of the way. Get out of my bar and out of our lives and don't come back, you conniving bitch. Enjoy your P45, and if I ever see you in Didsbury again, I will make your life hell."

Amber unlocked the door and threw it open.

"I'm really sorry," Bel said to the still-impassive Rick, and Amber said, "Yeah, yeah. Bye, now."

"Bye, Bella!" Ted called innocently as she swept past, and she managed a tight smile.

Bel was marching down the street, grim-faced, when she saw Connor emerging from a minicab a few yards away. She wanted to run to him, except when she told him what they were facing, he would have every right never to speak to her again.

He was jacket-less and had clearly raced over. He frowned at Bel, ducking his head down to tell the driver to wait.

"You're all right?" he said. "That wasn't a nice few minutes for me."

She could see he had been deeply worried and some part of her would feel gratitude if there were any non-terrified part of her left available to feel that.

"Kind of. Thank you for coming to rescue me."

"It went all right? When you didn't reply I thought—"

"Not really, no. They know who we are."

"*What?* Are they going to the police?"

"Nope. Worse. The editor and IPSO."

"What?! Fuck!"

"Yep. Shall we?" Bel gestured at the taxi. "I think we're best off doing this elsewhere."

"Should've enjoyed my not-nice few minutes more," Connor said, opening the car door.

55

No matter how many times they ran the sums, no matter how many times they looked for the ingenious way out, they came to the same conclusion: royally screwed.

And no matter how many times they watched film of the mundane comings and goings in a doorway in South Manchester, Glenn Bailey stubbornly failed to materialize.

"I can't blame Amber, can you?" Connor said, as they abandoned the laptop for softer seating and outright despair. "We've treated her and Rick as collateral. It must feel absolutely soiling to know that everything we did and said was to get into that iPad."

"Yep. When I started this I thought she was a willing, knowing handmaiden to a major bastard, and now I wonder if Amber might be more unwitting than that. They have to have deleted him, though."

"We can't know for sure without cross-referencing the Airbnb bookings and I deliberately didn't look at anything other than the footage. That might've been stupid, but principles, huh? Principles while you're hacking someone," Connor said.

"If you want to know why we'd be kicked out of MI5—they had location tracking turned on. They knew the iPad was here the whole time."

"Fuuuuu . . ." Connor put his hand on his head. "Of course! Oh man, that is the stupidest, dumbest, most obvious . . . I was lost in the mechanics of the Ring Video."

"I'll call Toby first thing. He's sacking me either way, but if he's called in to see the big editor without warning, it will be an extremely vitriolic meeting."

"He's sacking *us*—don't act like you're special and different."

"You can stay here rent-free for as long as you like, you know," Bel said, and Connor smiled.

"No offense, but I'll be leaving Manchester with such force it'll leave scorch marks all the way to Knutsford."

Bel had been astounded and so, so grateful that Connor's response to her imminently losing him his employment and ruining his prospects had been gallows humor and not inchoate rage.

"Why aren't you angrier with me?" Bel said. "You'd be justified in screaming. No apology could atone for what I've done. You save me from Anthony and this is how I repay you."

"You saved you from Anthony, I only had to make sure the video was running and hold my phone level. Also, I think I've evened out now, post-citalopram."

"Seriously, Connor. You have a mortgage. This is indefensible."

"In my last career, a man jumped out of a third-floor window, which has given me perspective about how much you can let a pay slip matter," Connor said. "I knew this might go sideways when I decided to take part. You said I could walk away yesterday too and I chose not to. I'm not a fan of blaming other people for my decisions. And what would be the point? We might as well have a laugh when there's nothing else to be done."

"Brokenly grateful for your generous Zen," Bel said, as she paced the sitting room and Connor lay across the sofa. "The sacking isn't even the worst part. It'll be ringing Ian and telling him that I have completely failed him and Erin."

"He can hardly blame you for the edited video and you've lost a lot, following his lead. He'll feel bad about that."

"Oh SHIT," Bel said, stopping in her tracks. "If Amber's told her mum, and her mum tells Glenn, then they could figure out from the details I've provided that Erin's the whistleblower. She saw Amber with the iPad the night that Glenn panicked. Which also means Glenn could well figure out Ian's involvement."

She put her palm over her face. "I've got to warn him. He could walk into . . . actually he told me he's walking Hadrian's Wall next week."

Bel foraged for her phone in her pocket to confirm.

"Leave it until you know what happens with Toby," Connor said. "No point decimating other Sundays with speculation."

Connor had mumbled he could go back to Salford, but as the day wore on, he said, "We'd only exchange morose WhatsApps all evening. I'm thinking we could lean into this with a last meal on Death Row Deliveroo energy."

"Yeah. You're welcome to stay here in industrial-luxe purgatory. I know a hangover tomorrow will be horrific and yet I'm feeling 'wine' too?"

"Wine for sure," Connor said. "Anesthetic."

Bel lit candles, they ordered takeout and spread it out on the vast dining room table, under the looped cord lights.

"The contrast is like that portrait of the matriarch and the manufacturing smog in your nookie lair," Connor said, shaking Sarson's malt vinegar over a heaped plateful.

"My 'nookie lair'!" Bel repeated shrilly, and Connor gave her a cheeky look as he licked vinegar from his finger.

"All right, Austin Powers. *Nookie*, not heard that word in a long time," Bel said.

"It's a good word."

Bel refilled their wineglasses and they took their dinner to the coffee table, saying, "Here's to celebrating when you have absolutely nothing to celebrate and have made a complete pig's ear of your assignment."

"Look at us," Connor said, "like *Waiting for Godot* with sausage."

"Anticipating our inevitable downfall does have a certain 'sparse theater production' feel, doesn't it?" Bel said. "Jodie Comer and Aaron Taylor-Johnson give career-best performances in *Fucked* . . ."

"Are you Jodie Comer? Jodie Porn Star Martini Coma more like."

Bel threw a cushion at him.

Full of fried food and numbed by Merlot, unable to concentrate on anything, they both lay across the sofas and listened to rain on the windows.

"Connor, can you tell me about your dog? The one you loved enough to have a photo of him on your desk? Was he called . . . Mosley?" Bel said.

"Mosley? Named after the fascist leader Oswald Mosley?"

"Oh bugger . . . Mo . . . M . . . Maurice!"

"The night before I get sacked and possibly criminally charged, why don't I discuss my much-missed dead dog? After that let's revisit the times I have been laughed at while naked."

"Have you been laughed at while naked?!" Bel said.

"No," Connor said, sitting up, pointedly contemplating the remainder of a battered sausage and making Bel honk. "My bare form has inspired only awe."

He ate it, brushed his hands and lay back down again.

"I bought Maurice as a puppy for fifty quid from some sketchy guy in the pub in Dagenham who clocked I wasn't going to let him leave in charge of an animal. I'd never had a dog and had to google what to do. I was only mid-twenties and it was like having a baby overnight, in terms of responsibility. Then Maurice became the making of me. We went everywhere together, except when he was with the dog sitter from eight to six that cost as much as a nanny. I realized I could actually really enjoy routine and responsibility. I was a bit of a pointless lad at the time, treating everyone and everything like it didn't matter."

"I can imagine a lot came easily to you," Bel said.

"Yeah, it kind of did, if I'm honest," Connor said.

Bel realized this was a different era between the two of them, because she could pay him a compliment and he didn't react defensively.

"Maurice bore witness to a lot in my life and gave me so much more than I ever gave him. The day I lost him . . ."

His voice thickened and he stopped. "Nope, still can't do that without weeping."

"I'm so sorry, Connor. I wish I'd met him."

"I wish you had too," Connor said, wiping a tear from his cheek.

Their livelihoods were about to be detonated but they were fully healed as friends.

There was a just slightly concerning brief memory fuzz for Bel in the middle of yesterday evening, like losing your central field of vision. And whatever had been said . . . why did it feel as if it had made him gentler with her?

She hoped to hell she'd not told Connor he was fit.

"I've said to Toby we need an urgent Teams and he's offered us ten a.m.," Bel said, handing Connor a black coffee at eight the next morning. "Not too long to wait."

She'd been awake since five. Bel had entered the phase of thinking the prospect *had* to be worse than getting it over with, fanciful self-soothing which was no doubt about to be corrected.

"Urgh." Connor rubbed his eyes. "That's going to be a real treat of an hour."

"It won't be an hour. I'm taking the view this is at least a guillotine execution. As soon as Toby hears I robbed the iPad, that's it, mission disavowed, contract terminated. *You* are negotiable."

"I'm not. If I scoured the RingVideo from it, I'm a full accessory."

The doorbell sounded. Bel couldn't remember if she'd ordered anything.

"Ant, great to see you again!" Connor muttered, and Bel said, "Don't."

She opened the door to Amber, in a faux-fur bomber jacket and Lululemon leggings.

"Morning, Becky Something. You look like shit. Did you not get much sleep?"

56

"It's Bel," Bel said.

She couldn't see what Amber needed to add to yesterday's diatribe but perhaps there was a further raft of inventive punishments. She agreed with Connor, she couldn't blame Amber. The only point of reference Bel had for how it must feel was when a mean girl infiltrator at school had pretended to warm up to Bel, purely to get an invite to her house and gather fresh material for the core gang.

Had this comparison occurred to Bel earlier, she might've never engaged the subterfuge at all.

"If you say so. Can I come in?" Amber said.

Bel stood aside. She couldn't judge her mood, not after having had a demonstration of Amber's world-class poker face yesterday.

"Oh hi, Connor. We meet again."

"Hi," he said, pushing his hands into his jean pockets.

"I'm not here to make friends," Amber said, arms folded. "What you did was unforgivable. We can miss the part where you bootlick. I'm sure the only thing you're sorry about is you didn't find what you were looking for."

She took a breath and Bel tried not to let her hopes go wild, because while Amber wasn't here to make friends, she'd surely not be here at all if there wasn't a deal to be made.

"I want to know more about Glenn. The nudes and the blackmail and so on. Do you know that's true?"

Bel described her meeting at the cemetery and all that followed. She took a gamble that only all cards on the table would do—vagueing out wasn't going to work. Surely only one of Glenn's female guests had seen that iPad, so Amber already had enough to trace this back to Erin, and subsequently Ian, anyway.

"He did what? She was *asleep*?" Connor interjected.

Bel was pleased he'd given her an opportunity in front of Amber to demonstrate she was the lead. If Bel couldn't extricate herself here, she might still secure a pardon for him.

"I didn't tell you about that, did I? I only found out when I met her in Sale. Yeah, it was worse than screenshotting onetime-view photos. She felt totally violated. As you would."

She turned back to Amber. "I don't know that it's happened that way more than once. I do believe Erin completely, and I also know men like Glenn will have many, many more skeletons. My contact works for him and said there were organizations that had stopped projects with the Mayor's office for reasons unknown. But it's buried deep. As I said, there will be a tipping point, it's a case of when. And who."

"Hmmm . . ." Amber said, newly cropped hair falling over her ear as she shuffled her feet. "You want your name up in lights, right?"

Bel shrugged. "To be honest with you, given the doorstep footage has been deleted, we're a long way off catching him. The story is not going to be broken by us. It'll probably take one of the women going public and risking being turned into a piñata."

Amber paused. "Is this girl a redhead? Very young-looking?"

"Yes and yes," Bel said.

"My bar has got nothing to do with this. Ci Vediamo is totally financially, legally separate from that house. The only connection is that I managed the bookings. I've taken the Airbnb listing down . . ."

Bel held her breath.

"If I help you, I need you to promise me that my name and my business would stay out of it," Amber said. Her face was stony and tone assured, but for the first time, Bel sensed her nerves.

"We could promise that. Definitely," Bel said, looking to Connor. "Your bar isn't relevant to what the Mayor's doing and nor are you. Your mum's name would come up, though."

She held her breath.

"Well, that's on her. I'm gonna speak to my mum—she can know what I've done. I'm not being a property pimp with her sex-case friend, but that doesn't mean I want my name in the papers."

"Understood, and we could keep your name out as a condition of the story. You'd be a protected, anonymous source."

Amber sighed and moved her weight from foot to foot.

"I've got the unedited Ring Doorbell. I kept it for a rainy day, as insurance. He stayed in February, then April, the last time was in June. Younger women every time. I don't know who they are, though you tell me the one in spring was this redhead."

"OK. Wow." Bel looked to Connor, having stifled an *oh my God* yelp.

"What will you do with it if I give you the film? Give me the step-by-step," Amber said.

"We'd check it ourselves and then send it to editors and lawyers at the paper to be sure it's him. We'd tell them you're co-operating on condition of anonymity. I'd interview Erin on the record this time, we'd get our story together and then call Bailey the day before it's going to run and tell him we have this proof, and does he want to comment. Obviously, he knows you had those files in your iCloud so it's up to you what you want to tell him about how we obtained it. But we won't tell him who our source is and only my and Connor's names will be on the story in public."

Amber blew air out.

"I curse the day you sashayed my way, Bella. Bel, Becky, what the fuck. All right. Text me your email address and I can text Rick on my way back—he's in the office. You'll have it in fifteen minutes."

"Than—" Bel began.

"Don't thank me. Don't you dare. I am up a fucking tree because of you and this is my best way down, that's all," Amber said.

Bel nodded.

As Amber left, she turned to Connor.

"I shouldn't be this much of a stupid romantic, but FYI: she was always telling me you two were dynamite in bed and that you were The One. I thought Bella might be bragging. But when she begged me to incriminate her and let you off yesterday, she properly *pleaded*. I don't trust her as far as I could throw her, but you should marry her. I've never seen a girl more smitten."

The door closed and Connor said, "Thank you, Bel," and she muttered embarrassedly, "Oh, no need, did what I could. She was fucking with us, with me, there, wasn't she? Amber figured out we're not a couple either."

"Yeah, most likely," Connor said.

Despite the extreme cause for jubilation at this miraculous turn of events, it was five minutes before either of them could fully look the other in the eye again.

AT TEN—HAVING SEEN FILM WHERE THEY BOTH SHOUTED, "Shit, it's him, it's really him!"—they were ready for a wholly different sort of meeting with Toby than the one envisioned.

He appeared on Bel's laptop: "Morning, my favorite folie à deux! What news? Are we toppling the leader of the north this week, in our little remake of *House of Cards*?"

Bel looked to Connor.

"I'd have thought so, Toby, yes."

57

No low was lower than thinking she'd have to ring Ian and tell him the story was sunk, and possibly him with it. No high was higher than battling through a dropping-in-and-out 4G connection to Ian at the site of Roman archaeological remains in Northumberland to say "We got him."

"It's fair to say I don't regret meeting up with you in Southern Cemetery. We were surrounded by illustrious personages that day but little did I know I was meeting a living VIP too," Ian said.

"That's very kind but far too much, I'm only doing my job. And thank me once GB's safely resigned," Bel replied.

"Admirable caution and restraint from you, as always. I think you should accept the applause and take a bow."

"Ian, you're the only person on this planet who thinks I am cautious and restrained, so thank you for that alone!"

After agreeing he'd liaise with Erin, and Erin and Bel could use his house to meet, Bel got off the call and Connor said, "You're not wrong there, Irene. You've taken years off my life."

He grinned and chewed on his pen, looking considerably handsomer and fresher than someone on little sleep, in yesterday's clothes, deserved to. Bel thought how pure the politics of this win was, between the two of them. Connor had been so philosophical and willing to shoulder blame when it was a catastrophe, that it all coming good at the last minute was something he'd earned, many times over. She liked sharing it with him. The hot resentment at his intrusion felt like another lifetime.

"I don't know how much praise I deserve for the blind luck of Amber's change of heart. I feel like I'm getting back slaps for finding a winning lottery ticket in a hedge after gambling the house away."

"You're too modest. Not only did you do the legwork to get here, you pointed out to Amber and Rick they'd be implicated. That was wily. If they'd caught me, I'd have said fair enough and burst into tears. I'd say you bet on yourself and won."

"Amber being disenchanted with her mum is what did it, I think. She was subconsciously or not looking for a big point of difference between them and here it is."

"Yeah, the fact it'll put her mum and dad's convictions back in the news says a lot. Amber must've decided that Christmas dinner is going to have to be strained this year."

Bel shook her head.

"I can't believe it. I keep trying to process that instead of spending today in the pub, doomscrolling Monster.co.uk, searching for a new job, we're going to be working until midnight."

"God, way to kill the buzz."

They laughed.

"Right," Bel said, grabbing her laptop, bag, keys, "let's do this."

They'd agreed they'd work from the Deansgate office. They burst through the door, unselfconsciously chatting and joking, to Aaron's stunned revulsion.

"Oh wow, look at you two both rolling in at"—Aaron checked the wall clock—"quarter past eleven, *together. What are the chances*, it's almost like you've been in the same place . . ."

"We have," Bel said. "Connor stayed at mine last night."

"Oh BARF, I don't want to know." Aaron glowered. "When I said we should be open with each other, I didn't mean it."

"In my spare room, because we have been working on our

big scoop which is going to come out this week. Which I'm sure you don't want to know about, now we're free to tell you."

Aaron twiddled his pen.

"All right, you fuckers, let's hear it. Have Oldham Council been putting prostate massagers on expenses?"

Bel outlined the tip, the Ring Doorbell, Erin's testimony.

"Fucking hell," Aaron said, mouth hanging open. "Fair play, Macauley, I'm in awe. You went for Shagger Bailey and got him?! Do you know how many people in this city thought that was only ever gonna come out after his obits? Me included. You rock up here and catch him in *months*?"

Bel knew how big this had to be for Aaron to be non-sarcastically fanboying.

"With help." She nodded at Connor.

Aaron clapped. "Honestly, hats off to both of yer. We'll be picking up Northern Media Awards next year. With you on FaceTime," he said to Connor.

"No telling anyone until we've filed," Bel said. "I don't know what defense Bailey could scramble to get us super-injuncted, but we'd rather not find out."

Aaron made a mouth-zipped gesture. "I'm not gonna be the guy who sinks this. I want to read it myself."

"You do the splash and I'll do the backgrounder with Erin's interview," Bel said to Connor. "I'll share any relevant quotes from Erin for your story once I have them."

"It doesn't really work to shadow investigations, you once told me," Connor said. "Look at my workload now."

They smiled at each other, with a unique understanding of the roller coaster of the last forty-eight hours that had led here.

At lunchtime, Bel left for Sale. She met the agency photographer, Theo, at the end of Ian's road. They were sort-of colleagues who'd never met before, Bel filling Theo in on the story as best she could before they both adopted full professionalism mode in front of Erin.

"You don't have to do this, you know," Bel said to Erin, as Theo set up his kit in the natural light of the back garden. Bel knew on this occasion at least she was putting being a better human before being a better journalist, and she was fine with that. "We have enough without you doing this interview. Don't feel obliged or trapped."

"I know I don't, that's why I want do it," Erin said. "People can say whatever they want about me for doing it. But they can't say it didn't happen." She hesitated. "Last time I met you I was going to pull out of the story. Ian said meet you face-to-face and make my mind up then. I'm glad I did. Glenn is treated like a god in that office and out with the public and I didn't think anyone would believe me or take my side. You being in my corner, and reacting the way you did to his taking photos of me, made me think it was worth doing. You second-guess yourself so much you go mad. I'd started to think maybe I was a prude. Glenn even called me—what was the word?—*unworldly*."

Bel shook her head in disgust.

Forgive me for being a little starstruck here, your voice has been the only sound in my ears . . .

He got such a kick from controlling perception of himself. Charisma used as a gateway drug. When people fell for it, some part of him must feel contempt, she realized.

"You reminded me there are people who don't think men behaving the way he did is OK. I started to feel like I'd slept with him so it was all my fault."

"Men like Glenn change the weather, they create a microclimate, don't they?" Bel said. "You think because they get away with it within that, they'll get away with it forever."

"Forever ends today," Erin said, getting a foundation stick out of her bag. "When's this coming out? Wednesday?"

"'Forever ends on Wednesday' sounds less cool, let's go with your first version," Bel said. Erin looked gratified.

As she sat with her notepad and her Dictaphone and a nervy raft of questions via Toby, watching Erin being asked to tilt her chin or unfold her arms, Bel thought about how Glenn had underestimated Erin.

As she'd said, his behavior had gone unchallenged for so long he thought there was no reckoning ever coming. Here was his reckoning, in nose stud and flatform sandals. Her hitherto hidden superpower, courage.

58

Bel got back to the office and found a half dozen Post-it notes on her desk with questions from the head office.

She and Connor barely looked up from typing and fielding calls, as the sky, through grimy windows, turned to dusk and then to night. Aaron left them at six.

"All right, kids, have a good one. Don't have been here overnight when I get in tomorrow."

He loitered by the door. "Watch your backs, after this goes live. Remember, in our job, it's never about the treasure, it's about the enemies you make along the way."

Bel made a small *got ya* salute.

"I can rest easy now," Connor said, as they heard the door close. "Until Aaron found a wise old grizzled Manc Yoda negative, this was too good to be true."

"He's more of a Baby Yoda, surely?" Bel said. "The Mancalorian. You've not seen him in winter but he's got the beige coat."

"You find the perfect nickname to annoy him, *in my last week*?"

They ordered pizza, Connor nipping out to Marks & Spencer's for a fresh shirt, as he'd not changed his clothes since the lock-in.

"Underpants too, all the mod cons," he said, slinging a plastic bag onto his desk.

"Let me cue up some music on my phone and you can change in the middle of the room," Bel said. "How about 'Pony,' Ginuwine?"

"You see, if I said that to YOU," Connor said, "you and your, as a great man said, 'feminist persona.'"

"We've been through this. If you said it to me you'd be implying you wanted to see my arse. Because it's me saying it to you, I'm turning the tables on objectification while satirizing your male vanity. And implying I want to see your arse. Which is obviously nonthreatening humor, because who would?"

"We can let HR adjudicate," Connor said, disappearing off to the loo.

They both read each other's copy before hitting Send.

"You should have your name alone on the backgrounder, none of that is my work, really," Connor said.

"I like the joint byline as a statement of unity and pride," Bel said. "Also, never give away a byline, Connor, have I taught you nothing?"

"I could accuse you of a lot but never that," Connor said.

Bel had never thought they'd get on, let alone have a rapport. All it took was multiple crises and bonding over men who should have their hard drives seized.

By half nine, they were both pale, shadowed under the eyes and agreeing they'd handle the fresh influx of queries, legals, deadline drama and last-minute checks at first light the next day.

"I couldn't have done it without you, Connor," Bel said, snapping the buzzing lights off.

"Thanks, that's really generous but it's not true. You could've done it all without me, minus the cock-up with the photo of my girlfriend on my phone."

"All right, please accept that you made *almost* every moment of it better."

Bel was as surprised and touched as Connor looked to find that this statement was wholly true.

They shook hands, warmly. When they parted outside, Bel looked over her shoulder at Connor walking to his Metrolink in the dark, just to record one of their last moments in her mind on a historic day. She turned away quickly as he turned back too.

THE FOLLOWING DAY there was a phone call to the Mayor's office, outlining the evidence, and the content of the interview with Erin, made by someone more senior at the paper than Bel or Connor. They asked if Glenn Bailey wanted to comment. After what was reportedly a flurry of activity at the other end, an assistant confirmed he did not.

Ian messaged Bel:

Apparently Glenn went ballistic, ranting and raving about shadowy forces conspiring to bring him down. Then put his coat on and marched out, that was it. No one can get their heads round the idea that he's not coming back—they're wondering if it might be a George in Seinfeld beat where he turns up like he never got sacked, next Monday—but equally, no one can see how he CAN come back.

Official word arrived via press release to all outlets, first thing on Wednesday, the morning their story was running. The Mayor of Greater Manchester, Glenn Bailey, had checked into a private clinic on the recommendation of his doctor to treat "sex addiction issues." He would not be returning to the role of mayor for the "foreseeable future" and "no further statements will be made while he addresses his mental health."

"My God," Bel said, as they all stared at the news break on their phone screens. "He's the victim, then? No accountability."

"Nice try at spoiler-ing your story too," Aaron said.

"Too late, fucko," Bel said, hitting refresh on the paper's website again; they were publishing at 9:00 a.m. "You're only going to drive more traffic to us because people want to know why he's gone. And every subsequent story for the next few days will have to quote us."

This was what it had all been for. Bel acknowledged her vicarious "gotcha" energy, alongside the nobler sense of having done something to right a wrong. She tried to make sure righteousness did not become gloating. A journalist like Aaron had no problem admitting his glories were others' horrors, and laughed at Bel's bleeding heart twinges. *Bless yer. Should've become a Macmillan nurse if you'd wanted the love of strangers, Macauley.*

Would she feel anything if Glenn Bailey came for her? Or the Kendricks? No, she'd take her lumps. Aunt Tessa said in life you needed a strong stomach and a strong lipstick. Bel was thirty-four and she had a bird's-eye view of herself today, working out what her job was going to mean. What she was going to make of it.

Bel's mobile began ringing nonstop as other outlets picked up on it, social media a choppy sea churn of outrage, conspiracies and bad-taste memes with coffee cups. Bel had broken stories before, but never one of this size.

More women started coming forward via Twitter to share their Handsy Bailey (and worse) anecdotes—secretaries, nightclub hostesses, even a cancer survivor he'd met at a tree planting ceremony. Tales of love bombing, lying, brief relations, silence and threats and a theme of wheedling to receive nudes that turned into a stash of ammunition.

Erin had never been alone, just isolated.

The Kendricks' convictions were rehashed, as MPs and commentators agreed that Bailey's position was "untenable" due to his taking favors from fraudsters. Bel was nervous in case some enterprising reporter named Amber, but deleting the Airbnb listing seemed to have done the trick of scrubbing her from the record. The ownership of the Didsbury sex den was the issue, not its administration. She wondered what Team Ci Vediamo were making of it all and was highly unlikely to find out.

She and Connor stared at the hard-copy stack of papers with their names on the front page.

"Funny sort of souvenir, isn't it? But I'll keep one for my parents," Connor said.

Aaron stagily shook the paper out like a stockbroker father in a 1950s film, and read aloud: "'Glenn Bailey's down-to-earth manner and approachability made him immensely popular in his native city. Yet persistent rumors swirled that there was another side to the former "nighttime czar" who'd done so much down the years to reinvigorate the fortunes and image of his beloved Manchester . . . One person who met "the other Glenn" was 24-year-old Erin Howitt, who interned in the mayoral office at the start of the year . . .'"

"You know what I'm taking from this?" Aaron said.

"That career abusers in positions of power should never relax?" Bel said.

"Knock on the back door instead."

59

Bel was walking home on Thursday, having spent the day negotiating interview access to Erin a dozen times. Bel had insisted Erin was the appropriate spokeswoman, and with Bel's guidance, Erin was very willing to do the interviews.

Bel would go so far as to say she'd seen Erin grow in stature and confidence hour by hour.

It reminded her of a James Baldwin quote: "The victim who is able to articulate the situation of the victim has ceased to be a victim: he or she has become a threat."

Bel was listening to a high-profile politics podcast analyzing Glenn Bailey's curtailed career—and what they coyly called in the introduction his "tragic, dysfunctional flaw." It prompted Bel to startle passersby outside Boots by bellowing: *"It wasn't a fucking chromosomal abnormality, it was a CHOICE!"*

Her progress was interrupted by an automated voice. She'd accidentally turned on the option that robotically related texts, in telegram-reading fashion. It was enhanced by the fact she had a friend called Miles so it had to differentiate between him and her brother in her address book.

MILES OPEN BRACKET MY BROTHER CLOSE BRACKET. *Mum incoming like Scud missile. Table stuff at wedding. Looking forward to seeing you. Been ages. Xx*

Bel scrabbled the AirPods out of her ears and panicked. Verity's wedding was this Saturday! She'd completely forgotten! Verity's wedding, Tim's sister. Tim and Rhiannon there together. Bel's sacred vow to her mother she'd not pull a disappearing act. Not only did she not want to renege on that promise, using an obvious excuse at the last minute, but she'd been planned and budgeted for, which would further make it a shit's trick.

Bel replied to her brother and seconds later, her phone flashed with MUM.

"There you are, you're rather hard to get hold of for someone in the communications business, Isabel."

"Sorry, I've been completely consumed by this mayor story."

"Oh yes, I read everything you sent me. That foul man. Why are there so MANY of them?"

"It's a sickness of patriarchal society," Bel said.

"I wanted to tell you that Verity's trying to pin you down to finalize her table plans. I know this isn't forefront of your mind but please be diplomatic and as helpful as you can—the final stages of wedding planning are awfully stressful."

As usual, her mother was laboring to smooth it over between her best friends and their former would-be daughter-in-law. Her mum and Miles thought no less of Tim, why couldn't the Hornbys be adults? Instead her mum, as interlocuter, was left constantly auto-tuning everyone's vocals.

She thought of Connor's views on the matter.

"Ah, that's Verity now," Bel said, as call waiting blipped at her. "I'll be sweetness and light, Mother. See you Saturday."

"Hi, Bel, sorry to chase you like this, some last-minute housekeeping," Verity said. "I've moved you to the table furthest from the top tables, as you wanted. I wondered if you're bringing a plus-one? I was sure you said you were on your RSVP and I've planned it in but Tim says you're definitely single."

"You've moved me like I wanted?" Bel said, brow furrowed.

"Yes—Tim said you wanted to be toward the back of the room. Giving you some space from each other."

Bel was stung, taking real offense at this. It wasn't the truce she'd hoped for, that was for sure. It was no longer excusable, as with a newly hurt person lashing back. Tim had moved on romantically and would be in the bosom of his family. It was becoming more like a nasty little vendetta.

How had she never seen the peevish side of Tim when they were together? She'd liked how loyal he was to his family and friends, how he firmly out-grouped the "dickheads" at work. It had seemed like integrity and unpretentious decency to Bel. She'd been one of the Good People in Tim's life, so she'd failed to notice how such tribal simplicities could also mask a childlike intolerance. Now she was labeled Bad People, she was learning the downside to the lack of nuance. No wonder he'd not known how to deal with her mum and Miles, who weren't by any logical stretch Bad People as a result of Bel's decision, but nevertheless "people Tim couldn't stand to be around."

It wasn't that Tim was a sinister person. Just a really petty, unimpressive one.

"Ah, I didn't say that, but wherever you put me is great," Bel said, breezily, quickly, before the pushback on Tim could be fully absorbed. "Really looking forward to it!"

"Only doing as I'm told," Verity said, in a tight, fatigued voice that conveyed *why the hell do I have to have my brother's ex there, I didn't ask for this.* Nor did I, Verity, thought Bel, but it's far too late to make up a phony holiday and be hated for that instead. She wasn't going to give Tim the satisfaction of a no-show.

"And is Tim right, you're single?"

Bel couldn't bring herself to say yes. For the first time she wondered if coupledom with Rhiannon had been . . . *time-led.*

"No, I'm bringing a plus-one," she blurted, defensively.

Uh, BEL, what the hell did you say that for?

"Great, see you on the day!" Verity said, ringing off so fast it was like crashing the receiver back into the cradle with a Bakelite phone.

Bel seethed. She messaged Tim.

Bel
Hi! Why did you tell your sister I wanted moving tables at her wedding?
Tim
Hi! She said she was doing a table of singles. I said I'd prefer it, she must have got mixed up.

Twat. The sullen, juvenile insolence of it. The assumption she was single.

Bel
Right, sure. This is very small person stuff, isn't it, Tim?
Tim
Does that mean you think you're the bigger person?

Bel drafted replies to this in her head and decided, as Connor had once said, silence was the most eloquent response.

Speaking of which, she had to do this before she could think about it too much. Connor was leaving this weekend. She knew it wasn't until Sunday, due to his dad's availability. She'd been about to offer Friday drinks, but instead she'd now be angling to drag him to a wedding full of strangers seventy miles away.

Bel
Connor, I have to ask a huge favor, and feel free to say "gross, no." My ex Tim's sister's getting married in York on Saturday, I have to go, and

Tim's being an arsehole about it. When I was put on the spot, I said I had a plus one. Don't suppose if you've got nothing on instead, you could come out of retirement for one last job, as my fake plus one? Warning: it's going to mean negotiated same-bed share again. Also, I am well aware I am taking the bare piss. Two days' notice, a wedding where you know no one—WHOOP.
Connor
Gross, no

Bel laughed and focused hard on the rippling "typing" dots. Hope bloomed in her heart and she thought about how much she enjoyed him.

Connor
Sure. I'd be offended if you asked anyone else, tbh.
You can't have a fake, fake boyfriend. I'm the real fake.

She wanted to let go an excited scream. Not for the first time, he had bailed her out.

Bel
CONNOR ADAMS THANK YOU SO SO MUCH X
Connor
How's Tim being an arsehole?

Bel felt a small glimmer of flattery that this was an authentically boyfriendish question. But she was kidding herself: Connor understood the assignment, that was all.

Bel
Lied to Verity (his sister, the bride) I wanted to be at a distant table.
Lied when I challenged him on why he'd done it. Took it upon himself

to declare me single on my behalf. Has gone fully cocky hostile dickbag, sadly.

Connor
I TOLD you he was immature. I've had enough of scorned Tim Hornby. Scornby. OK. Let's give them the biggest display of sparks since Burton walked on set to Cleopatra with Taylor.

Bel
You are 100 percent the Liz here.

Connor
Yep. Raven hair, violet eyes, London born. You are the craggy, very "regional pride" bellowing drinker.

Bel
Hahahahahaha - YES
(I will send you all the details)
(Thank you again x)

Dear Lord—this was almost flirty.

Bel squinted at her handset, wondering what was niggling at her, before a dazed smile settled upon her face. She'd never told Connor Tim's surname. Either Shilpa had mentioned it and he had a keen memory, or, OR. Connor had been interested enough in her life to do idle research?

She strained to believe it; could he possibly be that curious about her? Then again, he'd proved an instant hit at investigations.

60

Bel waved and watched from the back seat as Connor surrendered a brown duffel bag to the driver, a suit in a cover held by the hanger in his other hand. Bel was quite stomachache-y with gratitude.

"Hello," he said, climbing in next to her, "mind if I hang this up?"

"Pass it over," Bel said. "Room by me."

"No trains for Lady Macauley, then?"

"The hotel's in the middle of nowhere! One of those posh spa and golf places. We'd be on trundlers."

Connor smiled in an indulgent way.

"Who do your family think I am?"

"They have all your real biography except for the part where we're 'early days, having fun, nothing too serious yet' level dating," Bel said.

"Got it. Your mum is Bridget, your brother is Miles and his girlfriend is Yasmin?"

"Wow. Doing better there than some actual boyfriends I've had."

They started talking shop about the Mayor scoop fallout and Bel was surprised how fast the two-hour journey went. The car deposited them on a gravel drive that circled a dribbling fountain feature in front of a vast edifice of Grade II listed Jacobean gray stone.

Verity was marrying at 4:30 p.m., making their timing civilized.

They bumped into Bel's mother, Miles and his girlfriend straightaway, lounging on re-covered chesterfields in the Great Hall, all sipping Buck's Fizzes.

"God, you're not mucking around," Bel said, looking at her watch.

"They were complimentary! Did you want us to throw them back in their faces?!" Miles said.

She submitted to a hug from the rangy Miles, then Yasmin and her mother.

"Sorry to say these piss jobs are the Macauleys, Connor."

"I recognized the attitude to free alcohol," Connor said, shaking hands in turn. "Hi, I'm Connor, great to meet you."

Bel had to look away a little, feeling a pressure on her chest that must have come from the fact it was a deception. A necessary, small one, but a deception nonetheless.

She'd thought of explaining the backstory of Connor attending, and decided it would achieve nothing other than her family not knowing how to treat him. Her mother quite possibly objecting to the use of a decoy in case their hosts found out.

"You catch up with your family, I'll do the check-in," Connor said. "It's in your name, right?"

Bel nodded as he excused himself.

"Well, I never," her mum said. "Lovely manners and drop-dead handsome? Hang on to this one, Isabel."

Bel already knew what her fib about their "split" would be: *He hates the north and we couldn't make the distance work.*

Bel felt cheered by the sight of her family: today wasn't the easiest, but she had sound loved ones around her.

A porter led them to their room. Much deep pile carpet, the shade of a hamster, frilly pelmet floral curtains over fifteen-foot-high windows, Regency striped sofas facing off across a mahogany coffee table, and a canopied four-poster bed, in a space the size of a tennis court. Sharing a bed was still sharing a bed but Bel felt secret relief that, in this acreage, she and Connor were hardly on top of one another.

"It's like Balmoral. Before you call me Paris Hilton, I think they upgraded us," Bel said, after the door closed.

"Oh, I know they did. It was a woman on the check-in desk and she wanted to talk about how on earth I wasn't married, because I 'looked like I'd be married,'" Connor said, and winked.

"Blurgh," Bel said, but she was laughing. "What does 'looking married' entail?"

"It entails an Executive Suite. All right if I have first shower, then you can take longer at your leisure?" Connor said, pointing to the en-suite bathroom.

"By all means," Bel said.

She added the burble of the boiling kettle and *Murder, She Wrote*, volume low, to the offstage sound of running water. It didn't feel uncomfortable to share with Connor, Bel thought, but the not-uncomfortable had to be diligently maintained. With that in mind she opened her case, hung her dress up and made sure her knicker cache wasn't on display.

After a few minutes, there was a knock at the bedroom door. Bel looked over at the closed door to the bathroom and thought, Well, Connor wasn't going to exit unclothed anyway. So she was clear to answer it.

Bel was taken aback to see Tim: coordinated in a chocolate-brown suit with a pearl-gray tie and pocket square. Kind eyes, blond-brown hair and neat beard. Their coloring was similar enough they sometimes got mistaken for siblings.

His expression was neutral.

"Afternoon. Can I have a word?"

"Afternoon! Sure."

Bel had a hopeful premonition that they might be about to make friends at last. Despite the sniping she'd really like a burying of the hatchet. Bel wanted a redemption arc and a way for them to be around each other.

She stood aside and Tim passed her. She recognized his aftershave, a Proustian waft of Montblanc Explorer, and for a second it was as though the last year never happened. She pictured herself as Tim's date today, the *you next* entreaties. Time folded back on itself and, for fifteen seconds, they'd never separated.

"I wanted to let you know I'm here with Rhiannon. We've been seeing each other for a few months."

"Oh yes, I know. From Instagrams. That's nice. Rhiannon's great."

"I didn't think you were on there anymore."

"I'm not. Shilpa told me."

Tim's eyes widened. "Oh right, of course."

Bel genuinely couldn't tell if he was having her on. Of course Shilpa would tell her. She supposed male thinking might not have got that far. She'd assumed Tim had wanted her to find out that way to inflict pain, but if that was the general intention, Verity's wedding was more painful still.

"Yeah, Zack's with Nicky. He's a lot happier," Tim said.

Bel didn't expect that jab.

"Good for him. That was the idea."

"Whose idea, Shilpa's? No, it wasn't."

"You think she divorced so they could both be unhappier?"

"I think she wanted one so she could be happier, sure."

"There's nothing wrong with that. Women don't owe men staying in unhappy marriages."

"Ha, sure. Funny that she isn't, though, eh?"

"What?"

"Happier."

"How would you know?"

"Stuff Zack says about her response to Nicky. She unfollowed him."

Bel's apprehension increased. This didn't feel like an amnesty. More of a buildup.

"Probably for the best. All I know is she wishes them well," Bel said.

"That's a lie, but then you're very comfortable with those."

Bel took a moment to catch up with the savagery, as it was spoken as a casual observation.

"Erm . . . what?"

"Why did you come off social media right after we split up?" Tim said. Oh. *This* was why Tim was here: settling scores.

Bel was sweating now, her underarms hot. There was no shower running and Connor could hear everything.

"Needed the head space and I realized it worked well for the Manchester job."

"You didn't get offered that job until months later. Another lie."

"I said I 'realized.'"

"You also changed your mobile number," Tim said.

Oh God. Not today . . .

"Yes. I was getting loads of spam callers and as I'd deleted my apps, I thought, Fresh start . . ."

"Lie number three. Racking up."

"What is this? Why are you having a go at me?"

"It wasn't an Anthony Barr that made you do all that?"

Bel's heart was pounding so hard it must be audible. Had Anthony contacted Tim? Despite knowing Bel had the video? Was this his coup de grâce?

"What? No!"

"You weren't shagging this bloke when we were together?"

Time momentarily ground to a halt for Bel in the stark horror of receiving this long-overdue, assumed-never-arriving j'accuse.

"No?!"

"Yeah, I'm afraid fucking muggins here finally worked it out, Bel. Couldn't understand why this random guy was the first view on my Stories for months, turned up as visiting my LinkedIn too. Got stalker vibes, but why would a man I didn't know stalk me? Then he's sending me a weirdo message trying to find your new number. I couldn't place where I knew the name at first. You were shagging him when we were together and ghosted him, right?"

"No and no."

"Who is he, then?"

"An ex-colleague who developed a thing about me."

"Developed a thing without you doing anything to encourage a thing?"

"Yes."

"While we were still together?"

Bel licked dry lips. *Fail to prepare, prepare to fail.* "Overlapped slightly, yes."

"Why not tell me about him?"

"We were splitting up, it wasn't your worry."

"Haha. I've lost count of the number of lies we're on now. Is he why you moved to Manchester?"

"Of course not."

"'Of course not' from someone intimidated enough to change their mobile number. No one does that without a reason, Bel. They don't do it because they're getting PPI calls. You must think I'm an actual idiot."

"Why are we doing this on your sister's wedding day?"

"We didn't do it at the time, did we? When I was crying my heart out, trying to work out why one day we were suddenly done, no discussion. When I asked you, swearing on your mother's life, to tell me if there was anyone else . . ." Tim paused. "Oh. *Wait.* You said there wasn't anyone because you'd dumped him by then. You were playing word games with me when I was having the worst day of my life!"

The most shameful episode of her life, in turn, and Tim was absolutely right in all details. Bel hard-swallowed while her skin prickled.

"I'm so sorry I hurt you. But it wasn't due to—" Bel said.

"Don't bother carrying on lying. All those months I knew you were off with someone else and when I begged for the truth, you let me think it was all in my head," Tim said. "Bel Macauley, this firebrand journalist doing her big exposés of wrongdoing that end other people's careers, lying your tits off in your own life. Nice. You're the fakest person I've ever met."

61

"Tim, we were over because we were over, not because of anyone else. I wasn't sleeping with Anthony."

"You're still playing the word games? Did he not actually put it all the way in or something so you stayed technically in the clear to say that?"

The door from the bathroom opened, jolting both of them. Connor emerged, still buttoning his shirt.

"Hi. You must be Tim. I'm Connor," he said, extending his hand to a stunned Tim, who shook it. It was like someone had sprung from an empty cupboard in a conjuring trick. Did Tim not know she had a plus-one?

Bel fleetingly wondered if Verity had deliberately omitted that Bel was bringing someone to avoid Tim having a tell-her-she-can't temper tantrum. Actually, that was *definitely* what had happened, she'd sidestepped it and thought, He can't have a go at me on my wedding day and Bel's unpopular anyway.

It had inadvertently put Tim on the back foot when he'd presumably been planning this showdown for some time. Learning of the existence of Connor at this moment was suboptimal for Tim.

"I don't want to disrespect your history together, or cause any difficulty on a happy day, but equally, you appreciate there's a limit to what I can listen to someone say to my girlfriend?" Connor said.

Tim was completely blindsided and apparently speechless.

"You didn't say you were bringing someone!" he said to Bel, so taken aback he sounded astonished.

"This was going to be where I mentioned it. Like you with Rhiannon," Bel said.

She had him there. Sauce for the goose all over his gander.

"Right. Good luck to you," he said to Connor, recovering his acerbic attitude.

"Thanks, and you," Connor said, refusing to mirror the intonation. He was a class act.

"See you later," Tim said to Bel, and walked out, the door snapping shut behind him.

There was a tense pause.

"Was that the right thing to do?" Connor said. "I didn't want to undermine you but I put it to the What If This Actually Was My Girlfriend test, and did that. It's what I'd have done if it was Jen."

"Oh God!" Bel burst into a sob, putting a hand over her eyes.

"Wait, this is today's . . ." Connor said, stepping back, hurriedly unbuttoning and turning away. The last thing Bel saw before her eyes swam with too many tears was Connor throwing his wedding shirt over the back of a chair like a cape so it didn't crease.

He clasped her in a bare-chested hug which Bel was too destroyed to slyly appreciate.

"Should I have . . . told him . . ." Bel choked out in hiccups between waves of crying. "What was . . . the point . . . of even carrying on dodging . . ."

Connor accurately judged that shushing was the only option until it subsided. When she'd regained enough self-control to make conversation possible, he said, "Honestly? No, I don't think the precise mechanics of what you and Anthony did and didn't do needed discussing right now."

"I was such an arsehole to Tim, Connor. Everything he said was right. I am a piece of shit!"

Connor squeezed her supportively. "You fucked up, agreed. But you are *not* a piece of shit."

"Thank you," Bel said, looking up with a bleary face.

"Bel," Connor said, "I've been one of your harshest critics—"

"You're only scraping into the top ten at this point, I think," Bel said, wiping under her eyes.

"Therefore you can trust my judgment. Something can be not your finest hour without defining you."

"I should've told Tim everything on the day we split up."

"Except that would've made a horrible day of his life even more horrific, and as you said, it would've probably stopped your families staying friends. If it was an ex who you were never going to see again it would've been different. You two have different responsibilities to each other. You did what you thought was right. When people say you should tell the truth at all costs, they forget it's also about *who* pays the cost."

"Thank you. You're so wise. But I did do what Tim said. Who am I if I could do that to someone who loved me?"

"You're human."

"A shit human."

"A superlative human. Look it up, it means 'really good.'"

Bel smiled into his bare shoulder, damp with her tears.

62

"You know our prior deal about not taking things the wrong way?" Connor said.

"Oh God, WHAT?" Bel said, barefoot in her dress and having only lip-linered her lips, stopping still in the middle of the room. "We established that only ever means 'bullshit incoming.'"

"You look incredibly nice but also not you–ish, somehow."

"Because I look incredibly nice??!"

"NO, oh God, I knew I shouldn't have tried 'nuance,'" Connor said, and their warm bickering felt couple-ish as hell.

Bel had tried to stifle the up-down swoop of her heart at the sight of Connor in a dark, ink-blue suit: the man was custom-designed for suit tailoring.

Bel was in a dress with a black bodice and an off-white tulle skirt. It had reminded her of ballet lessons as a kid.

"You look absolutely lovely, OK? Just not as Bel as Bel usually does."

"Hmmm . . ." Bel hooked a black suede peep-toe sandal over her foot. "I admit it was an Undercover Bella purchase."

He could never know this but she had started to worry she was subconsciously dressing for his gaze.

"See! I could tell! I am fully exonerated."

"I'm not sure about 'fully.' I still recall the *recoiling* from me you did on your first day."

"Hahahaha. You have to admit your look that morning was very 'Helena Bonham Carter via the police drunk tank.'"

Bel mimed throwing her other shoe at him and he ducked.

THE PEACH-THEMED CEREMONY took place in a plush drawing room with a solo violinist, the reception moving to the ballroom for a wedding meal of shepherd's pie and mashed potatoes because the groom, David, loved pies and hated fuss and it was one of those weddings where it was a series of bride versus groom trade-offs. Such as speeches, but no first dance.

During the groom's ode to his new bride, Bel saw Tim giving her a steady poison glare, pointedly holding it for several seconds when she met his eyes. Rhiannon had seemed embarrassed around her, not surprising when they'd spent villa holidays and Christmases together and Bel had a few years ago coached her through a breakup with a man they came to call Snide Clyde. Bel didn't resent Rhiannon whatsoever, but given she'd be entitled to feel very strange about Rhiannon and Tim's relationship, she wanted to know why she was the only bad guy in it all.

And, *suck it, Tim*, the "social North Pole" table was great. They had nice dinner conversations with an assortment of people attending solo and making an effort. Now that the dance floor was thronged to Spiller's "Groovejet," she and Connor could sit chatting among the detritus, surveying the whole room, with no fear of being overheard.

"Connor. I've got a proposal. It's confrontational but, I think, workable," Bel said, in a rush of unchecked goodwill. He was so easy to be with, so grounded, so trustworthy. The cheekbones no longer made her think otherwise. "Accept what's happening—we've actually become friends. Would you like to stay friends?"

Connor leaned back, elbows resting on the table behind him. Bel had a moment of thinking about his body underneath the shirt, how his bare skin and muscles had felt as she'd sobbed on him. A bit lecherous, Macauley, she thought. Time to face the apps and find a boyfriend.

"What would that entail?"

"WhatsApps. Emails. Story tips. Drinks when I roll into Euston. You're welcome to come stay here from time to time, though I know that's like being offered detainment in Abu Ghraib to Adams. Let's stay accomplices."

"That's a lovely thought. Yes, I would like that a lot."

Bel leaned over and proffered her hand to shake. Connor smiled his beautiful smile, and shook it.

"It's been quite the distance traveled, you and I, hasn't it?" Bel said. "Who'd have thought we'd end up here?"

"It feels like a small lifetime," Connor said. "Guess what, after all my homesickness about the north, I'm dreading London. Jen's not found a new place yet. She's in the flat's spare room, but still . . . Could do without it. And I can't get my croissants from that bakery anymore."

"Could a reconciliation be in the cards?" Bel said, teasing, and as she did, she heard herself. No, worse, she *knew* herself.

Her voice, taut as a drum, straining for casual, when in fact she'd experienced an acute and unmistakable stab of destabilizing jealousy.

It's what I'd have done if it was Jen. Bel discovered she had even noted and filed the fact he said "photo of my *girlfriend* on my phone" last week, not his *ex*.

She wasn't OK with Connor moving back in with Jennifer, not at all . . . Whoa, what was going on? It was akin to feeling a little off and peaky, suddenly a wave of unnatural warmth coming over you, and realizing you'd definitely caught a flu bug. Except the flu was Connor Adams.

Weddings could make the sternest happily single a little forlorn, Bel knew this. Connor had dug her out of a mess of her own making—for the fourth or fifth bloody time, no less—by attending, and he was very easy on the eyes.

Some sentimentality was to be expected.

Yet it didn't feel like that. If that was all it was, Bel could imagine herself calibrating it differently on Monday, having washed the mood of the occasion out of her hair. Instead the only thing she forecast feeling, seeing the new girl at Connor's desk, was bereft.

Did she . . . ? Was she . . . ? Bel swallowed hard. Had she fallen for Connor?

The answer came back at her without hesitation. All she'd needed to do was ask the question. Heavily, thoroughly, ardently and completely.

What the fuck.

"Um, no, not in a million years, I thought I'd been clear on that," Connor said. He seemed a little put out that she'd said it and Bel wasn't immediately sure why. "This sounds like the Undercover Connor you constructed."

"He was only out of order because he was with me while keeping the door ajar with his ex. You're free to do that," Bel wittered.

"You've heard enough about how Jen's behaved—would you not think that was weak and two-faced of me?"

"Erm . . . I don't think she sounds your equal but also I'd reason it was your choice and not for me to judge."

Connor frowned.

In painting herself as angelically tolerant, Bel had a distinct sense of her own goal.

You're the fakest person I've ever met.

Oh God, Bel, she thought, dispense with this teenage tic of trying to act cool, like he doesn't matter to you. She'd thought the worst thing in the world would be if he could read her mind, but perhaps it was significantly worse if he couldn't.

63

Bel left the dry ice and hubbub of the reception disco and walked into the calm oasis of the lavender-scented, pink-plastic-filled ladies'. As she checked which stalls were free, she saw two cubicles at the far end were in use, one clearly by the bride: a swath of ivory shot silk poked out from under the door. An alcoholically amplified conversation was in progress.

". . . seen the guy Bel is with? Oh, my life. He's stunning!" Bel heard Verity say. She held her breath.

"Yeah, though Tim says he's blatantly a colleague she's roped in as a favor so she's not here alone," Rhiannon's voice replied.

"Really?"

"Oh yeah. Tim says look at their body language, they aren't a couple," Rhiannon said. "It's all very hands-off platonic."

"Oh wow, I'll be studying them now, hahaha."

Bel broke into a self-conscious sweat.

"Would Bel really do that, though? She never seems very bothered about appearances to me," Verity continued.

"Tim says Bel was definitely seeing someone behind his back toward the end. He thinks she left him for the other man, and it didn't work out. She's got to repair her self-esteem by asking this implausible hot guy to pretend to be Mr. Bel today. Tim's conclusion is he's a killer good-looking gay."

Implausible hit Bel like a roundhouse kick to the chin. It was a Tim word, she could hear him saying it. And once again, Tim was cruel, yet right in almost every respect.

Bel rapidly exited the facilities, feeling like a spectacle, a foolish one. *Implausible.* It wasn't credible that Connor would punch below his weight to be with Bel? Or perhaps it referred to Connor being implausibly attractive, full stop. Either way, it made her worry that Tim had spread this word and everyone had been snickering at her. And it had arrived at the very worst possible moment in regards to her feelings for Connor; it couldn't have hurt as much, even an hour ago. This was *drone strike* precise. Tim's greatest revenge and he'd never know.

Her ego was part architect of her downfall. She had initially expected to attend this event single and been pretty fine with that. It was the specific one-two punch of Verity putting her in social quarantine on Tim's orders, and mistakenly thinking Bel had a plus-one, that had impetuously provoked her. Now she was a target for mean-spirited sniping, when Tim was happy with a mutual friend and Bel had turned up in good faith to a Hornby mob celebration.

She knew the root of it was Tim still being wrecked over her finishing things, and knowing she wasn't in the same way. Her crime wasn't Connor, or even Anthony: it was being fine.

But Tim had exhausted her sympathy, and her guilt.

Despondent, she found Connor chatting to her brother by the dance floor. His ease with her family was so rewarding.

"Can I have a word?" she said, through her teeth.

Connor leaned in and she updated him on what had been said. He laughed heartily at *killer good-looking gay.*

"That's flattering, at least. I'm not well-dressed enough; my best wedding suit is in Stoke Newington."

"As long as your ego got stroked," Bel said, pulling a sulky trout face.

"You know what pisses me off?" Connor said. "I've actually been conscious that he was in love with you, probably still *is* in love with you. Pawing you in front of him felt like gratuitous cruelty. That's where this has come from."

Bel was extremely grateful for this reading, when hers was: *Should've picked a fake date that wasn't a whole division different.*

"You all right?" Connor said, quietly, studying her expression. "Tim has a grudge; he was never going to give your attendance a good review."

"I know. But I feel like everyone's laughing at me."

"Because they don't believe we're together?"

"Yeah. That I couldn't stand on my own two feet."

Connor gazed at her.

"There's an obvious fix if you want to shut them up, but I don't know if you've got the stomach for it."

"Oh?"

"We could kiss. I don't think anyone thinks you'd do that with your gay stooge workmate, especially if you do it right."

Connor looked at her steadily. Bel swallowed, her heart pumping faster. She had to say a quick yes and not think about how overwhelming this would feel. *Do it right.*

"I'm up for it if you think it'll do the trick."

Cool Girl indifference, when she was crucified by its secret appeal. What if he thought she was a bad kisser? She abruptly had the worries of a fifteen-year-old.

"Not here, then," Connor said.

"Why?"

"Too obvious. It'll look like we're kissing to be seen kissing."

"We *will* be doing it to be seen," Bel said.

"Duh! My point is, it needs to look spontaneous and like they're spying on us when we feel like we're alone." Connor listened to the song change. "This'll do. Follow me."

In her mid-thirties, Bel was humiliatingly forced to Shazam the music more often than she'd admit to, but she recognized it:

FKA twigs, "Two Weeks." It was intense and carnal and she was now scared shitless at what she'd set in motion. She wanted to kiss Connor so much it was like every cell of her body was ablaze, but in the act of kissing him, she couldn't have him figure that out. It was a logic pretzel and a phenomenal task, and frankly, so impossible she'd just have to try to enjoy it.

Bel was glad it was happening too rapidly for her to properly break a sweat.

Connor stopped, stationing them by a pillar.

"Let me check we're in their sight line. You keep looking at me," Connor said. ". . . Yep, they'll probably see us."

"I'm actually scared. Is it normal to be scared?" Bel babbled.

"Is this your first time kissing someone?" Connor said.

"I've never snogged the intern for a dare."

She had to be self-protectively dismissive or she'd not be able to do this.

"Don't be sick in my mouth, that's all I ask," Connor said.

"I have better control over my gastric contents than to—"

"Bel. Stop talking."

Connor pushed his fingers into her hair, hand clasping the side of her face, and moved in, but not without a split second of hesitation as he looked into her eyes that was somehow the most heart-jolting moment of all. As their mouths met, Bel thought if she'd not already admitted to herself how she felt about him, she'd have had no chance of her avoidance surviving this experience.

It was easily the greatest kiss of her life, slow but purposeful, hard but gentle, her hand on the back of his neck as she stood on tiptoes. It shouldn't be legal to kiss like that when you looked like that. The man was a dangerous intoxicant.

For a few seconds after they parted, they gazed into each other's eyes. Bel's powers of second-guessing Connor disappeared entirely. She was momentarily too lost in her own response to even begin to gauge what his might be.

Where I come from, that was a once-in-a-lifetime kiss; is it where you come from? Or do you call this "having to work on a Saturday"?

"Are they looking over?" Bel whispered, and Connor replied, in a low voice that turned her insides upside down: "I have no idea."

64

"Are you off the fake boyfriend clock?" Bel said, trying to dispel any awkwardness, as she kicked her shoes off in the room.

She'd hoped the fading inebriation would carry her through the awkwardness of the Post Kiss hours without a hitch, yet it being the two of them alone already felt intimate.

They'd left the reception's fading hours for television, caffeine and complimentary biscuits, to underline the fact they were unbothered jocular pals, yet now it felt like the opposite statement.

She'd never been in Lure Mode with Connor in all the time she'd known him. Now Bel knew what she wanted—him, in every way and at all costs—and had the forced proximity of their king-size bed and no idea if she should use it. It felt like an opportunity—but equally she was scared stiff of misreading it. The stakes were suddenly Burj Khalifa high.

"Depends. Am I still being paid or not?" Connor said.

"You're getting paid?" Bel said.

"As it's no longer possible to pay me in bylines I was assuming I could invoice, yes," Connor said, frowning. "I hope you don't think this sort of service is *free*?"

"Mmm," Bel said, regarding him, and a distinct tension, that might be of a sexual nature, joined them in the room. "In that case, keep the tab open and bill me for 'watching television together.'"

"Netflix and chill, is it? You are a predator."

Bel chortled, positioning herself against many pillows, and commenced channel surfing. She lucked out with the opening sequence of *Point Break*.

"What a film! And about going undercover! This is fate," she said to Connor, who joined her on the bed.

Bel leaned against his chest, her head under his chin, saying, "Charge for whatever this is."

She had to safety-proof him from flinching away, yet it didn't feel as if he would. Instead, Connor slid his arm round her middle. The hair at the nape of Bel's neck prickled: it felt as though they might be playing a game. One person pushed their luck a little, and the other responded.

"Nice watch," she said, looking down at his rolled-up shirtsleeve.

"Thanks. Gift from Shaun."

"I liked Shaun."

"He liked you, I'm dismayed to say."

Keanu Reeves was learning Bodhi's stoner philosophies and Bel impulsively put her arm over his arm, her hand over his. No doubt their not looking at each other was emboldening her.

Connor interlocked their fingers so they were holding hands. *He'd* done that, hadn't he? That wasn't her. That was definitely him.

Bel's heart was pounding now because it *had* to be a game of chicken. *Had* to be. There were no witnesses and here they were, in loving and wholly voluntary embrace.

What did she do to signal she wanted more still? Did he want that?

"If it's useful information, you kiss really well, by the way," Bel said. Sod it. Subtle was for people with more than twelve hours left, and he could hardly object to a compliment. It felt as if his embrace got tighter, after she spoke.

"Thanks, so do you."

"You have to say that."

Honestly, Bel, teenagers would think this embarrassingly clumsy.

"I probably would have to say that, but it's true anyway."

This was as easy as it was going to get. Bel took a deep breath, turned her head and kissed him. There was an agonizing split second when Connor seemed unresponsive, and then the message got through to Bel: *He's kissing you back*. It was more tentative than before yet still felt like all her birthdays come at once.

As it progressed, she pulled the strap on her dress down her shoulder, proving she was right to wear one of her nicest balcony bras for this event. She moved his hand onto her breast because her nerves couldn't cope with any more ambiguity, she had to know this was reciprocal. Connor didn't move his hand away, under hers, and they carried on kissing. She didn't know what to make of that. She was kind of hoping to be seized. She'd have to do the seizing. Bel squirmed against him. Her hands went to the waistband on his trousers as she fumbled with the buttons, without his help.

"Bel," Connor whispered, staying her hand, "I've really liked fake dating you. You've been the greatest girlfriend I've never had. But I draw the line at fake sleeping with you."

Bel stopped, nonplussed–stupid. "Given no one knows, I was thinking that we were real sleeping with each other?"

Connor let go and moved back.

"But we're only here because of all the pretending today. I don't think it's enough reason to trash a great friendship with a one-night stand."

Great friendship. One-night stand.

Bel knew "I do not want to do this because I am not sufficiently attracted to you" reworded when she heard it.

Why kiss her like that?! She'd never have been this foolhardy if she'd not thought that two incredible kisses, one entirely by choice, indicated some willingness.

She must've pounced, British-embarrassed, and stunned him into auto-responding before sanity reasserted itself. It felt incredibly like that, in fact. Connor thinking, Whoa there, I thought that was a moment of wine-fueled silliness, but you really mean this?

The only way to make this rejection a notch less excruciating was to act as if she was all "OK, thought this was casual, NBD, I do this all the time."

"Would it ruin it?" Bel said, aiming for a throwaway inflection.

"Are you in touch with any of your past one-night stands?"

It was on the tip of her tongue to say *no idea, I'm a serial monogamist*, except that might scare the living shit out of Connor. She hastily redrafted: "Honestly, I've never actually had one before. Unless you count . . . *that* incident, which I don't. Are there rules?"

Superb smokescreen that she was an experienced, do-this-all-the-time sex person; 5/5, no notes. *Idiot*.

"Not exactly . . . but weren't we staying friends?"

"Friends can't ever have done this?"

This sounds hideously like pleading, Bel.

"In theory, yes, but in practice we'll feel strange about it and never know what the subtext is if we get in touch, and therefore won't get in touch."

Translation: My next girlfriend will do thorough background checks and you won't survive the cull.

"Yeah, I see your point. We don't want to be sharing beers and getting involuntary flashbacks to the sight of each other writhing around naked. Like prisoners of war with PTSD."

Irreverent humor was full masking. When their being this close felt narcotic to Bel, when she'd discovered he held her heart like a newly hatched bird in his hand, it was weird indeed to be chatting potential intercourse through like it was whether they took the A640 or A642 tomorrow. But Connor was making his disinclination clear in very feeling-sparing terms, for her sake. It was ungrateful and self-sabotaging to insist he outright say, "Look, you're not really my type. The gig was 'pretending.'"

"Bel, this is because I want to stay in touch so much. I haven't said it before because I worried I was being . . . what do the kids call it? . . . *extra*. But I'm really going to miss you. Some serious bonding has gone on."

"Sure! I get it," she said, thinking there was no way of making And I Don't Want to Do It Enough not hurt. She thought it might be time to stop having her chest hanging out as untaken bait, and humiliatingly pulled her dress back up and into place.

Later, after lights out, while wondering if Connor was also wide awake in the dark, Bel tried very hard to see positives. You couldn't lose what you'd never had.

If he didn't want to sleep with her, that was a pretty conclusive answer to the question: Do I tell him I've fallen head over heels in love with him?

She'd gotten an answer—the answer she fully expected—without the agony of ever baring her soul, or her body.

Why, then, was this such agony?

65

I can't leave, I don't want to leave, Connor had thought while "The Queen Is Dead" thundered in his ears on his final morning run around Salford Quays, except this pervasive ennui made no sense because he absolutely did want to leave.

When he was comforting Bel, without his shirt on and somehow unselfconscious about the fact, what was going on came into very clear focus: he didn't want to leave *her*.

It wasn't the moment he'd have chosen to fully understand himself. After Psycho Tumnus and Bitter Tim, Connor was supposed to be the reliable pal, not the next applicant.

After "you're human" he'd wanted to add *the only one I lie awake at night thinking about, possibly my favorite one* but it definitely wasn't the time. Sadly, time wasn't something they now had much of.

Worse, it seemed this wasn't merely "fancying" Bel. He could tell his symptoms were not going to abate if they had a night together, or even a fling. It would probably make his suffering even more acute. It was as if Connor had put off seeing the GP until he was an urgent Accident and Emergency case. Except the dangerously high fever was Bel Macauley.

If it wasn't simply fancying her, he asked himself what word he might use instead to sum up the combination of adoration, fascination, tenderness and fierce desire he felt toward her. It had one syllable and, as soon as he spoke it in his head, he knew it applied.

What practical use was this surreal revelation? He couldn't disgrace himself and embarrass her by revealing that their game of splashing around the shallow end for show had seen him accidentally drown. Falling for her was, apart from anything else, idiotically suggestible.

Of *course* he got on famously with her family, who were a total delight, a demonstration to him of things that would never be. Her mother had short gray hair and an aristocratic bone structure, very well-spoken but entirely friendly. Connor had briefly worried if Miles was a to-the-manor-born Guy Ritchie film character, but he was a great laugh, and Connor genuinely felt that in different circumstances they'd be friends.

As he embarked on a wedding day with Bel at his side, he thought, Is there the smallest chance she has started to feel feelings for me? Unfortunately, paying closer attention suggested: LOL, no.

When Bel said she'd love them to stay "friends," then teasingly inquired if he and Jennifer would be back on in London—as if he'd do that, and as if she'd not care in the slightest!—Connor could see that while her regard for him had soared, when it came to attraction toward him, nothing had changed. To be fair, why would it have? It still hurt.

Then came the catastrophic wonder of there being a legitimate reason to offer to kiss her as a favor. The opportunity served up to him as if a benevolent god decided Connor should have a wish granted before his life continued on its doomed trajectory.

Obviously, circumstances conspired to force it, but if Bel was willing to do it, she couldn't find him wholly off-putting.

It was strange, auditioning for a role he so badly wanted, trying to communicate passion in a way that would make her think, Whoa, maybe I'd like to do this for pleasure as well as business. Connor thought he'd go all in, give it his best shot. He feigned confidence he didn't have in response to her nervousness and just kissed her like she'd asked him to do it for real.

And, oh God, of course it was shockingly perfect: compatibility and chemistry and the sweet softness of her. It felt like confessing everything, nonverbally.

He could see the surprise on her face afterward that surely he wasn't *that* good an actor. It somehow affected his vocal cords when he tried to speak to her. She said, "Are they looking?" and Connor was momentarily completely unable to wrench himself out of the fantasy and simply said, "I have no idea." He could've just as easily said "I don't care," and in a way he wished he had and then it would be done, dealt with, out there.

Although unfair on her, given they still had to share a bed.

Connor tried to detect if they'd shifted gears, yet Bel seemed more insouciant than ever. As soon as they were back in the room, kicking her heels off, putting *Point Break* on.

Bel was still in the floofy feminine dress, like a bedraggled Tinkerbell. Something about the layers of froth in her hitched-up skirts, her bare legs stretched out beneath, made Connor think unclean thoughts. He could grab her waist, pull her down the bed toward him . . .

She began joking about paying him gigolo cash and once again Connor thought, Are you hinting that you're authentically enjoying this, or are you reminding me it's pragmatism?

Either way, he wasn't going to say no, taking his own shoes off and pulling himself up next to her. She leaned back on his chest, and Connor did what felt natural and put his arm round her.

Bel vaguely chattered about what was happening on-screen and he wondered if she, like him, could only think about the way it felt, wrapped around each other. It was difficult to care about Johnny Utah infiltrating the coastline community.

"If it's useful information, you kiss really well, by the way," Bel said. Connor twinged with pleasure and held her tighter.

"Thanks, so do you."

"You have to say that."

"I probably would have to say that, but it's true anyway."

She turned her head as if to say something, he turned to listen, their lips right by each other. Like it wasn't a big deal, as if what he'd said was an invitation, as if it was the natural thing to do, Bel kissed him. Reality raced ahead, Connor's executive function in breathless pursuit as he kissed her back.

Bel pulled her dress down, a black lace bra underneath, and plonked his hand onto the pale skin of her right breast, her hand clasped over his. Connor couldn't move, frozen in a virginal fright. His brain played him a supercut of all the times he'd been interested in Bel's chest and in lofty denial of the fact. Now he was being asked to reveal that enthusiasm and he was in terror at finally making his feelings known. His mind left his body as they carried on kissing and he watched himself from the outside. This was his dearest wish, wasn't it? But what *was* this? Apart from what it was, obviously.

Bel started fumbling with his fly and his stomach flipped. There was no more messing around, Connor had to decide. He'd have no willpower to call a halt if she got any further.

"Bel," Connor blurted, his hand over hers to stop her, "I've really liked fake dating you. You've been the greatest girlfriend I've never had. But I draw the line at fake sleeping with you."

Bel looked justifiably confused.

"Given no one knows, I was thinking that we were real sleeping with each other?"

Connor let go and pulled back a little. How did he navigate this, stand her down without saying why?

"But we're only here"—he gestured at their surrounds—"because of all the pretending today. I don't think it's enough reason to trash a great friendship with a one-night stand."

Connor wished he'd anticipated *Bel initiates sex*—he might be handling this better. You didn't tend to disaster plan for best-case scenarios.

This is the part where you reassure me it doesn't need to be a one-night stand.

He knew this wasn't going to happen; of course it was a one-night stand. That's why she'd launched it when they had one night left.

"Would it ruin it?" Bel said.

"Are you in touch with any of your past one-night stands?"

Connor wouldn't have said this if he'd thought it through. Apart from anything else, he was jealous enough that he didn't want to know.

"Honestly, I've never actually had one before. Unless you count . . . *that* incident, which I don't. Are there rules?"

"Not exactly . . . but weren't we staying friends?"

"Friends can't ever have done this?"

"In theory, yes, but in practice we'll feel strange about it and never know what the subtext is if we get in touch, and therefore won't get in touch."

"Yeah, I see your point."

No no no, you don't "see my point."

"We don't want to be sharing a beer and getting involuntary flashbacks to the sight of each other writhing around naked. Like prisoners of war with PTSD," Bel said.

It would be absolutely fine if the burgers and beer was a date were the words that wouldn't leave his mouth. *In that context, my memory could play any X-rated highlights reel it liked. But the fact it hasn't crossed your mind it could be a date is a massive clue.*

"Bel, this is because I want to stay in touch so much. I haven't said it before because I worried I was being . . . what do the kids call it? . . . *extra*. But I'm really going to miss you. Some serious bonding has gone on."

"Sure! I get it," she said, with a robust indifference, with no *I will miss you too*. Bel pulled her dress back up and Connor inwardly winced. To call declining her offer *counterintuitive* was a hilarious understatement.

But in her uncomplicated eagerness to shed their clothing, she'd been offering all and nothing, Connor felt sure of it. He sensed the limits of her feelings for him and faced the extent of his own.

He'd handled that with effortful restraint and qualified honesty, so he didn't wake the next morning to the sound of a shower and lingerie strewn on the floor and the sensation that he'd gambled any future away to have her one time.

Why, then, did it feel like he'd handled it really badly?

66

It was an irony that Bel couldn't share with Connor, that only once the fake dating was over did their interacting feel fake.

They patched up the aborted sex with a lot of suddenly forced buoyant normalcy and humor and the end of *Point Break*.

They discussed anything and everything, like old friends, while YOU MADE AN ABSOLUTE SHIT SHOW OF YOURSELF thundered in Bel's mind.

Bel skipped the hotel breakfast—all things considered, she couldn't face it.

"I don't think I want to run the gamut of the Hornbys enough for eggs Benedict."

"Mind if I go?"

"Not at all."

He left Bel listlessly playing with her phone in its charger.

Shilpa
Reviews are in! I've had a message from Zack saying you are insensitive to "flaunt" new man in front of Tim without "doing him courtesy of warning you were seeing someone" and "it was really unnecessary, Tim says they were all over each other."

Bel thought of Tim's swipes at Shilpa yesterday. A lot of wingman-ing advocacy going on.

Bel
WHAT?! I thought me and Connor "weren't real"? If I'd told him I had a plus one I guarantee I'd have got rank-pulling "it's my sister's wedding so please leave the piece of boy ass at home." I couldn't win and unlike him I'm not allowed to move on. My two options: pitiable, or a bitch.

Shilpa
One hundred percent. I told Zack they've turned into the Brewdog Andrew Tates.

Connor returned, reporting her mum had said, in full hearing of the Tim-Rhiannon table, that she couldn't wait for Connor to visit. "And Miles is in London soon for a party and we've swapped numbers to go for a pint, hope that's OK?"

"Of course," Bel said, bloodlessly.

"I honestly don't think the fauxmance charges are sticking at all."

Bel smiled and said *brilliant*. Shame she'd had to be told it was one too.

She desperately wished she'd not gotten overexcited and tried it on with him. They could've salvaged the friendship she'd outlined. The Big Other Irony was that Connor had pretended that sleeping together would spoil it, but her trying to make it happen and his resisting had much the same effect.

There was now a ghostly question mark hanging over why she'd ever proposed their staying in touch at all, and she'd not be trying to arrange any meetups. She had a solid premonition that Connor wouldn't either.

As their car approached Ancoats and Bel knew that this was it, goodbye, more or less forever, she was incredibly glad of her large "hangover" sunglasses.

Connor asked the driver to wait a second, heaved Bel's case out of the boot and stepped up to the pavement to say goodbye.

"Nothing I could say to thank you would do justice to the support you've given me," Bel said.

"Are you kidding? Bel, you got me on the front page in less than twelve weeks. Toby wants to see me on Monday. I have gone from Total Nobody to Rising Star and it's one hundred percent down to you."

"You were never a total nobody," Bel said, trying to keep her voice light. "And career favors and personal-life favors aren't the same. The second is far more valuable and meaningful and you've done me those in spades."

"It was nothing."

Yes, Bel feared that for him, in the nicest possible way, it was. Connor leaned over and hugged her, and Bel threw her arms round him and closed her eyes and fought to stay in control.

"See you at the Christmas party, I guess?" she said, for a carefree parting line, wanting Connor to disagree and insist no, they'd organize something in the autumn.

"Guess so. In our antler deely bobbers."

Bel imagined seeing Connor across the room and realizing from a stray hand-touching that he and another colleague were seeing each other. She would honestly rather make up an excuse than witness that; it'd feel like gazing at a hangman's noose on a deserted moor.

Bel would have to phish with him beforehand to try to make sure he was single. *Look at him, he'll be single for about as much time as it takes an avocado to go gray!*

Bollocks to it, she'd eat microwave Christmas dessert from the tub and scroll it all online instead, searching for a glimpse of his face.

"You bet," Bel said. "Bye, Connor."

"Bye, Bel."

She turned and busied herself with getting through her door, as watching the taxi turn the corner was too much.

As she ditched her luggage and flopped onto the couch, she got a message from her mum.

Isabel, what a thoroughly delightful young man Connor is. Your father would've adored him. I have a very good feeling about you two. I'm already working on an itinerary for showing him around here—he seemed extremely enthusiastic about getting to know York/becoming acquainted with your origin story. I am afraid a viewing of the "nude toddler crabbing in Cromer" photos has been offered and accepted, haha! Hope you got back safely xxx

Bel burst into tears.

"At least it's not chucking it down like it was in May," his dad said. "You're getting out at the right time, if that was Manchester in the good months. Imagine November."

"Ha, yes," Connor said.

He was leaving her behind.

Soon he'd be staring out of windows at Pret Charing Cross, listening to songs about her, wondering what other bastard might be getting close to her. Grit-smiling through the rigmarole of dates that made him feel existentially lonely, and living for the funny debrief WhatsApps with Bel when he got home. Trying to avoid hearing about hers. Ugh. He was too old to find the tragedy of the loss of her poetic. He didn't want to wallow, he wanted her back in his arms.

See you at the Christmas party, I guess. Not if he was going to watch other men circling her and then overhear her say, "That's what my boyfriend says . . ." and feel like he'd bruised his ribs. Realizing any chance with her he might've ever had, had been comprehensively missed. He'd have to try to suss her romantic situation out ahead of time and cry off if needs be. *Crying* being the operative verb.

Could he have just bet the house, and told her? What would he have said? More to the point, what would Bel have said? Last night proved he wasn't friend-zoned, but there was still a yawning conceptual leap in wanting anything serious. Not so long ago, he was her hemlock.

"Got all your things, then?" his dad said, and Connor thought, Well, no. A massive sodding chunk of my heart is bleeding everywhere, forever stuck somewhere north of Manchester city center, but it is what it is.

"Yeah, I'll follow you down."

He heavy-sighed and did a last wander round, doing the visual sweep of the bathroom, the bedroom side tables. All he'd wanted when he got here was to go home again and all he wanted, on going, was to stay.

He was halfway down the stairs to the car, about to put the keys into the lockbox and make them irretrievable, when he remembered. He bounded back up the stairs and unlocked the door, walked over to the mantelpiece and picked the envelope up from behind the candlestick.

He ripped open Shaun's card. It was two sentences long. Connor read them and reread them and said aloud, in a disbelieving and somewhat choked voice, "Smart-arse bastard!"

He locked up again, bounded down the stairs with a new vigor and found his father fiddling with the car radio.

"Dad, would it be all right if we made a small detour? I have something I absolutely have to do before I go."

"As long as it's not too far. What's the address for the sat nav?"

Connor folded the card he was holding and put it in his jeans pocket.

"It's in Ancoats."

67

There was a ring at the door and Bel thought, I hope it's Anthony, I could do with some free violence.

She answered it combatively, not caring who saw her eyes pink and puffy like this. She was confronted with a deeply apprehensive-looking Connor, hands thrust in the front pockets of his jeans.

"Hi . . ." he said.

"Er . . . hi!"

Bel wiped at her face as she stood aside. She did care if *he* saw her like this! Shit. She'd not anticipated it might be him for a single second.

Connor fully focused.

"Wait, are you OK? What's wrong?"

He stepped forward, possibly to put a consoling hand on her arm, and she stepped back as if he were contagious. *No more physical affection, please, it's sent me a bit mad.*

"Bel, what's the matter?" Connor said, leaving the door open behind him, too disconcerted by what he must think was Bel's bad news.

"Uh . . ." Bel couldn't think of what she could invent as a cover story, or more to the point, if she should bother. She could also feel the risk of tears restarting if she started talking.

Confessing to him was a humiliation, but last night couldn't really be topped anyway.

"Would you believe me that you're the one person I can't

tell?" she said, stalling, trying for a playful tone, but she was already floundering.

"I would, but I'd really like to be someone you can tell anything," he said, with a vulnerability she'd not heard before.

On his head be it, then, Bel thought.

"It's this guy at work," she said.

"Oh?" Connor said, frowning.

There was a long pause while Bel summoned the courage and Connor added, "One of the ones I know, or someone I would be happier not knowing about? How many are in the Bel metaverse?"

"No need to make me sound slutty." She smiled weakly, and Connor said, "I'm just anxious."

Bel couldn't make sense of that and plowed on: "He's . . . someone I couldn't stand at first, and he didn't like me either. We were thrown together by a job and got to know each other, and at some point, really hit it off. He stood up for me, again and again, in a way I don't think anyone ever has. Somewhere along the line, the closeness we'd imitated became genuine for me . . ."

She paused, unable to read Connor's shell-shocked look. Bel hoped he wouldn't think this was supposed to make him feel guilty.

"When I realized how I felt, I threw everything at it on the last night I had with him, made a clumsy attempt at seduction. He told me he didn't want me that way. He saw us as friends. I know, so cringe. Except it turns out cringe was the least of my problems. Now he's going back to London forever, and it turns out I had in fact"—Bel cleared her throat—"fallen in love with him. I can tell, because my heart is broken and I can't eat anything. Unusual for me, as you know."

Bel wiped at her face and steadied her breathing. You could cut the air with a rubber knife.

She waited for horrendous, shriveling regret at saying the L word, right into the face of the man who had made her feel it, to arrive. It didn't. It turned out she'd grown so close to him, she wanted Connor to know. His insights were unmatched. Maybe Connor could tell her how to get over Connor.

"That's why you think he said no, he wanted you as a friend?" Connor said.

"Yeah. He said as much. I mean, it wasn't a surprise. I would hate it if the big-headed bastard ever knew I said this, but when all's said and done, I think he's out of my league."

"No one is out of your league. There is no league above you."

Bel smiled gratefully and couldn't answer him or she'd bawl. *Don't be lovely and kind, honestly.*

"Is, um . . ." Connor cleared his throat. "Is this guy at work me?"

"Yes," Bel said, one flat syllable she'd never forget having uttered.

"Wow!" He looked at her intently. "You and I have had some misunderstandings but we saved the biggest and best until last."

She smiled and shrugged. Bel didn't need him to let her down gently, she was already there.

"Why are you here?" she said.

"Remember my brother left me a card, with strict instructions not to look at it until today?" Connor said. He pulled it out of his pocket and handed it to Bel. She opened it and read:

You're in love with Bel. Do something about it.

Bel looked up in surprise.

"Shaun wrote this? About me?"

"Yep. Can you *believe* his presumption? Based on one evening's observation too? I mean, for my brother to work it out I'd need to have been unable to tear my eyes away from you that night or stop talking about you. Maybe it was me pathetically criticizing you for wearing 'unprofessional knitwear' when he asked what your supposed faults were, as he thought you were amazing . . ."

Bel was speechless, heart thudding.

"Bel, I have something to tell you . . ." Connor paused. "Shaun's right, I'm in love with you."

"Really?"

"Yes. I didn't think you felt anything like I did, so I've been trying to pretend I wanted to keep you only as a friend. I just wanted to keep you, full stop. Very much not as a friend."

"But you rejected me!" Bel blurted, half in tears again, half laughing. "I tried to grope you and you were all *no lustful hoes, thanks. One-night stands are bad news.*"

"They are, with people you haven't told you're mad about."

"But it only being a one-night stand was your premise, not mine."

"I was hinting that was what I didn't want, so you could reassure me it wasn't that."

"So, while being rejected I was expected to risk saying the thing you wouldn't say?"

"Yes. Shame on you."

Bel burst out laughing. "I know you like an abundance of caution but arguing the case for the outcome you didn't want, to test me, is next level."

"I know. No wonder my brother's had to deal me an Oblique Strategy card to break my own deadlock."

"To be fair, I did a version of this with your moving back in with Jen. That was the moment I knew that you were mine, and she couldn't have you, and there I was, wisecracking lightheartedly that maybe you weren't over her."

"At least I strongly contradicted that."

"I had no way out of the stupid flippancy I'd started. How did I switch to 'you know how once upon a time, I didn't like you? Well, now not only do I like you, I like you more than I've ever liked anybody'?"

At this declaration, Connor's face was suffused with a happiness she'd never seen before.

"Exactly the bind I was in. It's almost like spending months pretending didn't put us in the greatest place to start telling the truth."

"OK. Well, to put it all fully unambiguously out there, last night I was hoping one time led to lots of times," Bel said.

"Now I know that, it changes everything. It's quite life-changing information."

"Connor . . . Oh, hello?" Bel said, over his shoulder.

They turned and Connor's dad was in the doorway.

"Sorry, you weren't answering your phone and I'm bursting for a number one!"

"Sorry, Dad, big conversation here . . . this is Bel. Bel . . ."

"Hello, Mr. Adams," she said.

"Please, Stuart," he replied. "It really is quite urgent, if you don't mind. It'll happen to you too one day, Connor, your warning zone just disappears."

"Thanks, Dad."

"Let me show you where the loo is—use the downstairs one through here . . ." Bel ushered him through the guest bedroom and into the en suite.

She was dazed, occupying two time zones—some part of her was still sobbing on the sofa. Connor was in love with her too?

"Bel . . ." Connor caught her on the way back and pulled her into a kiss. Their first kiss as themselves, with the intensity of total sincerity and nobody watching. It was better than the first time.

"God, I hope my dad has got a whole Lucozade Sport bottle's worth," Connor whispered in her ear as he kissed her neck, and Bel shook with laughter.

"Can I come back next weekend?" he said, one hand on the side of her face.

"I feel like I'd die if you didn't," Bel said, looking into his eyes.

Just as she felt regret at being so purple, Connor said, "Same here."

They were going to be like this now? They'd flicked a switch to total candor and it was the greatest turn-on in Bel's life to date.

"What about you hating Manchester?!"

"It turns out I really don't."

They were interrupted by Connor's dad saying, "Oh God, that's better. I had a bladder the size of a haggis."

68

Connor got back into the car, somewhat delirious. He had to remind himself to put his seat belt on. His father looked at him curiously.

"Nice girl. Is it serious, then? Is she your girlfriend?"

"I hope so."

"Didn't I tell you women would be queuing up?"

"Bel isn't women, Dad," Connor said.

"Oh? Who is she, then?"

"She's . . . everything."

He'd turned up to say *I've fallen in love with you if that changes anything other than your respect for me* and she was in tears about Some Man and Connor was ready to take up bare-knuckle boxing and "howling into the eternal void" as hobbies, except the man was him and he could scarcely believe it.

His inability to accurately read Bel Macauley had been the most mind-blowing, humbling and rewarding misjudgment of his life.

"Hoo hoo, someone's got it bad," his dad said. "Oh, another bloody berk trying to cut me up! Look at this clown in the Beamer. This city. The grim north. Is Bel a Manchester lass?"

"York."

"I'll warn you that soon as your mother finds out about this young lady she'll be searching the bride-to-be's hometown wedding-venue options. She says you're thirty-five this winter and she's getting desperate."

"Tell Mum she can look at anywhere other than Hotel Du Vin."

"Good grief! Where is my son and what have you done with him?"

They drove on, the car full of his father's amused disbelief and Connor's newfound bliss.

"This Bel's got my full approval," his dad said.

"Based on that long in her company?" Connor said.

"Based on the fact I've not seen my younger son this happy in a very long time. Possibly since Christmas mornings of his childhood. Welcome back, we've missed you. Bel's cost me less than that Phantom Menace tat too. Good on you, Bel. Isabella? Isabel, ah. Pretty name."

Connor's phone lit up, and then his face.

"WHY ARE YOU CALLING ME ON A SUNDAY? Come to that, why are you calling me at all when there are messaging options?"

"Shilpa," Bel said, her voice cracking, with the weight of happy tears behind it.

"Fuck! Are you OK?"

"I'm fine. I'm great."

"What's happened?"

"Connor happened."

"Oh my GOD," Shilpa said, and there was a rewarding volume of crazed shrieking. "Did you? Have you TOUCHED IT?"

"No," Bel said.

"Oh," Shilpa said, crestfallen.

"But 'touching it' appears imminent and welcome."

"OH MY GOD! WHAT?! YOU'RE TOGETHER? LIKE . . . *a real couple*?"

"Uhm . . . yes," Bel said, tucking her hair behind her ear and for some reason, blushing crimson. For two people who'd been behaving like they were together for months, it was all so new.

"I'm coming round right now for the full version. This is too large to be digested in a call."

"Agreed," Bel said.

"Can I tell you something without getting mad at me?" Shilpa said, hesitantly.

"Oh God, Shilpa, what did you do?"

"On the night we went out with his brother, somehow we got into what the deal was with Tim. I said you'd wanted to end it but you were broken by it and told me afterward no one would ever love you as much as he did. And Connor got this faraway look and said, 'Hate to blow smoke but I've never met anyone where that's less likely to be true.' Then he seemed proper mortified and said, 'Don't repeat that.'"

"The incredible thing here is, you didn't tell me?! Since when did you become discreet?"

"I could tell he hadn't worked it out yet and then you were being weirdly catty about him too and I had an intuition that if I didn't interfere, something incredible would happen. Which was disappointing because interfering is my favorite thing in the world. But now it has. Get off the phone, I have to book my Uber!"

Bel stood in her kitchen, her head spinning and her heart full.

She scrolled to his name in her phone book.

69

Bel

FFS do you realize we could've done it last night if you'd not turned me begging for your body into "not liking you that much"? I was really going to put some effort in too. You are extraordinary.

Connor

Believe me, I hate myself more than you ever could right now.

Bel

Makes a change.

Connor

Doesn't it?

(can I say I'm almost high with the feeling I can be totally honest with you?)

(also strap in, I've now got four hours in a car and Dad's blasting talkSPORT)

Bel

Same, so I can ask you anything?

Connor

Absolutely

Bel

Without Shaun's card, would you ever have told me?

Connor

I refuse to give my brother that much credit. I think I'd have WhatsApped you to death and you'd have started to have suspicions. If I hadn't come round, would you have told me?

Bel

I think I'd have made up a reason to travel down for a meeting just so I could see you. But I was so scared of successfully "staying friends" then accidentally shooting myself in the face by having to meet your next girlfriend 💀

Connor

Oh God same re: next boyfriend. I HATE THAT GUY.

Bel

(He's you) x

Connor

Worked myself up into such a state about him that even though he's me, I can't immediately forgive myself x

Bel

What if we'd gone the rest of our lives, both feigning indifference to each other, never knowing we felt the same way? I bet that's how our bleak two-hander play "Fucked" ended, you know. Critics Circle Awards all round.

Connor

No chance. I thought of it as more of a sitcom. I would've eventually got trashed and messaged "can't stop thinking about ur boobs" and then had to investigate assisted dying.

Bel

HAHAHAHAHA (can't you? Last night I was worried you liked my great personality but I was physically as alluring as a urinal cake)

Connor

Yes it's like a sickness. Your fault for relentlessly flaunting them at me. (Don't be insane. I was that close to asking my dad if he could wait in the car for an hour.)

Bel

Wait for nine to ten minutes, surely?

Connor
Sassy. I promise you that you will regret sassing my prowess.
Bel
<3 This week's going to last forever, Connor x
Connor
My thoughts exactly x

Acknowledgments

So, special thanks, even more so than usual, go to my publisher Lynne Drew and agent Doug Kean, who both bore my lengthy and tedious plot wrangling with stupendous fortitude. It paid off later, I hope, but my God, I was a high maintenance pain in the arse. Thanks, both, for your humor, positivity, encouragement, calm, and bright ideas. And for your faith.

Assistant editor Olivia Robertshaw, thank you. You are a pleasure to work with and endlessly patient in the face of my "whoops, and also" requests. And thanks once again to the whole HarperCollins team for turning my sketchy ideas into a beautiful thing.

Praise, as always, to my trusted first-draft readers—Tara, Katie, Kristy, Sean, my sister Laura—who say, "More, please," and reassure me it's not a stone-cold career ender.

Thank you to my friend Helen for grasping the ins and outs of Ring Video and its theoretical theft. Glad one of us paid attention at school.

I'm further very grateful to journalist Maeve McClenaghan, who answered many of my dumbest, most basic questions about the practicalities of working the investigations beat. Any errors and all wild flights of fancy in this fiction regarding the realities and mechanics of the job are mine, but it was so useful to have your knowledge as a grounding. (Oh, and also, I'm confident your office environment is pleasant and not a Slough House.)

Gratitude also goes to author Emily Henry, whose "fist squeezing my heart" analogy I pinched, and for her huge generosity toward me in general.

Fellow writers/authors/booksellers/publishing people whom I speak to regularly, usually via social media and often via memes (you all know who you are), thank you for being one of the most supportive, witty, and friendly communities anyone could hope to be part of. Writing can be lonely and riddled with insecurity, and you fix that.

And thank you to the readers for the gift of your valuable time. Every time I start a first draft, I'm so excited to think I will eventually get to share my story with you. If that ever changes, I will do something else.

ABOUT THE AUTHOR

Sunday Times bestselling author **Mhairi McFarlane** was born in Scotland in 1976, and her unnecessarily confusing name is pronounced Vah-Ree. After some efforts at journalism, she started writing fiction and her first book, *You Had Me at Hello*, was an instant success. She's since sold more than two million copies of her books. *Cover Story* is her eleventh novel. She lives in Nottingham with a man and, sadly for the time being, no cat.

READ MORE BY INTERNATIONALLY BESTSELLING AUTHOR
MHAIRI McFARLANE

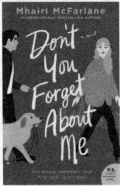

DISCOVER GREAT AUTHORS, EXCLUSIVE OFFERS, AND MORE AT HC.COM.